Olivia Northman's wc
to a drunk driver. Thi .... wiul
grief and the demands ui being a single parent to their autistic son, Ben. After her first attempt at a new relationship
crumbles, Olivia retreats to the simple, the predictable. It's
what's best for her son and her heart.

Ellie Vasquez isn't simple or predictable. In fact, she's
charmingly impulsive, as well as gregarious, confident, and
attracted to Olivia, which she reveals in an unguarded moment. Olivia doesn't know what's more surprising—Ellie's
interest, or her own—but a quiet conversation over drinks
soon spins into something more. As Olivia's caution gives
way to hope, she sees another chance at love, both for her,
and for Ben, who takes to Ellie with a tender openness. Ellie
is fearless about love in a way that makes Olivia want to be
brave, but the deeper their passion, the closer she gets to
drowning—in grief, in fear, in guilt. To have a future with
Ellie, Olivia must come to terms with her past. If she can't,
she risks losing the second love of her life.

Anne E. Terpstra's *Beyond Any Experience* is an intimate,
emotional debut that explores grief, parenting, neurodiver-
sity, and the vulnerability of love after loss.

Beyond Any Experience

Anne E. Terpstra

A NineStar Press Publication

www.ninestarpress.com

Beyond Any Experience

© 2022 Anne E. Terpstra
Cover Art © 2022 Jaycee DeLorenzo
Cover Photo by Anne E. Terpstra
Edited by Elizabetta McKay

ISBN: 978-1-64890-487-5

First Edition, May, 2022

Also available in eBook, ISBN: 978-1-64890-486-8

CONTENT WARNING:
This book contains sexually explicit content, which is only suitable for mature readers. Warnings for references to an auto accident/collision; PTSD/past trauma; loss of and grieving for a loved one; loss of a family member; discussion of suicidal ideation; ableism; fat phobia.

For Joanne

my always, my everything

Chapter One

WHEN FRUSTRATED, OLIVIA'S son doled out words the way a miser handed over coins—one at a time, and with a begrudging curtness—so she read him by the semaphore of his body and the tenor of his movements. Today, the angry clatter of silverware sounded the first warning. Setting the table usually soothed Ben. He loved a fork lined up on its napkin, a plate rim unmarred by chips. This chore needed no prescribed checklist, no adult confirmation. He could see for himself it had been done correctly, and he orchestrated it to the particular rhythm of his internal metronome.

A cabinet door slammed, and she twitched. Chair legs growled against hardwood. Huffing through his nose, Ben fussed with his glass, centering it on the line where the table leaves met. Even the way he flopped into his chair—toes scraping the floor in irritated sweeps—broadcast his discontent. She piled fettuccine Alfredo on his plate and sank into her seat.

Silence settled around them. Tempting. Easy. They had passed wordless meals more times than she liked to admit in the three years since her wife's death. At first, quiet dinners provided a fragile oasis after hours of grief-fueled rages. Now, on some days, speech was simply beyond them, Ben drained by the cajoling at school and therapy to "use his words," and Olivia numbed by phone calls and meetings at work.

The empty chair across the table chided her with memories of Sophia's gentle but determined efforts, the artful way she could coax Ben from a gloomy mood. His head hung low, dark bangs skimming the bridge of his nose, and he poked at his pile of noodles.

"Wasn't art class today?" Olivia started with a direct question to keep him from sinking beneath a sea of possible answers.

Ben ignored her, nibbling on a single strand of pasta.

"It's the big end-of-year project, right? Everyone works on the mural?"

"Murals are stupid."

"You didn't think so this morning. You were excited."

"They're stupid!"

"Did Jamal think they were stupid?" How his best, and only, friend took things often set the tone for how he handled them.

"He was sick." The first clue to his mood tumbled from his lips. Seeing Jamal was the main reason she could get him out of the house in the morning.

"I'm sorry. I know you hate it when he's not there." She chewed slowly as Ben pushed his fettuccine into clumps, tines screeching across the plate. "How's the Alfredo?"

He dropped his fork with a rattle.

"I need words, okay? How's dinner?"

"I don't like it."

"But it was your request. Because you liked it so much last week."

"It feels funny on my tongue."

"Funny?"

"Too thick."

"It's the same recipe. Same everything."

"It's too THICK!" His eyes snapped up for a burst of contact. An ugly flush crawled across his pale cheeks.

"Hey! Your attitude isn't appropriate."

"BUT I HATE IT!"

"Remember our agreement?" She fought to keep her voice even. "If you choose the meal, you have to eat it."

Tears welled in his tea-colored eyes. "You don't understand!" He ran from the table and bolted up the stairs. The hollow thump of his steps rattled the old house.

Olivia rubbed her face, then dropped her chin to her palm. A long, slow sigh leaked from her lips. This was a too-familiar choice. Allow Ben to lose a meal to the consequences of his own rigidities and boiling emotions, or erase the tenuous line she had drawn, hoping to pack more calories onto a thin frame that some days didn't seem strong enough for the double demands of autism and grief.

She got up from her plate and climbed the stairs, taking them two at a time. A wet snuffle sounded from Ben's room, where he hunched in a crouch between his bed and the wall. Her back twinged as she squeezed her long frame next to him, but she ignored the warning spasm and tapped his knee.

"Seems like you had a tough day."

He jerked his leg away.

"I know it's hard when Jamal is absent. That part I get. But art class doesn't make sense. Can you help me understand?"

He tapped thumbs to fingertips in quick succession, pinky to index, index to pinky.

Hoping to catch his eye, she leaned forward, but her overgrown hair spilled across her face. She raked it back impatiently, then played her only hand. "If you tell me about art class, we'll discuss a different dinner option."

He froze, index fingers to thumbs in a weak suggestion of the okay sign.

"But they have to be your words. No making me guess."

"I don't know where to start." The mumbled admission signaled his acceptance, and her shoulders relaxed. She would trade food for information any day, given how little he revealed at times.

"Start at the beginning. That's always easier. You ate lunch, then you went to art." She knew his schedule cold. The moment her caller ID flashed his school's name, she could guess the problem from the time. Tuesday at 11:13? Gym class. His aide forgot his noise-cancelling headphones, and overwhelmed by the ricochet of sound, he exploded halfway through a game. Thursday at 2:32? He refused to eat lunch, and in a moment of hunger-exacerbated emotionality, he burst into tears during a dreaded spelling test.

"I went to art...there was a substitute. She was mean! I hated her!"

"You hated her immediately, or—"

"No! Mrs. Garibaldi promised I could paint trees, not cars, on the mural because cars are hard. I like trees."

"I know you do." She had a drawer full of trees—tall, thin trees with lacework branches, broad trees squatting under a crown of heavy limbs. The form calmed Ben, a succession of orderly lines forking across the paper. They looked like trees when he finished, as opposed to cars or people, which his crude attempts couldn't approximate.

"The substitute said all fifth graders had to draw cars. And I couldn't help if I didn't. It was so unfair. Mrs. Garibaldi promised I could help with Lincoln Park!"

Making a vise of her thumb and middle finger, she squeezed her throbbing temples. His educational team had discussed this weeks ago. The entire school was painting a mural of the Chicago skyline, and while Ben's class was assigned a traffic scene on Lake Shore Drive, his teacher had agreed he could work on the park in the background. "Where was your aide?"

"At lunch."

"But another woman helps during Ms. Rickard's lunch."

"She was sick. They said to do art by myself. But I couldn't make the substitute understand, she didn't let me help, and now everyone but me will be on the mural!"

"Okay, okay, buddy. It must have felt terrible to be left out." When she slipped a cautious arm around his shoulders, he collapsed against her, crying harder. The unrestricted contact said more than his tears about how devastated he was. Times like this were the worst, when what should have been the highlight of his day turned sour. "Did they finish the mural?"

"No. It's really big."

"So next week, when Mrs. Garibaldi is back, the class will still be painting it?"

His head popped up. For the first time, his face lost its tight, strained look. "Yes."

"Maybe you can add trees then?"

"Yes!"

"I'll email your teacher, okay?"

"Okay. I used my words. I did!"

"I believe you." She lifted her arm as he squirmed free. "But remember how I said that even when you use your best words, some adults still might not understand?"

"If I'm using the best words, they *have* to understand."

They had circled this issue so many times, but it still eluded him. "The important thing is, you tried as hard as you could. The trying makes me proud."

"You can't be proud. It didn't work!"

"You never know if it will work. Which is why trying is the brave part, the proud part."

He wiped his face on his shirt, tears staining the fabric.

"You know what else I'm proud of?"

"What?"

"All the words you gave me right now. Good words that helped me understand."

"So, I don't have to eat fettuccine?"

"Not tonight. But remember, it's unfair to ask for something and then not eat it."

"Can I have applesauce?"

"Yes, but not just applesauce. You need protein."

"Ice cream!"

She stifled a grin at his hopeful expression. "Do you think after refusing to eat what I cooked, you're getting ice cream?"

His lower lip budged out, and his shoulders slumped. "Probably not."

"How about cottage cheese?"

"Okay." He scrambled across the bed. "I'll get the applesauce packs!"

As he tore down the stairs, she thumped the back of her head on the wall. Ben's emotions surged and retreated so rapidly, leaving her exhausted from picking her way through the minefield of his day. This time, at least, her patience had been rewarded with clarity. She puffed out a sharp sigh and pushed to her feet.

OLIVIA SLIPPED BETWEEN the sheets, groaning into the silence. She had stabbed at the cold remains of dinner during Ben's bath, then labored over an email to his teacher. Too polite, and the email might be ignored. Too firm, and she became the problem parent. Again. After the fifth revision, she had slammed the laptop shut. She needed rest, and coffee, before she gave it one final check in the morning.

The thermostat in the hall ticked, and from the attic, the air conditioner huffed to life, a cool waft skimming the hairs on her arm. Nights were the hardest. For all the attention Ben required, at least he provided a focus. Now, only the muffled dark and her aimless thoughts kept her company. She reached for her phone, squinting at the bright rectangle. Her thumb hovered over the message app, but she clicked the phone off and tossed it on the nightstand. Two months since she'd seen Jen. Two months since she'd held her ground during their last fight—no contact unless Jen was ready to be out. Since then, nothing.

She cursed herself again for succumbing at the reunion a year ago. A sympathetic conversation with an old classmate—she still mourning Sophia, Jen reeling from her divorce—had spiraled into surprising but passionate sex. Even now, after everything had fallen apart, that night hummed within her. Jen had been new to sex with a woman but uninhibited and keen.

Memories shuffled through Olivia's brain, like postcards from an impulsive vacation she still couldn't believe she'd taken. The soft slump of a breast. Silvered stretch marks undulating beneath her lips. Tongues, slick and urgent. These were the safest moments, well-worn and thumbed through. Others were still crisp, lightly fingered, too intense to bear much scrutiny. Sincere brown eyes inches away. Sun-streaked hair whispering down her stomach. An eager mouth bringing her to release, her orgasm a messy mix of relief and regret that opened the door for old needs to become new again. Sex had been the only thing they did consistently well, and now the need for it wouldn't abate.

She slid her left hand down her belly into soft curls, her middle finger passing over her clit in long strokes. It swelled beneath her touch as her right hand pinched her nipple, hard. Her brain resurrected the sensation of lips gliding up her thigh, a tongue lapping at tender places, wet spaces. Every pass stoked the slow fire until it spilled over in a rush, her hips twitching with each wave. But still she craved more, and she fumbled in her nightstand for the familiar tube.

Buzzing filled the room, which quickly muffled when she slipped the vibrator between her legs, her wetness smoothing its passage. In, out, in, out—the soft but relentless pistoning nudged her closer to the edge. She drove it faster, harder, needing it full and deep and long. Tension spooled low in her pelvis, winding tighter with each stroke, before finally snapping. She arched as a groan leaked from her clenched teeth.

Her hips fell to the bed, and she dropped the vibrator to the floor. As she rolled to face the empty space beside her, a snake of pressure coiled around her sternum. She brushed her wife's pillow in mute apology for bringing new memories and fresh needs to their bed. For two years after Sophia, she felt nothing. No real desire, no strong response. It had been easier, somehow, to float in a fog of grief and pretend this part of her was gone.

But since Jen, she couldn't retreat to that quiet absence, and she grieved again for what had been lost after Sophia's death. Passion that rattled her teeth and drove deep into her bones, followed by languorous sessions of touching and laughter in the relaxed haze of two bodies knowing the intimate cartography of every slope and curve.

She hugged Sophia's cold pillow, her mind muddy with grief and guilt and desire. She wanted to hate Jen for abandoning her to wallow in this half-life, her body reveling in the possibilities, her heart grasping at nothing. But she'd never been capable of hate. Jen was wading through her own pain, and neither of them had been strong enough to pull each other free. So she did what she had done for more than three years—huddle in the stark silence of her bedroom and wait for morning to arrive.

Chapter Two

FIREWORKS EXPLODED ON the television as a brassy march drilled into Olivia's brain. Stabbing the mute button, she turned from the raucous display, her mood more suited to the weak reflections blooming in the picture frames that crowded the fireplace mantel. She had sprawled on the couch after rolling Ben into bed, too exhausted by tonight's Fourth of July disaster to do anything but dangle her feet over the arm and wait for Arti, who had texted her arrival with vague hints about some drama.

A key rattled in the front door, and Arti shouldered her way through. She closed it softly before dropping her purse onto the coffee table. Glints of fireworks picked up the sleek blonde streaks in her dark hair. "This is still on?"

"It's a replay."

"How's Ben? I haven't seen him so upset in a while."

"He passed out the minute we got home. Tell your mom I'm sorry we left the picnic early."

"She doesn't care. She's just happy to see you two, for however long." Arti leaned her elbows on the back of a chair.

A gold pendant spilled from the fleshy confines of her cleavage. "Poor guy. I know he wanted this to be the year he saw the fireworks in person."

"I've never understood why he's so fixated on the Fourth when he hates everything about it—large crowds, flashing lights, loud noises. Makes me miss the days when all he wanted was to watch it on TV. On mute. Over and over."

"You're a good mom to let him try."

"Or a glutton for punishment."

"Aren't they the same?"

A soft laugh bubbled up, but it turned into a ragged sigh. "I really thought he'd make it. We talked it through, brought his favorite headphones and blanket, and then the first huge firework filled the sky and—"

"He lost his shit."

"I could see it on his face—the brightness registering, the size, how close it felt, and before he even burst into tears I thought, *I have made a terrible mistake.*"

"He begged to go. Pleaded. You have to let him take risks."

The finale erupted, and Olivia tilted her head to watch the explosions throw themselves against the screen in a thickening blizzard, their blinding frenzy in furious opposition to the muted sound. Was this Ben's world, rising churns of emotion without the words to express them? She groaned and rubbed her eyes. "I'm never sure what will be just challenging enough for him without being too much."

"Well, file this in the definitely-too-much category."

"You think?"

"Listen, you can't read the future. So stop beating yourself up." Arti shoved one of Olivia's overhanging feet to the side and perched on the couch arm. "Remember when we finally went to the fireworks by ourselves?"

"Summer before seventh grade."

"My folks only let me go because 'steady, responsible Olivia' would keep me in line. Plus, your amazing growth spurt made you so easy to find in crowds. It was the first time I truly felt American."

"Seriously?"

"Eating lukewarm hot dogs and drinking flat Coke with a blonde preteen? That's American, baby, all the way."

"Forty years of friendship, and you found something I didn't know."

Arti polished her long star-spangled nails on her dress. "I have untold depths."

"Depths? Sure. Untold? Never." She poked Arti's hip with her big toe. "What's up? I thought George had grand plans—the whole post-fireworks dinner and hotel."

"Oh, there was a post-fireworks dinner, followed by post-dinner fireworks. But this story requires booze." Arti grabbed Olivia's hand, hauled her to her feet, and led them to the kitchen. "What do you have?"

Olivia dug past the milk cartons and yogurt containers to find a lonely bottle tucked in the corner. "Champagne?"

"Really? Not that I'm complaining."

"Mom left it here last week. A friend gave it to her when her results came back benign, but she isn't a big fan of carbonation."

"Well, cheers to Alice!" Arti grabbed flutes from the cupboard, blew out the dust with two sharp bursts, and set them on the island. "I still can't believe a woman who never talks got a damn vocal cord polyp."

"My mom talks."

"Please. She was put on vocal rest for three weeks, and no one noticed." Arti plopped on a stool.

Olivia didn't bother protesting. Arti used exaggeration the way she used jewelry, for conspicuous and extravagant effect. Mom was quiet, but it was an expansive quiet, one that gave both of them room to breathe. Olivia settled on her own stool, then popped the cork. She filled Arti's glass to the brim. "What's the story? Late night stress texts are my thing, not yours."

"George proposed."

"What?" Champagne sloshed over the edge of her glass. She sucked the fizzy liquid from her thumb.

"I should've guessed. He'd been fidgety all night, and then dinner took forever. I mean, it was already late after the picnic, we hadn't had sex in a few weeks, and I wanted to get to the room and use the damn bed, but he begged to stay for dessert because the fucking cake had twenty layers or some nonsense. Turns out he'd had a ring put on top of a slice."

Olivia couldn't imagine what George had been thinking. Nothing was less likely to appeal to Arti. Or more likely to drive her away.

"My first thought when I saw it was, 'Fuck me!' And right behind it was, 'Getting chocolate out of a dense setting of diamonds? What a pain in the ass!'"

"How was the ring?"

Arti waggled her hand. "Sparkly, but not my taste. Expensive, though."

"It can't be easy choosing an engagement ring for a jewelry designer."

"You know what's not easy? Giving a ring to a woman who doesn't want it." Arti's breezy tone couldn't mask the disappointment shadowing her round face, more familiar to Olivia than her own reflection. Arti dunked her fingers in her glass and flicked champagne. "Stop looking at me like that."

"Like what?" Olivia wiped the damp splatter from her neck.

"Like you can pull my soul out through my damn chest! God, it kills me every time. All I ask for is monogamy and a little personal space. Why is marriage so important?"

"Maybe your company is more charming than you realize."

"Oh, I'm perfectly aware of how charming I am." Arti emptied her glass. "I told him no, of course."

"Where did this change come from?"

"He said he'd had an epiphany. He did want marriage. And kids."

"But you've never wanted kids. Or marriage. He knows this."

"Yet there he sat, with a ring half buried in chocolate, blathering on about 'even at our age' and fertility drugs and IVF and God knows what else."

"IVF? Really?"

"I'm fucking perimenopausal, for Christ's sake! I told George I didn't drag my financially solvent ass all the way to middle age just to bankrupt myself coaxing the last eggs from my shriveled ovaries for *kids I don't even want*!" Arti snatched the champagne and streamed it into her glass.

As the churning foam neared the rim, Olivia pried the bottle from her. "So this is when the post-dinner fireworks started."

"I reminded him I'd made my expectations for our relationship perfectly clear. He sputtered nonsense about assuming it was something women said so they didn't seem needy."

"Oh shit."

"I shoved the cake at him and said the next time a woman tells him something, he'd better assume she fucking means it!" Arti drained her flute, then sighed. "I shouldn't have dated a Greek guy."

"How did it end?"

"I dumped him. Actually, I let him dump me. If I dumped a guy from my parents' church, I wouldn't hear the end of it."

"I'm sorry. He was decent. And funny. I know you're going to miss him."

"Yeah, well, I guess we're both hard up for sex now."

Olivia scowled into her half-finished glass, her easy humor vanishing as the flip comment dug like a thumb on a bruise.

"C'mon. It can't be too soon for that joke. It's been three months!"

Irritation crawled under her skin. It shouldn't be too soon, but regret and loneliness continued to dog her. "I still hate how it ended. Walking out on Jen—"

"—was the right thing to do."

"Maybe this is all I should expect now, casual sex and casual affection."

"You're only saying this because Jen's the first person since—"

Olivia pushed away from the counter, away from Arti, from her words, from the truth. She turned and leaned on the sink, the cool porcelain soaking into her palms as she stared out the window into the backyard. Inky shadows lurked beneath the yellow haze of alley light. A neighbor launched bottle rockets, and their sound popped dully against the glass.

Arti's resolute reflection, distant and small from the other side of the island, came into focus on one pane. "I know you hate unresolved endings, but it's time to move on."

"You don't think she'll change her mind?" The question sounded pathetic the moment it left her lips.

"I think anyone who lets you go without a fight doesn't deserve you." Arti made a three-fingered throwing gesture, disgust plain on her face.

"I still can't believe we're even talking about this."

A broken tile, its crack like a frown, scowled at her from the backsplash. They'd delayed renovating the kitchen, waiting for more money, more time. Now she was both grateful and guilty they hadn't. Guilty because Sophia had spent hours planning a design she would never realize. Grateful because her wife's touch still permeated the room—the sticky drawer they had to rattle free, the crooked cabinet door that thwarted every cursing hinge adjustment, the chip in the island Sophia worried at with her thumb during conversations about Ben. Imagining a glossy magazine kitchen devoid of her wife's presence made Olivia's stomach turn.

Arti's reflection wavered, disappeared, reformed as she shifted off the stool to come stand beside Olivia, dark head hovering at her shoulder. "I'm sorry to push—"

"No, you're not."

"You're right, I'm not." She slipped Olivia's phone from her back pocket and opened the text messages. "Well, this is a long list. Me, Ben, Alice...Jen."

Arti didn't mention the final name, the one Olivia skimmed past because deleting it would carve away a piece of her heart. Sophia. Even now, Jen's name next to hers churned a horrible guilt. Sophia had meant everything to her, and to see her name the same size, in the same font as Jen's, impersonal, indistinguishable...

Arti tapped on Jen's name. Her gray text box sat on the left. *Did you get to your mom's okay? Excited for tonight. Feels like months, not weeks, since we've seen each other. Can't wait.*

Olivia's last reply sat in blue below. *Traffic was bad. Here now. Glad your boys are with their dad so we can have a longer night. Be there soon.*

"The surprise reservation was a mistake. It was too much."

"Because dinner out is the new edgy lesbian alternative to sex? Please. If she's fine trading secret hotel liaisons for months, a restaurant should be no big deal. It's not like she needed to buy a Pride shirt or swear a blood oath to lesbianism. Or bisexualism. Or any ism! Women have dinner together for all sorts of reasons."

"But her sons—"

"Are going to college soon. They're old enough to deal. Look, it's done with Jen. And you need to let it be done. Which is not your skill set, I know." Arti swiped Jen's name in the text list. The red delete box popped up.

"What are you doing?"

"You gave her the ultimatum—contact you when she's ready to date openly. You don't need to see her name every time you check your messages." She tapped the delete square, and Jen vanished.

It brought relief, not having the name there as a nagging reminder of her failure, but it stripped away a bit of hope as well. Olivia grabbed the phone and tossed it facedown on the counter.

"Why is this still eating at you?"

"Doesn't matter."

"Olivia, whatever words are stuck in there, spit them out."

She clenched her fingers around the edge of the counter. Hiding the truth from herself was one thing. Hiding it from Arti was almost impossible. "Until Jen said no, I didn't realize how much I needed her to say yes."

"You and your big tender heart." Arti nudged her with a gentle shoulder. "I knew this wasn't as casual as you said."

Guilt lodged in her chest like a stone. "What does it say about me that the first person I slept with after my wife died was the wrong person?"

"It says you're human, nothing more. At least you tried."

"Trying was my big mistake."

"Don't use Jen to shut down again." Arti grabbed her forearm and forced Olivia to face her. "It's okay that you wanted to feel something with a woman other than Sophia."

"You're very sure of yourself."

"It's easy when I'm always right." Arti patted her cheek and smiled. "I know this hurts now, but when it hurts less, you can try again."

"What if I don't want to?"

"You will. Trust me."

Chapter Three

ELLIE STEPPED FROM her office and made a quick left toward the noise rolling down the hall. She'd gotten turned around several times during her first week at The Therapy Center, but today, the swell of high voices led her straight to the large but crowded lobby, which sagged under the August humidity. Her new boss leaned on a column near the reception desk, and Ellie threaded her way over.

"We'll collect our boys in a minute. I'll introduce you to the parents as we go—a quick meet and greet for the first day." Rita grinned at the scrum. A harried father rushed through the doors, dragging a reluctant child by the sleeve. "Fall session is always a struggle. The kids aren't ready to be back. The parents are desperate to have them back. And no one is ready for the school-pickup-to-therapy scramble."

"Thanks again for putting me on your social group. It's nice to have the mix with individual sessions."

Rita waved off her words. "The job's not new for you, just the place. I would've given you your own if we hadn't already made those assignments."

The pale-blue shirts of TTC staff bobbed between pockets of families. Rogue toddlers pinballed everywhere. To the side, a lanky white woman, her skin dusted with freckles, listened intently to a boy with chestnut hair, who bounced as he recounted a story. Her eyes never left his, even as his gaze caromed around the room.

"Who's the brown-haired boy with the tall blonde?"

Rita turned in the direction of Ellie's nod. "Oh, he's one of ours, Ben."

"Isn't he too young?"

"He's eleven. Just on the small side. That's his mom, Olivia. Terrific parent. Very organized."

Ellie hid the smile creeping onto her face. It had taken less than a day to recognize Rita's favorite parents had one trait in common—organized.

"Sad story actually. Her wife died three years ago. Terrible car accident. Almost killed all three of them."

"Jesus."

"Yeah. Ben went off the rails for a bit. I'm hoping he's ready to tackle this group." Rita clapped her hands, then rubbed them briskly. "Let's go get our boys."

The crowd parted for Rita, Ellie trailing in her wake. She snuck glances at Olivia as they approached, Rita stopping every few feet to greet someone. Olivia was beautiful in an austere, angular way, and she held herself erect, not one of those women to stoop in apology for her height. Shaggy golden curls brushed her shoulders. That shimmer of blonde, and the placid face it framed, hovered at the edge of her attention each time Rita introduced her to another parent.

OLIVIA LEANED CLOSE to Ben's ear. "You got this."

He flinched, gnawing on a thumbnail. "You said that already. Twice!"

Her hand floated above his shoulder, ready for an encouraging pat. She pulled it back and shoved it in her pocket. This social group was important, and her nerves kept bleeding into her supportive attitude.

Rita plowed toward them, collecting rumpled, distracted boys like mismatched ducklings. Six feet tall and broad-shouldered, the director was unmissable. Although Olivia stood just an inch shorter, the imposing woman seemed to tower over her.

"Ben! I'm so happy to see you!" Rita's booming words cut through the din. Ben buried his chin in his chest, tapping an alternating rhythm with his feet. She squatted to catch his eye and lowered her voice. "I need help setting up chairs in room B. Will you organize a circle for eight? You remember the way?"

He darted off without a response, his thin scrap of a body disappearing into the crowd.

"He does love a task, our Ben." Rita sighed as she stood. "Olivia, I want you to meet Ellie Vasquez, our newest occupational therapist. We stole her from a city clinic. She's helping me in Ben's group. Ellie, this is Olivia Northman."

"Nice to meet you." Olivia extended her hand.

Ellie reached out at the same time, a dazzling smile streaking across her face. She was nearly Olivia's height, her riot of black curls wrestled into a thick ponytail. "You as well. I can't wait to work with your son."

"Have fun with these guys." She nodded at the mob of skinny arms and legs dragging half-shrugged backpacks behind them.

"I will." Ellie's dark eyes sparkled. A dimple appeared, like an apostrophe over the right corner of her mouth. Ellie held the handshake a beat longer before letting go. When she turned to follow the boys, Olivia noticed two pencils stuck at different angles into her ponytail. For some reason, it made her smile.

Chapter Four

ELLIE HISSED AS she scalded her thumb on the hot plate in the microwave. She grabbed a paper towel for protection and transferred the enchiladas to the opposite counter, then snagged a beer from the fridge. Her Skype screen chimed, and she spun to her laptop. These weekly talks with Claudia and Marisol were her lifeline now that their relationship straddled oceans. Sketchy internet and group texts were poor substitutes for two decades of inseparable friendship.

"Finally, the fucking connection works!" Marisol's voice punched through the speakers a second before her face popped into view. "Sorry about missing last week. Half a billion dollars for an oil rig in the Gulf of Mexico, and the satellite hookup is for shit. I could get serviced faster by a puta than our IT fuckups."

"Have you tested that theory?" Ellie pressed her tender thumb against the cool condensation on the bottle.

"Hell no! I'm too cheap to pay for it."

"Not to mention your sexy painter husband jumps your bones whenever you're on the mainland." Claudia, still in her fatigues, waved into the camera as she joined the chat.

"Artists are passionate. What can I say?"

"Why are you there on Friday night?" Ellie took a swig of beer and leaned on the counter.

"Maintenance issue. Don't ask. How's Germany, Claudia?"

"It's tense with all the refugees. Makes me appreciate what our parents went through."

"We were some of the lucky ones." She stabbed a forkful of enchiladas. The sharp heat and cilantro tang of Abuela's mole filled her mouth.

Marisol sketched a cross over her chest, then squinted. "What are you eating?"

"Abuela's enchiladas. My brother delivered a tray yesterday," she mumbled around another mouthful. "Traffic from the suburbs is a bitch. I barely made it."

"With her mole? Oh God, is it the verde or the negro? Ooh, or the rojo?" Claudia clasped her hands in front of her face. "I might cry. It's just as good, right? Tell me it's just as good."

"It's the verde. And it's perfect."

"I can't fucking believe you're eating in front of us." Marisol sank back in her seat and groaned.

Claudia's indignant squawk exploded from the speakers. "You live in freaking *Mexico*! What are you complaining about? You should see what the Germans do to Mexican food."

Ellie waved her fork at the screen. "You should come home for a visit if you want the real deal."

"Stop talking about enchiladas, or I'm seriously going to cry!" Claudia said. "How's the job going, Ellie?"

Footsteps drummed to a halt in the hallway. "Hang on." High voices hissed furiously, and a white envelope swished under her door. The flurry retreated.

"What was that?" Marisol asked as Ellie returned to the screen.

"The Hernandez sisters. The postal person mixes up our mail, and their mom sends them down. They race to see who can get to my door the fastest." She tossed the bill on the counter. "The job's good. My schedule filled up quick. And the bigger paycheck is nice."

"Can't fool us, chica. You're still wearing a guilty face every time you talk about it." Marisol's tsk-tsk made her sound just feet away. The illusion of closeness tugged at Ellie's heart.

"You gotta let this go," Claudia said. "There's nothing wrong with taking a new job."

"But the kids are so *white*."

"The kids need your help, no matter what color they are," Marisol said.

"But why can't they have a facility like this in the city? The space at TTC, the equipment, even the smoother insurance process, it's night and day." She knew when she took the job the demographics would change, but it still jarred, monochrome faces dominating the halls, the obvious jump in income and access.

"That's the 'burbs. What do the gringos call it? White flight?" Claudia fluttered a hand in the air. "When they fly away, the money flies with them."

"They would've cut your position at the other place sooner or later," Marisol said. "You left on your own terms. No guilt. No apologies."

"And no burning yourself out because you feel bad," Claudia said. "Once was enough."

"Basta ya! I give up. No more guilt."

"I'll pretend you mean that so we can talk about your love life. Any prospects?" The fuzzy connection couldn't hide Claudia's curious grin.

Ellie grabbed the beer and her laptop and moved out of the kitchen to the couch, balancing her computer on her legs as she settled in. "Define 'prospect.'" An ambulance squalled past her window, its dizzy pulse of blue-and-red light streaking the glass.

Marisol tapped on her camera, making the image jiggle. "You're hiding something."

"It's too early to be anything."

"Shit, you move fast! New job, new chica!" Marisol snapped her fingers. "Who is she?"

"One of the moms at TTC."

A month of Tuesdays had crawled by since she first met Olivia, but their interactions had grown increasingly scattered after the first week, when a coworker's early labor forced Ellie to cover a different group. It had been a mixed blessing. The separation from Ben lifted a professional concern, but it left her without an obvious reason to approach Olivia. She tossed in small talk when they happened to run into each other, but it never worked. Olivia seemed impervious to it.

"A mom? How old is she?" Claudia interrupted her musings.

"I'm not sure. Fortyish?"

"Rubia or pelirroja?"

"Rubia. Very blonde actually." She grinned. "Am I that predictable, guys?"

"Sí." They answered in unison.

Her laugh caught her mid-swallow, and she choked on her beer.

"Why the hell is she single if she has a kid?" Marisol had never met a direct question she wouldn't ask.

"Her wife died several years ago."

"Never date a viuda. Shitty mojo."

"What are you talking about?"

"Can't compete with a dead woman. She always wins."

"Someone older might be nice," Claudia countered.

Marisol snorted. "Says the woman with the geriatric husband."

"He's only five years older!" Claudia wagged a finger at the camera. "And he could bench-press your man."

"Chicas, chicas, both your husbands are pretty."

"Mine's prettier than hers." Marisol muttered the line.

Claudia rolled her eyes. "Can you date a parent?"

"I was looking for a subtle way to check, but then last week at work, I stumbled on old gossip. One of the therapists is married to a parent. The parent was already divorced—I didn't catch all the details—but they did meet at TTC."

"Was she the kid's therapist?" Claudia asked.

"No. And I'm not Ben's therapist. I was only the support staff for his group the first week. I've barely interacted with him since."

"What's wrong with this kid anyway?"

Ellie leaned into the screen, stabbing a finger at Marisol's face. "Did you just ask me what's *wrong* with him? Seriously?"

Claudia clapped a hand to her forehead. "Marisol!"

"Disculpa! Disculpa! You know what I meant. I'm an idiot! But if you date this woman, you're basically dating her son too. You want to take on something like that?"

"Like *that*? What the hell? He's a child, not a damn puppy!"

"Marisol's an ass, but she has point." Claudia jumped over Marisol's second wave of sputtered apologies. "You pour your heart into your work, cariño. I'm sure he's wonderful, but what if his needs ask too much of you?"

"What she said! I am an ass. Listen to Claudia."

"I know why you're worried, but it's not the same. I was a lot younger, it was my first job, and those kids—" She chopped the air with her hand, slicing through old regrets. "I've learned a lot since then."

"But she's still an older woman with a son. Does she have time to date?"

The clumsy restraint in Marisol's tone made Ellie smile. "You sound so white when you're trying to be tactful."

"I am sorry. I didn't mean—"

"Look, I haven't even asked her out. Let me see what's possible before you pile on with all the reasons this is a bad idea."

"I can't believe you have the hots for a suburban mamacita!" Marisol said.

"She lives in the city. She just drives to TTC for the services. It has the best autism clinic—"

Claudia clapped to interrupt them. "Who cares where she lives? Tell us what she's like. We've been too busy arguing to hear the good stuff."

The couch creaked beneath Ellie as she shifted deeper into the cushions. "She's quiet. Serious. Intelligent. She has a sly sense of humor, but she's hard on herself, I can tell, about Ben, meeting his needs. She's very intent."

"Intent?" Claudia asked.

"When she looks at me, nothing distracts her. I have all her attention."

"Is she tall or short? What color are her eyes? You stink at the details!"

"She's taller than me, surprisingly, but not by much. And her eyes..."

"You don't know what color her damn eyes are?" Marisol squinted at the screen.

"They're hazel! But the colors shift depending on the light. It's fascinating."

"God save us from white women with fascinating eyes." Marisol sighed, leaning back in her chair. "Well, she doesn't fit your usual type."

"What does that mean?"

"Cálmate." Marisol held up her hands in supplication. "I meant the quiet, intent part."

"Angie did rate higher on the bubbly scale," Claudia said.

Angie's energy, her restless, moving nature, felt so alive when they first started dating, but by the end, it exhausted her. Olivia's calm, steady confidence was the counterpoint to that. "I'm getting older, ladies. Maybe what I want is changing. I don't know. When I saw Olivia, there was just—"

"—something about her." They answered in unison again.

She laughed and heaved herself off the couch. "All right, enough of this, tontas. Tell me what's up with you two while I get more enchiladas."

Chapter Five

ELLIE SHOVED ONE arm into her coat, feeling for the other sleeve, which snagged on her office chair. Yanking herself free, she gave the chair a hard kick. It slammed back under her desk. Pencils rattled, and the photos pinned to her cubicle shivered. She blew a loud raspberry through her lips.

"Sounds like a tween-age sigh if I ever heard one." Shelley popped around the corner, cherry-red reading glasses perched low on her nose.

"Sorry, Shel. I didn't know you were there."

"No worries. Tough day?"

"More like tough evening." Ellie finally wrestled her other arm into her parka. "They're good girls, but..."

"So. Much. Crying."

"It's not just me?"

"God, no! When Rita assigned you the group after Jane's early labor, I about wept in relief. I raised four girls—middle school is the roughest."

"In my last job, I didn't have many girls. The sheer numbers amp up the emotions." She stuffed her phone in a pocket, then yanked on her zipper. It snagged halfway up.

"The holiday gauntlet doesn't help. They've barely worked off the Halloween candy buzz. Now Thanksgiving's coming to mess up their schedules. Hang in there."

"I will, thanks. See you tomorrow." Ellie fought with the zipper down the hall, past the receptionist, and right up to the main doors, which slid open as she approached. November was in a raw mood—low, brooding clouds and air so sharp it tasted of chrome. Just as the cold started to claw at her neck, the zipper took pity on her and released. She snugged it tight under her chin.

In the parking lot, at the edge of a pool of light, sat a faded Subaru, its left taillight edged in duct tape. Condensation billowed from the exhaust, blurring the solitary figure leaning against the driver's door. The person's frame was only an inky contour—dark slacks, black coat—but the bright tumble of hair... Ellie stuttered to a stop. Pulse high and tight in her throat, she watched Olivia tip her head back and stream a long, white sigh to the cloud-clotted sky.

The past few months had been more of the same: fly-by greetings and brief hallway chats, the sparse contact frustrating in its blandness. Now, alone among snow-dusted cars, Olivia was tantalizingly available. Ellie pivoted toward that forlorn figure and then away in an awkward half-turn before relenting to the pull of her heart.

"Olivia?" she called out as she approached.

Olivia twitched, hunching deeper into her coat.

"Sorry. Didn't mean to surprise you."

"It's fine. How are you?"

"I'm good, thanks. You?" She stood opposite Olivia in an empty parking space. A yellow line slashed between their boots. The overhead light daubed thick shadows on Olivia's sharp features, but it didn't diminish her lean beauty, or dull her hazel eyes, glimmering with so many colors Ellie couldn't tease them all out.

Olivia shrugged, her coat rustling with the movement. "I'm fine." Her tight expression said otherwise.

"Where's Ben?"

"Checking in with the psychologist. There was an incident during group. He kicked a chair across the room. Not at anyone, thank goodness, but still..."

"I'm sorry. He must have been really frustrated."

Olivia dragged a hand over her face. The movement wiped fading tear tracks from her skin, but it didn't erase the vulnerability beneath. This was the danger Ellie had sensed initially when she almost turned away. Olivia's emotions hovered near the surface, her self-effacing manner ruffled, messy in a way that was transfixing. Here was the woman she wanted to know, truly available for the first time, and she had no plan for what to do.

"So why are you standing outside a running car?"

"I like the fresh air." Olivia rapped the window with a knuckle. "I'm warming it up for Ben. He hates the cold."

The safe route beckoned—benign sympathy, a wave, and then a walk to her car. But the strain in Olivia's demeanor was too much. "You seem stressed, if you don't mind me saying. What's going on?"

"It's nothing."

Ellie's snort of disbelief sent a white puff into the air.

"Nothing new anyway."

"C'mon." In her best perky voice, she parroted the new promotional slogan plastered around the lobby. "Remember, TTC's a space for kids *and* parents!"

A half-smile tugged at Olivia's lips. "Ben's showing an interest in more group activities, which is great, but he doesn't always have the tools to handle them. This past

Sunday..." She shook her head. A thick curl spilled loose from behind her ear.

"What happened?" Ellie's fingers itched to tuck the blonde spiral back.

"There was a birthday party at a kids' arcade. He had a huge meltdown, tokens everywhere."

"Those places can be rough. Talk about overstimulating."

"I usually avoid them, but Ben *never* gets asked to parties. You should've seen his face when he showed me the invitation." Distress rippled Olivia's features, revealing again the woman beneath the polite tranquility. "Anyway, I carried him out screaming while the entire place watched. And now tonight with the chair. It usually rolls off my back, but there are moments I—"

When Olivia didn't continue, Ellie drew her foot along the line separating them, its crisp edge a warning. But this quiet intimacy she had stumbled upon was impossible to ignore. She pushed a boot across and nudged Olivia's toe. "Tell me, please?"

"Sometimes I wish...that it wasn't this hard. For him. Or for me." Olivia's low admission wrenched itself free.

Ellie couldn't let the pained words float there, isolated, in the space between them. Leaning forward, she tugged on Olivia's sleeve. "His needs can ask a lot of you, especially alone. It's okay to crack under the strain."

"No cracking allowed. It's on the first page of the autism parent manual."

"Your copy's out-of-date. I'll get you a new one."

Olivia tucked her wayward hair behind her ear, and then her hands dropped, twisting together. "Thanks." Her melancholy smile snagged hooks into Ellie's heart.

Her other foot scuffed the line as she stepped forward. She clasped one of Olivia's hands—their first contact since their introductory shake several months ago—and a fuse lit, racing up her arm to explode in her chest. Her breath sharpened. Clouds from their mouths mingled as their eyes met. "Are you always this hard on yourself?"

"Wait until you get to know me better."

"I'd like that, getting to know you better." She cupped Olivia's cheek, her thumb brushing soft, cool skin—

Olivia drew away gently, confusion coloring her features. Ellie's hand hung in the air.

"I'm sorry. I'm so sorry. I can't believe—" She snatched it back. Embarrassment boiled up her neck. "I didn't mean— good night."

She spun on her heel, winding through the last of the parked cars. Numb fingers fumbled with the fob before the lock finally clicked. Yanking open the door, she threw herself into the driver's seat. *Fuck, fuck, fuck!* She pounded a fist on the steering wheel. All her patience, all the waiting for the perfect moment, wasted because she couldn't stop herself when she saw the pain scrawled on Olivia's face. She stabbed the key in the ignition. The car chugged to life, and she sat while it idled, mind scrambling for the words she would need the next time she saw Olivia.

Chapter Six

SHOULDERS HUNCHED, BEN followed his OT out of the lobby, and Olivia allowed herself a slow, leaking sigh. He had been stuck at a sullen simmer since Tuesday night. If the "ch" in chair even crossed her lips, he scowled. After cycling through her usual tactics—encouraging, sympathetic, stern—she was stuck waiting him out.

She stalked to a deserted corner, tossed her backpack on a seat, and sank beside it. Her phone chirped. Tapping the work email, she skimmed the words while her mind wandered to Ellie. Their brief contact had consumed her. In the parking lot, lost in her self-recrimination, she was startled enough to draw back, but the echo of Ellie's fingers clung stubbornly to her cheek.

Did you get a picture yet? Arti's text popped up.

She stabbed at the phone with her thumbs. *I'm not sneaking a picture!*

I need to see what this woman looks like!!!

Not even sure I'll run into her.

No way that woman doesn't seek you out after hitting on you.

She didn't hit on me. Go away!

She scowled at Arti's characterization. It cheapened the moment. Hitting on someone was a deliberate act, but Ellie's hand on her face felt spontaneous, and her earnest admission was even more intimate than the touch.

"Olivia?"

The phone almost slipped from her hand when Ellie manifested in front of her. She chose to blame her accelerating pulse on surprise and not proximity. Ellie was the kind of woman anyone would notice—gregarious and confident, beautiful in a relaxed, uncalculated fashion—but Tuesday's moment amplified those qualities from the abstract to the personal in a way that glued Olivia's tongue to her mouth.

"Mind if I sit?"

Olivia moved her bag off the chair, and Ellie perched on the edge. When their knees brushed, Ellie jerked her leg to the side as if any contact might be unwelcome.

"I'm sorry about Tuesday night. It was completely inappropriate to touch you. Seeing you hurting...it was instinct, reaching out. I would hate it if anything I did made you uncomfortable at TTC. I'm so, so sorry."

The apology was sincere—Ellie practically vibrated with regret—but she didn't disavow any interest. Her lack of a denial lit a small flame Olivia tried to stamp out.

"It's all right, don't worry."

"You're sure?"

"Yes. Thanks for the apology though."

"Thank goodness. I haven't stopped thinking about you, and I wanted a chance to clear the air."

"You've been thinking about me?" Olivia didn't fight a smile.

"I meant thinking about what happened with you. I'm sorry. I didn't want this anywhere near Ben or TTC."

Ellie's flummoxed distress was so keen it tempted Olivia to reach out in comfort. It would be simple to end it here. A final lighthearted assurance, a quick thanks-but-no-thanks, and they could move on. The receptionist's phone trilled from the other end of the lobby, triggering a wail from a nearby stroller. Olivia grabbed her bag. "Let's step outside."

The hollow thump-thump of car doors closing bracketed the silence as they hid from the wind in her car. She turned toward Ellie. Through the window, she could see the light pole they had stood under two days ago. A giddy impulse took hold to bring Ellie's hand to her face, to reenact the moment and not pull away. Ellie followed her stare. Pink stained her cheeks.

"Honestly, I'm not upset." She had planned an easy excuse about not being ready to date, but in these close confines, Ellie's warm presence overwhelmed her. The tiniest details captured her attention—the way Ellie worried at her lip with the edge of her tooth, the curl escaping her ponytail, the mole below her left ear. "Tell me what you're thinking."

Ellie's mouth opened, then closed. Her sudden speechlessness was endearing.

"Pretend Tuesday didn't happen. What would you say?"

Ellie rubbed her palms on her thighs, the scrape of skin against fabric mingling with the muffled wind outside. She lifted her eyes. Hope and nervousness merged into one disarming expression. "I want to ask you out. On a date. Properly. I was waiting until...I guess until I could find a way to not have this conversation at TTC." Her hands lifted in a helpless gesture. "Which obviously didn't work."

"Waiting since when?"

More pink bloomed across Ellie's cheeks, and she buried her face in her hands. "Since the first day I saw you." The words leaked between her palms.

Delight and consternation danced in Olivia's chest. This woman had waited months to ask *her* on a date? She tugged Ellie's hands down. "Really?"

"It wasn't fair to Ben to approach you here. This is his space. If I'd met you at a bar, the gym, anywhere else, I would've said something sooner."

"I'm flattered you liked me enough to be so patient." She *was* flattered, and touched Ben had been so much in Ellie's thoughts. Then Jen's stunned, tear-streaked face came into focus. She rubbed her eyes to dispel the image.

"It's fine if you need time. This happened faster than I planned."

"It's not that." Three more days or three more weeks wouldn't change the fact that Ellie's touch had cracked open a door, one she hadn't been able to close again. "Getting time alone..."

"I can do whatever's easiest. Maybe a quick coffee while he's in therapy, or a lunch date during school, or—"

"You've been thinking about this." Olivia smiled as Ellie's natural enthusiasm rebounded.

"A little."

"Can I ask how old you are?" Their age difference hadn't registered before, but she wondered if Ellie had considered it.

"Thirty-five."

"The big age gap doesn't bother you?"

"Five or six years is nothing."

"You made my week! I just turned forty-five."

Surprise splashed across Ellie's face, and insecurity pricked at Olivia. She had half hoped to scare Ellie with her age, so why was she upset it might have worked?

"I don't care. At all." Ellie grabbed her wrist. "You're breathtaking."

Olivia blushed at the compliment and the spark of contact. She had built a wall of objections to protect herself from what could go wrong, but in this moment, she couldn't stop thinking about what could go right. Ellie's fingers, soft on her pulse, supplied all the force needed to collapse her carefully constructed arguments. "Okay, let's have a date."

"Really?" Ellie squeezed her wrist harder. "What do you want to do? Pick whatever's easiest."

All she wanted was quiet conversation, enough to see beyond the fizzing attraction that crackled along her skin every time Ellie touched her. "How about you come over on Saturday after Ben's bedtime? We'll need to hang out on the front porch so he doesn't hear us and wake up. He'd be confused if he found you in the house."

Ellie's exultant dimple popped for the first time. "Yes! What time?"

"Nine-thirty? I'll text you the address."

They exchanged numbers, and Ellie touched her knee. "I'm sorry about how this all came up. I never wanted to interfere with Ben's world here at TTC. Thanks for being so understanding."

"Thanks for being considerate of Ben."

"He's a great kid. You're an amazing parent."

Olivia found herself blushing for the second time.

"You're also the kind of person who doesn't give herself enough credit." Ellie's lips curled into a smile she hadn't seen before, soft and tender, the kind that whispered secrets across pillows and shimmered beneath a fluttering sheet. Olivia's heart surged against her ribs, desperate to embrace the promise in that smile.

Ellie stepped out of the car, a gust of cold rushing to fill her spot. The rearview mirror framed her as she broke into a quick jog to escape the wind. When the sliding doors opened, she spun around, waved, and then did a small skip into the lobby. Olivia stayed fixed on the mirror even after the doors closed, resting her hand on the passenger seat to catch the last of Ellie's warmth.

Chapter Seven

OLIVIA CROSSED HER ankles and sank deeper into the ragged wicker chair. Orange light from the heat lamps dusted the front porch, and warmth trickled down her hair and over her shoulders to pool in her lap. But the cold wouldn't be tamed completely. It seeped from the concrete to soak her booted feet. She hoped Ellie wouldn't mind. Weather had never been an issue for her or Sophia. Fall winds, spring deluges, the whip-crack of a summer storm— through it all, they filled this brick refuge with dreams and confessions and laughter and pain. The porch had seemed perfect when she suggested it, private and quiet, but now it roared with the undertow of memories.

She picked at a broken piece of wicker, twisting the stiff strand until it snapped. A dime-sized hole glared at her from the arm. Snorting, she flung the scrap over the wall. She'd ridden an emotional seesaw all day, dreading Ellie's arrival one minute, vibrating with anticipation the next. More than once, her thumb tapped out an apologetic cancellation text, then deleted it. A few moments from this week held her steady—Ellie's warm hand on her cheek, the quirk of a dimple, fingers light on her wrist. Tiny gestures with exponential promise.

A car door thumped, followed by the chirp of a door lock. Footsteps crunched on rock salt. The low brick wall blocked her view, but as the crackling steps slowed, she pushed out of her seat. Ellie's head appeared, breath filling the air around her beaming face. It was the kind of smile that couldn't be refused, and Olivia grinned despite her nerves.

"I brought hot toddies!" Ellie held up a thermos and two mugs as she climbed the stairs. "If you don't drink, there's hot chocolate in the car."

"A toddy's perfect." Fumbling for a greeting without the clear rules of TTC, she settled for brushing a light kiss on Ellie's cheek. Her lips barely touched skin—it was more an exchange of heat in passing—but her body hummed in response. Inky curls spilled over Ellie's coat collar, trailing the faint scent of coconut. A furious hissing erupted from Olivia's pocket, and they both started.

"Sorry." She set the monitor on the window ledge. It spat static once more, then quieted.

"You still use one?"

"In case of a nightmare. He gets disoriented."

White clouds streamed languidly from Ellie's mouth, where a scar marred the full curve of her lower lip. It was a faint pucker against the dark pink swell, but it held a story, and suddenly Olivia wanted to learn it, to trace the narrative of Ellie's skin. The strength of the impulse surprised her, given how new this all was, but not the source. Touch had always been her most cherished language. But here, warded in their jackets and boots and gloves, it was denied her. A twisting started in her chest. It screwed tighter with each breath, apprehension battling eagerness. How could she want to crush Ellie to her and push her away in the same moment?

"If I'm intruding with Ben, or..." Ellie glanced at the monitor.

"You're not." Olivia realized how she must look, feet set a bit too wide, screening off the sitting area. She took the thermos and mugs and set them on the side table. "Come sit down."

Ellie hesitated a beat, her expression mild but curious, then took a seat. "How's Ben?"

"Better, thanks." Olivia sat next to her, one knee almost brushing Ellie's long leg. "The school concert was yesterday. He usually watches with me in the audience because being onstage is too scary, but this year, he was asked to turn sheet music pages. The pianist thought having his back to the crowd might help."

"And it did?"

"Yep. He pumped a stress ball with his free hand like he was trying to inflate a tire, but he pushed through the nerves."

"That's terrific! You must have been proud." Ellie removed her gloves and stuffed them in her pocket, then grabbed the thermos.

"So proud. And relieved. He's riding this wave of motivation for new experiences, but the results resemble an EKG. He needs the highs to get him through the lows."

"I imagine you both do." Giving the thermos a brisk shake, Ellie filled the mugs. The sharp tang of lemon wafted on the steam.

"The tough part is when I see a low point coming. Should I step in? Will he learn more if he handles it on his own? It's a tricky balance, validating who he is while still acknowledging the world won't change for him."

"He has to adjust, but you want him to do it as authentically as he can."

"Authentically is the right word. He has his own way of seeing things." Olivia lifted the mug to her lips, blew across the surface, and took a cautious sip. The toddy traced a river of warmth down her throat. "We went out for hamburgers the other day, and I handed him the noise-canceling headphones because the restaurant blares their music, and he said, 'Food places shouldn't have music. Food is quiet fun. Music is loud fun. They don't go together.' And you know, I think he's right."

"I'm amazed by the kids I work with, the stuff they pick up on." Ellie cradled her own drink and shook her head. "We miss so much, being neurotypical."

"I wish everyone saw it your way." The rumble of an approaching plane had been building, and its melancholy doppler finally peaked as it passed low, headed for O'Hare. Olivia waited for it to recede, leaving space for her words again. "Some days, I think if I can just find the right plan, I can carve out a corner of the world where he'll be happy and understood. One little corner is all he needs."

"It's not about you carving out space. It's about giving him the tools to do it himself." Ellie winced over her mug. "Sorry. I switched into professional mode."

"Don't worry about it. Happens to me too. And I'm sorry to go on about him." Arti's warning echoed: *Do not talk about Ben all night. At least pretend you have something else you do with your time.*

"You're not 'going on.' You're passionate about seeing him happy. What is your professional mode anyway?"

"I'm an RN—a nurse manager, these days. Would you like me to look at your unusual rash or lecture you about the importance of vaccines?"

"If I have an unusual rash, maybe I need a lecture." Ellie quirked a wicked grin, and Olivia wondered how many alluring smiles she had. "Why the switch to management?"

"I needed more regular hours." The reason for that hung in the air, but Ellie didn't take the bait.

"So when you're not anticipating and planning and scheduling for Ben, you're doing the same for work."

"Pretty much." Olivia stretched her legs and tapped Ellie's boot with her own. "How are you with the cold?"

"I'm fine. The heat lamps make a big difference."

"Sophia surprised me with them because we loved chatting here after Ben went to sleep." Their casual energy stuttered. She hadn't meant for Sophia's name to even cross her lips tonight. "Sorry, I shouldn't have mentioned her."

"Talk about her whenever you want, especially here of all places." Ellie's furrow of sympathy was far too familiar, but somehow, on her face, it was easier to take. "I'm sorry about what happened. Rita told me there was an accident."

"I assumed you'd heard. We were quite the story around TTC at the time."

"She said the three of you…"

"I was driving. The drunk driver hit us head-on." The flat, numb sentences were less than Ellie deserved, but when Olivia tried to push more words out, they wouldn't come. Talking about Ben, about the present, flowed easily enough, but the past strangled her.

"Jesus. Were you and Ben okay?" Ellie flushed. "I mean, I know your wife—I'm sorry, that was—"

"Ben and I were pretty banged up, but it all healed eventually."

"I'm—" Ellie's dark brows pinched together. "Sorry feels like such a useless word right now."

"There aren't many useful words for this kind of thing. Trust me, I've heard them all." She looked away as Ellie's compassion finally pierced too deep. The house across the street peered at them through a lattice of scaffolding, a half-ruined face waiting to be made whole.

Ellie followed her gaze. "That's a big job."

"It's nice because they could've torn down and built new, but the work is taking longer than expected."

"Restorations are tricky. There's always a hidden problem or two. But it'll be worth it, in the end." Ellie sipped from her mug, then balanced it on her chair arm. "I'm sorry about bringing up the accident. I wanted you to know that I knew."

"No, it's okay. I'm sorry for being so..." She waggled her hand back and forth.

"Is it me, or have we each apologized ten times already?" Ellie's wry grin took the sting out of the question. The knot cinching Olivia's sternum loosened. "Can I ask two things, and then we'll move on to whatever people usually talk about on a first date?"

"Sure."

"How long were you and Sophia together?"

"Almost twenty years." Olivia twirled an invisible wedding ring with her right hand. When she caught Ellie watching, she picked up her mug, letting the heat soak into her cupped palms. After the accident, she'd stopped wearing the ring, its weight too much to bear, but her fingers still sought it out. "Second question?"

"Did one of you carry, or is Ben adopted?"

"Sophia carried. Which is why he's Ben Northman. Whoever carried, the other one got the last name. We used a sperm donor who's open to contact when he turns eighteen."

"Was it a hard decision—known versus anonymous?"

"Nope. Half his genes come from the donor. Why would we deny him his own history before he's even born? It's his decision to make." She held out her cup when Ellie offered a refill. "This toddy is delicious. Different, somehow."

"I used Calvados instead of whiskey. I tended bar during grad school, and I still enjoy mixing drinks."

"What kind of bar?"

"This fratty sports bar in River North and a gay bar in Boystown."

"No lesbian bar?" It was easy to picture Ellie behind a set of taps, charming a line of interested women.

"Not enough turnover. Lesbians love chitchat, so once they camp out on a stool, you're stuck with them for the night."

"Maybe they camp out because they can't resist the beautiful bartender."

Ellie's blush glowed in the light from the heat lamps. Her shy smile didn't highlight her dimple, but it was no less charming.

Olivia nudged her with the toe of her boot. "One compliment and you're all tongue-tied?"

Ellie fumbled her mug, sloshing liquid on her coat. "Jesus, you're distracting." She clapped a hand over her mouth. "I can't believe I said that out loud! This isn't how I imagined this going."

"How did you imagine it?"

"I was much suaver in my head."

"Aren't we all?" It was nice not being alone in her nervousness. "Can I ask you a personal question?"

"Anything to help me string a sentence together."

"How do you identify? Sexually, I mean?"

"Why?" Ellie's smile twitched.

"Sophia was bisexual, so I never assume."

Ellie opened her mouth, then closed it, cocking her head. "I figured, considering how long you were together...I should know better. Bisexuals get erased enough as it is."

"It's okay. Lots of people make the same assumption." The surface of her drink rippled as she shifted in the chair. "I didn't get a read on you, at TTC. I had no idea you were interested until the parking lot."

"I'm glad I kept it under wraps. Each time we talked, I worried the attraction must be all over my face."

"You were extremely professional. So professional, in fact, I thought you might be, I don't know, not straight, exactly, but... What do they call it now, questioning?" After Jen, she had to be sure where Ellie stood.

Ellie choked on her toddy. "God, no, I haven't been questioning since I was five! For the record, I'm a lesbian. Are you bi?"

"No, but one hetero moment hides in my past."

Ellie's brown eyes glinted with curiosity. "Do I get to hear the story?"

"It was a one-off college thing with a friend. Very boring." She hadn't meant to discuss herself again. Ellie pulled words from her before she could stop them. "Have you been married?"

"No." Ellie rested her elbows on her knees, her bright expression shifting to bemused confusion. "Why?"

"Sorry, that was clumsy. I haven't been on an actual date since college. We were all so young then. Nobody had a life yet to ask about."

"Since I know a little of your history, you'd like to know some of mine?" Ellie jostled her from her embarrassment with a playful bump of her knee. "I've dated several women, but I've only been serious once. We were together four years."

"Recently?"

"It ended six years ago. Wow, it's weird to say that. I haven't added it up in a while."

"What happened?"

"You want to hear about my biggest relationship failure right out of the gate?" Ellie leaned back in her chair and unzipped her parka at the neck. "Quite the screening process you've got there."

Heat crawled up Olivia's chest. She couldn't find a flow in this conversation when curiosity and caution wrestled for control of her tongue.

"It's okay. I was teasing. Mostly." Ellie winked and took a long drink from her mug, but the gesture, and the humor behind it, felt forced. For a woman as open as she was, any deflection glowed like neon. "When we met, I was a grad student. Jill was in her first year of medical school."

"Tough time for a new relationship."

"The schedules were hard, but we understood. When I got a job, we moved in together. The plan was to match in Chicago for residency, but then she was accepted to Stanford."

"Why apply there?"

"Her mom was a Stanford alum, and her dad went to Northwestern, so it was expected she'd apply to both. I knew Stanford was her dream school, but she played it cool, like they'd never accept her." Ellie's mobile features stilled, a rueful nostalgia papering over a faded pain. "How do you tell someone you love not to pursue their dream?"

"You don't." Olivia brushed her fingers against the back of Ellie's hand. She'd made a similar choice once. That kind of sacrifice—ending a relationship *for* someone, not *because* of someone—left a mark.

"There were Chicago offers as well, at Northwestern, U of C, but Stanford was it for her."

"You didn't want to tag along?"

"I thought about it for weeks, torturing myself. I love Chicago. My family's here, friends, and I didn't want to bail on my first job so early. I suggested long distance, to give myself time to establish a good work history, but she turned me down flat, said the demands of residency were hard enough."

Headlights spilled a bright wash down the street as a car searched for a parking spot, and Ellie tracked its progress. "If you'd asked me six months before we broke up, I would've said I was certain we were both committed. To be wrong about that...you don't just question the relationship, you question your own judgment, your ability to read people." The mug trembled, and Olivia leaned her knee into Ellie's in a silent show of support. "I was too attached to making it work, so when she turned me down cold on the long-distance thing, I didn't handle it well."

"I wouldn't peg you as the type to lose your cool."

Ellie set her mug on the table and shoved her hands in her pockets. "Jill saw this as a painful but rational conversation, but I wanted to fight for her, for the relationship. When I realized she didn't feel the same... I know 'emotional Latina' and 'repressed WASP' are stereotypes, but honestly, in the moment, I felt the cultural dissonance so strongly. How could she be this controlled while I was coming apart?"

Recognition welled in Olivia. "I understand. Sophia was Italian. Her family held nothing back. My parents were extremely reserved, so that volatile energy was another world. For good and bad."

"You two had intense moments?"

"Not many, fortunately. I can count on one hand the truly hurtful things I ever said to her. I haven't forgiven myself for any of them." She took a large swallow of her drink. Most of the warmth came from the Calvados now, not the tea. She swerved from Sophia again. "So you're a Chicago lifer?"

"Just about. My family came from Mexico when I was two, piling into the top floor of a three-flat my cousin owned. My brothers were dumped into school as soon as we arrived."

"How many?"

Ellie held up four fingers. "All older. Alberto and I are closest, both in age and personality. He's forty-one."

"Is Ellie a Mexican name?"

"My given name is Isabella, but only my family uses it."

"Isabella." She savored the way the *l* rolled off her tongue. "It's gorgeous, just like you." Ellie's self-conscious blush made her breath hitch. "So why the nickname?"

"Kids at school started it because Isabella was a mouthful, and I liked it. It made me feel like an American, not an immigrant most people thought was illegal."

"You got a lot of that?"

"Not as much once my accent faded."

Olivia guessed Ellie's casual shrug glossed over a history of slurs and snide remarks, and her fingers curled into a fist.

"That's a serious expression," Ellie said.

"What?"

"Your face—it's like you wanted to punch someone."

Olivia forced a smile and unclenched her fist. "Old memories. Arti, my best friend, was in kindergarten when her family moved here from Greece. She got so much shit, not knowing English. I hate thinking of you in that situation."

"You were Arti's ally?"

Now it was Olivia's turn to shrug.

"With your protective streak, I bet you're fun at Ben's IEP meetings."

A bitter laugh escaped before she could catch it. "The fucking IEP. What is it with acronyms and special education? IEP, FBA, BIP, RTI. Some schools forget there's an actual kid buried under those letters."

"Ben's school?"

"His previous one, yes, but he's in a better spot now. I'll spare you the ancient spleen venting." She inhaled through her nose and let it out in a long breath. "Tell me about your family. Are you tight-knit?"

"I'm closest to my abuela, my dad's mother. She came to live with us when Abuelo died. I was seven." Ellie's grin said everything about their relationship. "She's the most positive person I know."

"That means something, coming from you."

Ellie pinked again, and she laughed. "How many times are you going to make me blush tonight?"

"How long can you stay?" A charged silence vibrated between them.

"Now see, that was suave." Ellie's words were light, but there was a hiccup to her delivery, as if she'd pivoted from a different response.

Olivia shrugged, embarrassed by her smooth line, which had popped out before she could think about it.

"Okay, your turn." Ellie slapped the arms of her chair. "Close family?"

"Arti and I have been best friends since we were five, so she might as well be family. I wouldn't have made it through the last few years without her."

"What's Arti short for? I've only known Indian women with that name."

"Artemis, but she got sick of the Greek goddess jokes in school and shortened it. It's not traditional, and it irritates her mother, which pretty much sums up Arti."

Ellie's laugh burst into the night. She laughed so easily, like it hovered right below the surface, waiting for its chance. "What about your parents?"

"It's just my mom now. She's amazing with Ben, but we don't share personal details."

"Is it the gay thing?" Ellie's grin softened into concern.

"Oh no, that's fine." She stacked her empty mug inside Ellie's. "We're not a chatty bunch, I guess. The first time I brought Sophia home, they learned more about me than during all of college."

"She ratted you out?"

"No, but my parents are quiet, and Sophia got nervous they didn't like her, so she kept talking and talking to fill the silence. My dad was in awe the whole evening." She cut herself off, exasperated at how Sophia kept sneaking into their conversation.

"What happened to your dad?"

"He died six months before the accident. We knew it was coming though. Cancer." An empty sadness overtook her, the way it often did when she thought of her father. She'd been steadily picking her way across the landscape of his absence when Sophia's death obliterated everything. With no path to follow, she was forced to simply let him go.

"You lost your dad, then you lost your wife?" The chair creaked as Ellie shifted forward, resting a hand on her leg.

"It was a bad run." Olivia's shrug was quick, rote, a reflexive response to a line of sorrys trailing behind her to infinity. "After the accident, Mom rented a condo nearby so she could help out with Ben and not have to drive back and forth every day. But now things have settled, she's back full-time where I grew up, outside of Joliet. It would be too isolating for her in Chicago, stuck with me and Ben."

"No other family?"

"Sophia's family lives in the suburbs—her mother and sister. But as far as my family, Mom's it. I'm an only child."

"It must be hard, doing so much on your own."

Olivia chewed on the corner of her mouth. Part of her ached to talk about the strain and loneliness, to unspool her tightly wound pain. Instead, she reached out and took the hand on her leg. "I'm glad you came."

A softness smoothed Ellie's features, and her smile burrowed into Olivia, curling around her heart. "Me too. I'm relieved I didn't blow it the other night. I got caught up in the moment."

She traced the lines in Ellie's palm. "You weren't the only one caught up."

"What do you mean?"

"I thought about your hand on my cheek the entire drive home."

Boots scraped, and Ellie shifted out of her chair to kneel between her legs. That solid presence anchored Olivia even as her heart stuttered in her chest. When warm palms cradled her face, she sank into the gentle comfort and closed her eyes. Calvados and honey hung on their shared, shallow breaths. Gentle lips brushed hers, hesitant at first, then deepening into an exquisite, tender pressure that squeezed the air from Ellie's lungs.

Ellie was the one to break the kiss, stroking Olivia's cheeks with her thumbs and touching their foreheads together. "I've been waiting to do that since the day I met you."

Pulse thrumming, Olivia parted her lips for another kiss when a loud snore erupted from the monitor. Both of them jumped. A jittery laugh bubbled out of Ellie.

"I'll have to roll him off his back, or it will never stop." Another snore rumbled from the speaker. When Olivia reached to mute it, Ellie's palms slipped from her face, and cool air bit her cheeks. She ached to feel that caress again.

"I guess that's my cue." Ellie sank onto her heels, and her hands landed on Olivia's thighs, the warmth bleeding through her jeans. "Can we do this again?"

"You're okay, meeting here for now?"

"Absolutely." Ellie squeezed her legs. The pressure sent a charge through Olivia, one she tried to ignore.

"I can't promise more than this. Moving too fast can have consequences."

"I ask for nothing but time to work my charms on you." Ellie stood and spread her arms wide. "See? No hidden agenda."

Olivia chuckled, standing as well. "Thanks for the toddy. It was delicious." She stopped, absorbed by Ellie's twinkling brown eyes nearly level with her own. "Your height... It's funny to look straight at you and not down."

Ellie's flirty smile sent the floor sliding sideways. "Could have its advantages. Text you soon?"

Olivia nodded, and Ellie grabbed her thermos and mugs before hopping down the stairs. She turned and smiled once more, throwing her dimple back up the steps before crossing the street to her car. Olivia almost called out, wanting her to return, to stay longer, but the words lodged in her throat.

Ellie waved through her window as she pulled away. Olivia returned the gesture and then, with shaky fingers, traced her lips, still tingling with the echo of their kiss. She sank to the top step. The empty silence pressed heavy against her shoulders, and she buried her face in her hands while her breath collected around her in the cold.

Chapter Eight

ELLIE'S BOOT BROKE through the crusted ridge of snow separating her parked car from the sidewalk, and she sank up to her knee. A chuckled curse puffed from her lips. Yanking her foot free, she stumbled into a giant inflatable Santa wearing a Pride scarf. She grinned and patted his belly. Next door, a neon Feliz Navidad sign glowed, and past Olivia's bungalow, a Greek flag rippled over an elaborate nativity scene. She loved the street's hodgepodge decorations; it was as if the United Nations had crashed the set of a Capra movie. Even the wind tasted like the holidays, the cinder smudge of woodsmoke in the back of her throat, cold air glassy on her tongue.

Only a simple green wreath marked Olivia's front door, but scalloped snow carved its own whimsy along the dark brown brick and beige gutters. She stomped up the stairs, knocking white clumps from her boots. The porch had started as a practical necessity, but now, several dates in, she embraced its spare yet cozy quality. The last time she'd seen a brick wall over a date's shoulder, it had been splashed with a lurid mural, the centerpiece of a restaurant flaunting a trendy vibe. Olivia's brick had no vibe. It barely had mortar in a few weathered spots. But it was the perfect backdrop for the measured, thoughtful conversations they shared.

Ellie had never been in a relationship that started this slowly. There was an unexpected intimacy to it. Sifting through Olivia's history required patience, but the knowledge felt earned, coming from a place of trust. Previous women she'd dated often blurted their full stories on the first meeting, their openness a too-bright signal flare of interest, but Olivia listened more than she talked. She expressed her interest by being...interested. In her romantic life, Ellie had never been the center of someone's consideration in this way. She would have said otherwise, before meeting Olivia, and she would have been wrong.

The front door creaked as Olivia stepped through, all loose curls and long limbs and nonchalant grace. She wore what seemed to be her weekend uniform—broken-down jeans with cuffs frayed at the heels and a faded Henley under her half-zipped coat. Olivia managed to be both maddeningly self-possessed and completely unassuming. Desire shivered up Ellie's spine. She almost laughed out loud at the juxtaposition. Her mind reveled in this slower intimacy, but her body had its own opinions.

"Thanks for coming over in this weather," Olivia said. "How is it?"

"Messy, but the plows are starting on the side streets. Yours is already in good shape."

"The woman down the block works for a snow removal company. She always gives us a pass before heading out."

"Nice. I brought cocoa. It was too perfect with the snow."

"I like the way it sparkles in your hair." Olivia ran her fingers through Ellie's curls, trailing a tingling heat, and then her forehead furrowed. She touched the scar on Ellie's lower lip. "I keep meaning to ask about this."

"Pitched face-first over the neighborhood bike's handles."

"Neighborhood bike?"

"Nobody could afford their own, so all the kids fixed up one we found in the alley and shared it."

Olivia's lips skimmed the old wound before capturing her mouth in a tender, unhurried kiss. Ellie's lungs swelled against her ribs, and she leaned into the sensual pressure, tipping forward when Olivia broke it off.

"What was that for?"

"To say thanks. I know it's strange, sitting on my porch in this weather."

"Strange? You've got outdoor seating, heat lamps, and a brick accent wall. Buy some Edison bulbs, and you're a hipster hot spot in Logan Square."

Olivia chuckled. The low rumble made Ellie want to press an ear to her chest to find its source. "My wall doesn't accent anything other than a need for tuck-pointing. Come sit down."

On their first date, Olivia had receded physically, folding inward until she became a silhouette of the woman Ellie first met. But visit by visit, her body had unfurled, and tonight, they settled on the loveseat to huddle under a blanket. Fat white flakes swooped beyond the low wall. The small square of porch felt timeless, as if they were figures in a snow globe. At their backs, a tiny sealed-off house. Beyond the slurring snow, a sphere of glass. Ellie removed her gloves and slid her left hand into Olivia's right, lacing their fingers. The quiet suspension was intimate, seductive, but more and more, she wondered what existed for them beyond the fragile border of this enclosed world.

"This is the most dates I've had without trading coming-out stories." The statement landed in her lap like a rock, and she gritted her teeth at her own diversion. Concern about appearing overeager made her clumsy with caution.

"You know, I can't remember the last time I shared mine," Olivia said. "I was eighteen, and honestly, it was a relief. I always felt out of place or...I don't know, different, but I didn't know *why*. Was it my height making guys uncomfortable, or because I was serious and studious and terrible at flirting?

"I mean, don't get me wrong, I *liked* being tall. I *liked* schoolwork and skipping parties to hang with a couple of friends. I just assumed liking those things was why I felt different, when really, it was this aspect of myself I didn't understand. By the time I figured it out, high school was almost over. It was easier to crush on movie stars and masturbate until I could get out."

"So no high school romance for you?"

"Nope. I was a freshman in college when I got my first kiss. I told my parents the next year, over Christmas break." Olivia drew away, and disappointment stabbed Ellie, but she was only shifting so she could lean against Ellie's shoulder. Ellie lifted her arm to make room. The layers of their coats didn't diminish her thrill at this casual intimacy.

"How did they take the news?"

"Fine. They said they'd 'discussed it circumspectly.'"

"I can't imagine my parents discussing anything circumspectly." Ellie sifted Olivia's long curls through her fingers. Distinct lines of gray streaked the pale honey color.

"Well, Scandinavians don't get worked up about much." Olivia draped a hand on her knee. "How about you?"

"Short or long version?"

"Long, please."

"I always knew. Always. I had so many innocent crushes, but if I did anything in my neighborhood, everyone would find out. I discovered my brother's porn magazines in junior high. The girl-on-girl section was cheesy, but it gave me a sense of what was possible."

"I know what you mean. I was at a sleepover once, and we stole her dad's porn tapes, which now that I'm saying it out loud is a little gross, but anyway, one scene featured two women—candy stripers getting it on in a hospital."

"Inspiration for your future nursing career?"

"Ew, I hope not. But I was glued to the screen. It was the first time something clicked. Now, it's obvious, but at the time, I'd never heard of two women together." Olivia slapped her leg. "Back to you. Always knew, crushes, porn—go!"

Ellie's heart stuttered at the playful smack. "Summer after my junior year of high school, I attended this leadership camp for immigrants. Kids came from all over the city. Most were 'kids of color.'" Olivia's hair slipped through her fingers as she made air quotes. "But I was fascinated by this Polish girl with long blonde hair."

Olivia's hand started a slow circle, coasting down Ellie's thigh, across her kneecap and back up.

Ellie stifled a moan. She loved this looser physicality, but it sent her thoughts skittering like marbles from a bag. "We were assigned to the same work group. She'd emigrated when she was ten, and she hated getting teased for her thick accent. I offered to help with her pronunciation. During lunch, we'd sit on this stone bench hidden in an alcove, practicing words."

"What was her name?"

"Karolina." Her awkward smile quirked in Ellie's memory. "For two weeks, I stared at her lips as she repeated my words. One day, I leaned in and kissed her."

Olivia's short nails dug into her thigh. "What happened?"

"She kissed me back."

"She didn't!"

"Swear on my abuela's life! We dumped the language lessons and spent the last week kissing every lunch. We'd find these times during the day to touch hands, just the sides of our pinkies so it looked unintentional."

"How did it end?"

"The last day, I got some cojones and kissed her neck." She dropped her hand to Olivia's ear, tracing its curve with her middle finger. She smiled when Olivia took a deeper breath, her shoulders pressing into Ellie's chest. "Her nipple was hard, poking through her shirt. I cupped her breast and ran my thumb over it. When she moaned, I thought I might explode."

"Now you're messing with me."

"It's all true. I kept going, squeezing, caressing. Anything to hear another moan. Then a kid came crashing through the trees. We didn't get caught. Nothing bad happened." The clumsy thrill of adolescence ran through her. "I can still feel her breast in my palm. I wish I'd been brave enough to go under her shirt. I masturbated to that for a long time."

"Who wouldn't?" Olivia snorted. "What happened to her?"

"I don't know."

"What?" Olivia sat up, eyes wide.

"It was the last day! They put us into groups for the bus ride to our own neighborhoods, and I never saw her again. I have this weird fantasy where's she straight, but when she's masturbating, she remembers that moment." The older Ellie got, the more she cherished the protective bubble fate had put around her and Karolina. If they'd been caught, if her sexuality had become an ugly smear on a teenager's tongue...

"Who'd you tell first, about being gay? Friends or family?"

Ellie patted her chest, hoping to lure her back. She grinned when Olivia tucked into her again. She loved the weight against her, and her fingers resumed their slow journey through Olivia's hair. "Friends. Claudia and Marisol."

"Best friends?"

"The best. They already knew, of course. Why do best friends figure it out first?"

"Arti said it would've stolen my fun to spoil the surprise."

"Marisol had been dying to bring it up for months, but Claudia made her keep her mouth shut until I was ready. Which, if you know Marisol, was no small feat." Ellie rested her cheek on Olivia's head and let out a long breath. Her friends' absence cut deep in these early days, when she longed to share her giddy joy over late-night empanadas and stale churros.

"Such a heavy sigh. Do you guys not get along anymore?"

"Oh, no. We're close. But Claudia's in the army and got stationed in Germany two years ago. Marisol took an amazing job in Mexico. If you're a bilingual petroleum engineer, you can pretty much write your own paycheck, FYI. We Skype once a week and group text, but—"

"It's not the same." Olivia draped a hand across her leg again and squeezed.

"It's still weird, not seeing them. In middle school, we promised to buy a three-flat and live on top of one another our whole lives." A wistful lump lodged in her throat. "We never could agree on who would get the third floor."

"I assume they know about me?"

Ellie's pulse quickened. "They do."

Olivia tapped her knee. "You can tell me."

"Claudia's an incorrigible romantic—she married her husband four months after meeting him. But Marisol is more cautious."

Olivia glanced up from her shoulder with a smirk. "I like Marisol."

"This is a woman who made her husband sign a prenup."

"Why?"

"Marisol grew up poor. I mean, we were all poor, but she was the kind of poor where whatever she ate at school might be her only meal, or she couldn't shower because the water got shut off. In high school, she found a list of the highest-paying jobs and picked one. It helped she was super smart."

"And super determined, sounds like."

"She fell hard for a painter. Does these huge abstract canvases." She sketched the air with an imaginary brush. "Pretty cool, if that's your thing. Anyway, she promised to support him, but she said she didn't scrape her way out of abject poverty just to pay him alimony if he left her for a twenty-year-old performance artist."

"Was this before or after you and Jill?"

Ellie shivered at the question, at Olivia's talent for quietly unearthing more. "During. And after. We always expected Claudia would get hitched first, and Marisol said she would never marry, so when I got serious with Jill and Marisol got engaged, we laughed about how the script had flipped. But then Jill left, and a few weeks after Marisol's wedding, Claudia started her whirlwind engagement. Within six months, I was maid of honor twice."

"And you were single."

"I was so happy for them, but their lives took this huge leap forward while mine just...stopped. It didn't help that it took me several years to date again. I didn't trust myself after misjudging Jill."

"Well, I must ring all kinds of alarm bells."

"They—"

"Want you to be cautious. With an older widow. With a disabled son."

The words hung there, but she refused to pick apart Olivia's history in any way that might threaten their early connection. "They want me to be happy in my dating life. Which I am." She planted a kiss on the top of Olivia's head and held her breath.

"When did you tell your family?"

The fluid change of topic was a relief. "I told Alberto when I was a freshman in college. I had a girlfriend I wanted him to meet, but we broke up after I introduced them. Evidently, my version of Latina was okay, but when she met 'Berto, who has an accent and darker skin, she wasn't too sure about *his* version. I think she was embarrassed by him."

"I'm sorry. For the record, I think it's sexy when your accent creeps in."

"I'll keep it in mind, cariño."

Olivia grinned at her. "And the rest of your family?"

"Ooh, that's a story, but first, could I use your bathroom?"

"Sure. It's in the back by the kitchen."

The casual answer surprised her. It was a mundane request but a new one. It would be her first time in the house. Was Olivia simply comfortable, or was she avoiding any conversations a tour might spur? Ellie got up and hesitated at the door, looking from Olivia to the snow swirling in the dark. It was as if she suddenly discovered the tiny house in the globe unlocked.

She entered and unzipped her boots, leaving them in the entryway that sat between the living room and darkened stairs on her left. A tall brass lamp glowed, and through a plaster arch, light streaked from a half-open door. The message was clear: start here, finish there. Olivia must have done this each night she visited. It didn't prevent her from scanning the rooms—the spillover light made each space visible, if muted—but the boundary was obvious.

After finishing in the bathroom, Ellie kept her curiosity at a simmer, walking by the blank slate of a kitchen, but the fireplace in the living room beckoned. Pictures crowded the mantel, each a window into Olivia's past. The Ellie of ten years ago would have peeked. Maybe even five years. But seeing the photos without Olivia's words to give them context would be worse than not looking at all, so she slipped on her boots and returned to the porch.

"I've been out here worrying I picked an old scab, asking about your family." Olivia tipped herself forward, patting the empty space behind her, and Ellie eased back in, unreasonably happy that Olivia wanted the contact as much as she did.

"Oh, no, it's fine. My last year in undergrad, Mamá had been on me for months, dragging me to church to find a man, inviting random guys to dinner. One Sunday, my arranged date groped me under the table, and I snapped. I smacked him and told the entire room I was a lesbian, thank you very much, and I liked sex with women so get off my fucking back."

Olivia curled into a ball of laughter. "Did you really say that?"

"I might have said I like *fucking* women so get off my *damn* back, but I'm not sure. You'll have to ask 'Berto. I stormed out to the yard."

"And?"

"There was a lot of yelling. Mamá blamed Papá for giving her a daughter after four boys. I must have been tainted by the testosterone. Papá blamed my brothers for dragging me around with them. Then it got quiet." She would never forget that silence, the way it thickened into a mist that threatened to suffocate her. "Finally, the screen door squeaked. It was Abuela. She slapped my face and said I knew better than to curse in my mother's house. Then she patted my cheek and told me you can't control love. That was that. Abuela had spoken, and everyone else fell in line."

"I see why you're so fond of her. It's okay now?"

"Mamá swung from ambivalence to denial before finally landing on resigned acceptance." Her mother didn't wear happiness comfortably. Worried and wary were the twin pillars of her world. "It was uncomfortable in the neighborhood for a while, but now I'm old news. A younger cousin is gay. The barriers break down little by little."

"Thanks for the long version. You tell it well." Olivia tipped her head and smiled.

Ellie dragged her fingertips across a pale cheek, those thin pink lips, the long sweep of neck. "Ask me anything. I'll tell you all of it." She leaned over for a gentle kiss, but Olivia clutched her hair and rose into her, mouth open and hungry. Ellie burned with the slick, urgent contact and this first real taste of Olivia's desire. When Olivia's tongue stroked hers, she poured a moan down her throat. The moment they broke the kiss, both gasping, Ellie wanted to devour her mouth again.

"What are you doing to me?" She couldn't breathe through this need in her chest.

The desire in Olivia's hazel eyes softened into longing, and Ellie thought she might cry. Olivia kissed her again, the passion still there but now tender, less desperate. The earth tumbled away, leaving only the press of Olivia's lips and the painful throb of her own heart. When Olivia pulled back, the storm in her eyes had passed. She painted Ellie's face with light fingers. The intensity of her study made each stroke feel like an act of memory.

"Tell me what you're thinking." Ellie whispered her plea.

"How beautiful you are. And I needed to feel you, to make it real."

The earnest scrutiny stilled her tongue.

"What is it? I'm sorry if I—"

Ellie touched Olivia's lips. "What you said is wonderful. You're wonderful. It just caught me off guard."

"I hate that those words would ever catch you off guard. You deserve to hear them every day."

Grabbing Olivia's face, she kissed her, quick and hard. "Jesus, you are so—" She ached to kiss her again, but if she started, she might never stop. "I should go before it gets any harder to leave. I need to be awake early. The commute's going to be awful."

Olivia sighed, then nodded. She handed Ellie the thermos as they stood. "We forgot the cocoa."

"The company was too distracting."

A blush tinted Olivia's cheeks. "It's been great having you visit, this past month."

"I've loved every minute." Ellie hesitated, then plowed through the sliver of opening in Olivia's words. "Are you coming to the TTC fundraiser? The swanky bar one before the holiday break?"

"Seems like it. Arti found the invitation on my counter and signed us up. Said I owed her a fancy night out." Olivia's coat swished with her shrug. "Are you going? I thought it was organized by the nonprofit foundation, not the clinic."

"They asked for volunteers to help staff it."

"Is that weird for you? I don't have to be there."

"No, it's not weird." Ellie almost lunged at Olivia in reassurance. "I'll be busy during, but maybe we could hang out after?"

"Ben will be at my sister-in-law's, so as long as the event doesn't last too long, it should be fine. It's a trial run, to see how he does, and I'm not sure how he'll—"

Ellie interrupted Olivia's fumbling explanation with a kiss. "Whatever happens, we'll make it work."

Olivia rested a hand on her face, stroking one eyebrow with her thumb. "Thank you. For this. For everything." She grazed a return kiss across Ellie's mouth, her soft sigh swirling between their parted lips.

It was all Ellie could do not to shove her against the brick column and drown her in a kiss that would last all night. When she forced herself back a step, she didn't need words to know Olivia felt the same. The dazed, hungry expression on her face said it all.

"See you on Tuesday." Ellie planted fervent lips to Olivia's palm, then picked her way down the snowy steps and marched into the cold. As she reached her car, she gave Pride Santa a high five.

Chapter Nine

THE BROWN LINE shuddered beneath Olivia's feet as the side-to-side shimmy gave way to a gentle forward press of brake. Doors shushed open, and two young men tumbled in, their cold-slapped cheeks red and glossy. They collapsed in the seats behind her, bursting with chatter, and she picked out kolacja, the Polish word for supper. The doors hissed shut, sealing off the outside world again, and through her own pale reflection in the window, she watched the lights streak past as the train left the platform.

The 'L' had sold her on Chicago. She was eighteen when she went to the Loyola college tour on her own. The Metra in Joliet had dropped her at Union Station, and then she'd navigated through downtown to catch the Red Line. Once those train doors closed, she became part of the city, first underground, barreling through the dark, then ascending into the light below Fullerton. Obvious landmarks—Wrigley Field, Graceland Cemetery, the Aragon Ballroom—flew past, but she'd spent most of the trip absorbed by the people. That mix of faces and ages and languages was the world she wanted, a diverse stream flowing along 220 miles of train tracks.

It had stayed her world for two decades, the borders drawn in Red, Brown, Blue, Purple, Green, Orange. She shared it with Ben early on, taking him on the Brown Line on her days off to visit Sophia at work. He loved the last car's rear-facing seat, nestled in its own private cubby. He would stand in her lap, heels digging into her thighs, chubby palms on the window, and watch the tracks recede. But one day, something changed. He startled when speakers spat static. Clanking metal wheels made him flinch. If a forest of unfamiliar legs crowded his stroller, he swatted at them, crying. It all began to overwhelm him, and soon he feared a space he once adored.

She glanced around the car, at its mishmash of riders—men with slack ties and slack expressions; a woman hunched over a book, her long hair a curtain around the pages; three friends starting their night, all guileless smiles and sleek clothes. This ride had been Arti's suggestion, since she was driving from her parents' house to the fundraiser anyway, but it was a calculated risk. Ben had happily hopped into Christina's car when she came to pick him up, but not having her own car as the tether between them made Olivia uneasy. Checking her phone for the tenth time, she tried to ignore the twist of anxiety behind her sternum.

Harold Washington Library, State/Van Buren, a bland male voice announced. Wheels slowed their clatter, then stopped, and the doors opened. She stuffed her phone in her pocket and swung from her seat. A massive aluminum owl glowered at her from the library roof. The wind snapped and cracked on her walk to the club, but she ignored its icy lash and kept to a stroll. She'd fallen in love with the city's architecture in her twenties, spurred by a tour she and Sophia had taken. Downtown was where Chicago popped its skyscraper collar, puffed its architectural chest. It spoke of brute money wrestled from the land and thrust into the sky, a giant middle finger to the old-guard East Coast and the sun-soaked coin of California. She loved these burly, unpretentious buildings and the people walking among them, unbowed by the cold.

Rounding the last corner, she nearly took out Arti, who glared from under a faux-fur-lined hood. "We're not all Nordic warriors, you know. My Greek blood isn't designed for this."

"C'mon, you're not just Greek. You're Spartan."

"Spartans fight the way God intended, with their shirtless bronze chests gleaming in the Mediterranean sun. Too many layers diminish our ferocity."

Olivia showed her invitation to the bouncer. "Nothing diminishes your ferocity."

Arti cackled as they entered, funneling through the crowd to the coat check. A heavy beat thudded ominously. Bodies elbowed for room as everyone shed their winter gear, and the sudden press of heat drove the cool, clean walk from Olivia's bones. Sweat trickled down her spine. She and Arti squeezed past a cologne-soaked scrum of men and entered the main room.

"Stop squinting like a groundhog sticking its head out after a long winter." Arti smacked her arm. "When was the last time you went to a real club?"

Olivia flinched at the thrumming bass and rubbed the spot where a chunky ring had made contact. "Let's find the VIP lounge. Maybe it'll be quieter."

"Boy, you make a night out sound super fun!"

"I'm sorry, okay? This is more people than I expected."

Arti took her hand. "You used to be right in the middle, dancing through the night."

"It was a long time ago, and someone else led me out there." A petite brunette, hair flying, pulsed with the mob on the dance floor. It could have been Sophia in another life, and Olivia clenched Arti's fingers. The pangs of longing were less frequent, but their bitter intensity still stung. The music leapt to a new decibel, and the walls constricted around them.

"What is it?" Arti leaned closer. Concern creased her features.

"Maybe this was a bad idea."

"Are you kidding? It's the best idea I've had in ages."

The air, thick with sweat and booze, clogged her lungs. Lights swirled, and the floor pitched. "I'm not sure I'm ready for this."

"You've been talking with Ellie for weeks."

"But...being out—"

Arti yanked her so they faced each other. "You broke up with Jen because she wouldn't be seen in public with you. Now a woman asks *you* out—a woman you like well enough to spend hours talking to—and suddenly you want to hide? Stop freaking yourself out!"

The balloon expanding in her chest popped, and her shoulders crawled down from her ears. The Sophia lookalike was just a random twentysomething again. Olivia sucked in a large breath, leaned over, and kissed the top of Arti's head. "You make a lot of sense sometimes."

"Sometimes? All the time! You're just too stubborn to listen." Arti tugged her past the mayhem. "Where's the VIP lounge? I'm a woman who deserves a VIP experience."

They found it up a small ramp behind the dance floor. The bouncer checked their invitations and let them through a discreet door. Languid jazz dissolved the molar-rattling dance beat. Warm lights created pocket oases throughout the room. The people in this space moved with the sedate rhythm of money and maturity.

Arti sighed and gestured behind her. "They're having more fun out there."

"I assume the idea was to let donors feel young and trendy, walking by the dance floor, before having a drink somewhere they can think straight."

"Thinking straight takes the fun out of having a drink." Arti studied the crowd. "I knew your sweater wouldn't cut it. Thank God, I Facetimed you."

Olivia had originally thrown on a sweater with dressy slacks, but after one look at the outfit onscreen, Arti had verbally force-marched her to the closet. She had protested the shiny white button-down shirt Arti paired with her slacks because it was too snug across her stomach, but Arti assured her no one would notice because it was also snug around her breasts.

"Put this on." Arti dug a silver pendant from her clutch. "Your outfit needs a little bling."

Olivia knew better than to argue, so she turned to let her hook the clasp.

"I forgot how goddamn tall you are in heels." Spinning her around for a final check, Arti flipped the pendant over so the correct side faced out. "I'm staring right at your tits. Which look great in this shirt, as promised."

Arti, always a walking center of attention, had draped her full figure in a tight black dress. A loud necklace in bronze and agate started at her neck and didn't stop until it beckoned from her ample cleavage. A matching bracelet dangled from her wrist. She always wore black at events like these, the better to feature her jewelry. She often left without the necklace she wore, having sold it by the end of the night.

Olivia scanned the group for the real reason she stood here. When she finally spotted Ellie behind the bar, the air in the room thinned. A black leather tank top clung to every curve, and she'd pulled her luxurious curls back, exposing her broad shoulders and the sweep of her neck. She slid drinks to two men, then flashed a big grin as she tapped a glass jar. A sign on its front said, "Tips are DONATIONS, so tip GENEROUSLY." The men dropped several twenties into it.

"Where is she?" Arti muttered in her ear.

"Tending bar."

Arti let out a long wolf whistle. "Gynaikara. That is one voluptuous woman. You've been agonizing about going on a real date with *her*? As usual, you are seriously overthinking this situation."

"Shut up and behave. You promised if I brought you—"

"Yeah, yeah. Buy me a drink." Arti marched toward the bar, parting the crowd like a figurehead on a ship. As they approached, Ellie's gaze snagged on Arti before moving higher to meet her own. A radiant smile lit her face. Her obvious excitement soothed Olivia's nerves.

"Hi!" Ellie shifted to their end of the bar. "I'm glad you came. You look spectacular."

"Thanks. You look—" Words deserted her.

"Sexy as hell?" Arti's eyes took in all of Ellie at once. "That's what she means to say. It's not Olivia's fault. Her parents couldn't give an effusive compliment if they tried. Lovely people, but so taciturn. I'm Arti, the best friend." She offered her hand, bracelet jingling.

Ellie wiped her hands on a towel and shook it. "Nice to meet you. Can I get you a drink? It's an open bar, but tips go to TTC."

"You're doing well." Arti glanced from the jar to Ellie's cleavage.

"Arti—"

"It's okay, Olivia. I know the outfit's edgy, but the foundation complained about past fundraisers being stuffy, and they wanted to shake things up. When they booked the club, I offered to try out my best buxom barmaid routine on the well-to-do." She lowered her voice. "I brought a black button-down shirt in case anyone thought this was too much."

Olivia laughed. "I think it's just the right amount of much."

A blush bathed Ellie's cheeks. "So, what will it be?"

"I'm driving," Arti said. "How about a seltzer?"

"We can do better than that." Ellie's hands followed a fluid path between bottles before setting a glass on the bar. "An upscale cherry lemonade, without all the sweet. It doesn't have a name. It's just something I make."

Arti took a skeptical sip, and then her face brightened. "This is delicious. I almost don't miss the alcohol!"

Olivia coughed into her fist.

"I said almost!"

"And you?" Ellie's flirty grin drove every drink name from her brain.

"Surprise me."

Another quick set of pours, and she slid a tumbler to her. "A Manhattan. Classic. Unpretentious. Sexy. Like someone I know." Voices chattered from the other end of the bar, and Ellie turned in that direction before Olivia could respond. With a quick apology, she shuttled to her next customer.

"She's charming," Arti said. "Personality to spare. Amongst other endowments."

"Be good."

"I'm sorry, have we met?"

"Arti—"

"Fine. You sit here and ogle Ellie while I peruse the selection of single men."

"There can't be many. Lots of parents here."

"Maybe there's a wealthy husband who will buy his wife a necklace. I'll even donate the proceeds to TTC." As Arti shimmied through the crowd, Olivia shifted her attention to Ellie. She chatted with everyone—donors, staff, barbacks—flipping from Spanish to English as nimbly as she flipped the bottles to pour. She radiated ease and humor, even twirling a bottle when dared. Every so often, their eyes met, and her dimple appeared.

Olivia's first drink was nothing but half-melted ice and whiskey fumes when a parent from Ben's group sidled up and tugged her toward a table. A cold glass slid into her left hand, still resting on the bar. Fingers traced fire on the back of her wrist.

"Thought you might need a second drink." Ellie hovered close.

"I'm sorry—"

"Go. I'll be serving for a while anyway."

She let herself be dragged off, but each conversation was an exercise in focus. The room spun on Ellie's axis, and Olivia always found herself facing center—angling to spot Ellie or peek at her full-wattage smile over someone's head. She even missed several of Arti's quips, distracted by the music of Ellie's distant laughter.

Eventually, Olivia found herself shifting her weight from one throbbing foot to the other while the board's vice president droned on. Arti's bark of a laugh filtered through the din, and Olivia saw her shake Ellie's hand. She tried to escape the conversation to grab her, but all she caught was Arti's devilish wink as she left. Her phone buzzed in her pocket. She snuck a glance at the screen.

You're always too nice to cut people off. They already did last call. Dump the fucking bore, and go find Ellie! Do I have to do everything around here?

Biting her lip to hide her smirk, Olivia made a vague apology and stepped away.

Pushy broad, she texted back.

Yitha!

She laughed. Arti called her the Greek word for goat whenever she was being stubborn. The crowd was thinning, and she made her way to the bar, where Ellie was helping the staff clean up. Her grin sparkled over the taps.

"Arti dumped you with me." Sweat clung to her upper lip and ran a small trail between her breasts.

"I suspected as much."

"I'm sorry we couldn't chat more. I had no idea it would be this busy."

"It's okay. I have time for a drink, if you can drive me home afterward."

"Absolutely, but I'm dying in this leather. It does not breathe. My other shirt's in the supply room. Can you keep an eye out while I change?"

She tugged her gaze from Ellie's full cleavage. "Sure."

Ellie left the door open a crack. In the mirror above a sink, Olivia saw her peel the tank top over her head. *Gynai-kara.* She *was* voluptuous, all smooth skin over full curves. Olivia stayed glued to the reflection, absorbing Ellie's raw physicality. TTC's polo shirts and cargo pants hid her feminine contours under a neutral shell, and on the porch, her parka obscured everything. She imagined Ellie's damp skin against her palms. Desire slithered through her belly and curled deep in her pelvis, heavy, waiting.

Ellie had slipped the button-down shirt over her shoulders when their eyes met in the mirror. Olivia shifted, pretending to scan the crowd, but Ellie reached through the gap and pulled her inside.

"Like what you see?" Her breasts swelled over the cups of her bra as she pressed Olivia into the closed door. Ellie's height and size let her dominate the small space and Olivia with an ease that was new and incredibly erotic.

"Sorry, I—"

"Don't apologize. I want you to see me. All of me. Whenever you're ready." Ellie clasped her face and buried her in a bruising kiss, tongue slick and hot in her mouth. Their intense crush of lips released the breath Olivia had been holding since Ellie first touched her cheek. She'd tiptoed into this relationship to avoid the danger of her and Jen's headlong rush, letting each conversation inch her closer to the edge of possibility. But as she surged against

Ellie, taking all her ravenous mouth could give and demanding more, Olivia realized their time together had only deepened the chasm, leaving her even farther to fall.

Ellie ground her into the door and yanked Olivia's hands under her open shirt, plastering them to her sweaty back. When her splayed fingers sank into that soft expanse of flesh, Olivia groaned.

"Anyone in there?" A knock shattered the kiss, but their lips grazed as they gasped into each other's mouths. Ellie's breasts crushed Olivia with every choppy breath.

"Just changing." Ellie rested her forehead on the door with a quiet thump, melting into her.

Sweat and whiskey floated off Ellie's skin, and the tip of Olivia's tongue burned with salt as she traced the rapid pulse in her neck. She brushed Ellie's spine and followed the damp slope of her back before slipping under the waist of her jeans. Ellie moaned and arched into the contact. The motion sent Olivia's fingers lower, skimming her round ass. It was a matter of inches, a gentle sweep around Ellie's hip to the swell of her stomach, then lower, and she could stroke her, could find out how wet, how hot, how full and thick and luscious this woman was. Olivia was suddenly desperate to hear how Ellie sounded when she came—

A thud jolted the door as a loud voice issued instructions. She jerked her hand free.

"Jesus." Ellie pried herself off and fumbled at her buttons. Olivia stilled her clumsy hands, finishing for her, then painted the rise of those glistening breasts with her fingertips. Ellie shuddered. The need in her eyes mirrored Olivia's own.

When Ellie reached for the knob, Olivia slid to the side so she could open it, and their breasts brushed. She clenched her fists to keep from pulling Ellie back to her. They left the supply room without speaking and glided past the VIP doorman into the club. The music pounded with a carefree beat that matched her drumming heart. Ellie grabbed her wrist, leading them through the crowd until they reached the coat check.

"How much time do you have?" Warm lips brushed her ear.

The tickle of pressure made Olivia's pulse race, and she fought the urge to sweep Ellie into another kiss. She squinted at her watch, and her lust cooled. "Less than an hour."

Ellie's wistful smile couldn't mask her disappointment.

"I'm sorry. I wish I could be more spontaneous. You've been so patient, and I've—"

"Been completely honest about your schedule." Ellie laced fingers through hers and squeezed. "But I'm not ready to give you up. How about a quick bite? I haven't eaten in hours."

Olivia relaxed at her words. "Sounds perfect."

"GLAD YOU CAME tonight?" Ellie crossed her legs and popped another olive in her mouth. She focused on the earthy tang, the soft resistance as she bit down. Nothing helped. She couldn't clear their encounter in the supply room from her mind. The hunger in Olivia's kisses, the long press of their bodies...

"I am. Thanks for bringing it up."

"I had noncharitable motives, I must admit."

Olivia raised her eyebrows in question.

"I wanted a date that didn't involve parkas."

"I'm sorry. I know my porch is lame."

"No, no, no." She took Olivia's hand. "I love being with you anywhere, but it's not the same when we're bundled up. I needed a chance to see all of you."

"Arti picked this out. It's not too snug?" Olivia tugged at her shirt collar.

"Snug? Don't you know how amazing your body is?" Ellie had nearly dropped a glass when she'd spotted Olivia, sleek and tailored, her hair swept up. She shimmered like the pale edge of a sword, crisp and sharp and bright, pulling Ellie's attention wherever she moved through the room.

"For my age." Olivia gave a small half shrug.

"Please don't think because you're older I'm not super-attracted to you. Besides, you're in better shape than me. I've eaten too many of Abuela's tamales lately."

"I saw you in the mirror. You're gorgeous, full and luscious and... Is that a push-up bra?"

The way Olivia stared at her cleavage made Ellie want to crawl over the table and kiss her.

"Nope. These girls are all mine. So you're a boob woman, then?"

Olivia tipped her head in a playful side to side. "I'm a woman woman. There's something about the female body, the silkiness, the curves." Her fingertips ghosted the table-top, and the teasing lilt faded as she sank into her memories. "The feel of it on my fingers, my lips, it's intoxicating. I can spend hours touching someone. Learning them."

Desire licked every corner of Ellie. She clenched the table edge, aching to be one of the women flaring through Olivia's mind.

Olivia's hand froze. "Sorry. That was—"

"The sexiest thing I've ever heard. You should have been a sculptor."

Olivia drew back in surprise.

"Don't tell me you are!"

"I don't have an artistic bone in my body, but sculpture speaks to me. Sophia and I were in Paris, and we took a tour of smaller museums, including the Rodin. Some of his work was so painful and moving. Other pieces were incredibly erotic. Sophia went ahead without me. It was rare to be apart on vacation, but I needed time to absorb it all. I stayed for hours."

Ellie loved how sentimentality spilled from Olivia in odd, unguarded moments. "You're such a romantic."

Olivia's ears pinked as she straightened her silverware, rotated her glass.

"So, I'm not your type, because you don't have a type?" Ellie touched that restless hand.

"Oh, you're my type. I'm drawn to brunettes."

"Always?"

"One exception. It didn't work out. Am I your type?"

The swift pivot wasn't subtle, but Ellie let it go. "I've been known to chase blondes. And a few redheads. Better be a real blonde though." She winked to emphasize the joke.

"How about real blondes with a little gray, here or there?" Olivia smirked as her self-conscious funk lifted.

"Haven't tried it before, but it sounds fun. As long as I get to be here *and* there."

"It's a definite possibility." Olivia leveled her with a hazel stare, and lust bloomed in Ellie's chest. "So I'm not too old for this?" Olivia glanced from her own cleavage, where creases puckered, to Ellie's.

"Absolutely not." Ellie trailed a finger down Olivia's shirt. "There's only one problem."

"Which is?"

She popped the next button, exposing more of her bra. "Perfect."

Olivia's phone vibrated on the table, and her whole demeanor crumpled behind a veil of resignation. Rubbing an eyebrow, she put the phone to her ear. "Hey, Christina. What's—" A woman's apologetic voice murmured over Ben's distant wail. "It's okay. Tell him I'm coming." She hung up. "I'm sorry. A movie upset him—"

Ellie dug into her purse and tossed cash on the table.

"What are you doing?

"You need to get back, right? This is enough for the drinks."

"Stay here and order food. I'll take a cab home for my car."

"Don't be ridiculous. We'll pick him up."

"If we pick Ben up, he'll have a million questions. I can't deal with it this late at night."

"Then I'll drive you home. No arguments." Ellie hid her relief when, rather than bristling at her take-charge bravado, Olivia succumbed. She led them to the valet stand, and within minutes, the expressway thrummed underneath them. Olivia hunched in her coat and stared out the passenger window, her face bathed by passing waves of streetlights. All the energy from the evening had bled away. A fog of silence hung in the car.

"Can I ask something about Ben?"

"Sure." A muscle rippled in Olivia's clenched jaw.

"How old was Sophia when she had him?"

"Thirty-seven. The doctor suggested starting with me since I was younger, but Sophia was afraid she'd miss her chance if she waited."

"Was it hard for her to conceive?"

"We expected it to be. Everyone warns you about multiple trips, be ready for disappointment, but it worked the first time."

Another green sign passed overhead. Three exits to go. "When did you get the diagnosis?"

"Two and a half. I'd suspected earlier, but I thought my nursing background had made me suspicious." Olivia rubbed her face, leaving her hands on her mouth for a long moment until they dropped like weights into her lap. "Sophia blamed herself. Said she'd been selfish. That she should have let me carry. Ironically, I'd already been through a round of insemination when he was diagnosed. I stopped while we got a handle on things."

"You never tried again?"

"I wanted to give everything I had as a parent to Ben."

"And Sophia?"

"He was four when I got the courage to tell her I didn't want more kids. Sophia burst into tears. She felt the same but was afraid to tell me. She said she'd stolen my chance to be pregnant."

The physical separation grew too painful, and Ellie reached over and squeezed Olivia's left hand. "Do you regret it, not carrying?"

"Never. Sophia was so beautiful, pregnant. I couldn't stop touching her, mapping the changes. I loved experiencing it from the outside." Olivia streaked fingertips across the window.

"What is it?" Ellie brought the hand she held to her lips and kissed the back of it. During this entire conversation, Olivia had yet to look at her.

"I took so many pictures during her pregnancy, and I kept a few up after his birth. I loved remembering her that way. But after the diagnosis, they mocked her somehow, reminding her of how innocent she'd been, unaware. One day, she threw all of them out when I was at work."

Many families had shared stories like this with Ellie, even the ones who later were the most devoted, the strongest advocates. Autism, spina bifida, depression, cerebral palsy, Down syndrome, ADHD—the diagnosis didn't matter. The initial shock could rattle anyone. "You didn't hang more pictures later?"

Olivia frowned. "She was in enough pain already."

"You both had pain. It takes time to accept it. To adjust."

"It was harder for Sophia. She had an abortion during law school. She was always okay with it, very political about sharing her story if it broke the stigma, but after... She wasn't religious anymore, but the old Catholic guilt tugged at her." Olivia ground a fist into her thigh. "I hated how she felt. Hated that I couldn't make it better."

As they reached the garage, Olivia tapped a remote on her keychain. The door shuddered and clanked to life. "Sorry the night ended so abruptly. Still sure you want to date me?" The weak joke couldn't mask the fear beneath the question.

"This doesn't change how I feel about you." Ellie took Olivia's hand again, tugging on it. "Look at me, please."

A few beats passed before Olivia lifted her hollow eyes. The ease of their porch dates, with Ben already tucked in for the night, was an illusion Ellie had too willingly accepted. Tonight's call threw a harsh light on the truth—that Olivia was his sole comfort and her world stopped for his needs. And by putting Ben first, always first, she had buried her own pain far deeper than Ellie had imagined.

"I'm sorry to be so—" The key ring rattled as Olivia turned it over and over in her fingers. "I was having a good time, like a real woman on a real date, and when the phone rang, my carriage turned into a pumpkin, I guess. Big swings of emotion are hard for me."

"However it ended, I had an amazing time. There'll be other nights, other chances to make out in supply closets."

A small but genuine smile curled Olivia's lip. She unhooked her seatbelt and reached for the door, but Ellie didn't release her left hand.

"It's cold. Start your car and sit with me while it warms up."

Olivia hit the remote start. Tail lights flashed, and a white cloud rolled from the tailpipe.

"Come here." Ellie tucked Olivia into her shoulder and pressed a gentle kiss to her head. They sat in silence, watching Olivia's car idle in the brittle night air.

Chapter Ten

"I CAN'T BELIEVE you didn't tell me!" Ellie lifted her hand from Salma's round belly and grinned at the delight on her face.

Ahmad shifted closer to be heard over the din of the restaurant, his broad shoulders straining his crisp gray shirt. "I'm sorry. We hadn't cleared three months yet when you left for TTC, and when I realized I'd forgotten to text you the news—"

"We thought it'd be a fun surprise!" Salma laughed and squeezed her husband's forearm.

"I'm so happy for you both. I know how long you've been hoping for this." Ellie rubbed the corner of Salma's pale-blue hijab, stitched with delicate silver flowers. "Is the color a hint?"

"Oh, no! It just matched the outfit. We're going to wait to find out."

Ahmad flinched at a loud cackle from a nearby group and scratched under the edge of his knitted kufi. "Is it me, or is it loud in here?"

The restaurant oozed rote hipster cool—industrial light fixtures, faux tin ceiling, dark wood tables overloaded with small plates. The waitstaff slouched in low-slung jeans and canvas aprons while an emo soundtrack dueled with the boisterous chatter. It was a terrible place for conversation, but a wonderful place to be seen.

"Rachel has a nose for hot, trendy restaurants." Ellie tapped Ahmad's phone on the table to check the time. "And absolutely no concept of punctuality. How's the old place?"

"The hammer finally dropped. No more OT or PT services as of January. Social work and family services only. I hated to see you go, but it was the right choice."

With the rumored transition confirmed, the last of her guilt faded, and she released a sigh.

"Don't tell her that, Ahmad! I'll never hear the end of it." A four-inch black stiletto stabbed the floor by her chair.

"You gave me a lot of shit for leaving, Rach." Ellie grinned and stood to greet her old coworker. "A little payback is fair."

Rachel flung her arms around her. "Fine, fine. You were right. And I was too much of a bitch about it. What else is new?"

"It's good to see you." She sank into the enthusiastic hug. "Those heels, honestly."

Rachel released her and ripped a precarious twirl, her long hair a burgundy shimmer against her tight green dress. The sensual blur of color didn't go unnoticed by other patrons. "You should thank me! I save the stripper heels for a night out with friends. Aren't they worth it?"

"The question is, does Mara think they're worth it?" She reached past Rachel to give Mara a quick hug.

"As long as I'm the one she strips for, she can wear anything she wants." Mara's black faux-hawk arced over pale blue eyes, and the familiar tattoo of tree branches climbed up her neck from beneath a buttoned-up black collar.

They made quite a pair, the uber-femme showstopper and the petite punk butch. Several sets of eyes swept the table, trying to jibe the edgy lesbian couple with the Muslim headwear of Ahmad and Salma. Ellie, Rachel, and Ahmad had bonded early at her last job, united by their existence on the ragged edges of diversity. Mara, she had met later, on a panel for queer healthcare workers.

Mara slid a chair back for Rachel, then sat beside her and draped a hand across her taut thigh. Their dating was a more recent development. It unsettled Ellie. Rachel could be fun at work, but her high-maintenance personality often strained her dating relationships.

"So much for keeping in touch when you quit." Rachel shot her a prickly pout.

"I'm sorry. You wouldn't believe how fast my schedule filled up."

"How is it out there?" Ahmad tipped back on his chair legs.

"Very suburban." The group shared wincing nods. "But the equipment is great, and the staff are supportive."

Salma smiled as she tapped her husband's knee, and he returned the chair to four legs. "Ahmad said so many families use the bus to get to therapy. Where will they go now?"

"My place has taken a couple of referrals, but our focus on the queer community means we're not appropriate for everyone," Mara said. "They'll scatter around the city, but if public trans doesn't go where they need…"

She didn't have to elaborate. They had all lost patients to the vagaries of low-income healthcare. It kept Ellie awake some nights, fretting about the kids who had dropped out, their parents in a losing battle with insurance companies, or working three jobs, or the simple economy of no car.

Rachel stroked a finger up Mara's wiry forearm. "Can you work your voodoo, so we can order our drinks?"

Salma's deep dimples sank into her cheeks. "Voodoo?"

"It's the eyes. Servers, bartenders, hostesses, doesn't matter. They all come running at Mara's bidding."

Mara rolled those blue eyes and caught the server's attention, then murmured the order into the woman's ear.

Rachel scooted to the edge of her seat, closer to Ellie. "I need to tell you something."

"You better not be pregnant. Salma already pulled that one."

Ahmad chuckled, but Rachel didn't flinch. "I ran into Angie at my gym."

"Weird. She's pretty dedicated to the one by her place."

"She was doing her super-intense marathon thing—"

"Triathlon."

"Whatever."

"Wait, your ex is a triathlete? How did I miss that?" Salma asked.

Ellie nodded but didn't take her eyes from Rachel. "What's the issue?"

"Turns out she was at my gym because she lives nearby now, with her girlfriend."

"Whoever convinced her to shack up is a better woman than me." Ellie went for the easy joke, hoping to move Rachel off the topic.

"They're engaged."

An awkward silence draped over the table. Everyone knew they'd broken up because she wanted to get serious, and Angie's response had been to dump her.

"I'm sorry." Rachel's sharp features mellowed with a sympathy usually reserved for her teenage clients. "I didn't want to tell you like this, but I worried if I waited, you'd be blindsided randomly."

"You deserve better anyway," Ahmad said.

"Definitely." Salma patted her leg. "The perfect person is out there."

It should've stung, Angie shifting her stance on commitment, but they hadn't been a good fit. Her time with Olivia highlighted that fact. She winked at Salma. "I think you're right."

"Of course she is," Rachel said. "We'll have a girls' night, find new faces for you. There's a professional women's event downtown soon. Let me check my calendar." She dug around in her purse.

A tiny grin crept across Mara's lips. "You've already met someone."

Ellie cursed the smile that grew despite her efforts to smother it.

"Wait, what?" Rachel glanced from Mara to her, then tossed her phone onto the table and groaned. "No wonder we haven't seen you. Are you back in workout mode?" Her eyes drew a skeptical line down Ellie's body. "Please tell me not another gym rat."

She ignored the dig. "She's actually into rock climbing, but—"

"Rock climbing? You're terrified of heights."

"She does the climbing. I just enjoy the view." Ellie smirked remembering yesterday's date. They'd met at the indoor gym before lunch, and she'd caught the end of Olivia's final climb. The sport suited her—quiet, methodical, and cerebral. She hadn't appreciated Olivia's grace until she watched her ascent, a confident, balletic laddering of handholds and footholds.

The server brought Mara and Rachel's drinks, and she slid a fresh Coke to Ahmad, who accepted it with a toothy grin. "So how did you meet this woman?"

"At TTC."

Rachel's lips pursed. "Another therapist?"

"No."

"Good. Work relationships suck. If my girlfriend had to work with me *and* fuck me, I would have lost her ages ago."

Mara clicked her tongue at Rachel, who gave her a soft kiss.

"It's one of the moms."

"You're dating a parent?" Salma leaned forward to escape another rattle of laughter.

"Olivia's a widow. Her wife died more than three years ago in a car accident."

Rachel drummed her nails on the table, their glossy sheen flashing her disapproval.

"We met last August. Her son's autistic, and I was supposed to assist with his social group, but they shifted me to the tween girls. I didn't ask her out until last month." She sipped her whiskey to soothe her nerves. Part of her wanted to shout her joy, but another part hated exposing Olivia to the glare of Rachel's scrutiny.

Mara rubbed her chin, face thoughtful. "The relationship isn't a conflict of interest?"

"No. I cleared it with my supervisor. I guess it's happened before. But I won't be working with Ben, obviously."

"How old is he?" Ahmad asked.

"Eleven. He has solid language skills, but the nonverbal is tricky. His emotional volatility puts a big strain on Olivia."

"How old is this woman?" Rachel butted in. "I mean, if he's eleven?"

Ellie pulled the last pin and waited for the explosion. "She's forty-five."

Rachel ticked off a list, her voice rising with each flick of a manicured nail. "Middle-aged woman. Dead wife. Autistic kid! Seriously?"

"Easy, Rachel." Ahmad, always the peacekeeper, patted the table.

"What's she like?" Salma's question painted a thin veneer over the sudden tension.

"She's fascinating. She's taller than me, which is rare, and very striking. Intelligent. Sincere. She has this way of looking at you... I can't describe it, but I'd tell her anything when she does it."

"It's a lot of baggage for a new relationship." Mara's attention darted from Rachel to her.

"It doesn't matter. From the moment we met, I wanted to get to know her."

"And have you? Gotten to know her?" Rachel's attempts at humor often veered into the crass.

"We're taking it slow. A few amazing kisses and a lot of great conversations." The stolen moments at the fundraiser she kept for herself. They were too fresh and special to share yet. She hadn't met anyone who matched her physical energy the way Olivia did. Her skin tingled thinking of Olivia's hand cupping her ass.

"Ugh, old lesbians. Kill me now," Rachel said. "All they do is talk, talk, talk. I mean, they never even go out. What do they have to talk about?"

"I think it's sweet." Salma ran her fingers through her husband's curly beard. "I loved our early talks. How long have you been seeing her?"

"Almost two months."

"Two months and nothing more than a kiss?" Rachel tossed a red stream of hair over her shoulder. The edge in her voice redoubled.

"She's a single parent. She can't leave the house whenever."

"You're making my point for me! After Angie dumped you, all you could talk about was finding someone willing to put time into a relationship and be as serious as you were."

"Olivia is serious. More serious than anyone I've dated."

"But she can't possibly have enough time!" Rachel brushed off the hand Mara rested on her forearm. "Jill was obsessed with residency, Angie was obsessed with her training, and now Olivia's obsessed, and rightly so, with her son! Why do you always pick women who don't put you first?"

Anger churned her stomach. Rachel always picked apart her love life. "Just because Olivia has multiple priorities—"

"She has one priority. Her kid. You will never rate higher."

"It's not a competition! Millions of people manage to love their kids and their spouse!" She waved at Ahmad and Salma.

"So you want to marry this woman? After two months? How very lesbian of you."

"That's not my point, and you know it—"

"All I know is I was there the last time a woman broke your heart. I don't want to see it happen again!"

Ellie shoved away from the table, chair legs scraping the floor. "Keep this up, and you won't need to worry about it! I'm going to the bathroom. Can we have a new topic when I get back?" She threw down her napkin before her temper took full control of her mouth and marched through the tables.

She slammed open the restroom door and paced around the small space. It had been a mistake mentioning Olivia. Rachel had been so supportive when they first worked together, coaxing Ellie to full confidence after burning out at her previous job, making long meetings fly by with her wit. But discussing personal relationships had steadily become an exercise in frustration.

The door eased open, and Mara peeked around it. "Sorry. Rachel had a bad day."

"She break a heel?"

"Suicide attempt. One of her middle schoolers."

Sympathy muddied the waters of her indignation. "Fuck. Why didn't she say anything?"

"She doesn't want to talk about it. But since she unloaded on you, I thought you should know." Mara hooked a thumb on her tooled leather belt and leaned on the sink. "Plus, she'll never say it, but she misses you. Work isn't the same for her since you left."

"What was I supposed to do? Stick around until the bitter end, then scramble for a job?"

"Of course not."

"Then what?"

"She wants to see you more, but she doesn't express it well." A thin eyebrow canted upward. "Does she have a point, about falling for women who don't put you first?"

"No!" Ellie pushed the hair from her eyes and squeezed it into a ponytail behind her neck. "When she lists them off, I know it sounds that way—"

"Things often sound 'that way' because they are 'that way.'"

"Yes, Jill chose Stanford over me, but before that, the relationship was balanced."

"And Angie?"

Tonight was supposed to be about Olivia. She didn't want to pick through the wreckage of past relationships. "Angie didn't put me first because she never intended for us to be serious. I didn't recognize it soon enough. That's on me."

"Your explanations make sense. They do. But as a social worker, I've noticed people often react strongly to statements of truth. Or at least partial truth."

"How do they respond to stupid statements rudely delivered?"

Mara's laugh matched her smile, soft but genuine. "A lot like you did."

"You're much nicer than Rachel, you know?"

"Somebody has to be the nice one. Might as well be me."

Ellie leaned against the bathroom stall. The cool metal leached through her shirt, quenching her flare of temper. "I'm sorry. I shouldn't have made that crack. She's your girlfriend now. I'm just irritated. And feeling a little guilty about the suicide thing."

"All you knew was she came at you. Not your fault. Rach has a public and a private side. In a group, she tries to be the star of the show, and her worst tendencies come out. We've discussed it."

"Two social workers? And two lesbians? I'm sure you have."

"You really care for Olivia, don't you?"

"I do. More than I thought possible."

Mara's piercing eyes didn't waver. "Be careful. Rachel may have said it poorly, but a woman who's been through so much may have some sharp edges hiding in all that sorrow."

An image of Olivia surfaced—sitting in Ellie's car, tired and vulnerable.

"C'mon. Rachel will buy you another drink to make amends." Mara tugged on her wrist, and she let herself be dragged back to the table.

Chapter Eleven

THE SERVER SLID the champagne into an ice bucket, and Olivia stopped eavesdropping long enough to thank him. The young couple to her left were on their first date post-baby. The husband kept touching his phone, worried about the sitter, while the wife offered reassurances that seemed as much for her as for him. She remembered that stage—distracted and fatigued, but also slightly wonderous to be out in the world again. On her right, two men were decades past the starting point, wrinkled hands nested on the table. Their conversation, peppered with half-finished sentences and inside jokes, was harder to follow, and longing twinged at the private shorthand. She didn't know where she fit in this landscape. She'd been the one couple, had never doubted she would be the other. But now she sat, pockets heavy with endings and beginnings, waiting on a date. A shiver of anticipation arced down her spine. She was a woman who dated. A shiver of apprehension chased after it. She was a woman who planned to have sex with her date to-night.

Ellie appeared at the host stand, curls wind-wild and cheeks fierce with cold. Shedding her coat, she scanned the room, and the room scanned back, her gorgeous dishevel-ment drawing sly glances and a few bold stares. Olivia grinned at the extra height Ellie stacked onto her boot heels. No conciliatory flats for this statuesque woman, whose con-fidence was as alluring as her body. They made eye contact, and Ellie weaved through the tables. Olivia waited until the last moment to stand. Surprise flitted across a male face or two.

"You know how to make a woman feel special with that entrance."

"I took off my coat and walked across the room. How is that an entrance?"

"Because you're the one making it. You look absolutely stunning."

Ellie's bright eyes were twin chips of obsidian, their deep brown-black glinting with a secret translucence. "Is it too showy if I kiss you right now?"

"My feelings will be hurt if you don't." She leaned into Ellie, driving the cold bite of winter from her lips.

Olivia's phone buzzed in her pocket, and she ended the kiss with a wince. Ben's name glowed on the screen. When she sank to her chair, Ellie did the same. He'd been so ex-cited when she left him at his cousins' house.

"Hey buddy, what's up?" She skirted her voice beneath the cheerful murmur of the other diners. "You've won three games already? Great!" He chattered on, winding up for one of his rambles. "Ben? Ben? We agreed you would only call if it was important, right?" Her sister-in-law's voice echoed. "Sounds like it's time for popcorn and cartoons. Do you have your weighted blanket? Fuzzy the elephant? Then you're all set. I'm so proud you're trying a sleepover again. Have fun with your cousins. I love you."

Ellie settled back, draping her napkin on her lap. "I can't lie, I got a little nervous when he called."

"Me too. Turns out his checker game qualifies as an im-portant call."

"Sorry for being late. Train was stalled on the tracks."

"No problem. I've been people watching to pass the time." The server stepped over to fill their flutes. "I took a gamble and ordered champagne."

"Perfect."

Olivia lifted her glass. "Here's to our first full-blown, non-porch date. Happy New Year, a day late." The restaurant's understated energy burbled around them, absorbing the clink of their toast.

"Happy New Year. So, it's official? You're staying at my place tonight?" Ellie kept a neutral tone, but her grin betrayed her excitement. Olivia couldn't blame her. Making out at the fundraiser had struck a match neither could extinguish.

"Ben's determined to stay until morning, and I sweetened the pot by offering a new video game if he succeeds. Sorry about the short notice, by the way."

"Are you kidding? I was thrilled when you called last night."

"I didn't want to broach it until I knew Ben felt solid." Olivia rubbed a corner of the menu with her thumb. She organized tonight in a rush of anticipation, but nerves still frayed her confidence. The last time she'd tried a sleepover had been for the reunion. An image surfaced—Jen soaked in moonlight, eyes wide and lips parted.

Ellie reached over and threaded their fingers together. "Do *you* feel solid?"

Her jaw twitched. Sophia pressing into her thoughts was hard enough. She didn't need Jen doing the same. "I'll just feel bad if I have to bail."

"That's always a risk. It doesn't mean we shouldn't...expand our options."

The innuendo made her chuckle. "Options are good. Is the restaurant okay? I haven't been here in ages, but I remember liking the quiet vibe."

"It's perfect." Ellie's smile glowed in the candlelight. "I met friends last week at this trendy Fulton Market spot, and I could hardly hear myself. I'm getting too old for those places."

Olivia held up her glass again and gestured at the room. "Welcome to middle-aged dining."

"I'm a fan already."

The server came and went with fluid ease, and Olivia relaxed into her chair. She'd worried Ellie might want to rush dinner, given their plans, but they sank into a slow pace. Words and plates flowed. Light touches danced between them—fingers coasting up a forearm, a hand cupping a knee. She loved Ellie in the low light of the restaurant, the way shadows dusted her dimple with every laugh. She had never met someone who smiled the way Ellie did, so quick and broad, full of feeling.

"Olivia?"

"Hmm, what?"

"Where were you?"

"Sorry, I was thinking you have the most charming smile. What did you ask?"

An embarrassed pink shaded Ellie's cheeks. "Well, now it seems crass, but I asked about the guy you slept with in college."

"Darius? Oh, we were good friends in the same program. I wish it were more risqué, but we got tipsy one night and figured, what the heck?"

"Was that your actual pickup line? 'What the heck?'"

"I think it was more like, 'Are we doing this or what?'"

Ellie threw her head back and cackled. "Very smooth. So, how was it?"

"Ehhh. Honestly, the selling point was that he was six-seven. When would I ever have a chance to sleep with someone so much taller than me?"

"You slept with a dude because he was tall?"

"Do you think I'm the first woman to say that?"

"Fair point."

"I slept with him because I was curious, and he was game. Having a mat of black curly chest hair above me was weird, but otherwise it was fine. We both had orgasms." A mischievous impulse nipped at her. "That's how I got interested in dildos."

Ellie did a spit take. Most of it made it back in her glass. "Excuse me?"

Olivia trapped her smirk behind a bland expression. "I kept thinking, 'Penetration would be so much hotter with a woman.' I'd been hesitant about dildos. I was young and dumb, and I thought if I couldn't give my girlfriend an orgasm without props, I wasn't doing my job. But the shape, the size—you can't always duplicate it with fingers. If you want the sensation, why not?"

Ellie stared, like she didn't recognize the woman in front of her. Olivia grinned. People saw her as quiet and unassuming, so her comfort with sex, the fact that she was game, caught all her lovers off guard. Sophia had called her Clark Kent whenever she teased her about it.

The busboy cleared their plates, Ellie still staring, her cheeks crimson. It was fun, flustering her this way. Her speechlessness only made her cuter.

"You are so red!"

"I'm stuck between embarrassed and aroused. And the aroused is winning!"

"Have a drink. It'll help you cool down." Olivia bit her lip and waited for Ellie to take a sip. "So, I bought a dildo and experimented on myself. To get the hang of it."

Ellie coughed into her glass again. "You use a dildo on yourself?"

"Usually a vibrator these days. Don't you?"

"I've used them on my partners, sure, but I don't penetrate myself solo."

Olivia saw their server approaching. "Maybe one day I'll provide a demonstration."

"Is anyone interested in dessert?"

Ellie's face glowed like a firework.

"Sure," Olivia said.

"I'll give you a minute to look over the options." He handed them small sheets of paper and turned to the next table.

The menu fluttered from Ellie's fingers. She dropped her forehead to the table with a thud. "You're torturing me."

"What do you mean?"

"After your last comment, I was going to suggest we skip dessert."

"Do you want to leave?" Guilt plucked at her for pushing too far. "I'm enjoying this, the long dinner, no rush. I shouldn't have gone there, talking about the dildo."

Tipping her head, Ellie glanced at her from the tabletop. "When you look at me that way, I'll agree to anything."

"I'm not looking any particular way!" The waiter returned, and she lifted an eyebrow. "You sure, dessert?"

Ellie nodded as she sat up, her dimple popping above her smile, and they ordered. "So, you go for brunettes even with men?"

"Well, there's just the one example."

"But you said once you didn't. What's the scoop? A blonde turned your head in college?"

Olivia's stomach dropped. The story she had been avoiding was the one she most needed to tell.

"Why do I think I just killed the whole evening?" Ellie's smile faded.

The server interrupted with their desserts, and the question hung in the air while he set their plates down. She poked at her cake with her fork. Why could she talk about dildos and masturbation but get tongue-tied over this?

"Two years after the accident, Mom convinced me to go to my high school reunion. Ben refused to sleep alone after Sophia died, but I'd finally started transitioning him to his own bed. Mom offered to take him so I could stay in the hotel hosting it. I'd never attended before, and I assumed twenty-five years would make me forgettable." She set her fork on her plate. The scrutiny that night... Each furtive glance had pricked like a needle, stippling her skin until it crawled with the unwanted attention. "The whole evening was nothing but shallow hugs and pursed lips and 'I'm sorry.' Sorry you lost your wife. Sorry you were injured. Sorry you're a single parent. Sorry your son is fucking autistic. Who even says that?"

She twitched when Ellie took her hand. The warm grip pulled her from the chokehold of memory. "When it got to be too much, I snuck outside. A classmate followed me, and we started talking. She was recently divorced. I had lost Sophia. Before I knew it, we were kissing."

"Wait. Divorced as in husband, or as in wife?"

"Husband. He had an affair."

"Oh, shit." Ellie winced.

"I'd been so numb since the accident. To feel anything, even cheap arousal—" She scraped the hair back from her face. Nothing about that night was cheap, no matter how much she pretended otherwise. "We spent the night together."

"And she was up for all of it?"

"With the divorce, it had been a while. Jen was...enthusiastic."

"So, you had a one-night stand?" Ellie speared a bite of torte. "I mean, I'm a little jealous she got to you first, but why the serious face?"

"We kept seeing each other secretly. It was sporadic to start, but after Christmas, we met more consistently, once a month or so. Ben and I would visit Mom, and after putting him to bed, I'd make an excuse about going to a coffee shop or a bookstore. Mom was thrilled I was 'taking some time for myself.'"

"Where did you meet up?"

"Hotels, mostly. Once at her place when her sons were with their dad. After a while, the secrecy became suffocating, but she wouldn't talk about the next step. I thought, let's try being a couple. No big commitment, just dating, openly. This was last April, before you and I met."

"You gave her an ultimatum."

Olivia alternated her hands in the air, mimicking the movement of scales. "Ultimatum, lost my temper and shouted. You pick."

"Doesn't seem like you."

"It can happen." She hated those moments, scattered through her life. Each one stood as a mark against her character, and she never quite forgave herself for any of them.

"Good to know you're human like the rest of us." The gentle tease in Ellie's voice poked at her reflective mood. "I'm assuming Jen said no?"

"She couldn't take the next step. I hoped there was more to us than sex. That if she cared enough about me, she'd try." The shocked tears smearing Jen's cheeks still tore at her, but Jen's open, frozen mouth, empty of any of the words Olivia so needed to hear—that cut the deepest. She stabbed at her cake, smashing the crumbs on the tines of her fork.

"Moving too fast can have consequences."

Olivia looked up from her plate. "What?"

"You said that at the end of our first date. I thought it was about how I'd surprised you with my interest, but you were talking about Jen." Ellie pried the fork from her fingers before she could massacre the cake further.

"We started so differently, and I wanted it to stay different, to avoid the same mistakes." A rogue crumb flattened under her thumb. "I'm grateful about Jen, though, in an odd way."

"Why?"

Olivia stilled, searching for a way out of the conversation. She'd gotten comfortable and shared too much. Ellie had this effect on her. "I shouldn't have... Maybe it isn't the best thing to discuss on our first night together."

"Please don't hide from me."

"It's not hiding. It's just odd, bringing up sex with someone else when we—"

"I promise this won't change how I feel about you. Or this evening." Ellie licked chocolate from her fork. "Remember the dildo story?" The playfulness wasn't fake. Ellie was never fake, but she was working to absorb the Jen revelation.

It had been a mistake not mentioning it sooner. The least she could do was share all the details. She owed Ellie that much. "I hadn't had an orgasm since Sophia died. Ben was with me every night at first, and once I slept alone, I couldn't get anything to happen. I thought Sophia had taken that with her. That maybe I couldn't anymore. Does that sound weird?"

"No. You were grieving, adjusting to life as a single parent."

"Sex with Jen took the pressure off. I was buzzed, and I took the lead because, well, I knew the landscape. By the time she finished, my body had taken over for my mind, so when she reciprocated, I was able to let it happen."

"I'm glad you let yourself feel that again." Ellie touched her leg. "But I hate how she hurt you."

"I brought it on myself. I didn't see the warning signs."

"Do you always take some of the blame, protect your exes?"

"Arti would say yes."

An unfamiliar hesitancy blurred Ellie's face. "Have you and Arti—"

"No! She's just a terrible flirt, for the attention. She slept with a woman once, in college, but wasn't a fan."

"Why not?"

"She said, and I quote, 'There's only room for one queen in a bed.'"

Ellie laughed until her eyes shimmered. "You must have a thousand Arti stories!"

"A thousand would be lowballing it." It felt ridiculous now, hiding the story, given how generously Ellie had taken the news. Cradling Ellie's hand, she kissed her knuckles. "You deserved to know I'd been with someone since Sophia. I'm sorry I didn't mention it sooner."

"I'm not upset. Really, I'm not. But why wait this long to tell me?"

"My story is already so involved—losing my dad, then the accident, Sophia, being a single parent. I had nothing to share but these big, heavy moments. Adding Jen felt like too much, especially since I screwed it up—"

"You didn't screw up. You tried to connect after a horrible loss." Ellie wrapped both hands around her forearm. The sturdy grip centered her. "Your time with Jen changes nothing about tonight, but please know I want to hear everything, whenever you're ready."

The offer was earnest, but "everything" meant poking into corners Olivia had left dark for a long time. She scrubbed at her eyes and sniffed hard. "When did I get so bad at this whole seduction business?"

"Next time start with the ex and then close with the dildo bit."

"Good plan." A small grin broke through. "And also, I got tested after Jen and had no issues. Is that what people say now?"

"I don't know what 'people' say, but it's nice to have you mention it. I'm usually the one who does. And I'm all clear. How do you handle protection?"

"What do you do?" Olivia relaxed as the conversation returned to safer ground. When the server set the check down, Ellie reached for her purse, but Olivia stopped her. "You've traveled to me so many times. It's my treat."

Ellie let her purse slide to the floor. "If we're monogamous, then I'm fine with no protection."

"I've never been anything but monogamous, and whenever we get around to it, I want to be able feel, and taste, all of you." She arched her eyebrow and pulled Ellie in for a deep kiss. Those soft lips, the lush slickness of Ellie's mouth, brought her fully back to the present.

"Time to pay the bill so we can leave." Grinning, Ellie smacked her arm and stood up.

Chapter Twelve

ELLIE'S STREET WAS a typical winter scene in Chicago—salt-crusted cars packed between petrified piles of snow, the occasional shoveled-out dibs gap like a missing tooth. She recognized Mr. Pham's meticulously cleared spot. He always strung a ragged strip of caution tape from two stacked milk crates to an oversized garden gnome. Olivia had circled until she found a space a block away, but Ellie's simmering anticipation staved off the worst of the cold as they walked. Their breath danced in the windless night, and she relished their curled fingers, the lazy arc of their swinging arms. When they reached her building, she led them up the stairs, still hand in hand. In the heat of the hallway, Olivia's palm grew damp against her own.

"This is me." Ellie pulled her keys from her purse.

"It's a nice building."

"Yeah, I like it."

Olivia leaned a shoulder on the door frame. "How long have you lived here?"

"Four years. It's a short 'L' ride to where I used to work."

"Quiet neighbors?"

Ellie paused, the key halfway in the lock. Olivia's eyes flickered with an unsettled quality she hadn't seen before. "You don't make small talk. What's up?"

"What do you mean?"

"Don't do this. Don't go away. Tell me what you're thinking."

"I wasn't—"

The key jerked from Ellie's hand as the door swung inward. "Hola, 'manita. Did you—"

"Jesuchristo, 'Berto! What the fucking hell?"

Her brother's abashed face hovered in the half-open door. "I thought you were having trouble with the lock! I was letting you in."

"Why are you even here?" She wanted to strangle him for interrupting Olivia's thought.

"To discuss Mamá's birthday party?"

"Shit! I completely forgot." They'd set this up earlier in the week, but her excitement about Olivia's last-minute plans had driven everything else from her brain. "I'm so sorry."

"No es nada."

"It's not nothing, 'Berto. I should have texted you." She glanced at Olivia, who was drifting farther into the hallway. "Okay, hang on a second. Olivia, this is my brother, Alberto Vasquez. 'Berto, this is Olivia Northman, the woman I'm seeing."

"Nice to meet you." Olivia offered her hand, which Alberto took with his characteristic enthusiasm.

"You too, Ms.—"

"Alberto, I'm not much older than you. Call me Olivia. Please."

"Perdóneme, Olivia."

Ellie held her brother's gaze, willing him to catch her hint. "Ben is staying at his aunt's house tonight. It was last minute. I'm sorry about the mix-up."

Olivia stuffed her hands in her pockets. "I can go if—"

"No!" Ellie interrupted her more urgently than she meant to. "'Berto comes over late sometimes after his shift. We can do this another time."

"I hate to run you off," Olivia said. "At least stay for a quick drink."

A groan tried to escape. She wanted her brother gone and Olivia naked in her bed. Alberto sensed the trap, clearly reading her consternation but too polite to refuse Olivia. Plastering a smile on her face, Ellie pushed open the door. "Let's have a drink."

She shoved her brother in the shoulder as she passed through. "Una cerveza y te vas, hermano."

Alberto flicked her ear. "Tan impaciente."

"Tan cachonda. Keep it in mind, chatty pants."

Despite her brother's teasing, he kept to his one-drink promise, spinning funny childhood stories around carefully placed questions. Ellie had told him Olivia's general history, and she appreciated how he managed to appear the curious big brother without actually prying.

When she walked him to the door, she placed a grateful kiss on his cheek and threw her arms around him. "You're the best hermano I could ask for. Thanks. And sorry again."

"Me gusta ésta. Es amable." He winked. "Y caliente."

"Gracias, Alberto," Olivia called from the living room. "No estás tan mal, pero su hermana es más caliente."

Alberto's eyes widened in what must have been a perfect match for her own. "You didn't tell me she spoke Spanish!"

Olivia poked her head around the corner and grinned.

"How do I not know this?" Ellie asked.

"Tonight is the most I've heard you use it. I got a Spanish minor in college because it made sense with the nursing job."

"Any other languages in your secret stash?"

"I picked up some Tagalog. And there are a couple of Korean curse words I save for special occasions."

"I think we're busted, hermana." Alberto gave Olivia a quick wave and slipped out the door. He grinned as she closed it. "Me gusta."

"Yo también."

"I like him, too," Olivia said. "He's corto, though, more than I expected. Where do you get your height?"

"My mother's father was the tallest man in the village, and all of his height landed on me. I clear each of my brothers by a few inches. 'Berto's the shortest."

Olivia struck a relaxed pose, propped against a corner of the entryway, long legs crossed at the ankle, but her fists were buried in her pockets. The fabric rustled as she clenched and unclenched them.

"Why did you invite 'Berto for a drink?" Ellie asked.

"I was curious. You got to meet Arti already. Why? Should I not have?"

"It's fine, but I thought maybe by inviting him, you were avoiding...this." She pointed at herself, then Olivia. "Us."

Olivia sighed, her shoulders collapsing with the sound. "Not avoid, exactly."

"You're nervous." Ellie hooked a finger in a belt loop and tugged, placing a hand on Olivia's chest. Her heart drummed beneath the skin. "But you were so confident at the restaurant."

"I know, but with every step on the stairs—"

She'd never seen Olivia skittish, and a tender concern tamped the desire nipping at her heels. "If you're not ready, we can wait."

"I don't want to wait. But what if I'm not what you're expecting? What if—"

"I thought you were amazing from the moment I saw you. Nothing we do, or don't do, tonight will change that." She led Olivia to the bedroom. "We can stop anytime you want."

"Okay." Olivia's whisper fell into the sliver of space between them.

Ellie lifted the shirt over Olivia's head and kissed one wiry shoulder. The soft click of hooks releasing mingled with their uneven breaths, and then she peeled away the bra. Ellie had ached for this moment, when nothing separated her from the full expanse of Olivia's skin. Touching her forehead to Olivia's, she let her fingers trace twin lines across her collarbones to the sharp plane of her shoulders and down, ending at the knobs of bone at her wrist. She moved to Olivia's waist, was about to run her palms up that long torso, when Olivia grabbed her wrists. Ellie tipped back a few inches to meet her eyes. They were guarded, but they didn't break contact as Olivia lifted Ellie's hands and rested them on her ribs. A sharp breath expanded against her palms before it registered.

Ellie dropped to the edge of the bed on nerveless legs. It was obvious now, the web of scars on Olivia's left side, the biggest an angry serration marring the outer curve of her breast. The brutal tangle pulsed with each breath, and she looked up to find Olivia's face with that same flat, careful expression.

"The accident?"

Olivia nodded. Her mouth opened, then closed into a thin line.

Tears pricked at Ellie. To see these marks on Olivia, a physical scrawl of an old pain—it stole the air from her lungs. *Almost killed all three of them*. It seemed impossible she might never have met this woman.

Olivia tried to retreat from the scrutiny, but Ellie cradled her between her knees. If she wanted all of Olivia, it felt right to start here, to face this wound as she would any other—head-on, unafraid. She placed a kiss in the center of the cluster, and Olivia gasped. Ellie traveled each scar, planting kisses as she went as if she could remove the pain, the heartache, with every touch. She'd almost finished when Olivia rested a hand on her cheek.

"Please, Ellie..." The words were ground glass on her tongue.

Ellie stood and wrapped her in a tight hug. "I'm sorry, I'm so sorry." She couldn't tell if it was for the accident, the scars, or her attention to them. "This doesn't have to happen now."

Olivia drew back. Turbulent eyes pinned Ellie in place. "I want it to happen. I need this to happen." Then Olivia kissed her with a desperate passion.

The world narrowed to the urgent exchange of their open, hungry mouths, and the desire Ellie had, this terrible ache for Olivia, burst free. Spinning Olivia to the bed, she poured herself into the kiss. Ellie had never wanted to consume someone like this. Her teeth nipped that long neck and grazed angular shoulders. She licked the crook of an elbow, curled a tongue into the shell of an ear. Pressing her lips to one wrist, she absorbed its pounding pulse. When she sucked a pale pink nipple into her mouth, she moaned along with Olivia.

"Harder," Olivia rasped.

She bit with more force, and Olivia shuddered, grabbing her hair to drag her closer. No woman had ever let her attack her breasts with such aggression, and she grew wetter with each scrape of teeth across screwed-tight nipples. Breath pinched short by eagerness, she unbuttoned Olivia's pants and drew everything down her endless legs in one motion. She nuzzled her patch of curls—blonde mixed with gray—and inhaled her sharp, sweet scent. The urge to bury her face there nearly overwhelmed her, but she needed to be close this first time, face-to-face, so she kissed the soft dip of Olivia's navel and continued up.

Olivia's head was thrown back, eyes closed, fingers snarled in the comforter. Ellie was even with her now, and she spread Olivia's right leg open, pinning it gently to the bed with the weight of her hip.

"Olivia," she whispered.

Those beautiful eyes opened, filled with every color of wheat and gold and green and gray, and Ellie sank her fingers into that soft, wet heat. Olivia sucked in a breath as her eyes closed again. Exploring the length of her in long, slick passes, Ellie luxuriated in the sticky rhythm of their bodies, the clit swelling beneath her touch. Mumbled pleas and choppy gasps spilled from Olivia's mouth, and she opened herself wider, begging with her body as much as her words. Ellie skimmed her cheek along Olivia's, their breath hot and close, and quickened her strokes. Olivia came without warning, crying out and arching against her. Ellie captured her open mouth, swallowing the sounds surging from her throat. As they began to subside, she broke off the kiss but stayed close, Olivia's warm pants filling her mouth.

Without waiting, Ellie eased two fingers deep into her. Olivia buried her face in Ellie's neck, her growled *yes* stretching into a hiss. She started slow, but as Olivia's breath grew ragged, she increased the pace. Olivia bent her other knee higher, trying to take in more, and when Ellie added a third finger, a low, guttural groan rolled through her. The sound deepened when she came again, clutching Ellie, digging her right heel into her calf. As the orgasm finally quieted, Ellie started to pull out, but Olivia grabbed her wrist.

"Stay there."

She lingered in the velvet-sleek space. Small spasms still pulsed, but fleetingly. The lush folds began to soften, and through the thin skin, a distant heartbeat throbbed. When Olivia shifted, she eased out of her, bringing her hand up to run it through her long waves of hair. Olivia opened her eyes at the touch. When they met Ellie's, so close, a quiet sob tore itself from her chest. It startled Ellie, but she enclosed Olivia with her arms and legs to keep her from flying apart. Sobs wracking her body, Olivia tucked her forearms around her ribs as if she could do nothing to protect herself but curl into a ball. Ellie waited, running her palm along her spine until a muffled voice emanated from under her chin.

"I'm sorry." Olivia lifted her face, mapped with tears and wonder. "The way you kissed me when I came, when I saw you right there..."

"But Jen—"

"It wasn't...so intimate. I didn't think I could be this open again."

"I want to always make you feel this way."

Olivia hiccupped a laugh and rested her forehead on Ellie's cheek. "Oh God, if I come like this every time, I may not survive."

"I suppose you can have too much of a good thing." She lifted Olivia's chin. "I am grateful though. For all of this."

"Me too." Olivia placed a damp kiss on her lips, then tried to deepen it.

"Hold on," Ellie said. Olivia was a jumble of raw edges right now. She needed time.

"But what about—"

"You'll get your chance. Take a minute." Ellie tucked the comforter around Olivia and went into the bathroom. Humming to herself, she started a bath and lit candles, then returned to Olivia, who lay where she had left her, naked and spent. "Get ready for the best bath of your life."

"You're overdressed for a bath. In fact, you're overdressed, period."

"Once I got you naked, there was no stopping. Told you I can be impatient." Tossing her black sweater to the floor,

Ellie stood in front of Olivia in her black bra and jeans. Although she'd been wearing exactly this in the supply closet, now, in her own bedroom, painted by the gentle glow of a lamp, she felt newly exposed. She fumbled with the button of her jeans.

"Wait." Olivia crawled off the bed and stood up.

Ellie's pulse hammered in her ears. Olivia had flirted with her these past months, but she'd only seen that fierce desire once before, at the fundraiser. Gentle fingers eased the straps of her bra down her shoulders.

"You're so sexy. I haven't stopped thinking about you since our night at the bar." Olivia buried her face in Ellie's cleavage. "I love the way you smell."

A shiver tickled her neck as Olivia unhooked the bra and cast it to the floor. She cupped each breast, piling the flesh in her palms and brushing circles around the nipples with her thumbs. Bending to nestle her face under a breast, Olivia laved the soft skin with her tongue. "And you taste even better." Ellie's whole body sang with need.

Olivia's left hand skimmed her spine and slid under the waist of her jeans. "Here," she murmured against Ellie's neck. "I was here when that damn knock interrupted us." She plunged lower, palming one cheek, and Ellie groaned. Circling her hand around Ellie's hip, Olivia undid the button, then followed a faint trail of hair from her navel. "But I wanted to be here." Fingertips grazed the curls they found. "I wanted to know what you sounded like when you came."

Ellie's knees nearly buckled when Olivia stripped off everything to the floor. She fought the impulse to push Olivia to the bed, to straddle her face and show her exactly how she sounded, but the chatter of water reminded her of a slower pace, a different plan. "Now that I'm naked—" She rasped the last word and had to clear her throat. "—maybe we should get in the bath. Because I don't know what's going to overflow first, it, or me." She took Olivia's hand and led her to the bathroom.

"You have the biggest tub I've ever seen."

Ellie laughed and turned off the tap. "I love baths. When I bought this place, I had to move a wall to accommodate the tub. There's even an extra joist in the floor for the weight."

"You must have a water heater the size of Canada."

"Close."

They lowered themselves into the steaming water, Olivia running her legs along the walls of the tub. Ellie settled hers in the middle before pinching her nose and sinking below the surface. She emerged in a rush, water streaming through her hair.

"I'm going to enjoy baths if they always come with your own personal mermaid." Olivia radiated desire, and it made Ellie breathless to be the focus of it. She smiled and pushed sopping curls back from her face. The gesture raised her nipples above the waterline.

Olivia bit her lower lip. "Your breasts are amazing."

Ellie pulled her arms down to cover them, hesitated, then rested a forearm on each edge of the tub instead.

"I didn't mean to make you self-conscious. Am I...? I can't be the first woman to compliment them." Olivia's consternation would have made her laugh if she weren't so irritated with herself.

"They're bigger than they— Never mind."

"I don't understand."

"I was being insecure. I hate when I do that."

Olivia clasped her feet and shook them. "Tell me."

Ellie ground her fist into her forehead. This wasn't a story she'd expected to share. "I met my most recent ex, Angie, at the gym. I was in a dedicated exercise phase, trying to shake this depressive slump post-Jill, and Angie had started training to be a triathlete. She loved the workouts, the discipline. But it started to feel all-consuming. If we weren't there together, she was there on her own.

"As we got serious—as I thought we were getting serious anyway—I wanted more time for us. I cut back, focused on other stuff. I got heavier, and everything got bigger." She gestured toward her breasts. "I felt sexier actually. But Angie... I can see now, she probably resented the change in our dynamic, her shifting up a gear as I shifted down, but it came out as passive-aggressive comments. Covering myself, it's an old reflex. One I thought I'd left behind."

"You're a Renaissance painting. You're stunning. What could she possibly say?"

The obvious astonishment blunted the rough edge of memory. "It was never direct. Just toss offs about missing me at the gym or picking apart the health benefits of meals I'd cooked. All the faux health crap people throw at fat women. At the end it was hard, especially in bed, seeing myself through her eyes. I wanted her to be happy, and she obviously wasn't."

Before Olivia could protest, Ellie lifted a hand. "I knew it was her deal, not mine. And honestly, the weight issue was a symptom of other problems, but sometimes it still bothers me, even though it shouldn't. And then I'm mad at myself for letting it bother me." She grimaced and pinched the bridge of her nose.

"Ellie." Olivia tapped her knee. "Isabella."

She didn't like her given name. It was stuffy, formal. But when Olivia said it, low and sensual, it didn't sound stuffy at all.

Olivia lifted Ellie's foot and kissed the pad of her big toe. "There isn't a part of you I'd change." A tongue laved her arch. "There isn't a piece of you that doesn't take my breath away." Teeth nipped her heel. "And I will prove it by licking every square inch of your luscious skin."

The lust in Olivia's intent eyes scattered Ellie's response.

"Is it okay that I called you Isabella?"

"How you say it is really sexy, in moments like this."

"I'll save it for special occasions." Olivia winked and put her face close to the water. "Isabella, tell me about your first time."

The words skimmed the surface, sounding louder to her ears. "You mean having sex?"

"Focus on a happier memory. Lean back, close your eyes, and describe the whole thing."

"Okay." Curious, she settled against the tub, closing her eyes. Candlelight trembled faintly through her lids. "My sophomore year of college, I met a girl at a party. Well, I knew her from a class—" Strong thumbs dug into her arch, and a moan burst loose. "That feels incredible, but it makes it hard to talk."

"Focus. You can do it."

"Okay, focuuussssss." Thumbs pressed a line from her heel up to the ball of her foot.

"What was her name?"

"Shannon. Her name was Shannon. She had amazing red hair."

"Everywhere?"

"Yes, everywhere." She poked Olivia in the ribs with her other toe.

Olivia grabbed that wayward foot, following the same path of delicious pressure. "Keep going."

"Ohhhhhkay. She started talking about class, and I thought she was fliiirrrting." Ellie fought for a deep breath as Olivia stroked her calves. "It was hard to tell...oh God...but then she kissed me."

"A good sign."

"We made out at the party but left when it broke up. I lived at home, so we went to her place, some crappy apartment— Jesus, what are you doing?"

Olivia's hands slid to her thighs, spreading them. Water sloshed against her sensitive nipples, sending desire arcing to her clit.

"Who made the first move?"

"I don't remember." She could barely recall her own name at the moment. "We were kissing, rolling around on her bed—uhhhhh." Thumbs swept her inner thighs, brushed her labia, and slipped away. "I couldn't get her bra un-hooked!"

Olivia's laughed bounced off the tiles.

Ellie cracked an eye open. "It's not funny. I'm a woman, for christ's sake, and I can't unhook a bra."

"Close your eyes. No cheating," Olivia said mock-seriously, and Ellie grinned and put her head back. "It happens. Doing it in reverse can be tricky."

The water slapped the tub as Olivia knelt between her legs. Her palms blazed a path along her ribs, under the water.

"What are you—"

"Shhh. What happened next?"

"She straddled me and removed the bra herself. She was busty—oh God." Warm hands slid under Ellie's breasts. "So they fell toward my face when she leaned over meeeee." Fingers rolled her hard nipples, and her pulse pounded a drumbeat straight to her clit. "I thought I might pass out from excitement."

"I know exactly what you mean." The tip of Olivia's tongue traced slow circles around her areola.

"Uhhhh...I could have—" Ellie's breath snagged in her lungs. Her skin crawled with electricity.

Olivia lifted her other breast from the water, letting it cool and pucker in air. "You could have what?"

Ellie expected Olivia's tongue again, its slick, muscular attention. When teeth bit down, firm but careful, she yelped. "Icouldhavesuckedonherbreastsallnight!"

"Did you?" Olivia asked the question around the nipple in her teeth, breath tickling Ellie's skin. She tugged on it, a slow, erotic withdrawal, her teeth scraping with exquisite pressure until it finally popped free.

Ellie's shudder rippled the water. "It...felt like it. But we did a lot of things."

"Did she touch you here?" When Olivia drew a finger along her slick lips, Ellie almost levitated.

"Jesusssssssss."

"How about here?" Olivia's thumb circled her clit.

She arched into the contact, air leaking between her teeth.

"And here?" Olivia stroked each fold and tender lip while Ellie writhed. "And did she do this?" Two gentle fingers slipped inside her.

After the delicious, agonizing build, Ellie had expected release, but this tender penetration only wound her tighter. Olivia froze. A swinging strand of hair tickled Ellie's chest. Her own shallow pants grew louder in her ears. She was seconds away from begging. Or screaming. Or both.

"Uhhhnnn." Ellie arched again as Olivia began to fuck her in earnest. Those fingers now thrust with relentless intensity, curling to brush one spot over and over. She pulled her knees up to open herself, rocking against Olivia's hand, willing her deeper, harder, and Olivia responded, driving into her with pounding strokes that spurred her to the edge of climax.

"And did you come hard?" The words hovered in her ear.

Her groan exploded into a shout, and she plunged over the edge, the thrusting hand drawing out wave after endless wave. Olivia's thumb slid along her clit, strengthening the orgasm, prolonging it until a final crest crashed through her in a hot, pulsing rush. She had never heard the sounds bursting from her own throat.

Finally, Ellie's heart began to slow, and she lowered her knees. She peeled open her eyes when Olivia's head came to rest between her breasts. She hadn't had an orgasm like that...ever. Another minute passed as she sorted through her sputtering brain and found the power of speech. "Jesus, Olivia. I mean...I just...that was...without a doubt, the sexiest thing someone has ever done to me."

Olivia's low chuckle chased a shiver down her spine.

"Tell me about your first time, while I recover."

Olivia went still. Unsure about the shift, Ellie wrapped her arms around her shoulders.

"I was a freshman in college. I met this girl, a senior. She was the RA in my dorm. Cute, dark hair, great tits. Totally my type."

Ellie snorted and pinched Olivia's ear.

"Short though. Five feet at best. So funny. So smart. Just...brilliant." Olivia's wistful sigh flowed across her chest. "She was out, and she was the most spectacular woman I'd ever seen. I don't know what she saw in me, but she let me tag along when she made her rounds at night, up one stairwell and down the other. We talked about everything as we walked.

"After a month, she slipped her hand into mine on the first floor. It was perfect, like we'd done it a thousand times before. That went on for a few days until, one night, she stood on the first step and kissed me. I could taste the apple pie she stole from the cafeteria." A smile curled against Ellie's skin.

"She acted like nothing happened, and we started up the stairs. On each floor, she'd kiss me even longer until we finished her rounds back at her room. She took me to bed, as the stories say, and I was never the same."

"What was her name?" Ellie asked, entranced by the romance and Olivia's obvious warmth in telling it.

"Sophia."

Ellie's voice evaporated.

Olivia shifted to rest her chin on her chest. "I'm sorry. I shouldn't have brought it up right after we—"

"It's okay."

"It felt wrong to say nothing when you'd been so open, but I couldn't explain without...explaining."

"I'm the one who asked. Don't hide anything from me because you think I'll be upset. Especially about Sophia." She cupped Olivia's cheeks. "It just surprised me. I didn't know she was your first. You've mentioned several college relationships."

"There's more to the story, but we don't have to do this now."

"Give me the short version. I'm curious." Olivia hadn't hidden Sophia, exactly, but their history always felt curated, as if Olivia had stripped away the details to shield her. Ellie wouldn't lose this chance to learn more.

"We were together her whole senior year, but she went to law school at UCLA. The long-distance thing was a lot—I was only nineteen—so we decided to break up. Arti calls the rest of college my 'tepidly promiscuous' era."

"What does that mean?"

"I stank at getting laid on the first date. I wanted to know the women, so I had four girlfriends in three years, one at a time."

"Does it count as promiscuous if you're always monogamous?"

"It was the best I could do." Olivia's grin mixed the sweet and abashed in the most adorable way. "Anyway, Sophia returned to Chicago after law school. I was finishing college, getting ready to be a nurse. We were both invited to the same party and started talking. Turns out she'd also been tepidly promiscuous, with no success. We got together that night, and from then on, we were never apart."

"It's great you found each other again." She kissed Olivia's forehead to dissolve any stray tension. "Is it me, or is this water getting tepid?"

Olivia tickled her thigh. "Let's get dried off. We're not done yet." When she crooked an eyebrow, Ellie melted into her, stealing a fierce kiss before she could slip away.

ELLIE SPRAWLED ON her back, eyes unfocused, and let the sensations roll over her. In the bath, Olivia had promised to explore every square inch of skin, but Ellie hadn't realized how serious she was. She'd recalled Olivia's musings about the female form so many times, aching to be one of those women. Reality blotted out any whim of her imagination.

The singular attention made her newly aware of her own body—the backs of her knees, the crease where her thigh met her ass, the sensitive flesh under her bicep. Olivia had buried her face in the soft skin where leg met hip, murmuring about her smell, her taste. Now she straddled Ellie, and her tangled curls cascaded around them.

"Your body is amazing." Olivia nuzzled her cheek before capturing her mouth, lips parted, breath hot. When she broke away to look at her, Ellie sank into that intimate, desirous gaze. "You're perfect."

Tears leaked from her eyes, and Olivia kissed them dry. Lips skimmed her cheeks, her chin, before coasting down her neck and across her chest. Olivia kissed the side of her breast, then raked her tongue across an aching nipple. Ellie closed her eyes as Olivia worshipped her breasts. It was the only word that fit. Olivia made her feel worshipped. Tender but insistent, she moved from one breast to the other until something between a sigh and a sob burst out of Ellie.

The bed creaked. The sheets shifted. Then Olivia's lips closed over her clit and sucked, hard. Ellie's cry was so loud she was sure she'd woken her neighbors, but she was beyond caring. The orgasm ripped through her like fire. Gone was the slow, reverential Olivia. She devoured her now. When Olivia thrust her tongue inside her, Ellie lifted her hips from the bed and grabbed fistfuls of blonde hair, pulling her deeper. She wanted more. She wanted everything. She wanted this woman to climb inside her and never leave.

When the last spasms faded, she released Olivia's hair, and Olivia crawled up to settle on her shoulder, resting a hand between her breasts. The weight on her sternum was all that kept Ellie's heart from beating its way out of her chest.

"What have you done?" She didn't know whether to laugh or cry.

"I couldn't go to sleep without tasting you." Olivia's husky voice rumbled near her ear.

"You have ruined me, Olivia. Ruined me."

"Oh, we're just getting started. I have more where that came from."

"You mean now?"

"No, no. In the future."

She flushed at the word—future. "Good, because right now I can't feel anything below my neck."

"Thanks for letting me explore. I've wanted to do that since I saw you in the mirror."

"*You* are thanking *me*?"

There was a high, light quality to Olivia's laugh, one Ellie hadn't heard before.

"You don't understand how much I love it," Olivia said.

"Oh, I have some idea. Give me a sec, and then it's your turn."

"What if I can't wait?"

"Now who's impatient?"

Olivia lifted herself to a kneeling position. "I have an idea."

"Show me."

Olivia shifted to straddle her face, grabbing the head-board for support. As Olivia lowered herself, Ellie gazed up her long torso, the underside of her breasts, the sharp cut of her jaw. Her own words echoed. *You have ruined me, Olivia. Ruined me.*

Chapter Thirteen

OLIVIA YANKED ARTI by the elbow and steered her toward the pharmacy section. "No, no, no. We're not going any-where near the jewelry. It took me an hour to calm you down the last time."

"This crap is an insult to jewelry!"

"I know, mass-produced trinkets ruin the livelihoods of real artists."

"Stop pandering!" Arti shoved her sideways, hard enough she had to dodge a skin cream display. "Why are we running errands anyway?"

"You wanted the Ellie lowdown, and I need to shop while Ben is at Jamal's." Olivia tossed a bottle of ibuprofen into the cart. "Zariah and I have a firm 'no one deals with them alone for more than two hours' pact, and her hus-band's pulling the weekend shift."

"But there's a cute wine bar down the block!"

The back wheel of the cart locked up as they turned the corner. Olivia kicked it loose. "And when was the last time we met at a wine bar?"

"Exactly my point!"

"You're the one with the hot date. Otherwise, you could've had wine at my place later."

"Which reminds me." Arti threw a box of condoms at her.

Olivia plucked them out of midair and dropped them in the cart. "You're still buying these? If you can spring for the IUD, couldn't the guy scrounge some condoms?"

"I do not use any form of protection that has been *scrounged*. A woman should always take responsibility for her own safe sex."

"And if the guy isn't willing to do the same?"

"Then he may not be long-term material. But I've had a dry spell since George, and I'm horny. Besides, the men I'm dating these days focus on their Viagra prescription."

"File that under things I don't have to worry about."

Arti rattled the cart. "Are you going to fill me in on last night or what?"

"It was good."

"Good? You fucked a buxom woman ten years your junior, and you lead with *good*?"

A woman passing the other direction glared at them. Olivia waved a casual apology. Decades with Arti had numbed her to public embarrassment.

Arti slapped her hand down. "I need more. Let's start with this morning. Any panic?"

The resistance rushed from Olivia along with her sigh. This tug of war was as old as their friendship. While the subjects changed, the end result never did. "Nope. I opened my eyes and saw her, and it was like she was supposed to be there." Nothing about this morning mirrored her first time with Jen. Sex with Ellie had completed a circle they'd been drawing for weeks. She and Jen— It was like being woken from a deep sleep by a bucket of water, stimulating and disorienting all at once.

"What about the night before?"

"I was nervous." The swift departure of her confidence had surprised her as much as Ellie.

"Why? This slow build was your plan all along."

"Yeah, but I didn't appreciate how much falling into bed with Jen saved me from thinking."

"Well, if you need saving from something, it's thinking."

"What do you mean?"

"Please." Arti braced herself on the cart, halting their progress. "You think about everything. Ahead of time. All the time."

"I didn't think about these, about warning her." Olivia brushed her scars, the fabric of her shirt soft against them.

Arti's brusque expression melted into sympathy. "Since Jen avoided them, you worried how Ellie might respond."

"Jen didn't avoid them. Her hands would land there when we—"

"But she never asked about them."

The package of bagels was in Olivia's hand before she realized it wasn't Ben's favorite brand, and she stuffed it back on the shelf. Her scars were the one aspect of the accident that asserted itself as a presence, rather than an absence. Most of her loss came in the form of negative space, the painful emptiness of what used to be, but the scars were a three-dimensional reality she couldn't ignore. They tugged when she reached for something high. Water from the shower ran in strange zigzags along their fractured path. The only person who'd seen them, before Jen, was Arti. Even her mom, in the hospital, left the room when they changed her bandages, too raw from the recent loss of her husband to face the damage that had nearly stolen her daughter.

"What was Jen supposed to say?" Olivia finally spotted the bag she wanted and dropped it in the cart. "She's going to deal with my tragic scarring right out of the gate?"

"I'm guessing Ellie did."

That memory held a sweet pain. Ellie's gentle kisses had made the scars feel nearly as raw and tender as after the accident, but her attention also loosened the band they cinched around Olivia's ribs. "It's not the same. Jen was dealing with her own—"

"Enough with Jen already!"

Olivia turned at the end of an aisle and crashed into a pallet, which pinned her between a trailing Arti and a cooler of frozen dinners. The motion sensor kicked on and bathed them in a sterile LED wash.

Arti took a firm step closer. "I can tell from how squirmy you are it was great last night, but instead of focusing on that, you circle back to an unsuccessful eight-month, off-and-on relationship. Do you know why?"

"Because you compare people, relationships—"

"Bullshit. Ellie already blows Jen out of the water. There's nothing to compare. But you do, these last few months, because it's safe. Much safer than comparing Ellie to the only woman who will ever matter."

Olivia whipped the cart around and pushed by Arti, wheeling past a blurry scroll of condiments, the shelves closing in. She crossed a broader aisle and abandoned her cart to pace among the racks of dresses.

"In here." Arti tossed her into a fitting room.

Olivia flinched from her own tense expression in the mirror and backed into a chattering mass of hangers. Her gaze crawled the narrow walls until finally soaring to the ceiling tiles, far away and floating. The vertical column of open space gave her room to breathe, and the stricture in her body eased. She had been relaxed with Ellie, so different from Jen, but now...

Another memory from last night surfaced—Ellie's warm, open-mouthed kiss as she came. Longing knifed Olivia's chest. It was one of her favorite things. Sophia had done it, their first time together, and somehow Ellie thought to do the same. That single kiss had stripped her bare.

"What is it? Tell me." Arti took her hands in a tight grip.

"Ellie did something only Sophia has ever done." Olivia collapsed onto the small red stool. "It was wonderful. And so painful. The emotions...I thought sex with Jen moved me past that."

"I hate to get all Hallmark on you, but I think you and Ellie made love last night. Sex with Jen was just sex. Which I'm a big fan of, myself, but for you...it sounds like you finally got what you wanted." Arti crouched low to meet her eyes. "From now on, consider Jen your preflight check. Flipping switches, making sure everything's in working order, ready to fly. Good to have, but it's not the same as lifting your wheels off the ground."

A laugh punched through. "Where are you getting this terrible analogy?"

"The guy I'm seeing tonight is a pilot. He's chatty about his job. I'm hoping he'll shut up once I'm sitting on his face."

"And how do you know Ellie isn't another test run?"

"I don't. But I like the way you are since you've started seeing her. So stop using Jen as a screen for any conflict you're feeling about Sophia. I know you. I know it's still in there. For now, focus on Ellie. You don't need to solve it all at once."

She sagged against the cool mirror and lifted her eyes to the distant ceiling again. "Focus on Ellie. Okay. I can do that."

Chapter Fourteen

ELLIE LOVED WAKING up next to Olivia, loved the dense heat of her slumbering body, loved sinking into the well of her gravity. She lifted her head from its burrow against Olivia's back. Sun ribboned through her sleep-tumbled hair, lighting the honey color from within and turning the gray to silver. A bare shoulder, skin like cream splashed on the navy sheets, lifted and fell with Olivia's sigh, and Ellie rested a featherlight hand there. Warmth sank into her palm. The steady, gentle heat reminded her of the radiator she and her brothers huddled around on winter mornings, of Abuela's comal after a long Saturday of tortilla-making. Olivia blamed perimenopause, but to Ellie, it felt more elemental. It felt like home.

Spotting Olivia across the lobby in August had been a jolt of recognition, a "where have you been" moment. She was careful to set that aside as they started dating, but the intimacy of their first night wrecked any fragile walls protecting her heart. The old Ellie would have blurted out an "I love you" before Olivia left the next morning, but she bit it back. She might be ready to say it, but she knew Olivia wasn't ready to hear it.

The connection of their first night sustained her as they cobbled together porch dates and stolen hours at her condo, biding their time until Christina could take Ben for another sleepover. She'd thrown herself at Olivia last night when she walked through the door, and with the first-time jitters behind them, they spent the evening in playful exploration. Ellie was usually the more adventurous partner in sex, but Olivia was comfortable in a way even she wasn't. It reminded her of Olivia's rock climbing—an intimate interaction with the surface around her, and whatever came next, whatever opportunity presented itself, she flowed in that direction.

She kissed a trail along one naked shoulder. A murmur, thick with sleep, leaked from Olivia's pillow. Ellie ran her tongue down her long spine, and as Olivia arched into the contact, she snuck a hand between her legs.

"Don't you know I'm an old woman?"

"Don't old people enjoy a morning constitutional?"

Olivia inched her thighs apart, and Ellie kept stroking, fingers growing slick as she kissed her way along a hip and rolled Olivia to her back.

"What are you doing?"

"I'm having you for breakfast."

The first firm pass of her tongue coaxed a shudder, and she smiled against gray and gold curls before continuing, one demanding sweep at a time, Olivia's honey and salt taste coating her lips. Olivia dragged a pillow over her face, then wrapped her legs around Ellie's shoulders and ground into her as she orgasmed, wet and hot in Ellie's mouth.

Olivia tossed the pillow away. "Come here, on top of me."

Ellie scooted up the bed, first grinning, then confused, when Olivia stopped her.

"Hold on." With a long stretch, she yanked on the curtains and flooded the bed with light. "Straddle me. Here, across my stomach."

She settled onto Olivia, blinking against the flare of sun. Olivia sucked in a breath, and her gaze raked Ellie's skin like another hand, bringing gooseflesh wherever it passed. Ellie's own hands moved restlessly, and Olivia stilled them.

"Please don't hide yourself. You're gorgeous. Let me see you."

Olivia eased her fingers between Ellie's legs, stroking until she was so ready she couldn't focus. Then she slipped them inside. Ellie grunted, wanting to drop her hips, to grind down. But for the first time with Olivia, she hesitated, unsure in this new position.

"Do it." Olivia's low voice tunneled into her thoughts.

"What?" She gasped as Olivia slid a third finger in and drove deeper.

"Fuck my hand. I know you want to." The vulgarity on Olivia's lips sent fresh desire rippling through her.

"But am I too—"

Olivia cut her off with a shake. "I can take whatever you give me." A thumb coasted over Ellie's clit in lazy circles, and she let her head fall back, a silent moan trapped in her throat.

She sank onto Olivia's hand, slowly at first, then with more force. With each pass, Olivia's thumb stroked her clit, sparking like flint on steel. A rhythm developed, Olivia plunging deep with every fall of Ellie's hips, and she rode the delicious line between penetration and pain. Every time she closed her eyes, sun blazed red behind her lids. She didn't know what was more blinding—the morning light or Olivia's burning regard—but the sense of being visible, of being so urgently *seen*, turned her on in a way she'd never experienced before. As the orgasm began to roll through her, she arched hard.

Olivia drew her knees up. "I've got you. Let me see you come. I want to see all of you."

Gripping Olivia's thighs, she tipped back, the last of her self-consciousness dissolving as she cried out, fully exposed. Every tremble, every strain, every quiver—she let Olivia witness all of it, then collapsed onto her in a panting, boneless heap of astonishment and joy. No one had ever made her feel this beautiful, this sexy, this wanted.

"How do you do this?" Ellie clenched a handful of Olivia's hair in each fist.

"Do what?"

"Make me feel so fucking sexy."

"I don't understand why you don't feel fucking sexy every minute of the day."

Ellie's eyes watered despite her best effort to reign them in.

"Hey, what's going on?"

The words surged behind her lips. *What's going on is, I've fallen in love with you, Olivia Northman.* They sounded so clear in her mind she thought she'd said them out loud, but Olivia's expression didn't change.

"I'm emotional right now, sorry. The orgasm was intense."

Olivia quirked a half-smile that made her heart trill, then drew her into the warm cocoon of her arms. "Don't be sorry for what you feel. Ever."

ELLIE TRACED OLIVIA'S ribs in slow, repetitive strokes. The patch of sun that lit her aglow earlier had slid inexorably off the bed, a waterfall of light pooling onto the floor. Their skin was tacky with sex, the air thick with the smell of it, and still she wanted more. More time, more Olivia, more everything.

"Earlier, when you were on top...does it bother you, your weight?" Olivia's question slipped into the silence. She laced their fingers together and rubbed Ellie's palm with her thumb. "Because if you need anything from me, I want—"

Ellie squeezed their interlocked hands. "No, you make me feel amazing, but I haven't been this active in bed since I got heavier. Certain positions are different."

"But you and Angie?"

"Our sex life suffered when we fought, and honestly, I gained more weight after it ended. The post-breakup emotional eating struggle is real."

"I'm the opposite. When I get stressed, nothing tastes good. Arti's mom would throw food at me when I came home from college after finals. I would start eating again in self-defense." Olivia rolled on her side and touched their foreheads together. "You are beautiful. Breathtaking. Absolutely perfect. I need to know you hear me when I say that."

"These bursts of insecurity peek out, and I hate them, but I do hear you. And it means so much." Ellie snuggled her face into the curve of Olivia's neck. "Being on top is partly logistical. We're new together, and my body's different than it was."

"You're talking to a woman who can't get out of bed without a joint cracking. I understand different. Listen, I'll tell you if there's something my creaky old bones can't do, but until then, I want to give your body all it can handle. Please."

Olivia sketched a thumb along Ellie's eyebrow and down her jaw before pulling her in for a languorous kiss that made her teeth ache. Kissing Olivia filled her with a desperate joy, an urge to weep and laugh in the same breath. She almost did both when they finally separated, Olivia tugging her lip with her teeth as the last spark of contact.

Olivia's phone chirped, and her chest expanded with a sigh. "I should officially start planning to shower. Pancake Saturday at Christina's only lasts so long."

"I hate to sound needy, but it's never enough."

"I've been thinking about this. To have more time together, I need to integrate you into my life."

Excitement prickled, but she forced her hand to continue its casual stroking of Olivia's ribs. "What about Ben?" He was the reason for their measured pace, but this choppy intimacy wore on them both.

"If we want to see if this can work, he has to know. Anyone who's with me is with him. We could try a lunch firs—"

She stopped Olivia with a kiss. She'd been eager to talk about the next step, but bringing it up first was like treading on a frozen pond. There was no way to know when the ice might break.

Olivia pulled back and held her face. "I can't make any predictions. Things with Ben have a habit of going well, then erupting. What we do depends on how he's acting."

"I understand. I'm just happy you're willing, that you think enough of me to try."

"I think everything of you. Which is why I want to try." Olivia continued the kiss now, and Ellie poured all her gratitude, her happiness, her passion into it. Surging with desire, she worked her hand lower.

Olivia tore her mouth away to gasp a protest. "Shower... I have to—"

Ellie grinned. "There's time for one last orgasm."

A low moan rattled Olivia's chest as she opened her legs. "You know I can't resist your damn dimple!"

Chapter Fifteen

OLIVIA DROVE PAST split-level ranches, tidy blocks of beige, white, or gray set back from tidy blocks of weary winter grass. The streets were broad and the lots were wide, but the monotonous, placating openness reminded her too much of where she grew up. Her sister-in-law's house hunkered in the middle of the block. She pulled into the driveway and parked under a battered basketball hoop. The side door to the garage was ajar, and a shadow streaked across it as someone moved within. A dull dread settled over her. Sophia's family hadn't just welcomed her, they'd clutched her close, and she never questioned their effusive love, never wondered if it would hold. Until now. She peeled her clenched fingers from the steering wheel, then forced herself out of the car. The side door squeaked as she opened it fully, and Christina looked up from a pile of storage bins.

"Oh, hey, you got my text about the garage."

"I did." They exchanged kisses to each cheek and a warm hug. "But why are you out here?"

"I'm just getting these down while Frank and the boys clean the kitchen. We're finally putting the Christmas decorations away this weekend."

Olivia took the coffee Christina handed her. Faint steam curled around her cheeks with the first bracing sip. "Bless you."

Christina cleared a space on a wicker bench stored against the wall so they could sit. The last box she moved was for the family tree topper, an antique passed down from her father. They'd traded it back and forth, each year, until Sophia's death. Faded Italian scrolled along the battered cardboard sides. A cellophane cutout in the lid had been patched with yellowing tape, and through it, an angel-shaped depression stared out from faded green velvet lining.

"This time always hits hard for me." Christina set the box on a larger plastic bin and sat back, leaning against the garage wall. "Sophia told you, I suppose, how we fought about her liking girls in high school? I didn't understand. If she was attracted to both, couldn't she pick the easier one?"

"She mentioned a falling out." Olivia glided past the full truth of her wife's teenage devastation, which she'd learned of in college. Resurrecting that pain served no one.

"I was furious at her for changing things and scared it would ruin my senior year with gossip. We barely spoke for months. After the Epiphany service, I found her crying in our room. She'd kissed a girl—"

"I couldn't believe she got her first girl kiss in a Catholic Church!"

"That's our Sophia. Go big or go home." Christina choked, caught between a laugh and a sob. "The other girl confessed to the priest, and Sophia was terrified he'd tell our parents. Once I saw her fear and how brave she must have been to kiss her, all my anger disappeared."

Olivia knew the entire story, beat by beat, but grief had taught her patience when people shared their memories.

Everyone was crafting their own oral history of Sophia. Each retelling made it more indelible. "She said you made it possible for her to tell Nonna and Nonno before the priest did."

"I think of those months of silence and what a fool I was. I'd do anything now for six more months with her." Christina wiped tears from her cheeks. "Sorry for dumping this on you."

"It's fine, really." A muffled, playful shout echoed from the house, followed by a burst of several voices in laughter, Ben's high trill among them. The older he got, the more he could embrace the boisterous energy of Christina's house. For a time, at least. "Thanks again for taking him."

"Of course. Frank loves it, especially with Matteo living on his own. The more boys the better, as far as he's concerned." Christina twisted in place, a frown drawing twin furrows around her mouth. "He joked about wanting ten, but four was enough."

"Sciatica bothering you again?"

"When you ask me like that, I feel ninety years old."

"I hear you. My body doesn't bounce back the way it used to either." She hesitated at the shrewd look passing across Christina's face. "What?"

"Do you have something to bounce back from?"

Olivia huddled around her coffee and studied her sister-in-law. More salt than pepper wove through her hair, and at fifty-three, the crow's-feet never left. She didn't resemble Sophia, but the same intelligence glinted in her eyes. This woman had been part of Olivia's entire adult life. Facing their shared history, she fumbled for a way to show even a hint of a new future.

"You've met someone." Christina did the work for her.

Relief surged, along with shame in hiding from the words. "How did you know?"

"The sleepovers. And you seem happier, relaxed."

"Are you upset?"

"No." She ran a finger along the lip of her cup.

"Christina—"

"I'm not. At least, not with you. No one in this family expects you to be alone forever, but it's the last step to letting Sophia go, isn't it?"

Letting Sophia go. How did she let go of a woman she still saw every day? It might be the chestnut highlights in Ben's hair, or the way sunlight brought an amber glint to his eyes, or even the slant of his toes, but it was all Sophia. Still present. Still vivid.

"Ellie. Her name is Ellie." The world shuddered like a film skittering off the reel. With those five letters, Olivia transformed from a sister-in-law, a widow, a confidant in grief, into a woman creating a reality separate from Sophia. Silence throbbed. She had summoned Ellie into Christina's world, but she didn't know where to go next.

"What's Ellie short for?" Christina said the name carefully as if testing a strange sound she'd never associated with Olivia before.

"Isabella, but only her family calls her that."

"Italian?"

"Mexican."

"She has dark hair?"

The implication was hard to miss. "Yes, but curly, and she's almost my height."

"Really? That must feel different."

Ellie's sable eyes glittered in her mind. "It can be oddly intense. I'll turn to her, and she's right there. With Sophia, there'd be a beat as I looked down."

"What's she like?"

"She's very open and quick and sweet. She's an OT at the clinic, which is how we met."

Christina finished her coffee with a long swig, then squeezed the empty mug until her knuckles went white. "You've slept together?"

She thought of Ellie's tender, gentle face after her first orgasm. Emotion swelled—joy and regret so tangled she couldn't feel one without the other. "I wasn't sure I could be so open again. Part of me feels like I've betrayed Sophia."

"Absolutely not. You're allowed to be happy. Sophia would want you to be happy." Christina laid a hand on her arm. "I don't think I've said that yet. And I should have, a while ago. I'm sorry. I should've been the kind of sister-in-law who nudged you to find someone else, but...I was selfish. I wanted to keep her with us by keeping you with us, and—"

"I'll always be with you. With all of you. Me and Ben."

"And we'll always love you, no matter what changes, no matter who you open up to."

"Thanks, Christina." Tears stung, and she sniffed hard. "I'm such a mess lately. Emotional."

Christina dabbed at her own eyes. "Just wait for menopause."

"Oh, that's the craziest part. I forgot to tell you. Ellie's thirty-five."

"Shut up! You had sex with a thirty-five-year-old last night?"

Olivia let a tiny smirk slip out. "More than once."

Christina smirked back. "Keep that up, and I won't be the only one with sciatica."

The side door banged open as Ben charged through, face tacky with maple syrup. His jacket flapped wildly from one arm. "Mom! Frank said you were out here. We saved you pancakes. Come, come, come! I want to tell you about my checker moves!"

She tugged the coat over his other arm. "You can tell me all of them, but I need one more minute with Zia Christina. Will you make sure there's some syrup left for me? Because most of it's on your face." She regretted the crack the second he swiped at his sticky chin with his coat sleeve. The door banged open as he ran back through.

"You are definitely distracted, making that rookie mistake." Christina nudged her shoulder. "When are you going to tell Mamma?"

Olivia shrugged, her petite mother-in-law looming large. Their conversation...she needed more time.

"She'll be okay. I think." Christina patted her knee. "Did you really wait this long to tell me because of nerves?"

"MOM!" Ben's voice carried from the house. "Come see this selfie I took with Marco. Our milk mustaches are hilarious!"

She offered a hand to Christina as she stood, a little lighter as this first revelation fell away. "I wanted to be sure enough about Ellie to risk bringing her into Ben's world. Telling him is next on my list."

Chapter Sixteen

OLIVIA TOOK A last turn around the living room before Ellie's arrival, touching various objects—a photograph of Lake Michigan, Van Gogh coasters from the Art Institute, a garish rainbow mug. Their randomness camouflaged their true connection. The photo she took standing on the hood of Sophia's car to get the perfect angle, leaving a dent Sophia razzed her about for years. The coasters were a white elephant gift from Sophia's office holiday party. The mug Sophia bought at their first Pride parade. Every room in the house held items like these, innocuous on the surface but weighted with story. She'd tried to tuck some away, but when everything evoked her wife, it became too over-whelming to choose.

Ellie texted from her parking spot—part of their coordination to give Ben time to transition. She leaned on the banister and called up. "Hey, Ben, Ellie will be here in a minute. Can you come downstairs? Ben?" Shaking her head, Olivia climbed the steps and found him exactly where she suspected.

Flat on his belly among his Legos, he was building red walls four bricks high, blue walls five bricks high, and yellow walls six bricks high, a pattern he'd followed for years. A fierce protectiveness overtook her. He wasn't the kind of child the world expected. He wasn't even the child they had expected, back when she whispered knock-knock jokes through Sophia's growing belly. But he was exactly who he was meant to be, and he was *theirs*.

"Is Ellie here?"

"Any second now." She squatted low and plucked a plastic tree from a plastic lawn. "You'll have time for more Legos later, but right now, I need you downstairs."

He grabbed the tree and returned it to its spot, then rolled a tiny car back and forth.

"You were going to welcome her at the door, remember? We practiced this yesterd—"

The doorbell rang, and Ben sprang to his feet, darted past her, and drummed down the stairs. She scrambled to catch up. As she hit the top step, the front door swung open.

"Ellie! Welcometoourhome. Wouldyoulikeatour?"

Olivia reached the first floor to find Ellie smiling at Ben, who had issued his greeting but also parked himself in the doorway, blocking her entrance. She guided him back a step. "Buddy, put some pauses in there."

He pushed her hand away. "I said it like we practiced!"

"The words were great, but it was a little fast. Watch us." Ellie's cheeks glowed with contained mirth. "Hi, Olivia."

She smiled, playing along. "Hi, Ellie. Welcome to our home."

"Thanks for inviting me."

"We're glad you could make it."

Ben bounced on his toes, driving an overflow of energy into the worn hardwood. His shaggy mop of hair flapped with each movement.

"What a lovely home you have."

"Thank you. Would you like a tour?"

"It takes sooooo long! Come see my room." His eyes darted to Olivia. She raised an eyebrow. "Please," he muttered.

A laugh finally burst from Ellie, and she stepped into the house and closed the door. "I would love to see your room."

He spun and bolted up the stairs, rattling the old house with each thumping footstep.

"Sorry. He's used to flyby greetings with Arti or Mom. I should make him practice more."

"It's fine. Jesus, I thought I was nervous, but the two of you..."

"What do you mean?"

"Ben bouncing like a rabbit. You clenching those fists in your pockets. It's such a giveaway." Ellie stripped off her jacket and hung it on the coat rack.

Unlocking her fists, Olivia slid them from her pockets. "I'm sorry. Ben struggles with new people in the house, and I don't want him melting down, or—"

"It's his house. He should be comfortable. Don't worry about me." Ellie gave her a quick peck. "Can I ask you a super-important question before I go up there?"

"What?"

"Has a men's white V-neck replaced the Henley as your official weekend shirt?" Ellie tugged on the frayed edge of her T-shirt.

"I guess." Olivia never paid attention to her clothes. Sophia always threw something at her when she needed it. "I run hot, so I hate too many layers. Why?"

Ellie clenched the thin shirt in a fist and dragged her close. Her hand coasted along Olivia's forearm, trailing sparks as she went. "I love it when you're scruffy. It's hot as hell."

She cupped Ellie's cheeks. It was hard to stay nervous with her dimpled smile so close. "You're trying to relax things by flirting with me."

"Is it working?"

"You tell me." She captured Ellie's mouth and drank her in with a long, sweet kiss.

"ELLIE! UP HERE!" Ben's voice ricocheted down the steps and propelled them apart.

"Like our intercom system? It's very unobtrusive."

Ellie laughed and sucked on her lower lip, then released it with a soft smack. "You don't play fair. I'll be back."

ELLIE LOOKED FROM Olivia to Ben as he purred into his bowl of ice cream. It was the calmest he'd been this afternoon. His tour had been a dizzy whirl. First, his bedroom and its Lego sprawl. Then, down to the kitchen for a review of his snack cabinet before heading back upstairs. In his bathroom, he demonstrated his new soft-close toilet lid, followed by his battery-operated toothbrush. Olivia hadn't jumped in, even though it was clear none of this fit her idea of a house tour. Ben's version of guest appropriate was fun, but Ellie was disappointed he'd barely waved at the living room and its photo-laden mantel before going to the deck. His birdfeeder wasn't quite the family context she craved.

"I love ice cream." He had picked his way through a tuna sandwich and blueberries—he explained crunchy foods made his ears hurt—to get to the ice cream. The bowl fell somewhere between a treat and a bribe to keep him at the table. She shot another glance at Olivia, who nodded and touched his shoulder.

"Ben, now that we're set with dessert, we want to talk to you."

"No therapy. Ellie isn't in her blue shirt."

Ellie pressed a hand to her green sweater. "Nothing with therapy. But this is your first time seeing me without it, huh?"

He nodded with the spoon in his mouth.

Olivia kept her tone light, but tension stiffened her posture. "I told you how Ellie and I are friends, and we hang out, right? Well, sometimes adults decide they want to be more than friends."

He scarfed another spoonful. A long white drip splattered unnoticed onto his shirt.

"Ellie cares for me, romantically, and I care for her the same way. We've talked about this before, different ways to feel about a person."

"Yeah." He crammed in more ice cream, gaze fixed on the bowl.

Olivia tapped a finger on the table, close to his hand. "Ellie and I want to spend more time together, so she might come for dinner or hang out on a weekend. Would that be okay?"

His skinny shoulders lifted in a shrug reminiscent of Olivia.

"Ben?" Ellie's voice drew his eyes upward for a second before they skittered away. "I want to get to know you, too, when I'm here."

"You already know me."

"I do, but it would be nice to know you better."

"Can I show you my Minecraft world?"

"Sure."

"Are you okay with Ellie being here?" Olivia asked. "Do you have any questions?"

He shoveled in three huge bites, then dropped his spoon. It clattered to the table in a sticky spray. "I'm gonna start the computer." He darted from his chair before they could speak.

Last night, Ellie had rehearsed answers to dozens of possible questions, preparing to meet Ben's need for detail. His sudden departure threw her. "That was quick."

"Since he knew you from TTC, I hoped he'd be more relaxed, but—" Olivia poked a spoon at her own melting ice cream. She'd barely touched it. "Sorry it took so long for him to settle at the table."

"It's fine. Like you said, we should base what we do on how he's feeling. But did it go well, or not?"

"If he hates an idea, he has zero filter, so he's okay. For now, at least. But he takes forever to process. We'll have this conversation several times."

Ellie set his abandoned spoon in his bowl. "Are you okay?"

"Why?"

"You're distant."

Olivia finally looked up, a muscle in her jaw clenching. "It's just stranger than I thought, telling him. It felt so cut and dried when we planned it, but the reality is..."

Concern wormed its way into her brain. "Do you regret it?"

"No, but it's a lot to absorb. I didn't really let myself feel it because I was so worried about Ben—what to say, how to make him comfortable—and it all crashed down right before you came." She pushed her bowl aside and took one of Ellie's hands.

"ELLIE, I'M READY!"

They both twitched, but neither relaxed their grip. "Is that why you were so jittery when I got here?"

"Yeah. I'm sorry about—"

"ELLIE! MY ROOM IS UP HERE, REMEMBER?"

Olivia dropped her forehead into her other palm. "I have to get him to stop doing that."

They needed time to string together more than these choppy sentences, but Ben's patience wouldn't stretch much longer. Ellie pushed back from the table. "If you don't see me in fifteen minutes, send the Minecraft rescue team."

The stairs sighed and creaked beneath her feet as if protesting her ascent. The longer she stayed in the house, the more she sensed her own strangeness in it. Their time on the porch hadn't prepared her for the interior's intimacy, the way it cradled memories of a former life. She passed a closed door on the way to Ben. Olivia's bedroom. Their bedroom. Curiosity whispered, persistent and seductive. Her hand grazed the brass knob, rubbed by age to a soft finish. Then she turned away.

"All right, Ben, show me your worlds."

Without acknowledging her, he trailed description over his shoulder. Ellie knew enough to follow along, but as the minutes ticked by, the various worlds blurred. An ancient radiator, craggy with layers of paint, pinged in the far corner. Next to it, a huge painted tree scaled the wall and climbed onto the ceiling. Hand-painted leaves dotted half the branches, but the rest were unfinished. She tiptoed through the minefield of Lego projects to get a closer look. Whose idea had it been? Olivia's? Sophia's? She traced a thick ridge of paint on the trunk, but the tree didn't give up its secrets.

A bookshelf squatted nearby, and on top sat a dusty framed picture of Sophia with a toddler-sized Ben. When she picked it up, the backing fell off, and a second photo sailed to the floor. Olivia stared up at her, but it was an Olivia she'd never met. Ellie crouched and picked it up by a corner. This Olivia was younger, much younger, and she'd been caught mid-laugh, mouth open and eyes sparkling. Sophia, in profile, gazed at her with obvious devotion.

For the first time, jealousy knifed between Ellie's ribs. She'd never made Olivia laugh like this, had never seen her face so joyful. Tears stung her eyes. Was she not enough?

"You guys have been up here awhile. How's it—" Olivia froze in the doorway.

Ellie jerked to her feet, wiping her face. "This fell out of the frame."

Olivia took the picture from her with a shaky hand. "Ben, I'm borrowing Ellie for a minute."

He didn't even turn as she followed Olivia into the hallway, pitching her voice low. "I think it was stuck to the back? I didn't mean—"

"It's fine." Olivia's gaze scoured the floor.

"It doesn't seem fine."

"Years ago, Sophia put this one in Ben's room, and I changed it out for the picture you saw. It became a silly game. How long until the other noticed? I haven't seen it since..."

Before the accident, Ellie thought, when Olivia didn't say it. "I didn't mean to pry."

"You didn't." Olivia bit the words off as though she was convincing herself.

Jealousy still pricked at her, a stitch in her side. "How—"

"MOM!" Ben ran from his room and bounced into Olivia, who jerked in surprise.

"I'm right here. Why are you shouting?"

"My phone notification. It's time for Jamal's!"

"Ellie and I need a minute."

"You promised! Lunch with Ellie and Jamal's at three." A pink flush splattered Ben's neck, his agitation growing. "It's three right now!"

"He's right." The photo, and the interruption, had Ellie nearly as flustered as Ben, but she swallowed her discomfort. "You should go to Jamal's."

"No, wait—" Olivia took her wrist with gentle fingers, and the small contact, the fact that Olivia needed it, eased the worst of her tension.

"It's fine. We can talk later." She hated leaving, but they'd planned it this way to avoid overstaying her welcome the first time and to give Ben a chance to blow off steam afterward.

"Are you sure?"

"My shoes are untied. Fix them so we can go." Ben stomped a foot on the top step.

Olivia swung back to him. "Hey, how do you ask for help?"

He dropped his chin to his chest and changed his words to a question, tacking a half-hearted "please" on the end.

"I'm going to go. Ben, can I have a goodbye?"

His gaze skimmed hers. "Goodbye. We're two minutes late now, Mom."

Olivia slumped against the wall. Frustration carved sharp lines on either side of her mouth. "I'm sorry."

"It's okay. Call me later?" She squeezed Olivia's hand once, sending her own signal.

"Yeah."

Ben's timekeeping prattle followed Ellie down the stairs as she collected her things and let herself out the front door. The abrupt end to the visit had her off-balance, and she sank into a wicker chair. Brusque daylight stripped the porch of its romance, revealing it not as the sanctuary she'd imagined, but rather a gateway to a more complicated world.

ELLIE PEELED A long, damp curl from her 5 Rabbit label and slumped lower on her stool. Alberto had taken one look at her glum face, muttered "triste" under his breath, and banished her to the far end of the bar. It was where he sent all of his miserable customers. Twenty-five years at this place—from a chubby teen bussing tables to its balding manager—had made him an expert in people. Sad drunks brought the energy down. With a gloomy Eeyore at their elbow, customers might not order an extra round, share a second plate of fries. But he was too softhearted to send anyone away. So he culled the sad from the happy with his keen eye and gave them a home by the kitchen, where they could commiserate in peace. Tonight though, she was alone in her gloom, her only company a growing pile of shredded paper.

The bell over the front door jingled as 'Berto ejected a handsy customer, his squat bulk discouraging anything more than a snarled protest. Giving a thumbs-up to the server, he worked his way through the weekend crowd and settled next to her. "Fucking cagón. He's got enough machismo to grab the waitress's ass, but when I walk over, pfffffft."

"I promise she appreciates the support. Do you know many times I got grabbed waiting tables or tending bar? None of my managers did shit about it." The television overhead showed a soccer match from a fuzzier, pre-HD time. "Is that the '93 Copa América match against Ecuador?"

"Glad to see you haven't forgotten your roots."

"You guys watched that recording until the tape melted in the VCR. Besides, the running forward flip? Has to be Sánchez."

Alberto swept her label strips into a small pile, pinched them into a clump, and leaned over the bar to toss them in a trash can. "¿Isabella, qué pasó? 'Cause you're not here to talk about El Tri. Explain your text again. No entiendo."

"I messed up." She grimaced and rolled the bottle between her palms.

"How? You saw a picture."

"I overreacted, and now she must think…" Her stomach soured as she remembered Olivia in Ben's doorway. "I don't know what she's thinking, actually. Which I hate."

"Was she mad, yelling?"

"No. She seemed wounded, but right when I tried to ask her about it, Ben came flying in. It was like that all day. We'd get in a flow, and then he would act up or interrupt—"

"That's what kids do."

"I know, but—"

"No, no sabes." He leaned forward, elbows planted on the brass rail, and pointed a finger at her. "You work with kids, but you've never lived with one. Carmen and I can have a whole argument waiting for Pablo to find his phone or Alejandra to pick out clothes for school. Because that's how much time we get."

"But you two have fifteen years together. You were solid before the kids. I don't have that with Olivia, and it's the first time I've left with something unresolved between us."

"Explain again about the photo."

"It was Olivia and Sophia, but younger. And Olivia—" Ellie huffed through her nose. "She looked happy. Completely, utterly happy."

"She was happy, with her wife. You know this."

"I do, but *I've* never seen her that happy, and it hurt. Then I got jealous, ridiculously, stupidly jealous, and I started to cry—" She slammed her palm on the glossy wood. "Mierda!"

"You cried over a picture?" 'Berto's black eyes scrunched, his disappointed big brother face adding to her guilt. "Isabella..."

"I said I overreacted! You don't have to tell me. Jesus, I'm never jealous. I don't know what happened."

"You're not jealous, hermanita. You're scared."

"Scared?"

"Yes, that you will never make her as happy."

Bile wafted in the back of her mouth. She took a swig to drown the bitter flavor. "Why would you say that?"

"Because it's true. Olivia is a kind woman, but the sadness is still there. Maybe she can't be happy in the same way. Maybe it's unfair to ask it of her."

His words landed in her gut like lead. She never pressed for details about Sophia, telling herself it was out of respect for Olivia's feelings, but maybe she'd been protecting herself. From the full reality of what they'd meant to each other. And from the possibility she might never fill that role in Olivia's life so perfectly.

The Olivia in the picture was a casualty of the accident, along with her wife. Ben had lost two parents that day. One was gone forever, but the other was finding her way back. That Olivia was the woman she had fallen for. That Olivia was the one who mattered. Her phone chirped with a text, and she wiped away tears before digging it out of her pocket.

"Probably Mamá telling you to hit the bodega tomorrow before coming over." He always hid behind humor after dropping a piece of wisdom on her.

"I can't believe Manuel taught her to text. It was easier when she avoided the damn phone for fear of it cooking her brain." She choked on her beer when Olivia's text popped up.

Feeling unsettled about earlier. Is it just me?

Only Olivia would use the word "unsettled" in a text message. It helped, though, knowing she wasn't alone in her stewing. She held the screen out.

'Berto waved a meaty hand to show he'd been right all along. "If she's texting, she can't be too upset."

She ignored him and tapped a response. *Nope. Me too. R U OK?*

Was going to ask you. Can we talk?

Want me to call?

Getting Ben ready for bed. Would you mind coming back over?

What time?

In an hour?

C U then

She went to put the phone away, but it chirped one last time.

The way you text makes me feel old.

She laughed and stuffed it in her pocket.

"¿Todo bien?" Alberto took a sip of his water, a purposely bland expression on his face.

She hooked a thumb toward the door. "I'm headed out after this beer, 'Berto. I need to apologize to my girlfriend."

OLIVIA FLATTENED A bent corner of the photograph, falling through its window into another world—a world smoothed by the backward winding of time. Her curls hung looser with no coarse gray to twist them into crisper whorls. Tiny seams of crow's-feet had yet to unravel and expose themselves. She looked shiny and young in a way she couldn't remember being. Even her cheeks carried a softness that had been stripped from her.

Her house was crammed with pictures she didn't notice anymore. Ben needed them as touchstones, arranging them to suit the current logic of his grief. Early on, she'd studied each mercurial adjustment for a clue to his thoughts, but if there was a message, she never found it. Eventually, exhausted by the fickle shuffle, she stopped looking. Only the shifting outline of frames told her when something changed. But this photo's sudden reappearance gave it power. It forced her to see the woman she'd once been, reflecting the light of Sophia next to her.

The front door cracked open, and Ellie's cautious face peeked through the gap. "I know you said it would be unlocked, but I knocked softly anyway."

"Sorry. I was lost in thought. Thanks for coming over. I didn't like cutting things off earlier."

"Me either." Ellie hovered in the doorway, an odd hesitancy muting her normal confidence.

"Will you come in and sit down?" Olivia hated the relief on Ellie's face, as though she needed permission. Ellie turned the deadbolt, then crossed to the couch, and Olivia tossed the photograph onto the coffee table. "Arti took this the day we found out Sophia was pregnant. She goaded me into a laugh by making a lewd joke."

"How old are you?"

"Thirty-two. I haven't seen it in years, so it knocked me back. It was Sophia's favorite photo of me." Her jaw ached from clenching, and she forced the muscles to relax. "Why did it make you cry?"

"I haven't been jealous of what you had with Sophia, not once, but your smile here, seeing you this happy—" Ellie pulled the picture closer, then grimaced. "Jesus, this is hard to admit. It hurt, knowing you've never looked like that with me, and I got scared. Scared I would *never* see you like that. And I got way too upset. I'm so sorry."

"Oh, Ellie, it's only a moment. One moment." She tapped her smiling face. "This woman, she had no idea what it would mean to parent Ben, she hadn't watched cancer hollow out her father. I'm not sure she existed before the accident, much less after. I know I'm pretty serious, and I can be too quiet, but that's me. It's who I was when this picture was taken." A dark insecurity bubbled over. "If I'm not the person you... If I've disappointed you... Maybe who I am isn't who you want."

"That's not what I meant. At all." The words leapt from Ellie's mouth, and her hands latched on to Olivia's forearm. "I think you're incredible. I just want to be enough for you. I want to make you happy."

The intensity of Ellie's reply soothed Olivia's unease. She searched for a way to return that assurance. "You do make me happy, every time I see you, every time I think about you." With her free hand, she dug her phone out of her pocket and scrolled through her photos. She opened one and set it on the table by the photograph. "Here's Ben and I, six months after the accident. We were taking selfies again—it was something he did with Sophia, and I knew she wouldn't want me to let it go—and this was an early one. I've kept it as a reminder of how far he's come."

Ellie sucked in a breath, blinking back tears.

Olivia understood the reaction. Where age had scoured her features with its inexorable crawl, grief was a brushfire, a conflagration of change. Her guarded face wouldn't support the smile she tried to hang on it, and sorrow had picked her gaunt body clean. The Ben at her side was more empty vessel than boy. "The woman on the phone is numb, lost. Where I am now is so far from that empty place, and so much of it has to do with you. Please believe me."

Ellie turned the photograph facedown. She did the same with the phone. Then she cradled Olivia's face, her walnut-dark eyes misty but steady. "The woman I am looking at right now is everything I want. I love that you're serious, and quiet, and thoughtful, and I hate that my stupid overreaction gives you even the slightest idea I don't think you're absolutely wonderful." Her thumb stroked Olivia's cheekbone. "It's like with your scars, our first night. The accident was an abstraction, and then it was horribly real, how much you must have suffered, that you almost died. Today, in this house...Sophia felt real to me. Real in a way she hasn't before. And it made me scared I could never be enough."

"Ellie, you are exactly who I need you to be. Working through Sophia's loss is my deal, not yours. It shouldn't impact you in the slightest. You deserve something easier."

"Hard, easy, it doesn't matter as long as I have you." Ellie drew her into a strong hug, and she returned it with fierce intensity.

"You have me," Olivia whispered. "You have me."

Chapter Seventeen

ELLIE LET HERSELF into her parents' house, closed the door behind her, and threw the locks gingerly. She toed off her shoes next to her father's tattered boots. As she passed the stairs, she rubbed the worn newel post the same way she had when she was a child sneaking to her grandmother's room. A faint yellow strip glowed under the door, and she smiled. Abuela slept fitfully. If the light was on, she was happy to have visitors. Ellie visited like this often, keeping the old woman company in the dark, close hours before dawn. Occasionally, she would come across one of her brothers doing the same.

She opened the door to find Abuela propped up in bed, humming along with a Spanish music station while a veladora burned low on her nightstand. Its weak flame cast more shadow than light on the dozens of frames on the walls, crowded tight like three-dimensional wallpaper. Every new photo sent from Mexico got added, Abuela wanting her family close despite the distance. The black-and-white images were Ellie's favorite. She'd spent hours of her childhood in this room, hovering her finger over one face and then another while Abuela recounted their history. Their names sometimes slipped Ellie's mind, but their stories didn't. The mustached man on a horse was the cousin-who-fell-down-the-well. The dour woman making tortillas was the aunt-who-might-have-killed-her-fourth-husband.

Abuela's creased, wrinkled face burst into a smile. "Mi solito!" *My little sun.* She'd used the nickname the first time she saw Ellie smile as a baby.

"Hola, Abuela." She gave her a kiss on both papery cheeks, then held up a DVD case. "Guess what I found?"

"*El Bolero de Raquel*! I love Cantinflas in this one. The way his hips move..." Her own hips shimmied under the blankets, resurrecting the memory of a thousand dances.

Once, Ellie had been small enough to stand on Abuela's feet as they moved around the kitchen together, the rhythms sinking into her body. "I know how disappointed you were the last DVD got scratched."

"Will you put it in the player for me? To be ready for later."

"We can watch it if you want." She loaded the disc into the tray.

"No, no. Now is time for talking. It has been so long since your last night visit."

Abuela's gentle rebuke stung more than any scold from her mother. The dates with Olivia had absorbed her, and too much time had passed. "Perdona. I should've come sooner." Ellie climbed onto the bed, careful not to jostle her. Her petite grandmother held a wiry strength long into old age, but the last few years had whittled her to skin and bones. "How are you feeling?"

"Old. The same way I feel every day." The raspy chuckle made Ellie's heart ache. Abuela's laugh used to be loud and long.

Resting her head on one bony shoulder, Ellie stretched her legs well past the small lump where Abuela's feet rested.

She remembered, at ten, realizing she was taller than Abuela, how her excitement had turned to unease. Her grandmother had seemed ageless until that day, when Ellie's body signaled the passing of time for both of them.

"She must be special to have stolen your voice, mi solito."

Ellie snorted. She never needed to start a conversation with Abuela. Somehow, she just knew. "She is special. Very special."

"Is she as chatty as the last one?"

A loud cackle erupted, and Ellie clapped her hand over her mouth to avoid waking her parents. Abuela hadn't cared for Angie, the only time they'd met. It was right before the worst of their problems, and her grandmother's dislike signaled the end more clearly than anything else. "No. She's quiet. Much quieter than anyone I've dated."

"Good. You talk enough for two people anyway. What is her name?"

"Olivia."

"A gringa?"

"Yes. She's blonde, very striking, and tall."

"Striking?"

She'd taught Abuela English as a child, doing her school worksheets together, but certain words still stymied her. "It's like beautiful, but different. She has these sharp features. You notice her immediately because she strikes your eye in a specific way."

Abuela mused on the word as she rubbed her rosary. The click of the wooden beads blended with the maracas on the radio. "How tall?"

"An inch more than me."

"It will be like talking to a tree! You cannot find a shorter woman?"

"Angie was short." She lifted one eyebrow. "Which would you rather have, short and chatty, or tall and quiet?"

Abuela pouted for a second, then grinned. "Tall and quiet."

"Good, because I already made my pick."

"Is she kind to you?" Abuela's tiny hand, peppered with age spots, was swallowed by her own.

"She's kind and thoughtful. And serious. You'll like her."

"Is she serious in her heart, or serious because of life?"

"Both. But life has been particularly cruel to her."

"Tell me."

"She's a widow."

Abuela snatched her hand back and poked Ellie in the leg. "I told you when you were little not to sweep over your own feet. Now look!"

"Ow!" Ellie grinned at the old superstition. "I don't think my broom habits got us here."

"What happened?"

"Her wife died in a car accident, an accident that almost killed her and their son as well."

Abuela tsked and painted a cross over her heart, kissing her rosary at the end. "She loved this woman very much?"

"Beyond words."

"And you are not jealous of what was between them?"

"No, I'm not jealous." She could say those words and mean it now. Her overreaction to the photograph still bothered her, but the envy had disappeared. "What Olivia had with Sophia... If she loved that way once, maybe she can again."

"Good girl. You say she has a son?"

"Ben. He's eleven and sweet. He's also autistic."

"Like the ones you work with? Who don't have the words?"

"Some kids have trouble with words, especially in my first job, remember? But Ben speaks pretty well. It's understanding emotions, his own and others', that can be hard."

"Emotions give everyone trouble! Why do you need a name for that?" Her grandmother lifted a misshapen mug from her side table and took a sip of water. "Abeula" was spelled out in lumpy letters. Ellie had made it in school the year Abuela came to live with them. Seeing it cradled in her hands, still intact after thirty years—a mix of love and guilt swelled in her throat.

"I'm sorry I haven't visited lately. I shouldn't be so thoughtless."

"You are not thoughtless, cariño, but when you fall for someone, you fall with everything, and it is all you can see for a time. That's how I know you love this woman. It is the longest I have gone without a night visit, the longest I have watched you fall. I worry though. Olivia's story is not a simple one."

Ellie stepped carefully around the word—love. If she used it internally or with others, it might slip out with Olivia too soon. "She's an amazing woman. Her story, it's just a part of her."

"True, true, but her son is a child, not a story. How you feel about Olivia, it's easy for you, sí?"

"Sí." She shifted to meet her grandmother's rheumy eyes.

"Loving a child is easier and harder than loving an adult."

"What do you mean?"

"Think of your mother, and her love for you. You are simple to love, mi solito, but when you told her about your heart, the way it is drawn to women..."

The flame on the prayer candle guttered a fitful light through Our Lady of Guadalupe. Devout as Abuela was, she had accepted her granddaughter completely. It hurt, still, how her mother had to be scolded by her mother-in-law into following the same path.

"And Juan, he made it easy for your mother to love him when he was a child, but now, he makes it hard. He uses that easy love against her, knowing she cannot forget it."

A large family photo dominated the space above the nightstand. Juan's stony face glared back. She had no memory of her oldest brother as a happy boy. He'd been thirteen when they moved. By the time she was old enough to know him, he was an angry teenager, forever bitter about slights at school and the way his struggle to assimilate isolated him.

"It's early. Nothing's set in stone."

"Which is why you must be careful with this boy. His heart is the most vulnerable. He lost a mother, the worst pain for a child. If you enter his life, you must stay there at all costs, even if he makes it hard. Remember this when Olivia fills your thoughts—always leave room for her son."

Talking about Ben felt presumptuous, but Abuela was right. At some point, she would have to commit to him, as well as Olivia. "I will."

"Good." The radio switched to "Mi Gente," and Abuela's hips shifted minutely again, unable to resist the beat. "When do I meet this tree of a woman who steals mi nieta's tongue?"

"It makes me happy you want to meet her."

"Why wouldn't I?"

"Plenty of abuelas don't want to meet their granddaughters' girlfriends."

"Plenty of abuelas son estúpidas."

Two side-by-side photos from her high school and college graduations caught Ellie's eye. In each, she and Abuela hugged, their identical, wide smiles beaming at the camera. The young woman in green robes hadn't come out to her family. The woman in maroon had. Yet nothing about her grandmother was different; her fierce love radiated equally from both images.

"Why were you okay with me coming out?" Ellie hadn't asked this before, and Mamá's voice sounded in her head— *never question good news, just grab it and run.*

"If I were not okay, you would still be lesbiana, sí?"

"Yes, but—"

"My opinion cannot change who you are. It can only change how we are. So when you tell us, I must decide what is important—my opinion, or you? It is not hard when you think of it that way."

"And the church?"

"Pfffft, the church is wrong about many things. They just drag their feet like a stubborn burro. Look how long it took them to apologize to Señor Galileo! They will admit this mistake one day too." The radio changed again, energetic salsa giving way to "Por Fin" and its lovestruck lilt. "Oh, my favorite! Will you sing it with me?"

Vision blurry with tears, Ellie squeezed her grandmother's hand. "Of course."

Abuela's thin, reedy voice picked up the lyric, and Ellie joined her as she had so many times before.

Chapter Eighteen

"HOW'S THE WATER?" Ellie dropped Olivia's duffel on the bed. Through the open bathroom door, she could see her head above the tub, blonde curls stained dark with water.

"Hot. Glorious."

"Stay low to keep your shoulder warm. I'll be there in a second to work out the kinks."

"You're being very kind to a woman who showed up late for our Valentine's date."

"Technically, Valentine's Day is tomorrow, so you're four hours early. And it's not your fault your mom got stuck in traffic." Ellie shed her clothes, tossing them into the hamper. "How did she seem? Still okay with everything?" Olivia had told Alice about them last weekend.

"She's fine. Coming up for the night to be with Ben is her way of saying she supports our relationship."

"Scooch up. I want to sit behind you." She lowered herself into the steaming water and gathered wet strands of Olivia's hair behind her neck. "I just noticed...why do you never wear a ponytail?"

"Ben hates it. Reminds him of the hospital, when they tied it back to make it easier with dressing changes. The first time I put it up at home, he freaked out, so I stopped."

Olivia's life was filled with these asterisks on behaviors. The discipline to follow them astounded Ellie. "So what happened at climbing today?"

"My right hand slipped, and my left arm took all my weight. Something popped."

A faint scar marred Olivia's left shoulder, one Ellie had missed before. "Did you have surgery on this?"

"It was broken in the accident."

She probed the area, then manipulated the joint. It didn't take a goniometer to see the range of motion was affected. "Does this hurt?"

"It's stiff, but whatever you're doing feels good."

Digging into the muscles around the area, Ellie tried to release the tension. "Will you tell me about it? The accident?" She'd never asked this explicitly before. When only the lapping water filled the silence, she refocused her attention on the shoulder.

"The drunk driver was in our lane." Olivia's flat, terse words made her flinch. "This hill rose toward a bridge, and as we crested it, he just...appeared. He hit us, and our car clipped the railing. We rolled several times before landing at the bottom of a ditch."

Ellie shifted to the right shoulder to compare the range. If she kept Olivia moving, maybe more words would follow.

"I heard the accident before I felt it. The sound was incredible. When we rolled, it was like a giant dog shook me by the neck. By the time we stopped, my side door had caved in, and the steering wheel crushed my ribs." The water sloshed as Olivia gestured toward her side. "It's how I got the scars."

"Ben?"

"Concussion. Broken arm. Lots of cuts and bruises."

"And you?"

"Broken shoulder. Compound fractures of the ribs. They said I was lucky the ribs didn't cause more internal bleeding, or the lung didn't fully collapse. That was the worst of it. A nasty concussion, ugly bruises, whiplash."

Picturing Olivia trapped and bloody... Ellie's hands trembled too much to maintain the massage, so she wrapped her in a hug. The web of scars pressed into her right palm. "Sophia?" She took a risk, asking, but this was her best chance.

"Dead. Internal hemorrhaging. They said she never felt a thing." Olivia's voice cracked on the last word.

"How long were you in the hospital?"

"Five days for Ben. Ten for me. They wanted to move me to rehab, but Ben... Christina took him, but he kept begging for me, raging, crying, running out the door. They put him on sedatives to keep him safe. His blank stupor when I picked him up—" Olivia's shuddered sigh rippled through them both. "I stopped the drugs immediately. It didn't matter how bad it got for us, I never wanted to see him like that again." She splashed water on her face, rubbing it with rough strokes.

"And the other driver?"

"A twenty-four-year-old who'd been drinking all night with his girlfriend but hadn't slept it off before he drove home." No rage colored Olivia's tone, not even a streak of bitterness. Just weary, miserable resignation. "He survived. He got eight years."

Eight years. Ben's age when Sophia was killed. "So he'll be thirty-two when he gets out."

"Younger than I was when Ben was born."

Ellie shifted in the tub until she could see Olivia's face. It was as melancholy as her words. "You weren't—aren't—angry at him?"

"I don't do angry for long. I can't sustain it. Besides, I never had room for anything but grief, and more grief. This guy didn't stalk Sophia. He made a terrible, stupid decision, and she died. If I'd woken up five minutes sooner, if I'd stopped for gas the day before like I planned…"

"The accident wasn't your fault."

A harsh chuckle escaped. "It took a year of therapy to say that out loud." Here was the sharp edge Ellie had expected, but Olivia had flipped the blade, pointing it inward instead of out.

"How much longer to actually believe it?"

Hazel eyes lifted. The surprise in them, the pain… "I believe it now. Most of the time. How did you—?"

"You take everything to heart. I've known you long enough to see that." When Olivia dropped her face, Ellie tucked a finger under her chin. "I want to hear all of it, not just the fun, easy parts." She kissed her forehead. "How about we get ready for bed?"

Olivia rested a hand on her forearm. "I know it's Valentine's, but is it okay if—"

"We don't need to have sex every time we're together. As long as I'm with you, I'm happy."

A small smile dispelled some of the shadows haunting Olivia's face. Ellie wondered what would chase the rest away.

"Let's get dried off and snuggle. I've never been the big spoon for anyone taller than me. You keep hogging the spot. My turn."

THE SUN STREAMED through the passenger window, making Sophia's tea-colored eyes glow from within. Olivia's hands were steady on the wheel, her gold ring tapping in time to the music. Sophia was speaking, but there *was no sound, just a low droning. They were about to cross a bridge. A tree-lined river stretched to their right. Faster than thought, a black car appeared in front of them. She flinched. The bridge railing appeared.*

She jerked awake. Jagged pants scraped the silence. Unfamiliar curtains hovered in her vision. A warm body pressed close.

"Olivia? Are you okay?" Ellie's drowsy voice penetrated the fog.

"Just a dream." The words were a croak. She fought to clear her throat, but the residue of panic coated it like sand. "Go back to sleep." Another croak as she waved off Ellie's question and rolled from the bed.

The nightmare hovered at the edge of her consciousness, a shadow she couldn't shake, and she staggered to the kitchen. She yanked open the refrigerator. Jars clanked and chattered in the door, protesting her clumsy force. Squinting against the fridge light, she grabbed a water bottle, then stood in the open door and let the cold wash over her.

The compressor's droning hum. The snap-crack of the lid. Long, icy swallows. She focused on one input at a time until the nightmare was stowed away. Still too restless to face the tight circle of Ellie's concern, Olivia retreated to the piano in the far corner. Gentle pressure let her play without sound, a slow sink into resistance, then a silent settling at the bottom of the stroke. Her fingers walked a mute pattern across the board—resist, settle, resist, settle—until her heart found an even rhythm.

Behind her, a latch clicked. A hinge squeaked. Feet swished on carpet. The piano bench creaked as Ellie sat down.

"I didn't know you played."

Olivia stilled her hand. "I don't."

"It's a nice tactile sensation, isn't it? The first time I touched a piano as a child, I thought it was magic. You press here—" Ellie mimicked her silent stroke. "And sound comes out there." She pressed again, and this time a soft note trembled from behind the panel of the upright.

Sheet music lay open in front of them, the notes a black spatter. "Adele?"

"Her range suits my voice."

"Will you play for me?"

"Sorry. Condo rules. No instruments until nine."

The thin plastic of the water bottle crinkled as Olivia rolled it between her palms.

"Can you tell me about it? Please?"

The nightmare belonged to another time, another bed. To have it intrude now, in the refuge of Ellie's arms...the disorientation was too much.

"Hey." Lips brushed her bare shoulder.

"I can't. I'm not trying to be difficult, but...I can't."

"How often do you get them?"

"Varies. Not so much recently. Our conversation probably stirred it up." Olivia leaned forward and set the bottle on the piano, seeking distance from Ellie's warm focus.

"Is it just nightmares? Or is there more?"

"Only nightmares these days. I had a couple of panic attacks early on, but they stopped after I changed jobs."

"What do you mean?"

"I was an ER nurse, before. But when I returned to work, I couldn't handle it. The rattle of a crash cart, the smell of iodine, the beeping—" She shuddered at the memory of those attacks, the panic crawling up her throat. It was like drowning on dry land.

"So you didn't leave because of the schedule?"

"It was both. I needed different hours for Ben, but I also couldn't be the nurse I was before. The person I was before."

"I'm sorry." Ellie brushed a hand along her spine. The gentle touch was almost too much to bear. "I've never asked, but is Sophia buried somewhere? It might help to visit."

"She hated cemeteries. Didn't want to take up space when she was gone." Olivia closed the lid over the keys and pressed her palms to the cool, glossy wood. "We cremated her, and her mother kept the ashes. Ben couldn't stand the idea of her remains in the house."

"Were you okay with no plot? You sound ambivalent."

"At the time I agreed, but having lived through it with Ben, I think he'd like to sit near her stone and talk to her. He does it with my dad—the physical anchor is helpful. But I can't bring myself to violate her wishes."

Ellie ran a hand down her forearm, then slipped fingers through her own, splayed on the lid. "Why don't you come back to bed?" She curled around Olivia's hand, waiting.

"I'm not sure I can sleep."

"Let's try. Please."

If she resisted, Ellie would stay. If she stayed, they would talk. So Olivia squeezed her hand in return and let herself be led to the bedroom.

Ellie stretched out on her back, and Olivia tucked into her shoulder. The spicy tang of her skin mingled with the buttery scent of sleep. Ellie stroked her side in long passes, palm rasping her scars. Fearful echoes from her nightmare rushed to fill the silence.

"Sing something for me?"

"Any requests?"

"You choose."

Ellie began a low, soft melody. The confidence and emotion in her voice carried Olivia past the darkness.

"What's that song?"

"'Remedy.' It's the sheet music you saw on the piano."

"I love your voice. It's so effortless. Will you sing it again?"

"Sure. That was the chorus. Want to hear the whole song?"

She nodded against Ellie's chest. The gentle hover of her voice filled Olivia's last memory as sleep possessed her.

OLIVIA STRUGGLED TO wakefulness, alone in the bed. Sharp panic had faded to a twinge this morning, matching the one in her shoulder. A glass of water and two orange pills sat on the nightstand.

"Ibuprofen," Ellie said, entering the room. Her breasts swayed under a faded gray tank top. Desire flared in Olivia, then receded in a tide of guilt for an evening filled with old wounds and sad stories. She shifted into a sitting position, and Ellie perched on the mattress. "How are you?"

"Still sore, but not as tight. You have magic fingers."

"I meant about the nightmare."

The compassion on Ellie's face made her chest ache. "It's not how I wanted last night to go. You deserve more romance."

"I asked, remember, in the bath? I want to have every conversation, light and dark. Being with you is all the romance I need."

"Thank you." She leaned in and kissed Ellie softly at first, then with more intensity, until Ellie abruptly broke it off.

"Let me hold you."

"But last night, we never got a chance—"

"I don't care about the sex. I just want to be with you when you're hurting." Ellie crawled over to the headboard and drew her close.

Dappled sun danced across the sheets as Olivia let herself absorb the warm comfort of the embrace. "I'm sorry if I retreat or deflect. I've been doing this alone awhile."

"Why is that? I mean, I know there's Arti, and your families, but..."

"It's my fault." She paused, finding the words for that dark time. "After the funeral, all these people pressed in, wanting to help or talk or...I don't know, be close."

"It's a common impulse."

"I know, but I didn't want anyone close. I didn't want anyone there at all. Even Arti was too much, at first, but there was no way I was getting rid of her. She'd sit across the room and work on her jewelry or cook in the kitchen while I hid on the back deck. Friends did check in, but I ignored the phone, the doorbell. Eventually they gave up. I don't blame them." She nuzzled her forehead under Ellie's chin. "Anyway, that's a long way of saying old habits die hard, but I am trying."

"I'm glad you're trying with me."

"I'm trying *because* of you. Which reminds me, I got you a present. It's in my bag. Do you want to open it?"

"Sure. You can open mine too. I'll get it."

Ellie scooted down the bed and unzipped the duffel. "Hey, what's this?" She pulled a colorful sheet of paper from the bag, along with her present.

"It's from Ben. His social group made valentines for their families, but they also made one for a new person in their life, to show that it's good to be open to new friends."

"And he picked me?" Ellie's delighted face lifted Olivia's gloom.

"Yep. He really wanted the tree to have rainbow leaves, but TTC didn't have those stickers, so he settled on rainbow hearts. I'm pretty proud he made the compromise. A year ago, he might have had a meltdown about it."

"I'm super proud! And so touched." Ellie's eyes shimmered. "Open yours now. I need a minute." She set Ben's valentine carefully on her dresser and retrieved a wrapped box from her closet.

The box was heavier than Olivia expected. Inside was a small but substantial object encased in fabric. Peeling back the wrap revealed a sculpture of a reclining woman, her arms, torso and upper legs.

"The way you spoke after the fundraiser, about Rodin's sculptures, learning a woman's body. I couldn't get it out of my mind. When I saw this, it reminded me of our first night."

The figure was arched in passion, and one arm was thrown over her unseen face. Olivia followed the line of a hip with her finger. "'The Torso of Adèle.' It's one of my favorites."

"I see what you meant, about the eroticism and the emotion in his work."

"It's a beautiful present. Thank you. I love it." The words fought through the thick emotion clogging her throat. "Open yours. I hope you like it."

Ellie tugged at the paper. "I'll like whatever you give—" She froze, riveted by the black-and-white portrait. In it, Ellie lay naked on her stomach, propped up on her elbows, one hand tangled in her hair. A huge smile lit her face as she looked to the side. Her full cleavage peeked through the gap in her arms, and the sweep of her back accentuated the round curve of her ass. It was sexy but not scandalous, and the humor in her face added spontaneity.

"I brought my camera last month, remember? After our first night in the bath, when you talked about your body, I couldn't let it go. That you would ever feel anything but beautiful was impossible. I wanted to show you. This is how you look to me."

"Olivia, you said you weren't artistic, but this is art." Ellie stared at her own image in wonder.

"You are the art. I clicked a button." She took the frame from Ellie and set it aside. Drawing the tank top over Ellie's head, Olivia guided her to her back, then slipped the boxers from her hips. Morning sun drenched the lush landscape of her body. Every gilt rise and bronze hollow pulled Olivia farther away from the dark paths in her own mind. She trailed a hand between Ellie's breasts and over her stomach's lavish swell. Floating her lips next to Ellie's ear, she whispered, "I always want to make you feel beautiful."

Chapter Nineteen

"I REFUSE TO do homework on a Saturday!" Ben's red face glowed like a Christmas light, the veins in his neck bulging. "I REFUSE! I REFUSE! I REFUSE!"

Ellie twitched when Olivia smacked the dining table to jolt him from his tantrum. "If you say 'I refuse' again, you'll lose computer privileges! I am done with this! You wouldn't do the work this week, so this is your consequence. No Minecraft until the project is done."

"You NEVER understand! I. CAN'T. DO. IT!" His plate jumped when he pounded the table in return.

Ellie chewed on her lip as they faced off, hesitant to step in. It had been an edgy morning, Ben stacking grievances like Legos and Olivia biting her tongue so often she should've been spitting blood.

"Upstairs. Cool down time. Now."

Growling, he stomped to his room. When his bedroom door slammed, the house shook.

Olivia pressed a finger between her eyes, a sigh hissing through her gritted teeth. "I suppose that wasn't an OTapproved method for helping your son with his executive functioning skills."

"Because no parent ever loses their temper with their kid?" Her wry smile was matched by Olivia. "Natural consequences are the best kind. This is what happens when he leaves homework until the last minute."

"Bet you're glad you came for breakfast."

"I'm always glad to be here." She streaked her last bite of waffle through some maple syrup and popped it in her mouth. "This might sound strange, but it's reassuring that he loses it on occasion when I'm around. It means he's comfortable being himself with me."

Olivia stabbed at her own waffle, shredding it with her fork. "Oh, he's comfortable. No worries there."

"Is everything okay? You're both wound tight this morning."

Olivia's fork dropped with a clatter, and she stacked her plate onto Ben's. "It's been a rough week, homework-wise. They're piling it on as preparation for junior high. Then I have to email his teacher to remind her about his IEP and the limits to what she can assign. And then she tells me which busywork nonsense he actually has to do, and which he can skip."

"I assume this project is in the 'can't skip' category?"

"Yep. I've been trying to help him chip away at it all week, but—" A crash echoed upstairs. Olivia scrubbed at her face, a groan leaking from her hands. "I'll go check on him."

"How about I take a turn?"

"Be very sure when you make that offer because I don't have the strength to turn you down."

"Sit here and finish your breakfast. I'll give a shout if things go south." She planted a kiss on Olivia and headed for Ben's room. Her knock was met with silence, so she cracked the door. He sat in a rumpled heap, kicking a book with his toe.

"Hey buddy." When he didn't yell at her to leave, she inched into his room. "Mind if I ask what this project is about?"

Shrugging, he pouted his lower lip. "Thomas Edison."

"Like, a biography of his life, or—"

"His inventions."

"All of them? Because he invented a ton."

"I have to write about four. And I can't pick the light bulb. Which is the best one!" An indignant scowl creased his face. "It's not fair!"

"The light bulb is pretty awesome. I can see why that's irritating. But he invented other cool stuff. Do you have research materials?"

He kicked another book.

"If those books have the information you need, what next step makes the most sense?"

"I have to get the information out of them. But how do I pick? There's too much!" He made an exasperated sound in his throat, exactly like Olivia, and she fought a smile.

"I bet it feels that way. All the words, all the choices—it can get overwhelming. How many books do you have?"

"Four."

She squatted and lined the books up in a row. "What if you picked one invention from each book? Could you do that?"

"I guess."

"And from each book, you could pick five facts about that invention."

"Only five?"

"Five each, which would make…"

"Twenty."

"And they can't repeat."

Ben's voice rose again. "But I'm supposed to put them in a chart!"

"One problem at a time. First, collect twenty facts." Pulling out a pad of sticky notes she'd grabbed, she peeled them off in stacks of five. "I'm putting five notes on each book. Once you pick the invention for each book, write down one fact per slip. Stick them to the door as you finish them. When all the sticky notes are gone, then you'll know you're done. Now repeat it back, what's the plan?"

He took a big breath. "One invention from each book, five facts for each invention, put the notes on the door."

She gave him a thumbs-up. "Find me when you're done."

"MOM, ELLIE, COME look!" Ben bounced down the stairs, sticky notes drifting after him like falling leaves. "Come look, come look!"

"What is it?" Olivia asked. "Do you need help?"

"Just come! Come, come, come!"

"Okay, hang on." Ellie stood up from the couch, glancing at Olivia, who shrugged. He had only been at it an hour. Neither of them had wanted to jinx the silence by checking on him.

Blue notes flurried Ben's door, his terrible cramped writing filling each square. One came loose, fluttering to the floor. He picked it up and slapped it on the door again. "Twenty! Aren't these sticky notes awesome, Mom?"

"You did a great job!" Ellie was thrilled he'd taken so well to her plan. But Olivia stood mute, holding a blank sticky note with a strange expression. "Right, Olivia?"

Something shook free in her brain, and she gave him a tight smile. "Great job, Ben. You really worked hard."

"What's next, Ellie?"

"Can they go in a chart as they are?"

"Probably not." He scratched his head, launching an errant cowlick straight in the air.

"What does a chart have?"

"Columns?"

"Yes, and columns hold what?"

Thinking, Ben held his breath so long she worried he might pass out. "Groups of things?"

"How many groups do you have right now?"

He sketched a large circle around the notes with his hands. "One big one."

"Think about what belongs together, and arrange the notes into smaller groups. Then we can check in."

"Okay. This is fun!"

"Keep it up, buddy," Olivia said, finding her voice.

As they went downstairs, Ben's contemplative muttering fading behind them, Ellie tugged Olivia's hand. "You got kind of funny up there. What is it?"

"You're amazing with him, so patient and clear. I would have wrestled with this one step the whole morning."

"I did get a master's degree for this stuff. And thanks, but you still look..."

Olivia crumpled the blank note and shoved her fists into her pockets. "Sophia loved sticky notes. Used them constantly. When he was learning to sight read, she slapped words on everything, repeating them over and over until he got them." A wistful pain clouded her face. "I thought he would remember, but he acted like these were a new idea."

"Hey, I'm sorry." Avoiding Sophia landmines had become trickier lately.

"It's not your fault. They're a great tool for him. But it's hard seeing him forget." Olivia always minimized these moments, hoping to hide the sting of their melancholy nostalgia.

She cupped Olivia's face. "You'll remember for him." Her phone buzzed on the entrance table. "Mamá. Wonder what she wants?"

"My weight so she knows how much poison to put in my food next week?"

Ellie rolled her eyes and grabbed the phone. "Hola, Mamá." Spanish erupted in her ear. "¿Cómo?" The ground jerked under her feet. Her legs buckled. A hand clamped around her arm. Olivia, holding her up, leading her to the bench near the door. "Sí, sí. Pronto, Mamá, pronto."

The phone dropped to her lap. Numbness crept from her fingers through the rest of her body. Buzzing static filled her ears, and she choked out the next words. "Abuela died. In her sleep last night." Then grief closed her throat, and she buried her face in Olivia's shoulder as sobs overwhelmed her.

Chapter Twenty

OLIVIA LIFTED THE door knocker, its brass ring heavy in her hand. Her pulse throbbed in her ears as she held it, suspended, then set it down in silence. She stepped off the welcome mat and straightened it with a nudge of her toe. An elderly couple scooted by in the hallway, their faces tight with suspicion. Forcing a nonthreatening smile, she centered herself on the mat again. This time when she lifted the knocker, she used it—three quick raps. Ellie and her family were in Mexico, burying Abuela next to her husband, which left her with too much time and too few excuses to avoid this visit. A chain jingled, the latch snapped, and then her mother-in-law stood framed in the doorway.

"Hello, Nonna." She bent over and kissed Sophia's mother on both cheeks, which wrinkled deeply with her smile.

"Where is my beautiful grandson?" Iron-gray hair swept back from her face, settling around her navy turtleneck. She was a video of Sophia on fast-forward, small and elegant and trim.

"He's at school."

"I don't like it when you leave him behind." She scolded her with one crooked finger, the knuckles swollen with arthritis.

"I know, but I need to talk to you."

"Ooooh, serious stuff. We can't do this without espresso. And biscotti."

Olivia followed her into the compact kitchen. Adrianna lived by herself, a scandal amongst her friends, who had all moved in with their children years ago. Sophia and Christina had begged her to do the same when their father died, but she refused. She'd never lived alone her whole life, she said, and she wanted to try it. It suited her.

"Do you need anything opened?"

"Yes! My sister sent me several jars of my favorite Italian olives. Open two, please."

Olivia found them in a cabinet and cracked the seals. "Both in the fridge?"

"One. Leave the other on the counter. I'll have it for lunch. Then, sit...sit!" Adrianna shooed her toward the table, then fussed with an espresso pot on the stove.

Olivia tucked the jar away and lowered herself into a chair. She wanted to get this over with, but no one rushed Adrianna where espresso was concerned. "Do you need help with the cups?"

"The day I can't hold un caffè is the day you put me in a home." She carried the drinks one at a time, an arthritic hand clamped on each side of the saucer, but finally they were both seated. "Have a biscotti. Or two. You don't eat enough."

She shook her head in polite refusal. It would only glue to the roof of her mouth, already dry with nerves. She sipped her espresso instead, needing its bitter, bracing heat.

"What's so serious? Your face...are you sick?"

"No."

"Benjamin?"

"He's fine."

Clever eyes narrowed. Again, a future Sophia appeared. "Yours is a face of bad news."

"It's not bad news. At least, I hope not." Her lost wife's reflection in her mother-in-law's face choked off her words. Taking a deep breath, she tried again. "I met someone."

Adrianna's expression shuttered closed. She rotated her cup as she stared at Olivia, the ceramic scraping in rhythm with the ticking of her ancient clock.

"I didn't plan for this, Adrianna." Olivia switched to her formal name, one she hadn't used in years. "I assumed I was done with relationships."

"Tell me about this woman." The flat directive revealed none of her thoughts.

"Her name is Ellie."

"What kind of name is that?"

"It's a nickname for Isabella."

"She's Italian?" Adrianna's eyes brightened with interest.

"Mexican."

"Hmm. This Isabella, she's good for my grandson?"

Olivia risked a smile. "Ellie's wonderful with him. She's an OT, so she understands him better than most."

Nodding, Adrianna dunked her biscotti into her drink. "Was she married before? Does she have children?"

"No, she's never been married, and she doesn't have kids."

"Strange, at your age."

"She's thirty-five."

The biscotti wavered for the barest second, then Adrianna took a neat bite from the soaked end. She set the rest on her saucer and wiped her fingers on a napkin. "You love her?"

The blunt question stunned her. "It's serious, but we're not there yet."

"You love her. It's as plain as the nose on your face. Why do you trap your feelings behind a wall of silence?"

Olivia's ribs closed around her lungs like a vise. "I'm not...It's just..." She flailed for an answer while her mother-in-law waited with a familiar firm jaw and glinting eyes. "It feels like I'm betraying Sophia, like our relationship wasn't as special if I can care about someone else."

"My daughter was stolen from you, from us. The hole you have"—a gnarled finger pointed at Olivia's heart—"is an open wound. If this woman can heal it, you must let yourself love her."

Adrianna's response left her reeling, like she'd driven her shoulder into a locked door, only to discover it swung freely. "But when Nonno died, you said no man would cross your threshold again."

"Ahhh, I say a lot of things. And, I had my Antonio for fifty-five years. If I'm alone a little at the end, it's as it should be. But you would be alone another forty years! Alone twice as long as you were with my Sophia. My daughter did not want that for you, or Benjamin."

"This isn't what I expected." Olivia cradled her spinning head.

"You think I'll be upset with you for finding someone, but no. I am Sophia's mother, and I must speak for her. It is a hard burden sometimes." Adrianna lifted Olivia's chin. "She would not want you to suffer alone. There is nothing left to prove to her, or to me."

Tears slid down Olivia's face as she realized how much she'd held back from Ellie, afraid of what the next step meant.

"Bring her to me," Adrianna said, like the queen she was. "I want to meet her."

"Of course." Olivia wiped her face with her napkin.

"I will try not to scare her...too much."

"SO NONNA WANTS to meet Ellie." Arti cackled as she dried a plate. "Good luck. That woman may be tiny, but she radiates more authority than Berlusconi ever did."

Olivia plunged her hands into the soapy water to get another dish. "I still can't believe how easily she took the news. I prepped all these responses, and now they're bouncing around in my brain, unused."

"You almost sound disappointed."

The plate slipped away, sinking below the suds. "What does that mean?"

"I'm just wondering, with all the preparation, who you wanted to convince—Nonna, or yourself?" Arti grabbed her forearm before she could reach into the water again. "You've told everyone who matters, and we all support you. The only permission you need now is your own."

Olivia shrugged free of Arti's grip and rescued the plate, ignoring her aggravated snort.

"When is Nonna and Ellie going to happen?"

"No idea. I did not tell Nonna that Mom met her already, by the way."

"Smart choice. And Alice is still being okay about it?"

Handing off the rinsed plate, Olivia tackled the battered warhorse of a stockpot. It had been her dad's, his trusted companion for every experimental soup, but after he died, her mom passed it to her, claiming she couldn't lift the unwieldy thing. It was heavy, and cumbersome, and one of the handles was cracked, but she couldn't give it up. "Mom's fine, but she doesn't ask many questions for fear I might answer them."

"Story of your life. When will you meet Ellie's folks?"

"It should've been this week, but with the funeral, I'm not sure when we'll reschedule. Ellie was devastated I couldn't meet Abuela."

"Poor kid."

"Please don't call her a kid. She's thirty-five, not nineteen."

"Fine, fine. Although, technically, nineteen is legal, if it doesn't work out with Ellie."

She flicked water at Arti. "You're the single one. You try it."

Smirking, Arti stacked another plate in the cupboard. "When is she back?"

"In two nights. She extended her trip because family kept coming from all over, and her parents wanted to stay longer. She couldn't leave them."

"So why am I here? Other than my stellar conversation."

"I need your eye for detail." Heaving the pot upside down on a towel to dry, she leaned against the sink while water gargled down the drain. "Ellie flies in late on Thursday. I don't want her to be alone, so I was going to invite her to sleep here. And if it goes well, then maybe we can do it more regularly."

"Makes sense." Arti took two wine glasses from the cabinet. When Olivia shook her head, she put one back. "I'm guessing we should bring the Sophia level down?" She yanked the cork out of a bottle on the counter and poured herself a glass.

"The trick is, we can't get rid of certain things because they're part of Ben's routine."

"Up to the bedroom, then. Might as well rip off the bandage."

The bedroom was the last place Olivia wanted to start, but she swallowed her dismay and trailed Arti upstairs. After the door was shut, Arti turned a slow circle at the foot of the bed.

"I never noticed how spartan your bedroom was."

"Stop making that face."

"What face?"

"That 'you disgust me' frown your family's so good at. It makes you look even more like your brother."

"Ouch! And to think I plucked my chin hairs before I came tonight." Arti scratched at the underside of her jaw.

"Can we get started?"

Arti lifted two photos from the dresser and stacked them on the bed. "Ellie's very cool about Sophia, but if you'll be having sex in here, the pics have to go. Are her clothes still in the closet?"

"A few." Her faint hope Arti wouldn't check dissolved as she yanked open the door.

"Everything's still here! We discussed donating this a year ago."

"I don't need much space."

"But Ellie will. Unlike you, she has an actual wardrobe, from what I've seen. I'll get bags in a minute. Toiletries?"

A blush burned Olivia's ears.

Arti pushed past her to the bathroom. The medicine cabinet squeaked open. "You've never used hairspray in your life! This can't be yours." She popped her head around the door. "Is this her toothbrush? Never mind, I can tell by your face. Okay, all toiletries must go." She put a hand on Olivia's arm. "Am I being too casual? I feel like it's what you need."

"No, you're right. It's time."

"It's past time, but for you, that's on schedule."

Her jaw clenched as Arti moved to the dresser and opened Sophia's jewelry box. She took out a necklace, thin chains in gold, silver and copper intertwined. "I made this for her when Ben was born—a color for each of you."

"It was one of her favorites. You should keep it."

"No. It's for you, the family."

"You *are* family. She'd want you to have it. Please."

Arti nestled it gently in her pocket. "What should we do with the rest?"

"It's too personal to donate, but it hurts too much to wear any of it."

"Why don't we tuck it away for now? I'm sure Ellie would understand." Arti moved the box to a shelf in the closet, then walked over to Sophia's nightstand and opened the drawer. Smiling, she picked up a square blue pad. "That woman loved a sticky note."

"I still find them in random places. I stumbled on one in the glove compartment recently."

"What was on it?"

"A grocery list. It was nice to see her handwriting again."

Arti yanked the drawer open wide. "You've hidden a stash of these, haven't you?"

"No." She didn't mention the collection tucked into her own nightstand. On difficult nights she shuffled through them, tracing the looping, extravagant handwriting. The notes were relentlessly practical—*parmesan cheese, birthday present for Mamma, reschedule deposition*—but their digital lives made any tangible reminder more precious.

"And this?" A neon-orange ball the size of a quarter glowed in Arti's palm.

"Ben's. She would hide toys he left around the house in here, hoping he'd have to ask for them and learn to tidy his stuff. But he figured it out, and it became a game." An old memory shook free. "He opened the drawer once, after the accident. He saw the ball, but he didn't take it with him. He still checks on it sometimes."

"You're sure you're ready to see Ellie here?" Arti pointed at the bed.

Olivia shoved her hands into her pockets and nodded once. It was as much certainty as she could muster.

"Then it's time to empty this drawer."

The ball bounced bright parabolas across the floor. Olivia plucked it from the top of its arc, then dropped it in her own nightstand.

Arti raised an eyebrow.

"It's only a ball." Olivia shrugged. "Ellie won't even know what it means."

The detritus of Sophia's drawer began to collect on the bed next to the photos—the blue pad of sticky notes, along with an unopened yellow pack; a Sara Paretsky paperback, bookmark wedged halfway; eye drops; mismatched pens, all with the ends chewed; Costco reading glasses; a clatter of loose change.

"How is Ben with this idea anyway?" Arti tossed hand cream on the pile.

"I explained how Ellie would be sad about her abuela, and I didn't want her to be alone, so she might stay here some nights. She'd sleep with me because that's what adults do, when they're romantic with each other."

"Did he lose it?"

"No, but he was nervous. He did the thing where he repetitively touches his fingers to his thumbs."

"An oldie but a goodie."

"Turns out he was worried about not being able to come in the room if he had a bad dream. I told him that wouldn't change, and he felt better." Lip balm rolled onto the floor, and she tossed it back. "He didn't mention Sophia. I don't think he remembers her sleeping here as clearly anymore."

"It's supposed to fade, in time."

"But she carried him, gave him everything for eight years. To watch her be reduced to a collection of moments, not even a complete person..." Olivia slumped on the bed and picked up the sticky notes, fanning them. "It's my job to keep her alive for him, to press all the memories I have of her onto a record he can play forever in his mind."

"You know that isn't healthy, for either of you." The mattress sank as Arti joined her. "When he asks for stories, you'll tell him the best ones. Right now, it's enough you remind him how much she loved him."

She looked around the bedroom. Arti had called it spartan earlier, but every surface teemed with memories. "Do you think I'm doing the right thing, with Ellie?"

"Do you love her?"

It was the second time today someone had asked that question, and still the answer lodged in her throat.

Arti clucked her tongue. "You and the L-word. You make it so hard."

"It's the best I can do."

"Then, yes, I think you're doing the right thing. How will you know if you don't try?"

Olivia wrapped her arm around Arti's shoulder and hugged hard. "Thanks for this. And for everything."

Arti kissed her shoulder, then leaned her head there. "Always."

Chapter Twenty-One

A BELLY-DEEP groan erupted from Ellie as the rain showerhead wrapped her in delicious, drenching heat. Side jets pummeled her hips, stiff from hours in a cramped airplane seat. She pressed her palms to the cool tile and let Olivia's shower blast away the day's sweaty tackiness. It didn't quite match her steaming tub, but the invitation to spend the night had been irresistible. After two weeks in the tight quarters of her uncle's home, weeping relatives crammed into every spare corner, she craved the quiet peace of Olivia's arms.

"Mind if I join you?" Olivia stepped halfway in, naked. "I'll give you a tour of the shower, so you can adjust the jets."

"Whatever they're doing now is amazing."

"That's the massage setting. I changed it earlier."

She grabbed Olivia by the wrist and pulled her under the stream. "You're a very thoughtful woman."

A shoulder lifted in the deferential shrug Olivia always gave to compliments. Water soaked her hair to burnt honey, misted her eyelashes, strung beads along her upper lip. The town where Ellie had been was locked in a drought. Showers were rationed. A real bath, unthinkable. Most nights, she fell asleep with the heat of the day stuck to her skin. Standing in this column of water with Olivia, she felt like a pale Chalchiuhtlicue had summoned the rain, reviving her.

Olivia furrowed her fingers through Ellie's curls, drawing them off her face, then reached past her for the shampoo. Fingertips massaged delicious paths along her scalp, then soapy hands caressed her body, sloughing off the fatigue with their gentle attention. When she finished, Olivia enclosed her from behind and let the water rain down. The warm circle of those arms brought her fully back from the arid village and the sharp grief of the funeral, and she inhaled. Steam poured into her lungs. When she released the breath, a sob broke through, surprising her.

Soft lips hovered by her ear. "It's all right. Let go. I've got you."

With Olivia's tender words, she did let go, crying harder than she had all the days in Mexico, crying for the small but fierce woman who had taught her what it meant to love and be loved. And who had cherished her exactly as she was. Olivia kept a strong grip, holding her upright through the wave of emotion. When it finally washed through her, Ellie pivoted in Olivia's arms. Gentle kisses brushed across her forehead, her cheeks, her lips.

"Time for bed." Olivia kissed her forehead again.

Ellie let herself be dried off and led to the bedroom. New pajamas lay on the right side of the bed. Sophia's side. Now her side. Her thoughts tangled like so many threads, her brain too weary to pick them apart. So she smiled her thanks and dressed quietly before crawling under the covers. Sleep tugged at her as she settled in Olivia's shoulder. They should talk, check in about this change, but when Olivia's hand sifted through her hair in a slow rhythm, fatigue clutched her, and she sank into darkness.

OLIVIA HAD WATCHED Ellie dress—her height and size filling the small bedroom with an unfamiliar, disquieting dimension—while the space whispered memories of Sophia. But when Ellie stumbled getting one leg in her pajamas, her exhaustion obvious, Olivia stomped on her own discomfort and slid under the blankets to offer an open shoulder.

Full breasts pressed against her side, a round thigh settled over her leg, the damp weight of curls—these recently familiar sensations crackled in this old setting. Sophia had fallen asleep in this exact spot so many times, light but active, her fingers, a shoulder, a cheek twitching as if she kept part of herself alight, even in slumber.

Ellie was the opposite, a heavy, still stone undisturbed by the river of sleep rushing past. Olivia kept up her even strokes. She wouldn't let her unease disrupt the woman in her arms. Ellie's presence was comforting in the abstract, but a prickling tension grew as her form warred with Sophia's memory. Olivia glanced around the room, half expecting to find someone else in the shadows.

Chapter Twenty-Two

THE WEEKEND MORNING percolated around Ellie as she lay on the couch, a crocheted blanket heavy on her legs. Olivia had encouraged her to sleep in, but being alone in the bedroom Olivia had shared with Sophia left her feeling exposed and restless, so she'd dragged herself downstairs to doze through the domestic burble of breakfast. The whirr of the open refrigerator blended with Olivia's low murmur, then feet shuffled from wood to carpet.

"Mom said to cheer you up." Ben's hair, short from a recent cut, was a nest of sleep-tangled cowlicks.

An exasperated sigh came from the kitchen.

"Would you snuggle me? That always helps." It was a big request, one he might not grant. He pattered his toes, considering, then nodded once. She lifted the blanket so he could crawl under, and he curled up facing her, head under her chin.

"Are you still tummy sick, or just heartsick now?" Sticky-sweet maple syrup wafted up on his breath.

"Tummy sick?"

"When you're so sad your tummy hurts."

She stroked the hair at the base of his neck. He tolerated light contact the best. "I know what you mean. My tummy hurts when I'm sad, or mad, or scared."

"Me too!"

"Where did you get the idea to call it tummy sick?"

"After Mommy died, Mom said she was heartsick. That it was a real word." He rapped her sternum. "I asked if tummy sick was a word. She said no. But I was tummy sick and heartsick after Mommy."

Stretched thin by Abuela's loss, she couldn't stop the sting of tears, but she kept her voice level. "Which went away first?"

"Tummy sick."

"Do you still feel heartsick?"

He paused for so long that she worried he had shut down. She brushed his neck again.

"A little." His hand twitched, thumb tapping against his fingers. "I think I didn't love Mommy as much."

The faucet shut off in the kitchen.

"As much as what?"

A faint shadow hovered on the other side of the door-jamb.

"Mom. She's been heartsick way longer."

The breath she blew out ruffled his hair. "You absolutely loved Mommy as much as Mom did." Ellie took a careful step onto this new path. "Do you know the word grief?"

"It means super sad."

"Yes. And grief is different for everyone. So how you feel is right for you, and how Mom feels is right for her. It doesn't say anything about how much you loved a person."

"Okay." His fingers stopped.

"I was tummy sick about Abuela at first because it surprised me, but she was very old, and even though I didn't want her to die, I knew she would soon. Now, it's more about realizing we won't ever talk again." Her heart clenched thinking of their last chat, of Abuela's concern for Ben, and she drew him into a hug.

His wiry body stiffened. "Too tight!"

"Sorry." Loosening her grip, she brushed a kiss against his hair. "Do you want to hear a song Abuela taught me? It's in Spanish."

He gave a quick nod. As she sang, she tried to recreate the experience of her grandmother's voice. In her mind, she was Ben's age, snuggled next to Abuela, rubbing the worn fabric of her nightdress, jasmine soap faint on her wrinkled skin. The memory cracked her open, and she buried her face in Ben's hair.

"Ellie? Are you okay?" He patted her damp cheek. "You should feel better, not cry! Mom said."

Olivia appeared above them, leaning on the couch arm. "It's okay, buddy. Just being with someone while they're sad can help."

Ben's gentle pats continued as Olivia's forehead touched her temple. Blonde waves fell in a curtain around them, and Ellie sank into their quiet protection and let the grief wash over her.

ELLIE PUTTERED IN the living room, its light muted now as the afternoon sun drenched the kitchen. With the fog of travel clearing, she could absorb the changes. All the law books were gone. Their space swallowed Ben's clay sculpture and an old photo of Olivia's parents. Her father carried the same lanky limbs and proud posture, and although the image was black-and-white, she knew from Olivia his intent eyes were hazel.

Nursing books remained, along with an entire shelf devoted to autism and parenthood. Tattered spy thrillers sat at head height. Olivia loved to reread them, hunting for new hints in the familiar plots. Ellie touched three spines, only slightly creased. They were her Christmas gift to Olivia after a conversation about books and movies. Other gaps sulked, and she searched her memory. Mysteries. Sophia had loved mysteries. Guilt plucked at Ellie as she wondered where they had gone, and she turned from the accusatory glare of the hollowed-out shelves.

Olivia padded barefoot into the room, picking dried glue from her T-shirt. "Well, the diorama's finished." When their eyes met, her hand dropped, and she stepped close. "What is it?"

"You got rid of a lot. I hope it wasn't all...that I didn't—"

"It started small, making space for you in the bedroom. But then I came down here and looked around and...the timing seemed right, I guess." She touched the mantel. "This is still pretty cluttered, but Ben is so attached—"

"It's fine. You shouldn't pretend she didn't live here. And if you find yourself missing something, please put it back. Even in the bedroom." Ellie walked along the crowded mantel. It reminded her of an ofrenda, although the living sat side by side with the dead. She tapped a photo. Sophia and Ben's narrow faces filled the frame. "It still surprises me how much he looks like her."

"He doesn't have her olive skin, but otherwise, yeah."

"It must be hard, seeing so much of her in him." When Olivia didn't respond, Ellie took her hand and kissed it. "He has a lot of your mannerisms though."

"Nah, he's all Sophia." The discomfort in Olivia's posture was obvious, another thing she shared with her son, but those similarities were lost on her—she refused to dilute the influence of the woman who had carried him. He'd become a chalice, filled with as many of Sophia's attributes as his young body could hold.

"Where was this taken?"

"Indian Boundary Park. He and Sophia would visit the ducks and turtles. It was their special place."

"Do you still go?"

"No. He said it wasn't the same without her."

There was a pattern she couldn't quite pin down, but as she scanned the mantel again, it clicked. She chewed her lip, balancing the risk of this next observation. "There's nothing recent."

"After she was gone, I stopped taking pictures."

"What about Ben's selfies? You never wanted to frame one of the two of you?"

A muscle in Olivia's jaw twitched. "He had so many rituals after the accident, touching photos in a certain order, arranging them on the floor and leaving them for days. I didn't want to disrupt his pattern with anything new."

"I get that, but I've noticed, since I've been over here more, you two can be a bit...cloistered. Does it get hard—"

"MOMMMMMM!" Ben's scream sliced through the house.

Olivia bolted up the stairs ahead of her. They found him in her bedroom, looking in what used to be Sophia's nightstand.

"It's gone! It's gone! It's gone!"

"Ben—"

"YOU STOLE IT!" He charged at Ellie, his bony hands jabbing into her stomach. Caught off guard, she stumbled and landed on the floor. Rage smeared his features red. "MY BALL! YOU STOLE IT! STOLE MOMMY! I HATE YOU!" He lunged at her again, but Olivia grabbed him.

"Ben!" she yelled in his ear, over his shouting. "Ben! I moved Mommy's things! I moved the ball! I did it, not Ellie."

"WHY? You love Mommy!"

Olivia set him down and spun him to face her. "I do love Mommy, always, but she's been gone a long time. We can't keep everything the same."

"I want it the SAME!"

"I know you do, but Ellie is here now, and she needs space. I moved the ball to my side. It's right here." When she opened her drawer, he snatched up an orange ball.

"I WANT IT THE SAME!" He flung it at Olivia, who raised her arms. It caromed off her wrist and around the room. Ben darted past Ellie and slammed his door. The ball hit the dresser with a hollow thud, then rolled under the bed.

"Damn." Olivia dragged tangled curls out of her face.

Ben's fury, the ugly snarl twisting his sweet features— Ellie felt herself sliding into tears.

"Hey, he didn't mean it. Any of it."

"You don't know that."

"Come here." Olivia helped her from the floor and shut the door. "We knew this might happen. He was handling it too well."

"He said he hated me." She hiccupped a sob, fighting for control.

"Listen. After the accident, Ben said he hated me because I killed Mommy. Because I was driving."

The agony those words must have caused Olivia, so soon after Sophia's death— Ellie pressed her fist to her mouth.

"It was in the first month, and only twice." Olivia cleared the husk from her voice. "So, I get why you're upset, but he doesn't mean it."

"I don't want him hurt by us being together."

"I don't think we can avoid it. You were right, what you said about us being cloistered. I've been protecting him, probably more than I should. But change is inevitable. If not with you, then in some other way."

"Was it too soon, me spending the night?"

"Hard to tell. I'll talk to him. I don't want him thinking one good fit can scare you away." Olivia put a hand on each of her shoulders and squeezed. "By dinner, he'll chat with you like it never happened. Mom once said Ben's rages were summer storms—they come up fast and leave everybody but him picking up the pieces hours later."

"I should be telling you this." Ellie wiped her face with her sleeve, embarrassed by her reaction. "I mean, it's what I do for a living."

"Give yourself a break. You're off your game after a funeral and a long flight."

"When will you talk to him?"

"After he settles down." Olivia pulled her close, and she didn't resist. But no matter how deep she buried her face in Olivia's neck, she couldn't wipe Ben's angry face from her mind.

ELLIE CLICKED OFF the lamp on the nightstand, leaving the bedroom dark except for a sliver of light from the bathroom door. "You were right about dinner. It was like nothing happened."

"He flares so intensely, and then it's gone. Getting him to understand how he affects the other person is hard." The light went out, and Olivia stepped through the door like a shadow.

"I feel silly getting so upset." Ellie rolled toward Olivia when she slipped under the covers.

"It's not silly. Ben can give you whiplash. Everything's fine, and then it's a disaster, and then an hour later, it's fine again. It's hard enough when you're in a good place. When you're struggling, it feels impossible." Olivia said it offhandedly, in comfort, but Ellie heard the deeper truth, the reality of Olivia's life. She never had time to recover from Sophia's death alone, to crawl into a hole and wish the world away. Ben was her world. His needs didn't stop just because her life had been shattered.

"I want to handle things better than I did today."

"Do you know how many times I've said that in eleven years?"

"Twice?"

Olivia's chuckle vibrated by her ear. "Twice a week if I'm lucky. Twice a day if I'm not."

Ellie scooted even closer, crooking her leg around one thigh. "I missed this so much."

"Me too." Olivia mapped soothing rivers of touch along her side. "Is there anything else you want?"

"Earlier in the day, I thought maybe, but now, do you mind if we snuggle?"

"Whatever you need. But...is the room bothering you? Are you comfortable?"

She rested her hand on Olivia's sternum. "It's not about that, honestly. I'm tired from the trip and tender about Ben, and this feels—"

Olivia stopped her with a light kiss. "I don't care about the sex. I just want to be with you when you're hurting."

"No fair using my words against me," Ellie protested through a yawn.

"Shhhh, enough talking. We'll have time for more later."

Chapter Twenty-Three

ELLIE HAD WATCHED partners masturbate before, but never someone with Olivia's blunt physicality. She didn't shrink when Ellie clicked on the bedside lamp, soaking her in decadent light. And she wasn't shy about the thick black tube between her legs, a surprise gift Ellie had brought. They'd been finding their rhythm after her absence, and tonight Ellie had asked for that long-promised demonstration of vibrator prowess. The reality was far better than she'd imagined.

The vibrator plunged in and out of Olivia's dense curls. Sweat glistened on her splayed breasts, which rocked with each thrust, the pink nipples tracing erratic ellipses. There was a bold intimacy to this view. The rhythm Olivia set, the depth of each stroke, the minute clench of neck and belly and thigh, the hitched breath, even her scent—it all telegraphed her building intensity. Olivia was telling the story of her own pleasure, and she was letting Ellie watch.

The pace increased, the vibrator driving deeper, harder. A coarse groan escaped, and she arched in climax, her toes curling, her free hand twisting in the sheets. As she collapsed to the bed, she pulled the vibrator free.

Ellie crawled on top to plant a kiss on her dry lips. "Who needs porn when they have you? Want to go again?"

Olivia released a breathless laugh. "No, no, it's my turn. This is going right into you."

"What?"

"Hands and knees." A sly grin crooked Olivia's lips. "Please?"

"Well, when you ask so nicely." Ellie pushed to her knees, the mattress shifting as Olivia settled behind her and began to explore. Spine, shoulders, ribs, stomach, hips, thigh, ass—Olivia mapped them all with hands so electric it was like they ran beneath Ellie's skin. Her body expanded with every charged caress, offering up this inch of skin, that unexplored nook, until she threatened to splinter into tiny humming fragments of touch. At the precipice, when she was about to fly apart, Olivia slowly coaxed her back to center as if casting a fine net and gathering those scattered attentions into a solid form once more.

Now those hands coursed up her stomach, and Ellie arched, desperate for warm palms to finally take the heavy weight of her breasts. They were one of two places Olivia had yet to explore, and both ached for attention. But only a lone fingertip brushed each nipple. Olivia repeated the motion again and again, a delicate, barely-there contact that sizzled on her sensitive flesh. A thick moan spilled from her lips as she ground against Olivia.

"So impatient," Olivia murmured.

"You said—" She trembled with another pass. "Jesus. You said the vibrator...uhhhhh...was going right in me." When Olivia's hands moved away, Ellie uncoiled for a moment. Then Olivia stroked between her legs with both sets of fingers. "Fuuuuuck..."

"We'll get there, but you could...be...wetter." Olivia punctuated her last words with long, tender sweeps of every fold.

"I don't think it's poss—"

Another guttural moan escaped when Olivia returned to her nipples, coating a wet spiral from the engorged tips all the way around her breasts. Air licked those damp lines, and the musky cut of her own need mingled with Olivia's more mineral tang. Strands of hair tickled Ellie's back as Olivia leaned over her, pinching and tugging her nipples until she shuddered with unreleased desire.

"Jesus...I need...please."

Olivia circled her clit. "Definitely wet enough." She dragged the vibrator along the inside of Ellie's thigh, then thrust it into her. Bucking, she nearly came right then.

"Does it turn you on that the vibrator I just used is now inside you?"

"Woman, you need to shut up and fuck me with that thing."

Olivia laughed, low and sexy, then stroked her in leisurely passes. The vibrator wasn't on yet, but it didn't need to be. The pressure, the movement was all Ellie could take. Except for one small addition. Olivia's other hand rested on her cheek, the thumb near the crack of her ass.

"Will you..." The arousal choked off her words.

"Tell me what you need."

"Will you put your thumb in my ass?"

The vibrator paused as the lube top snapped, and Olivia filled her with more delicious pressure. "This okay?"

"Perfect." Ellie dropped to her elbows, and Olivia began pumping again. Tiny shifts of her thumb kept pace. "Faster with the vibrator."

The speed quickened, the vibrator skimming that perfect spot, a call-and-response she could never resist. Each plunge was a fist on a table, demanding now, now, now. She wanted to hold on, to stretch it out, but with one last pass, the orgasm exploded, and she bit the pillow to hold in a scream. The bright arc descended as Olivia slowed her thrusts, but now she turned the vibrator on.

Ellie unclenched her teeth from the pillow. "I don't know if I can come again. It's so intense."

"Let's see what happens, okay? If it gets uncomfortable, tell me." Olivia's thumb still worked with the relentless pulse of the vibrator. Each time it penetrated her, she opened more, trying to take all that Olivia could give. The pace increased gradually, nudging her closer to orgasm, but then it leveled off, leaving her suspended in glorious agony until a thin, wordless plea leaked between her teeth. Olivia responded, ramping up the speed, and now the orgasm roared at her like a train.

"Let it go. Feel all of it."

Olivia's words tripped the switch. She flew apart, screaming into her pillow. A ballooning pressure released, and liquid gushed down her thighs. Olivia slowed, coaxing a few final shudders before Ellie collapsed to the bed. She lay there, arms trapped beneath her, gasping. Then, like another orgasm, emotion rushed up her chest and burst from her in breathless sobs. Olivia spooned close, pulling the blankets over them. "It's all right. I've got you."

Words flooded Ellie's mouth, threatening to drown her from the inside out. She had no more control of them than she did the orgasm moments before. Now, they demanded. Now. Now. Now. "I love you." The admission ripped itself free. "I love you, Olivia. I love you so much."

Olivia kissed her temple. "I've got you. I'm here." The strength in her arms never wavered, but her fingers trembled against Ellie's scalp as she stroked her hair.

The shivers finally receded, and she could breathe again. There was a damp stickiness on her thighs and the sheet. "I don't know what that was."

"It's okay. It's happened to me before. You ejaculated."

"I thought ejaculation was a myth."

"Definitely not a myth."

"And the emotion, at the end—"

Olivia nodded. "It feels like if you don't release it, you'll choke."

She turned in Olivia's arms, her limbs heavy, clumsy things.

"Hey, what is it?" Olivia prodded her with her nose.

"Nothing."

"Is it about what you said after?"

"I didn't mean to blurt it out." She couldn't hold back the tears. "I've felt this way for a while, but I thought it might scare you."

"Hey, we're in this together. I want to know what you're feeling. Always."

"But you don't feel the same."

Regret dulled Olivia's eyes. "I care about you, which I know isn't the same. I care about you more than I imagined would ever be possible. Do you understand? I thought this would never happen again, so I'm still absorbing it. I care for you so much, but I'm not there yet."

Ellie tried to smile through the ache. "How do I say 'I love you,' and when you don't say it back, you come off as more romantic?"

"I'm serious. I want you to know where I am. And that I'm sorry I'm not where you are."

"It's okay." Ellie needed an escape from this conversation. The orgasm had left her exposed, like a raw nerve. "I'm sorry about the bed. Did I ruin it?"

"I use waterproof mattress covers in case Ben sleeps with me. He wet the bed, after the accident."

"How handy." She fumbled for a joke.

"Want me to start the shower? I'll change the sheets while you're in there. I don't care, but if Ben comes in the morning—"

"No, no. Let's clean up."

When Olivia rolled from the bed and left the room, Ellie buried her face in her hands. After all her caution, she'd said those three words in a spasm of emotion, completely unplanned. But it was true. Olivia had been honest and sweet, and Ellie understood where she was coming from, but it still hurt like hell she hadn't said it back.

OLIVIA ESCAPED TO the bathroom, desperate to put distance between her and Ellie. She turned the shower knob, then plunged her shaking hand into the spray. A cold stream ran down her fingers and dripped from her wrist. Her pulse slowed as the heat increased. She made a small adjustment to the temperature, then turned to the sink to clean up.

Their fun sexual lark had turned intense, and Ellie's raw declaration pressured Olivia to say something, anything. What Ellie deserved was an equal response, but she couldn't manage it. Meeting Ellie's eyes in that moment, knowing the last time she'd said those words had been to Sophia, in the same room...her tongue had turned to stone. Sheets shifted in the bedroom, and Olivia dragged the hair from her face. Ellie deserved everything, but she didn't know how to give it to her.

Chapter Twenty-Four

"I CAN'T BELIEVE you threw up on his fucking boots!" Marisol's laugh pealed over the Skype connection.

"Last time that corporal makes a crack about my pregnancy, I promise you." Claudia rolled her eyes. "Why do some guys get so freaked out by a pregnant woman?"

Ellie wiped tears from her face, the laptop shaking on her stomach. "I'm sorry you've been sick, but Jesus it's funny."

"I finally feel better, but now the cravings have kicked in. It's so weird—a week ago the smell of food made me puke, and today I could eat everything. God, if you handed me an elote right now, I might cry."

"Ooh, an elote," Ellie said. "That's tough to ship, even for your mom."

"She's trying to figure out a way."

"Hey, is it official—your husband's going to be a stay-at-home daddy?" Marisol asked.

"Yep, he filed the paperwork." Claudia's sweet grin lit up the screen. "He's so pumped. The guys give him shit, but he doesn't care. Being career military was always my passion."

"I'm so excited for him! Is your mom still planning to fly over to help?" Ellie's bottle tipped precariously as she shifted on the couch, so she took a swig and set it on the coffee table.

"I told her to stay home and take care of Papi, but you know how she gets." Claudia's sigh skipped as the connection lagged. "It's her first grandchild. She's a little loco."

"Abuelas always fuss. Don't be too hard on her."

"Oh Ellie, how are you? Is it getting any better?"

"It's getting less weird. Is that the same?"

"One step at a time, cariño. Grief follows its own winding path." Marisol sank into the hammock on her balcony, the world swinging gently around her, and Ellie smiled. Her friend's surprise appearance at the funeral last month had been a salve on a raw wound, her blunt practicality the perfect counterpoint to the flood of distraught visitors.

"How's your dad?" Claudia asked.

Her father was as he always had been—quiet and sturdy—but without the quick smile he usually carried. "He's sad, but he won't admit it. When people mention her, he'll talk about how lucky we were to have her so long, but Mamá says he still hasn't gone into her room. He won't even talk about what to do with her things."

"It's only been a month," Claudia said. "He'll get there."

"So are you doing the family dinner with Olivia soon?" Marisol's face slid sideways, then righted itself. "Sorry. Laptops and hammocks don't go together."

"Not this coming weekend, but next."

"Are you nervous?" Claudia asked. "I know your mom can be funny about your girlfriends."

"Mamá's off-balance because of Olivia's age and having a son. It never really sank in for her that gay marriage was legal and queer folks have kids—it seemed like a bizarre American fantasy. But Olivia makes it real. Mamá has to take her seriously."

Claudia ruffled her short hair, sending wayward curls in all directions. "What does Olivia say about it?"

"She's ready to meet them. She just wanted me to pick the time I was most comfortable with, especially after Abuela."

"And are you? Comfortable?" Marisol squinted at the screen, her scowl suspicious. "Because that face of yours doesn't look it."

Ellie pinched the bridge of her nose and grimaced. Her mind kept circling to the unanswered "I love you" no matter how she tried to avoid it. "I was when I set it up."

"But?"

"We had an awkward moment a few days ago. It's still bugging me."

Marisol moved her drink from her lap and set it out of sight, her scowl morphing into a growl. "What did she do?"

"She didn't do anything!"

"Then what did you do?"

Ellie puffed a sharp sigh. "I told her I loved her, and she didn't say it back."

Claudia covered her mouth with her hands. "Oh, Ellie!"

"You're not making it any better!"

"Lo siento, but I've done that. It's the worst. What did she say?"

"A lot of sweet things about how much she cared for me, but that she wasn't there yet. We spent the next day being super cautious with each other."

Marisol shook her finger at the screen. "You and Claudia are always too quick with the 'I love you.' You should be more careful. Make them say it first."

"I *was* careful. I've been sitting on this for two months. Do you know how hard it's been *not* to say it?"

"So why now? The sex was so fucking good you lost your mind?"

Ellie's hand froze, bottle halfway to her mouth.

"Oh shit, I was joking, but—"

"You said it during sex?" Claudia's question was more of a squeak. Her fingers were over her eyes, and she peeked through them at the screen.

Ellie groaned and let her head flop on a cushion. "Technically, it was after."

"Damn, woman. When you lay it out there, you really lay it out there."

"What will you do?" Claudia asked.

"Get over it and be patient. Jesus, I don't even want her to say it unless she means it."

"What if she never says it?" Marisol's frank question poked at her deepest fear.

Claudia jumped in. "It's too soon for that discussion."

"Hey, I'm with Olivia. I would never pull the I love you trigger so soon. But Ellie did, and now the clock's ticking. You're okay leaving your declaration sitting there for six months? A year?"

The thought of waiting months for Olivia to reciprocate made Ellie's stomach churn. After Angie, she'd vowed not to repeat this situation, but here she was, jumping first again.

"Marisol, stop freaking her out!"

"What? I'm being practical."

"Ellie, listen. You've only been dating five months, and there's her son to consider. Of course she's cautious." Claudia spread placating hands toward the camera. "You're the kind of person who says 'I love you' whenever you feel it. Which is why *we* love you. If Olivia knows you at all by now, she'll understand."

"Fuck." Ellie swung her feet to the floor as she sat up, then set her laptop on the coffee table. "Do you remember when our biggest worry was whether or not there'd be a second date?"

"Think about it this way—if Olivia was freaked out, would she still be up for meeting your family?"

Marisol tapped on her chin, her lower lip pouting in thought. "Claudia has a point. It'd be easy to put you off if she wanted space. The fact that she hasn't is a good sign."

Ellie picked at the label on her bottle. A wet curl gave way beneath her nail. "I hadn't considered that."

"You're still upset about Abuela, cariño, and this dinner is a big step with your family, so no wonder you're tense, but don't make extra problems for yourself, okay?" Claudia smiled sympathetically. "You keep talking about how she's quiet and serious, right? Well, it seems like that's what she's doing—being quiet and serious. You just be your wonderful self. Let Olivia be Olivia."

Marisol and Claudia's assurances popped her bubble of worry. She sucked in a big breath before releasing it in a rush. "Okay. It's official—I am done fussing about it. I said the words. I meant the words. And we are moving on. Now, let's talk baby shower. We might not get to Germany before this kid is born, but we can at least bury you in presents."

"Fuck yeah, we can!" Marisol grabbed at the subject change with her usual grace. "Do you know how much money I make? Other than keeping my husband in paint and canvas, I got no other demands. This baby will be spoiled rotten!"

She grinned as Marisol listed the gifts she had planned, one more ridiculous than the next. "Tontita, who are you fooling? You're buying that kid savings bonds and starting a 529."

Claudia's squawking laugh punched through the speakers. Her body shook so hard she almost fell out of her chair.

"She got you there. You already bought the bonds, didn't you?"

"I did not!"

"But they're an open tab on your browser, right?" Ellie tipped her beer toward the screen, then drained the bottle to the sounds of Claudia's glee and Marisol's sputtered defense. The fears fogging her mind had thinned, as they so often did after talking with these women, and she headed to the fridge for another drink while Marisol peppered Claudia with financial questions.

Chapter Twenty-Five

"I'VE ATTENDED PLENTY of art exhibitions, and honestly, this kid has a stronger point of view than most adults." Arti polished off her second mimosa as she considered the painting. "Whoever decided to host an opening during brunch hours is brilliant."

"I'll be sure to tell the organizer. It's their first featuring art by queer teens rather than adults. They wanted a family-friendly vibe." Mara snagged a champagne flute from a passing server and swapped Arti's empty glass for the full one.

Ellie grinned at the deft maneuver. Femme women brought out Mara's solicitous side. Rachel would be foaming at the mouth if she saw it, innocuous as it was. But a family issue had dragged her to the burbs, leaving Mara to meet Olivia on her own. The change hadn't been unwelcome. Rachel had squashed her worst critical tendencies lately, but a face-to-face meeting might have brought them out. If Olivia put her on the defensive, Arti would make her head explode. She wasn't used to being out-femmed or out-quipped.

Olivia studied the next painting, a vivid portrait of a young woman screaming, her exaggerated, wide-open mouth lined with all the colors of the rainbow. Ellie slipped her arms around her waist from behind and rested a chin on her shoulder. "I remember that feeling."

"Mmm." Olivia leaned into the contact, her body melting against Ellie's. "So full of this new realization, but not sure how to tell anyone."

Ellie cherished the return of their loose, easy physicality. Her conversation with Claudia and Marisol had been the nudge she needed, and once she let down her guard, Olivia did the same, as if she'd been waiting for a signal. She nuzzled Olivia's neck and inhaled. "You smell suspiciously of cinnamon."

"The French toast petit fours are addictive."

Through Olivia's jacket, a short vibration buzzed Ellie's forearm. Olivia reached around her and fished the phone from her pocket. Zariah's name appeared in the notification.

Jamal and Ben want to catch the paletas man before he leaves. Do you mind?

Ellie read over Oliva's shoulder as she typed. *It's fine. Remind him he didn't like the Spiderman face the last time.*

"Spiderman wasn't a hit?"

"It tasted—and I'm quoting here—'too red.'"

"Huh. What does red even taste like?"

"No idea. But too much of it isn't good, apparently."

Zariah's reply popped up. *LOL. Will do.*

"Must be officially spring if the paletas guys are pedaling around." Ellie brushed a kiss on Olivia's ear.

"All right, enough of the art on the walls. Let me see this piece on your arm." Arti's bossy request brought Olivia's head around.

"Arti—"

"What? No one gets a tattoo this big unless they're prepared to show it off."

"She's not wrong," Mara said with a smile, shedding her leather jacket. Arti dropped her rainbow-framed reading glasses from their perch on her head. She'd spent much of the exhibit peering through them at various pieces, and now she gave her full designer's attention to the intricate tree that sleeved Mara's arm and twined branches across the left side of her chest, neck, and shoulder.

"Nice glasses, by the way," Mara said.

"One for every occasion," Olivia teased. "Ask her how many pairs she owns."

"Ask *her* how many pairs she's lost," Arti muttered. "This tattoo makes me want to design an arm cuff to complement it. What does it mean?"

"It's a warden tree. The Swedes and Germans considered them guardians, protecting those who lived nearby from bad luck. I read about them in a children's book and loved the idea."

"Weren't warden trees green, even in winter?" Olivia asked.

Surprise ruffled Mara's quiet features. "How do you—"

"My dad read me myths and folktales before bedtime." Olivia touched a crisp branch cutting across Mara's shoulder. "So why no leaves?"

"I grew up in foster care—it's one of the reasons I went into social work—and at the group home where I stayed the longest, this huge tree dominated the front yard. I was always struck by how barren it was in winter, even though I knew by summer it'd be covered in leaves." Mara didn't often share the larger story behind the tattoo. Ellie was touched she showed this early trust in Olivia and Arti.

"During the hard times, I'd remember that dead-looking tree coming back, year after year. When I designed it, I wanted to represent both the warden and the promise of hope." Mara rotated her arm, exposing the inside of her bicep. "Which is why there's one green leaf tucked away, right here."

"It's a gorgeous piece," Olivia said. "And I should warn you now that Ben will ask all about it when he sees it. He loves trees."

"You could have brought him today."

"Crowds aren't his thing." Olivia's response dwindled as she stared over Mara's head. "I'm sorry, weird question—where could I find a few sheets of paper?"

Mara hooked a thumb over her shoulder. "Look for the rainbow suspenders by the bar. They'll know."

"Thanks. Be right back."

Ellie looked from Mara to Arti. "What was that about?"

Arti gave a "beats me" frown, then collared another server, this time for a bite-sized quiche. The three of them made small talk, but as the time stretched out, Ellie scanned the room.

"All right, I give up. Where is she?"

A strange smile curled Arti's lips. "Over there." She nodded toward a boy who was flicking his fingers and rocking his upper body. His stroller creaked as his stimming grew more intense. He wasn't too far from a meltdown. Olivia spoke to his parents, and after they nodded, she crouched to the boy's level and waved hello.

Unfazed by his lack of response, she extended her other hand, revealing a small origami bird perched on her up-turned palm. He ignored it until she pinched the bird at both ends and tugged, making its wings flap. The motion captivated him. He inspected it delicately, shook it when it didn't work for him, then held it out in a "show me" gesture. Olivia guided his fingers to each end, pulling with him before letting go. He kept tugging, the wings flapping, his mouth a perfect *O* of wonder. She smiled, then stood and gave something to the parents before making her way back.

Before Ellie could even ask a question, Arti clutched Olivia in a fierce hug. "You old softie."

"I'm a little rusty. I screwed up two before remembering how." Olivia sniffed hard and wiped a wrist across her eyes. "He's the little brother of an artist. His sister recently came out, and the parents want to support her by staying for the whole event, but they're not sure he'll make it. I gave them extras. Hopefully, it buys some time."

Ellie exchanged a look with Mara, who seemed as impressed and confused as she was. "It was extremely sweet, but I don't understand...you're so emotional."

Olivia reached for her hand and laced their fingers. "Ben was six when we started eating out again. We'd bring sheets of paper so he could draw trees to pass the time. One day, a server made him a small origami bird that flapped. He loved it. The guy showed me how, and from then on, we had our routine. Sophia handled the ordering, Ben drew his trees, and I folded origami birds. Once the meal came, he'd fly the birds from branch to branch, giving us time to eat and chat a bit."

Ellie pulled Olivia close for a soft hug. There were so many stories they had yet to share. "How did you even know there was an issue?"

"I could tell his stimming was ramping up because of all the side-eye from the crowd. Folks think they're being subtle, but I promise you, the parents see it. It hurts to be so noticed and so shunned at the same time."

Mara frowned, a sharp furrow slashing between her brows. "This is supposed to be an inclusive space."

Olivia shrugged. "Queer or straight, people are uncomfortable with disability."

"Including some who should know better." A scowl creased Arti's mouth.

"That was a long time ago."

"And you're too forgiving. Grudges should be nurtured, clutched to your chest until the last breath leaves you."

"We're talking about Ben now?" Ellie tugged on Olivia's hand. "Who wasn't supportive?"

"Some friends stepped away after the diagnosis—"

Arti rolled her eyes. "That's one way to put it."

"To be fair—"

"Which you are, to a fault."

Olivia ignored the comment. "To be fair, nobody had a frame of reference for it. One day, we were the same as them—park meetups and playdates—and then suddenly, we weren't. Ben did best with familiar spaces, so we avoided restaurants, parties, even other people's homes, at first. We didn't go out as a couple because he was distraught if he woke up to anyone but us. We basically dropped out of the world. Not everyone wanted to spend time with us when we came back."

"Please, they acted like autism was contagious. Can't let precious Austin or sweet Madison stand too close, or they might start acting 'weird.'" Arti's bitter tone went arctic.

Ellie shivered. She hoped never to be the focus of that ire. "What about TTC?"

"We were all in the same boat, living by a schedule, struggling to find babysitters. Made socializing hard. Honestly, being a parent to a disabled child is far more isolating than anything I experienced as a queer person." Olivia cocked her head, the small twitch that happened when her phone went off, and she pulled it from her pocket. "It's work. Let me step outside and take this." Tucking it to her ear, she made her way to the front door.

"And I'm going to find the restroom." Arti hitched her mammoth purse higher on her shoulder and sashayed through the crowd, her bright swirl of a dress dancing around her hips.

Ellie lifted an eyebrow at Mara. "I think that was her not-so-subtle way of giving us space to dish on Olivia."

"Does Arti have a subtle way?" Mara grinned, then tipped her glass in Olivia's direction. "And there's not much dish-worthy, especially after her bird move."

"I don't know what impresses me more—that she noticed him escalating, or that she found a way to help which involved *freaking origami*."

"It was pretty nifty. Seriously, she's a great person. And she and Arti together are a trip—a middle-aged angel and devil perched on your shoulders." One of Mara's clients came up and whispered in her ear, and she excused herself.

Ellie drifted to a nearby sculpture, using it as cover while she observed Olivia through the window. She paced up and down the sidewalk, gesturing with her free hand.

"I heard it went well with Alice." Arti's voice hovered by her ear.

"Jesus! I thought you went—"

"Long line. Decided to wait."

The affected casualness in Arti's expression made Ellie suspicious. "Yeah, it seemed like a good visit. She's quiet though. Even more than Olivia told me."

"As a kid, I didn't know that kind of silence was possible. I mean, if my mom stopped talking, I'd probably call 911. Alice is a cakewalk, though, compared to Adrianna. You got off the hook with her last-minute trip to Italy."

"It's too bad her sister broke her hip, but I can't lie, a reprieve is nice. Meeting Olivia's mother is one thing. Meeting Olivia's mother-in-law is..."

"Next-level stuff, for sure."

"How is Adrianna, really?" Ellie still didn't know where Arti was headed, but if she was in a sharing mood, it paid to take advantage.

"She's sharp as fuck and stealthy about it—like an assassin but with questions. The two of you are chatting along, then suddenly, you're revealing details you would never expect."

"Now I'm even more relieved."

"It'll be worth it." Arti watched Olivia through the window. She was still on the phone, leaning on a bike rack as she hunched against the wind. "Because she's amazing."

"She absolutely is."

Now Arti nodded at the boy, still happily playing with his bird. "Remember this the next time she clams up. She's always been more of a show-than-tell woman."

Ellie's pulse quickened.

"Yes, I heard about the 'I love you' situation."

Ellie had tucked that moment away, resolving to be patient, and here was Arti, of all people, resurrecting it. A flush stung her neck. She bit her lip to stop it flattening into a scowl.

Arti surprised her with a smile. "I knew you had a temper in there. Don't be mad. I forced it out of her. Forty years of reading Olivia, I can tell when she's upset." She sketched an apologetic wave, her thick gold ring winking in the light. "It sucks to put that out there and get crickets back, but it might help to know I've had this exact conversation before."

Intense curiosity muffled Ellie's defensiveness. "Sophia?"

"For most people, the first 'I love you' is a way of saying you matter to me, I'm serious about this, there might be more for us down the road. It's an indication, if you will."

"Okay." The sentiment didn't encompass the emotion roiling her heart, but with a story hovering on Arti's lips, she didn't quibble.

"Olivia doesn't work in 'thinks' or 'mights.' Those three words have a special power for her, almost like a marriage proposal. It took her forever to say it to Sophia, but after she did, she said it all the time. And remember, she didn't expect to ever say it again for the first time."

Irritation bled away, and Ellie slumped. With her fixation on the words Olivia hadn't said, she'd lost sight of how tied up they must be in memories of Sophia.

"How's the sex?"

The blunt question knocked her sideways. She studied Arti's face for a hint of a trap.

"Fine, don't tell me."

"Amazing. Intense." The words rushed out. She was desperate to keep the thread going.

"You're okay, then. She isn't truly intimate unless she feels strongly about a person. Sophia told me once when Olivia needed to talk, she poured her energy into the sex, trying to say physically what she couldn't emotionally."

"So this silence isn't new?"

"God, no. Olivia's reticence goes back longer than you've been alive. Her whole world can be summed up in six words—feels so much, says so little. Once you're in, you're in, but getting in takes patience."

"Every time I think I'm in, something else proves I'm not."

"You're getting there. Just look at the house. I've pestered her to get rid of stuff for a year, but nothing changed until you came along." Twirling the golden rope of her necklace around her hand, Arti scanned the crowd. The unease in her posture didn't match her typical confidence.

"Why are you telling me this if it makes you so uncomfortable?"

"I generally steer clear Olivia's love life—it's one of the reasons we're still friends. Consider this my rare moment of playing Aphrodite." The necklace finished its loop around her fingers, encasing them, and she made a fist. "But keep in mind, if you anger the Greek gods, they will have their revenge."

"What do you mean?" The coiled necklace reminded Ellie uncomfortably of brass knuckles.

"We're getting along, which is great, but if you use what I've told you to hurt Olivia, I'll hit you with a mati so hard you'll spend the rest of your days regretting it." Arti made a sharp gesture with her other hand, as if throwing something away in disgust.

The word mati meant nothing to Ellie, but she knew the threat of a curse when she heard one. With that, Arti winked and strode toward the bar.

Chapter Twenty-Six

"DO YOU MISS being a nurse, Olivia?" Ellie's father collected the dinner plates. Thick fingers, scarred from a lifetime of welding, handled each dish with a deceptive grace, nestling them on top of one another.

"I miss the patients, but not the hours. What I do now is easier on my schedule, which helps with Ben." It had been decades since Olivia's last meet-the-family dance, and it was all the stranger as a parent herself. The night seemed to be going well, although the mood was subdued with Abuela's absence still keen.

"Isabella says you climb rocks?" Alberto had been a gem throughout, asking questions at the right moment and filling the silences with funny stories about his sister.

"I climb in a gym. They line the walls with holds shaped like rocks. It's great exercise."

"You should see it," Ellie added. "At the top, she's six stories up."

"You pay to climb fake rocks? Why not the real thing?" Juan had spent most of dinner in sullen silence, which, according to Ellie, was the best-case scenario where her oldest brother was concerned.

"I would, but Chicago's pretty flat, and it's hard to get away with Ben's schedule."

"Americans are ridiculous with their exercise. Who needs it if you do real work?"

"Juan, help me with the café," Ellie's mother said. He dismissed her with a curt wave.

"What do you do?" Olivia forced a bland smile.

"I manage a bodega." His broad face mirrored Ellie's, but without her sparkling warmth. It was eerie, this cold, bitter reflection of a woman she adored.

"Which one? There's a few I hit on my way home from the hospital."

"Nowhere a pretty white woman would shop." He sneered. "Solamente la gente."

"Juan." Ellie's sharp voice cut through the awkward silence.

He was picking around the edges, looking for a fight. Olivia slapped on a thin smile, determined to let his insults shoot past her.

"Tu hijo, he goes to Ellie's work for help?"

Olivia's pulse whooshed in her ears. Juan could dig at her all night, but he didn't want to get any closer to Ben.

"He's one of these, yes?" He flapped in a grim parody of an autistic kid, and a cold rage poured through her.

"Juan!" Ellie shouted.

Indignant Spanish drummed across the table.

"¿Qué?" he shouted at Ellie, then whipped to Olivia. "Did she tell you if she had a son like yours, she would kill herself?" He sat back, smug, splaying his hands across the table. "Saint Isabella, helping the poor fucking retards."

Thud! The steak knife bristled in the wood an inch from Juan's hand, Olivia's fingers wrapped around the handle.

"Fuck!" He recoiled. "You could have stabbed me!"

She lashed him with a flat, icy tone. "If you ever refer to my son in ANY fashion, if his name even begins to cross your lips, this knife will be the least of your problems. Do you understand?" Pinning him with a glare, she released the knife. It vibrated as she pushed away from the table, the scrape of her chair shredding the silence.

She stalked through the front door, then sank to the porch step. Rage boiled up from her gut, hot and sour on her tongue. Rage at Juan and rage at herself. She hadn't lost control like that in years, but Juan's cruel dismissal of Ben... Her only thought had been to rip the belligerent satisfaction off his face. Her fists clenched and unclenched as his last words ricocheted around her brain.

Spanish exploded from the front door as it opened. She fixed her gaze on the street, not ready to meet Ellie's eyes. The door closed with a click, muffling the tumult of voices.

"Olivia, I'm sorry. I'm so sorry. I had no idea. Juan can be...but even for him it was..."

The anguish in Ellie's voice cracked her. Anger drained away, exposing a raw insecurity that had flared at Juan's cruel words. She patted the space next to her. Ellie's feet scraped on the porch, then a loose floorboard creaked as she settled by Olivia's hip.

"I don't care about your asshole brother, but what he said about you and kids..."

Now, Ellie was the one to stare across the street, the flush on her neck betraying her. Juan's words had hit home.

"I wouldn't blame you, being an OT, if you didn't want this in your personal life. But Ben, he's—" Olivia's heart thudded dully. She had avoided this conversation for too long.

"I would never have asked you out if I wasn't comfortable with Ben." Ellie laced their fingers together and squeezed hard. "Never."

"But something about what Juan said bothered you."

Ellie pressed her lips to the back of Olivia's hand and sighed through her nose, her breath a warm gush. "My first job was in a residential setting, which was always my goal. I'd been there a year when Jill and I broke up. I buried myself in work. We were always short-staffed, so I'd take extra shifts, do whatever they asked. I told myself it was because I was the newest therapist. I needed to show my dedication.

"I realize now I wanted to prove I'd made the right decision with Jill. If I could make a difference, it'd be worth it, you know?" Her shoulders heaved with a rough sigh. "One day, I took four kids to the play yard, as part of their OT. They liked a chance to be outside. But on our way back in, one boy slammed his head against the wall. It was intentional. He just whipped his head sideways and..." A shudder ran through her. "Jesus, there was so much blood..."

"Head wounds can be—"

Ellie dismissed her consolation. "He needed stitches. We sent him to the ER. The whole time we waited for the ambulance, I kept replaying it, searching for the sign I had missed. It was my job to help him, my job to keep him safe. As they drove away, I thought, 'I failed him.'

"I came to my parents' house after work a complete mess. I don't even remember Juan being there. I broke down, talking about how I couldn't take it anymore. I said something like the job was making me not want to have kids because if I failed my own child like I failed that boy...it would kill me."

Olivia released Ellie's hand and wrapped an arm around her shoulders. There was resistance, and then Ellie leaned into the contact.

"I gave my notice the next day. I still feel guilty I didn't stay, but I was so burned out. Which is no excuse for thinking such horrible things."

"All parents think horrible things." She and Sophia had breathed those dark, sticky thoughts to each other in bed, hoping confession could soothe the shame at their existence. "And all parents torture themselves with 'What if I' and 'Why didn't I'. The good news is there are always positive thoughts waiting to drown all of it out." She kissed Ellie's temple. "I wish you had told me sooner. I hate the idea of this causing you stress."

"I was afraid you'd have too many doubts. About me. About me and Ben. I mean, how do you tell a parent of an autistic child you cracked in your first job with autistic children?"

"You didn't crack."

"I did. I was completely overwhelmed at the end."

"It was your first job, and in a really demanding setting. Patient care is tough, full stop. And if they have communication challenges as well... People who haven't done it can't really understand. Have you experienced anything similar since?"

"No, not even close. Honestly, after the shock, the hardest part was accepting I wouldn't be doing the work I originally planned, that I *didn't want* to do that work." Ellie tipped her head until it rested against Olivia's. "I'm sorry. I should have told you earlier, when I talked about Jill."

"We all have stories that are hard to share." A thread of guilt spun into the recesses of her mind. She wasn't ready to follow where it led. "Since we're here, can I ask..." Olivia wrestled with the question that had always hovered over their relationship. Either answer would bring its own struggle. "Do you want to be a parent? At all? Because I know Ben has always been part of the deal but—"

"Ben is wonderful. Challenging at times, but wonderful. I haven't brought him up before because...how do you even start the conversation? Ben is your son, and Sophia's, but yes, I'm willing to be more to him, eventually. If you and he will let me."

The bravery in Ellie's words, and the acceptance beneath them, untangled the dread knotting Olivia's chest.

"You amaze me." There were other fears—shadowed, shape-less—but she forced them aside and kissed Ellie tenderly, putting all her gratitude into it.

In the distance a door slammed. The sound broke them apart.

Ellie rolled her eyes. "There goes Juan storming out the back door, per usual."

"Is it this dramatic with every girlfriend you bring home?"

"Jill never got the full brunt because Mamá didn't take my relationships as seriously then. I brought Angie once, and she never returned." Ellie nudged her with an elbow. "Your move with the knife was much cooler. Now Abuela won't be the only one with a knife story."

"I didn't even know what I'd done until the knife was in the table. I'm so embarrassed."

"The one who should be embarrassed is my son." Ellie's mother appeared behind them like an apparition.

"Jesus, Mamá!" Ellie said. "Make a sound, something."

Somber creases painted Rosa's thin features. "I need to speak to Olivia."

Ellie's eyes slid to hers, and Olivia nodded. "Good luck." Ellie brushed a quick peck against her cheek and scrambled inside.

"Luck? Why does she need luck?" Rosa scolded her daughter's retreating form. "What am I going to do? Nothing." The door clicked shut, and they were alone. "Sit with me on the swing, please. My old bones cannot get down that far." She patted the bench, and Olivia joined her.

"Rosa, I'm sorry about your table. I can have it refin-ished—"

"Our table has seen much worse. My son's behavior, for one thing. I am the one to apologize. I am his mother. I told him tonight he is not welcome in my house until he can keep a tongue in his head."

"I don't want to come between—"

"No more excuses." Rosa chopped the air with her hand, a gesture Olivia had seen from Ellie dozens of times. "I have forgiven him too much over the years. He is not the same since we left Mexico. He was a teenager and happy there. You have one child, yes, and you make decisions that are best for him alone. When you have five, a decision may be good for many, but not all." She made the sign of the cross. "It's not true, what he said about Isabella and your son. He twisted her words."

"Ellie told me. We're okay."

"Isabella, she has gone through life..." Rosa held her palms up. "Light, empty. No, not empty—"

"Unencumbered?"

Rosa shook her head at the unfamiliar word.

"She's not burdened."

"Yes! She is always an open, happy girl. She loves easily and very much, but she has never carried many things at once. You carry many things. You have carried heavy things for a long time." Rosa's stare bored into her. "Now Isabella carries her love for you and your son. Love is a weight. A beautiful weight, but a weight just the same."

Olivia creaked a stiff nod. Rosa's eyes, and her words, froze her in place.

"Loving you comes with an extra weight. Isabella doesn't see it, but I do. I fear she may be crushed by it."

Dread tightened a band around Olivia's chest. "I have no intention of hurting her."

"You cannot promise her a life without pain. You of all people know this. You carry your own weight, and that of your son, but you also carry the weight of your wife. I ask, as Isabella's mother, that if you find yourself drowning one day under the weight of all you carry, do not drag my daughter with you. Please, if you love her, release her before you both are lost."

"Mamá!" Ellie threw open the front door. "What the hell is wrong with you? First, she gets attacked by Juan, and now this?"

"You do not protect yourself. You are too much of the heart—"

"Stop! Please go inside."

Rosa threw up her hands, as though she had done all she could, and it was up to God now. The screen door bounced behind her.

Ellie dropped into the swing with a rueful grin. "You're getting every intense family element in one night." When their eyes met, the smile dropped. "Jesus, what did she say?"

"She looked right through me, talking about Sophia."

"Hey, she does this to everyone." Ellie cupped her cheeks, the gentle touch breaking the spell. "None of us take it seriously, so I forget how freaky it can be. Ask Manuel. His wife didn't come back for weeks!"

"What?" With Rosa gone, the night air lost its thick, choking quality.

"It was all the same. 'Don't drag him into darkness. Promise me you'll release him so he may live a happy life!'" Ellie's impersonation spun humor through Olivia's bleak fears. "I figured she'd leave you alone because of Sophia. Jesus, I could strangle her."

Olivia stopped her with a kiss. That yielding, tender pressure blunted the sharp edges of her mind, and she deepened it until swallowed breaths and slick tongues dissolved every creeping thought.

When it ended, Ellie touched her forehead to Olivia's. "What was that for?"

"I had to banish the last of the heebie-jeebies."

"She really did get to you. I'm sorry."

Alberto poked his head around the door. "I'm guessing Mamá did the bruja trick?"

"How did you know?" Olivia asked, trying to sound game.

"She had the face." His brown eyes lingered on her. "Come inside and let Manuel tell you his story. We'll push the ghosts away."

"Can you take a bit more?" Ellie asked. "Mamá makes the best tres leches cake."

"Besides, we can't stop talking about how rudo you were with the knife! Que chévere!"

Olivia glanced at Ellie as the Spanish stretched past her abilities.

"They think you're a badass."

A voice drifted through the doorway. She couldn't tell if it was Manuel or Hector. "It's going to be leyenda in the village. Legend!"

Embarrassment pricked at Olivia again, but the siblings' buoyant humor tempered it. She allowed a small grin to escape when Ellie slipped a hand into hers and led her back inside the house.

Chapter Twenty-Seven

ELLIE DUG HER palms into her sockets, scrubbing the sleep from her eyes as she padded down the stairs. A crick seized her neck. It had been a terrible night's sleep with Juan's hateful comments looping in her brain. Morning pushed its way in far too soon, but Olivia had nudged her back to sleep with a kiss on her temple.

"Hey, Ben, have you noticed Ellie's been around the house a lot recently?"

She halted midstride. Through a cracked-open window, she could see the outline of Olivia and Ben on the front porch.

"Yeah."

Bright fingers of sun flickered on the step below her. It was the first of several that creaked with the lightest pressure. One glowing line streaked across her suspended foot, which waited for her command. She returned it to her current step.

"Does it still feel okay, her being here?"

"I like it. Do you?"

A chuckle rumbled from Olivia. "Yeah, I do. Does it bother you when she sleeps over?"

"No, but I miss sleeping with you." His thin voice blended with the chattering of leaves in the spring breeze.

"We stopped doing that before Ellie."

"But I'm your son, and she's your... What is Ellie anyway?"

"I guess she's my girlfriend."

"She hasn't been your girlfriend as long as I've been your son!"

A silent laugh shook Ellie's shoulders. The kid had a point.

"It's not about length of time. You never slept with me and Mommy before."

"Except for a bad thunderstorm."

The curtain rippled a sigh, then fell slack. "You slept with me after the accident because you were sad and scared, but you're older now. You don't need to anymore."

Wicker creaked, and the shadow of Ben's head shifted. "Is it weird having Ellie in bed instead of Mommy?"

"Is it weird for you, seeing her in the bed when you come in the room?"

"Not anymore."

Ellie willed Ben to follow up on his unanswered question, but he didn't.

"If it ever gets hard with Ellie here, I need you to tell me. Okay?"

"Okay."

"You've got your thinking face on, buddy. Can you give me some words?"

"Do you love Ellie?"

She eased to a squat on the step. She wanted to be the bigger person. She wanted to be the person who could walk away from this private conversation. She was not that person.

Olivia's long sigh tapered into silence. "I might."

"I thought love was a yes or no."

Ellie would have kissed Ben's tousled, curious head if she could.

"It can be more complicated."

"Does Ellie love you?"

"Yes."

"How do you know?"

"She told me."

"Are you not allowed to love Ellie? Because of Mommy? Is it a rule?"

"No. It's not a rule." The smile in Olivia's voice mirrored her own.

"Oh, good. I might love Ellie, and I was worried it was against the rules."

Ellie bit her fist, trapping any sound she might make.

"Oh, no, buddy. Not at all." Through the gap in the curtain, the back of Olivia's head appeared as she leaned into Ben. "Mommy wanted your life to be filled with love."

"Does Ellie love me?"

"What do you think?"

"I don't know! That's why I asked you!"

His indignation almost made Ellie snort in laughter.

"You should ask her. She won't mind."

"I'll wait."

"For what?"

"To be sure."

"What do you mean?"

"If she said no, it would make me sad."

Ellie's heart broke open. *It does, buddy. It does make you sad.*

Olivia's exhale was more shudder than sigh. Her shadow leaned into his again, and her arm moved across his shoulders. "You really are the smartest, sweetest boy in the whole world." She must have hugged him too hard because he yelped.

"Too much hugging! Go hug Ellie instead. She likes it."

Ellie pushed to her feet and scooted upstairs before she could be discovered. Olivia's voice drifted behind her.

"Maybe I will!"

"YOU ACTUALLY STUCK the knife between his fingers!" Arti's shriek drew stares from half the patio. A server froze, coffee pot suspended above a white tablecloth. Another server set a plate of donut holes down and retreated.

"*Next* to his fingers. I got closer than I should have." Olivia threw a dagger of silence with her eyes. Arti batted it away with a nonchalant wave. Ellie's offer to hang with Ben while she and Arti grabbed a bite suddenly seemed like a bad idea.

"Oh, when I tell it, it's going to be right between his fingers!"

"You can't tell anyone! It's embarrassing."

"Embarrassing? Olivia, it's amazing! It's the most amazing meet-the-in-laws story ever. Nothing even comes close."

"I don't know what I was thinking." Olivia scraped the hair from her face. She was touchy lately, as if her skin was stretched too tight over her bones. "I've never done anything like that."

"Are you kidding? What about in kindergarten, the boy who made fun of my accent?"

"He made you cry!"

"He needed ten stitches. And lost a tooth."

"Just a baby tooth," she muttered.

Arti pushed the donut holes toward her. "You're telling me you remember none of this?"

"Two incidents forty years apart don't make a trend."

"What about Sophia at the bar, when those handsy creeps trapped her in the hallway?"

The memory exploded from a dusty corner of her brain, an uncomfortable echo of last night. "I haven't thought about that in years."

"Sophia said you looked so tough when you smashed your beer bottle against the wall and threatened them with the broken neck. Ooh, I can't wait to tell Ellie this story." Arti drummed the table.

"Don't. I already look like I'm wound too tight. And the conversation with Ellie's mom didn't help."

A tall man with a salt-and-pepper Afro sauntered past, and Arti twisted in her seat, craning her neck until he turned the corner. "God, I need to get laid." She bit into a donut, sugar sprinkling her cleavage. Brushing it off with a flick of her manicured nails, she nodded. "Go on. Ellie's mother what?"

"She apologized for Juan, which was fine, then went on and on about how I carry all this weight, and Ellie's so light, and I shouldn't hurt her."

"I'm not following. Because Ellie's bigger than you, by a bit. Don't get me wrong, she's gorgeous and you're gorgeous and everyone's just gorgeous and who am I to talk—"

"She meant psychic weight! I'm the yoke around Ellie's neck, what with being a widow and having an autistic son and all."

A grimace twisted Arti's mouth. "She went low, bringing Sophia and Ben into it."

"I don't think she meant it that way." Rosa's bleak eyes bored through her again. Anxiety surged, and she took a breath. "She begged me to let Ellie go before I drowned her. I'm not describing it well, but it was eerie."

"What did Ellie say?"

"She said her mom does this to everyone they bring home. Her brothers agreed, and they told me their stories. Still, it seemed so possible. That with Sophia, and the grief, maybe I would hurt Ellie." She searched Arti's face for the reassurance she couldn't summon on her own.

"I'm siding with the girlfriend here. Her mother wants her babies close by, and she's using superstition to spook you. What's more possible? A random old woman can peer into your soul, or that she knew you had a past, including a tragic accident, a dead wife, and a 'touched' son. It was served up for her on a silver platter. I could spin my own version right now if you want me to prove it."

"No, thanks. 'Touched'?"

"I was creating a mood." Arti popped another donut hole in her mouth. "Look, you and Ellie are in a good place, and we're all happy for you. Don't torture yourself because it's going well."

Olivia dragged the tines of her fork across the white tablecloth. "You think I'm scared to be happy with Ellie."

"I think you forgot what happy was, for a while, and it's time to remember." Arti took the fork from her. "Now tell me the knife story again." She clapped her hands like a kid at Christmas. "This will never get old."

Chapter Twenty-Eight

THE LAST OF the rain pattered on Olivia's hood as she pulled the garage's side door shut. A soft snuffle from behind made her pivot.

"Hey there, Wrigley."

The husky wedged his nose through a narrow gap in the fence, and she squatted to scratch his black-and-white muzzle with a finger. She never did this in front of Ben, who was terrified of dogs, but he wasn't with her today. For the first time, he'd asked Ellie to get him from school, and other than a joint selfie sent from the pickup line, Olivia had heard nothing else.

His absence turned out to be more disorienting than liberating. Thursdays were Starbucks night, and when the barista handed her two drinks through the window, it took a long, awkward second to realize she'd ordered a lemonade for an empty seat. Then she was halfway down the exit ramp for the after-school center before she realized her mistake and had to circle back to the expressway. Even hearing Marketplace on NPR was strange. Ben always commandeered the stereo by the time it came on. The entire drive, she felt like she was missing a limb.

She gave Wrigley a final scratch, then straightened and turned toward the house. Her feet froze, one on the sidewalk, one in the damp grass. Dusk's gray edges were bleeding into blue-black, and the encroaching gloom coated the dark brick bungalow in felted shadows. The windows though— A bolt of nostalgia shattered against her chest. Normally, they were black hollows, the only greeting for her and Ben a solitary bulb above the back door. It was up to her to swipe wall switches, to tug lamp chains, to summon the light that turned their shell of a house into a home. But along the first floor, cheery squares blazed, welcoming her in a manner she hadn't seen since her wife's death. Sophia had always soaked the house in light to ward off memories of a frugal childhood spent hunting for bulbs her father would unscrew to keep the electric bill low.

As Olivia cracked the door, garlic leaked through the gap. The decadent smell was so Sophia that her head spun. Then piano chords bounded into the room, dancing with Ellie's vibrant voice, and the illusion collapsed.

Consumed by the past, she had let her present blur—the lasagna was her own, frozen for easy reheating. And the lights— Not all of them were on. Only their unexpected appearance had made them glow so brightly from the yard. Easing her backpack and coat onto a hook, she slipped across the room and peeked around the corner. Ben and Ellie shared the piano bench, her son listening in rapture as she played for him. He interrupted the song to ask a question. From Ellie's patient smile, it wasn't the first time.

"What's a warm embrace?"

"Embrace is another word for hug."

"But how can a hug be warm?"

Ellie tapped a single key, thinking. "It could mean warm like someone's body warming you up when it's cold. Or warm like you feel happy inside when you get the hug."

"I hate when a word means different things!" Ben kicked the piano with a hollow bang. "How do you know which is right?"

Olivia smiled. She'd had countless similar conversations, trying to satisfy the literal logic Ben craved.

"With songs, there isn't a right or wrong, most of the time. Just a way it makes you feel."

"Feelings are hard."

Ellie nodded. "They can be."

"Do they get easier when you're an adult?"

"Sometimes, yes, but other times..."

Ben scowled his disappointment.

"Should I keep playing?"

"Yeah."

Ellie started at the same line, her vibrant alto weaving through the spare music of the keys. When Ben rested a hand on her forearm, regret pierced Olivia's heart. The piano was a rare failed experiment of Sophia's. The delight on Ben's face as Ellie dusted off his mother's dream— Resentment flared, a hot coal lodged behind her sternum.

"What does black and blue mean?" he asked.

The music stilled. "It describes the color of bruises on your skin. But here, it's another way of saying to fight hard to protect the person you love."

"Oh. That's Mom!"

"What do you mean?"

"She fought the principal at my old school!" Ben vibrated with excitement, as if he was describing a scene from a favorite movie. "He was being mean after Mommy died, and Mom yelled at him and hit his desk super hard. It made him jump. It was awesome!"

Olivia bit back a groan. She'd always regretted letting her frustration spill out in front of him that awful day.

"Is there more fighting in the song?" he asked.

"No more fighting. There's not much left actually." Ellie finished with a flourish, the last chord lingering. "What do you think?"

"What does 'ends of the earth' mean? The earth doesn't have an end. It's round!"

"It means the person would go anywhere on the earth to be with someone she loves."

"Oh." Ben's face softened, and his right hand twisted around his left wrist. It was an old gesture from a time before their world fell apart.

"What is it?"

"Mommy would've liked your song."

The house plunged into silence. Ellie's mouth worked for a response as Olivia struggled to drag air into her lungs.

"And she would've liked your singing. It's nice." He didn't recognize the simple truth; Sophia could never have heard Ellie sing. The two women existed in separate universes, the presence of one predicated on the absence of the other. Each breath Ellie took in this house was one fate had stolen from Sophia. The dichotomy left him unblemished, but it slashed a bright line through Olivia's soul.

Ellie trembled as she touched his shoulder. "What a wonderful compliment."

"We're practicing compliments at school!"

"Well, you did a great job."

"Is your song a lullaby?"

"No, but it could be, I suppose."

His feet swung small arcs beneath the bench. "Would you sing it for bedtime?"

Olivia twitched at his shy request. He had a lullaby. Two, actually, although Sophia's hadn't been sung since her death. A snarl of protest fought to claw its way free, its vehemence blindsiding her.

"Anytime you want." Ellie pressed a kiss to his forehead, and he didn't pull away.

"Let's do a selfie here, by the piano!"

Ashamed by her bitter melancholy, Olivia started to sneak back to the kitchen, but Ellie spotted her.

"Hey there!"

Ben whirled on the bench, nearly upending himself.

"Mom! Doesn't Ellie sing nice?"

"Nicely. Yes, she does."

"She said she'd sing it for my lullaby!"

Her heart seized at his obvious happiness. "Go wash up for dinner."

"I have to pee!"

"Do that first," she called out as he darted to the bathroom. When she turned around, Ellie threw herself into her arms. Olivia hugged her reflexively and stared at the empty piano bench over her shoulder.

"I know it's a bad idea to expect validation from any kid, autistic or otherwise, but it's the most he's let me in." Ellie pulled back, cupping her cheek. "Did I do okay? With his Sophia comment? He's never brought her up with me before."

"You did great." She pushed the words out, then hid from those searching brown eyes by giving Ellie a kiss.

"Kissing! Gross!" Ben interrupted them, hands dripping water onto the floor.

"Gross is the mess you're making. Use a towel!"

He wiped them on his shirt. "I want to eat!"

Olivia stepped toward him and dropped into her stern tone. "Ben, here are the steps. First, get a paper towel. Second, wipe up the drips. Third, wash *and* dry your hands again. Then we'll eat."

"It's water!"

"I don't care. Clean it up!"

"Mom!"

Ellie put snap in her own voice. "Ben, don't argue."

He slapped a foot in a wet splatter and stomped to the kitchen.

Olivia rounded on Ellie. "I've got this."

"I was just backing you up." Ellie's startled flinch cut through Olivia's mood.

"I'm sorry. I shouldn't have—" She didn't know why Ben's acquiescence to Ellie rankled. "I'm really sorry. Let's go eat." Olivia kissed her in apology and headed for the kitchen.

"SERIOUSLY, THE THINGS you do to me." Ellie sprawled stomach down on the bed, sheets tangled around her calves.

Olivia ran her hands over Ellie's ass. "I'm not done yet." She licked the salt-tinged sweat from her glistening skin.

"What? I'm going to need a minute."

"Relax. This is an apology massage for being short with you earlier." Olivia craved these intimate physical moments lately. They were the only times her mind held a clean focus. All of her other thoughts brushed against Sophia, or Ben, or the changes rippling through her quiet world, until her mind became tangled in sticky webs of emotion and memory.

"What was that about anyway?"

"The day ended with this crappy meeting, and I—"

"Don't." Ellie twisted to look at her.

"What?"

"Don't push away with a vague excuse."

Ellie's determined stare pinned her in place, but Olivia

couldn't explain the wrenching mix of happiness and resentment Ellie and Ben's moment stirred. She settled for a half-truth instead.

"Ben brought up the school story, and it took me back to a rough time. One I'd rather forget."

Sympathy replaced Ellie's scrutiny, and now Olivia choked on another emotion, guilt, as her deflection worked. "Did you actually punch the principal's desk?"

"It was either the desk or him."

"What happened?"

"Some bullshit after Ben returned to school. I knew he would struggle, but he needed to not sit around the house and be miserable with me. We redesigned his IEP, organized more supports, but the school— My phone was a bomb, always blowing up with a crisis. I lost it one day when the principal said the next time Ben was too difficult, he was calling the cops."

"What?"

"On a fucking nine-year-old! And the school wasn't even following their own protocols! I was so livid I pulled him. Which is how he ended up in his current school." Resurrected anger thudded in her veins. "The principal was a jerk, but I hate that it happened in front of Ben."

"He sees you as the hero. What's wrong with that?"

"After all the lectures about controlling his emotions, I go off—"

"You showed him that you'll fight for him. Which he needs more than any executive functioning lecture." Ellie took her wrist and drew her down. "You never told me this."

"Talking about it gets me agitated, so I don't. But I shouldn't have snapped at you earlier, no matter the reason."

"Is everything okay? You've been a little short lately."

Kind brown eyes offered tender intimacy, the safety to

whisper fears into the scant inches separating them, but Olivia had already picked at one old thread tonight. She couldn't follow another. "I have to be so direct with Ben. I don't realize how I sound. I really am sorry."

Ellie kissed her chin and dragged knuckles across her ribs. As her hand drifted lower, Olivia's stomach clenched. She couldn't be the focus of Ellie's intensity right now. She needed to feel less, not more.

"Can we just hold each other for the rest of the night?"

"Don't you want—"

"I'm fine, honestly. Can I spoon you?" She turned off the lamp before pressing herself to Ellie, scooting her hips to close the last breath of space between them. The rise and fall of Ellie's ribs slowed, and her muscles unspooled as sleep dragged her away. Olivia lay silent, lashed to that steady presence while murky thoughts whipped through her mind.

Chapter Twenty-Nine

BANQUET HALLS, WITH their cavernous ceilings and accordion walls, had been the backdrop to every wedding reception, bridal shower, and quinceañera of Ellie's youth, so despite the za'atar on the table and the pulsing Arabic music, the aqiqah for Ahmad and Salma's baby had a nostalgic familiarity. Ellie rubbed a thumb across her chair's sturdy upholstery, ribbed with two forgettable shades of beige. Each hall had its own peculiar blandness, adaptable to any culture, religion, or community.

Mara weaved through the tables, a slim navy dart in a sea of flowing abayas and khimars. Her rainbow bowtie bobbed at her neck. Teenagers clustered by the wall tracked her with obvious fascination.

"You were gone a while. Everything okay?"

"Bathrooms are on the other side of the lobby." Mara slid into her chair. "It's been a minute since I've walked past so many subtle stares."

"And not-so-subtle ones." Ellie nodded toward the chittering girls.

"To be fair, a woman in a hijab would get stares in Boystown. Context matters."

"I see those girls and remember myself at that age, knowing I was queer but pretending to blend in. I'd have passed out if you walked through the door."

"Fourteen-year-old you had a thing for short butch women?"

"Fourteen-year-old me would've thought you were amazing!" Ellie called out to Ahmad as he worked his way over. "Hey, if you'd seen adult Mara when you were fourteen, wouldn't you have thought she was the coolest?"

"The absolute coolest! Of course, back then, I was six feet tall and a hundred pounds soaking wet, so everyone was cooler than me." He squatted on his haunches next to them. "By the way, I've pointed out the pair of you to a few kids who've had trouble finding queer role models. Hope you don't mind."

"Point away," Ellie said. "Thanks again for inviting us. I've never been to an aqiqah, but it's way more fun than a baby shower. And this hall is a blast from the past! I've attended at least three wedding receptions here. My feet hurt just thinking about it."

Ahmad laughed and clapped his hands together. "Baba wanted it at the community center, but Mama overruled him. Evidently, when we added our 'American' friends to the total, we needed more room."

"I hope he forgives us for crashing the party," Mara said.

"Oh, it's fine. The more love around our new daughter, the better."

Ellie smiled at his enthusiasm, the way his face glowed as the word "daughter" left his mouth. "Amal is a beautiful name. What does it mean?"

"Hope."

"Well, you've been hoping for her for a long time, so I'm glad she's finally here." Mara craned her neck to see past the throng of women surrounding Ahmad's wife. "How's Salma feeling, really? We just talked for a second."

"Tired. Sore. Emotionally, she's still struggling with the emergency C-section. We spent months making this great birth plan, and in seconds, it fell apart. It was so scary—" He waved both hands, brushing away the memory. "But I'm not talking about that today. Amal is fine, tomorrow is Salma's first Mother's Day, and we're trying to focus on gratitude rather than fear." He pointed at the empty seat next to Mara. "So where's Rachel?"

Ellie had asked the same question, but Mara had deflected it until Ahmad was there—she didn't want to repeat the story. Her avoidance could only mean one thing.

"We're not together anymore." Mara's cool blue eyes didn't waver. "She sends her regrets, and she'll give you Amal's present at work."

"When did this happen?" Ahmad asked.

"After you went on paternity leave. She volunteered to skip today, instead of me."

"She could've come anyway," Ellie said. "You're both adults."

"It wasn't me she was worried about. Not entirely." Ice-blue eyes darted to her and then away again. It was the closest Ellie had ever come to seeing Mara squirm.

"What does that mean?"

"Did you ever wonder why Rachel was so dismissive of your girlfriends?"

"She told me I wasn't as good a friend when I was dating. I tried to be aware of it, but it didn't help. She'd still get snarky."

"She's in love with you."

The words spun on a loop in her brain. As much as she tried to get them to settle, she couldn't.

"I always thought something was funny there," Ahmad said.

"Wait, what?" Ellie rounded on him. "How did you know?"

Sputtering, he held up his hand in defense. "I didn't know. I just wondered. A vibe I got."

Mara scratched the tight buzz on the back of her neck. "It's more fair to say she's hung up on you. You were getting over Jill when you and Rach first met, right?"

Ellie nodded. Rachel was a good friend early on, using her snark to support, rather than cut, as she did now.

"It's why she didn't make a move, initially. Then she was with someone when you started dating again, and then there was Angie."

"She told you this?"

"I got it out of her. Honestly, I never noticed until you hooked up with Olivia. She became fixated on your relationship, how it wasn't good for you."

Ellie leaned her forehead on one hand, glancing at Mara from underneath it. "I'm sorry."

"We're good, you and me. It was Rachel's deal. She couldn't get past it."

"I feel like such an idiot for not noticing. You want to tell a woman next time?" She smacked Ahmad's arm.

"What if I was wrong? Now I'm the creepy dude pairing up his female coworkers. No thanks."

"I think she was playing it cool, hoping you'd make the first move," Mara said. "She wants to be pursued—sticking her neck out and risking rejection isn't her style."

Ahmad's mother came over and whispered in his ear. He nodded, holding up a finger in a "one second" gesture. "She needs my help, but I'll circle back." He placed his hand on his chest and smiled at Mara. "For the record, Rachel's the real loser in this equation."

"Thanks."

As he wound his way through the crowd, Ellie touched Mara's knee. "I'll admit, when you two started dating, I was worried it might get messy, but you seem okay."

"I don't do messy endings. Not my style."

"Yeah, but they are Rachel's style."

"I had a clear picture of who Rachel was when we started up. The surprise was you being in the middle. Not on purpose, obviously." Mara's edgy visual aesthetic was an incongruous mask for her steady nature. Even hurricane Rachel couldn't disrupt it.

"It's impressive how okay you are. You were together, what, a year?"

"Are you trying to make me feel less okay?" Mara's bemused smile gave away the joke.

"Jesus, no. Ignore me. I'm just dragging my baggage into your breakup."

"What baggage?"

Ellie put up a hand to screen Mara's face, which had dropped into a familiar, probing expression. "Don't hit me with your contemplative social worker eyes. I've seen too many people spill their guts when you use them."

"So there are guts to be spilled." Mara pulled her hand down. "Let's hear it."

She shook her head, grimacing. "Ever since Abuela died, I've felt unsteady. I overreact to stuff that normally wouldn't bother me. I'm extra clingy with Marisol and Claudia online, which they're fine about, but it's not who I am."

"Makes sense. It's a huge loss for you."

"But it's getting weird with Olivia, and I can't trust my own gut." Their encounter after the piano still lingered. The more Olivia pretended it was nothing, the more Ellie couldn't let it go. "We had a fight this week—not even a fight, really, just a tense moment—and I think there's more than she's letting on."

"Could it be Mother's Day weekend? Must be a complicated holiday for her."

"I wondered about that, but she's been pretty open about tomorrow being difficult." Ellie rapped her knuckles on the table. "It's the stuff she won't talk about that worries me. Our dating life started with these long conversations about everything and nothing. I've never had such a connection before."

"But…" Mara rotated her finger in a "go on" motion.

"I sleep there certain nights now, which is great. The sex is…it's amazing, honestly. The best of my life. But—" Huffing a sigh through her nose, she searched for the right words. Olivia's shift was subtle but unsettling. "Have you ever been with someone in bed, skin-to-skin, and still felt like they were a million miles away?"

The coolness in Mara's eyes wavered, then reset. "Yes."

"We still talk, sometimes, but other times there's a wall."

"You've told her this?"

"I have, but she either isn't getting it or won't hear it." The past few weeks, Ellie had sifted through slivers of stories, hunting for truths hidden in the scraps Olivia shared. "The longer I'm in the house, the more distant she keeps me."

"Are you looking for a way out?"

"I don't want out. I want in. I want in all the way."

Mara raised an eyebrow in her version of surprised. "It's only been six months."

"Six and a half, but it's different from Angie."

"It always is."

"Won't it have to be different for me to find the right woman? Why can't it be now?"

"It can be, but this relationship has so many moving parts." Mara drummed her fingers on the table. "Have you told Olivia? About being all in?"

Olivia's subdued reaction to the "love" conversation had stilled her tongue when it came to big emotions. "My relationships with Jill and Angie fell apart when I pushed for things they weren't ready to give. I won't make that mistake again."

"Asking for what you need isn't a mistake."

"I know, but I can be too impatient, which isn't fair to Olivia, who's juggling a lot." It grated on Ellie to be so hesitant, but each choice carried its own risk. "She's balanced on the edge of something. I'm afraid if I crowd her, she might fall away."

"Don't compromise your needs too far. You're both in this relationship."

"I hear you; I do. And it's not always like this. We have days where we're so close. Then other times, just lately, she retreats in pain. I hate seeing her struggle."

"You can't make her accept your help. You said you want in all the way, but what if she doesn't want to let you?"

Mara's question was valid. If the roles were reversed, Ellie would've asked it herself. But her brain refused to process any outcome that didn't include Olivia. "I don't know. I really don't, because I can't imagine life without her."

Chapter Thirty

OLIVIA TOSSED HER backpack on the kitchen island and cursed the freight train one more time. Long minutes had slipped by while it trundled past, long minutes where she chewed on her guilt for disrupting Ben's routine. Before Ellie, she wouldn't have scheduled a late meeting. Before Ellie, she wouldn't have cut her commute this close. Ben's anxiety spiked when she was late, and Chicago traffic was too unpredictable to chance a tight travel window. She shouldn't have accepted Ellie's offer to handle school pickup and dinner. She shouldn't have gotten so comfortable.

As her hand clapped on the railing, Ellie's voice slid down the stairs. She climbed the steps slowly, sticking to the quiet treads, then peeked around Ben's doorjamb. He lay flat on his back, weighted blanket tucked tight under his armpits, rubbing the worn ear of his stuffed elephant. His eyes closed and opened in slow, sleepy blinks. Ellie was curled on the edge of his mattress, close but not touching, and the song she'd sung last week hovered between them. The cozy scene cleaved Olivia's heart—one half embraced the sweet comfort he showed with Ellie, the other half recoiled. This painful fission had flared more and more.

"Hey guys," she murmured. Ben reached out a skinny arm to her.

"Now that Mom's here, she can sing."

He shook his shower-damp head. "I want to hear the rest of yours."

There wasn't room on the twin bed, so Olivia settled on her knees by his head. "Sorry I was so late."

"Ellie did the routine."

"With a lot of prompts." Ellie's dimple flashed her amusement.

"Sing, sing," he said.

Disappointment tugged at her. She'd missed her window to talk about his day. Sighing, she burrowed into his neck and smelled the mix of lavender soap and strawberry toothpaste. He was the most relaxed after his bath, the most receptive to her closeness, her affection. Ellie's voice faded as the song ended.

"Ellie?" Ben whispered.

"Yes?"

"Do you know Mommy's lullaby?"

Olivia clenched her teeth, barely holding in a hiss of surprise.

"What's the name of it?" Caution colored Ellie's tone.

"What's it called, Mom?"

The gap in his memory knifed through her soul. She swallowed hard. "'At Your Side.'"

"I don't know it."

Relief flooded Olivia. To hear Sophia's song coming from Ellie...

Ellie shifted on the bed. "Why don't I sneak out so you and Mom can talk?"

"Just stay like this," he said.

"Sure, buddy." The words were dust in Olivia's mouth. Including Ellie in the bedtime ritual should be welcome progress, but her heart thudded with a dull beat of discontent. When he dropped into a fitful doze, she slid from the bed, and Ellie followed. With soft steps, they shut Ben's door and crossed to the bedroom.

Self-recrimination drummed in her brain. It was her fault he'd forgotten. Her fault for avoiding the song and the pain it stirred. Her fault another piece of Sophia was slipping away. She ground her teeth and headed for the bathroom, but Ellie grabbed her wrist.

"Hey, why didn't you sing Sophia's lullaby?"

The question bristled, covered in so many wicked barbs that any answer would leave her bloody. "I didn't want to."

"Yeah, I got that part. But why?"

"The song is inappropriate now."

"How can a lullaby be inappropriate?"

"It's all about being supported, about having someone at your side." She yanked free and stalked to the closed bathroom door.

"Olivia, look at me."

She curled her fingers around the worn brass knob. Its cool weight pressed into her palm. Space, isolation beckoned, but she made herself turn around, her back flat against the door to keep Ellie's suffocating scrutiny at bay. "During preschool, kids were always excluding him, leaving him out of games, and he'd come home so upset. Sophia sang it to make him feel less alone."

Ellie stepped closer, filling the gap Olivia had sought, and placed a hand on her forearm. "So what's the harm in singing it if he asks?"

"Sophia's *not* at his side! Not anymore!" She jerked away, her elbow banging the door hard enough the knob rattled. "It's a bad idea!"

"For you or for him?"

"Ellie—"

"Don't warn me off!" She cut the air with a choppy gesture. "You're doing it more and more with Ben."

"Because you won't leave it alone! You're not his parent! I am!"

Ellie flinched like she had been slapped, icy shock wiping the concern from her face. "You think I don't know that?"

Desperate to snatch the words back, Olivia reached for her, but Ellie batted her hand aside and stabbed a finger in her chest. "Anyone who wanted to be with you, had to be with Ben. Those are *your* words! At Mamá's, *you* asked if I could see myself being his parent, and I said yes." Tears glistened in Ellie's eyes. Her voice grew thick. "You can't have it both ways! You can't demand I be a part of Ben's life, then cut me out of any discussions about him!"

Olivia's heart collapsed at the devastation on Ellie's face. She slid slowly down the door, landing on her ass. "I'm sorry. I'm so sorry."

Ellie's gaze lay heavy on her. "What is going on?" She sank to the floor. "Talk to me."

"The bedtime routine is our thing. Ben's and mine."

"I know, but you were late. He was tired and starting to lose it."

"Seeing him with you, not needing me..." *Not needing Sophia.* Resentment smoldered in her chest, an ember that wouldn't be extinguished. "Sharing him is harder than I thought."

"He needs you for everything, and you've handled it so well for so long. Let me help. I'm not his parent, but I want to participate."

She smothered her pain and took Ellie's hand. "I'm so sorry I said the parent thing. It was horrible. As soon as it left my mouth, I wanted it back."

"Thank you. Really." Ellie brushed a kiss on her knuckles. "But I can tell there's more. What is it?"

She closed her eyes and rested her head against the door. It echoed with a hollow thump. Ellie read her so easily. Too easily. The conflict she felt right now, the irrational resentment—it floated at the surface like an oil slick, but more was bubbling up from below. Until she understood what, she refused to burden Ellie with it.

"I feel terrible for being a jerk when you've been so wonderful. You don't deserve it." Leaning forward, she kissed Ellie, those full lips soothing her brittle emotions. "Let me make it up to you?" She started to tip them to the floor, to whisper regrets along Ellie's skin and kiss her full of apologies, when Ellie rested a soft hand on her chest.

"I'm not in the headspace for that."

Olivia sank on her haunches. "I just…wanted to connect a little, physically."

"Snuggles on the couch are more my speed right now."

"How about snuggles and apology ice cream?" It was a clumsy way to lighten the mood, and Ellie stared at her for long seconds, her brown eyes kind but firm. She was waiting for more—more explanation, more insight, more… Olivia scrubbed at her face and forced herself to string a sentence together.

"I'm working through some stuff, Ellie—nothing about us." Panic simmered with each halting word. "I've always been this way, processing in my own head first." It roiled, black and bitter in the back of her throat. "I'm sure it's frustrating to watch from the outside, but I need a little time." It sloshed into her mouth, swilled across her tongue. *Please be enough. Please be enough.* If Ellie asked for one more word, she didn't know what would spill out.

A small, forgiving smile tugged at the corner of Ellie's lips. "What kind of ice cream?"

She almost choked in relief. "There's a pint of peanut butter and chocolate in the freezer, too high for Ben to see."

"Baskin-Robbins?"

"Of course."

Ellie climbed to her feet. "Then come spoon-feed me all the apology you want."

Throat still tight, she stood and crushed Ellie in a fierce hug. "Thank you."

Ellie stiffened in surprise, then enveloped her in return. As they headed downstairs, Olivia brushed her hand along Ben's door. The hum of his noise machine must have been playing tricks because she swore she could hear the low strain of Sophia's lullaby.

Chapter Thirty-One

ELLIE STACKED THE last pan in the drying rack, then pulled the stopper from the kitchen sink. She grabbed a sponge and swept broad, sudsy circles across the island. The floor creaked overhead as Olivia checked on Ben. She hoped he was sound asleep. Romantic nights were always put on hold if he was restless, and tonight she had a specific plan.

The past few weeks had run hot and cold. She didn't doubt Olivia's regret about her blowup—the horror at her own words had been instantaneous—but still, the parenting crack left Ellie dull and tender like a week-old bruise. Olivia had soothed the hurt with tender caresses and long massages, spilling her remorse across Ellie's skin. They'd found their footing again, but the question of why Olivia had lashed out went unanswered. Ellie had tried, but every conversation seemed swept away by one breathless orgasm after another, almost all of them her own. She frowned, tossed the sponge in the sink, and grabbed a towel to dry the damp granite.

"Your sexy plans are still on."

"Jesus!" She jumped when Olivia's voice hovered in her ear.

"Sorry. I assumed you heard me on the stairs."

"No. Lost in thought. So he's asleep?"

"Out cold. A book slid off his bed onto the floor. That's what we heard. Thanks for finishing the dishes."

"No problem. Happy to be your kitchen wench."

"Wench, eh?" Olivia slid a hand into the front of her dress and cupped her breast.

"Hey, we agreed I'd be spoiling you tonight."

"Who says you can't?"

"Lately, you've been ravishing me, and—" She gasped as Olivia thumbed her nipple. "—by the time you're done, I'm too exhausted to do you."

"Do you hear me complaining?"

Olivia's pelvis ground into her ass, tempting Ellie to bend over the counter and let Olivia's free hand continue its journey up her thigh... She squashed the impulse and spun around.

"You're not taking me seriously. Tonight is about you."

Confusion furrowed Olivia's forehead, then her face rippled with an emotion Ellie couldn't name. Her body unwound, and she stepped back. "You're right. Sorry." The smile was quick, apologetic, but it didn't reach her eyes. "Where do you want me?"

"In the shower. I'll just be a minute."

"Meet you there." Olivia turned on her heel and left.

The abrupt departure threw her. It seemed silly to complain about Olivia's lavish attention, but she couldn't shake Arti's comment about Olivia substituting physicality for conversation. Ellie pinched the bridge of her nose. What she needed was a long, intimate talk, but Olivia had asked for time, and she wanted to honor that. If the physical world was where Olivia felt comfortable, Ellie would meet her there, but it couldn't be so one-sided. Their communication was already out of balance. She wouldn't let their sex life be the same.

She sucked in a deep breath, then released it. Time to focus on the positive. Upstairs was a beautiful woman in a sexy mood, and Ellie had a long, pleasurable evening planned. Maybe by the end, Olivia would be relaxed enough to share some of her internal world. The muted hiss of the shower started, and she smiled.

OLIVIA CRANKED THE shower on and dangled a foot in the water, testing the temperature. When it climbed to a steamy heat, she stepped in and buried her face in the powerful stream. The rejection downstairs stung, even though she understood it. She'd meant to honor Ellie's request, but the only time her mind quieted lately was when she focused on Ellie's body.

The shower door opened, and Ellie stepped through, naked and glorious. "Room for me?"

"How am I supposed to behave myself when you come in here all—?"

A finger pressed against her lips. "No talking. Got it?"

Olivia wanted to suck that wicked smile from her face, but instead, she nodded.

Ellie filled her palm with soap and rubbed slow circles across her chest. The tension locked there unraveled, and Olivia relaxed into the sensuous journey. Hands slid under her breasts, wrapped around her hips, stroked the backs of her thighs. As the water cleared a path through the bubbles, Ellie's mouth followed it. Tongue, lips, teeth—all found places to lick and suck and bite. After the last of the soap rinsed away, Ellie skimmed her glistening bronze body up her own pale one and slipped a hand between her legs. Insistent fingers teased her clit with soft strokes.

"Someone still needs a rinsing."

Arching her eyebrow, Olivia stayed silent, determined to follow the rules.

Ellie grinned, adjusted the jet controls and, in one quick motion, pinned her to the shower wall. Her nipples hardened on the cool tiles, and she hissed. Ellie had centered her in front of a pulsing jet. It throbbed against her clit, and she shifted slightly, finding the perfect spot. Why hadn't she thought of this?

"Don't move an inch." Ellie sucked on one earlobe, then stepped away. The latch of the shower door clicked. She returned in seconds, and Olivia whimpered as Ellie kissed a trail down her spine. Each hungry press of lips sparked a flare of desire.

When her mouth reached the curve of Olivia's ass, she plunged her tongue deep into the crack. Olivia slapped her hands on the tiles for balance. It had been a long time since anyone had done this, and never with such vigor. Ellie spread her cheeks apart, and her tongue thrust harder, working in delirious opposition to the pulsing water, creating a relentless throbbing rhythm. Olivia's fingers curled, slipping on the slick tiles. She needed to hang on, she needed—

The orgasm slammed into her, driving a long, low moan from her lips. Ellie didn't let up, pushing her harder against the jet. As the water pounded her clit, a low hum started, and then a vibrator eased into her. Its thickness filled the only space that still ached for release, and she moaned louder. Ellie began pumping it in and out, in and out, and suddenly, there wasn't enough space between sensations to breathe. The plunge of the vibrator, the water drumming her clit, the maddening pressure of Ellie's tongue... The second orgasm buried her in an avalanche of sensation.

She panted open-mouthed against the tiles as Ellie drove the vibrator deeper, faster, extending the climax and stretching her control to its thin, delicate limit. A final intimate thrust of that tongue, and she shattered. Warm liquid gushed from her, and her legs gave out. Ellie eased her to the floor. Emotion rushed into the vacuum created by the orgasm, all at once, assaulting her. Hot tears spilled out, unstoppable and unending. She curled up in a ball, Ellie wrapped around her protectively, as the water rained down.

THE SUN STREAMED through the passenger window, making Sophia's tea-colored eyes glow from within. Olivia's hands were steady on the wheel, her gold ring tapping in time to the music. Sophia was speaking, but there was no sound, just a low droning. They were about to cross a bridge. A tree-lined river stretched to their right. Faster than thought, a black car appeared in front of them. She flinched. The bridge railing appeared.

A thunderclap of destruction detonated in her brain, and the world shuddered, shattered. A nauseating kaleidoscope—blinding sun, green grass, achingly blue sky—spun in a fractured blur, her body pinned to the center of the maelstrom. Metal twisted and shrieked. Glass exploded into perfect diamonds of pain. Her skull cracked like an egg, and her thoughts spilled out into the darkness...

A high-pitched wail screamed her back into existence. Her lungs fought for air, two bellows full of sand. A fiery lance pierced her left side. She forced her eyes open. The car surrounded her, a cruel cubist painting of a vehicle, all sharp edges and broken angles. Again, that shrill, mindless keen of a wounded animal. Then silence. Ben.

Agony sank its teeth deep in her chest and shoulder at the smallest movement. She turned her head inch by excruciating inch until she saw a tousled head. She willed her trembling fingers closer, to wrap around one limp hand. As she did, the head turned to look at her. Ellie's eyes met hers. The younger woman opened her mouth to speak. Instead of words, bright red blood poured from her lips.

Olivia pitched upright. The room lurched in her vision as she clawed free from the dream. Her own scraping gasps punctured the silence. The woman next to her didn't move, long hair fluttering with every deep breath. With tentative fingers, Olivia moved dark strands to reveal Ellie's tranquil face, shadowed in the spare light from the clock.

A shaking possessed her fists, then her forearms, before swarming her shoulders and overpowering the rest of her. Desperate to feel warm, she staggered to the shower, turned it on full blast, and crawled under the stream.

A LOW HISS dragged Ellie from sleep. Her arm swept through empty sheets, and she turned to the clock—3:32. Four hours since she'd dragged an inconsolable Olivia into bed and curled around her. One hour since Ellie finally dozed, exhausted by the confused whirl of her thoughts. The shower fully penetrated her groggy mind, and she forced herself upright and shuffled to the bathroom. Steam roiled the small space. Olivia sat hunched on the floor of the open shower, the hot spray painting her an angry red. When Ellie shut off the water, Olivia broke from her trance.

"Couldn't stop shaking. Needed to get warm."

Ellie grabbed a towel, keeping her voice low even as her pulse raced at Olivia's vacant expression. "There's warm, and then there's hard-boiled." She helped Olivia up and dried her, then sat her on the toilet while she grabbed pajamas. Olivia said nothing as she got dressed.

"Back to bed. Come on." For the second time that night, Ellie spooned a despondent Olivia, drawing the blankets high. She finally got a response when one hand crept up and grabbed hers. Even as Olivia collapsed into sleep, her tight grip remained, clinging until the gray light of dawn seeped around the curtains.

Chapter Thirty-Two

OLIVIA PADDED DOWNSTAIRS in her robe, grateful to find Ben alone on the couch. She had faked sleep this morning, tracking the sound of Ellie through the house until she left for work. She was ashamed by the feint, by her distant behavior since the shower, but the image of Ellie's face, blood pouring from her lips, had hovered over every moment this week. Blaming her breakdown on the flu was a flimsy excuse. Ellie hadn't bought it for a second. But Olivia couldn't explain the dream without explaining everything. Her lie heightened the tension between them, and Ellie's concern had enveloped her until she could only breathe in the other woman's absence.

"Hey, buddy. Enjoying the in-service day?"

He didn't respond, mesmerized by the screen in front of him. The phone had been Sophia's idea, after he'd become fascinated with selfies. He'd always hated being photographed, but one day he saw Sophia fiddling with a camera function on her new phone. She showed him how the camera "flipped" to face them, and he was hooked. A selfie could never be a surprise. Framing, timing, the decision to smile—

it was all under his control. One tilting, listing, off-center selfie at time, he built a crude diary. *I was here. This happened then.*

It was only later they thought to incorporate it into his social life. When he floundered meeting someone, he could whip out his phone to break the ice. If he couldn't put a face to a name, a simple scroll reminded him. Kids loved selfies. Most adults loved selfies, Olivia not included. Lately, though, he played games on it, and she monitored his time.

She settled next to him, leaning against his shoulder while he scrolled through his photos. An imaginary Sophia wagged a finger to say *I told you so.* "Can you start at the most recent one?"

Ben tapped a couple of times and started again.

"Who's that?"

"Thomas."

"Why does he use a wheelchair?"

He shrugged a shoulder, immune, as always, to most social details, and swiped through more selfies. She hadn't registered how many new people he'd met, but in sheer number, Ellie dominated the screen. Every vibrant smile rebuked Olivia for closing herself off.

"This is my first one with Ellie," Ben said.

"When was this?"

"TTC, the day group started."

Ellie looked about the same, but the smile, while genuine, was smaller. Two eraser tips hovered over her dark curls. As Ben moved backward from Ellie's first picture, the number of photos shrank—a few with Olivia, some with his cousins, his friend Jamal. Finally, he reached the picture they had looked at a thousand times. Ben and Sophia huddled close, his mother smiling big and bright, unaware this would be her last photo, that in a week she would be dead. A sob choked Olivia. The desire to pull her wife from the image, drag her into the present with them, overwhelmed her.

"Where are we?" Ben asked.

She clenched her fists. How long had it been since they'd talked about this picture? "At Indian Boundary Park, near the fort. The wind blew your popcorn off the picnic table, and all the pigeons flocked to eat it from the grass."

"I remember! Mommy shared hers with me because I was sad." Ben set the phone on the couch and stood up.

"Where are you going?"

"I'm playing Minecraft with Jamal at nine." He clomped up the stairs without a glance.

His casual departure was a fist to her chest. Ben always scrolled to the first selfie he'd taken with Sophia. Always. She grabbed his phone and tapped on that picture. A muted wisp of a boy stared back. She scrolled forward, a flip-book through time, watching Ben open up. His flat affect in the early years made Sophia's smile seem manic by comparison, but right before the accident, he'd grown more comfortable. His eyes focused on the screen, and smiles crept in, even if they had the forced school-picture quality common to kids his age.

After the accident, his face closed again. Things shifted as she scrolled, small grins returning, a new classmate on the screen, but after the first picture with Ellie, his world exploded. More people, new friends, a goofy pose or two. She ended with a picture taken last night. His smile wasn't huge, but it was real, and Ellie had snuck in a kiss to his cheek.

Olivia flipped from the recent picture to his last one with Sophia until the images blurred. The phone slipped from her grasp. She wanted to be happy for Ben, happy that he was happy with Ellie, with life, but the crushing sadness that Sophia wasn't part of it suffocated her. Her head sank into her hands, and she shook with quiet sobs.

Chapter Thirty-Three

SALSA MUSIC LEAKED through the back window as Olivia put her key in the lock, and when she opened the door, Ellie's laughter cascaded through the kitchen. The music was louder inside. Every horn blast and cymbal crash rapped against her skull. She dropped her bag on the floor. Through the living room arch, Ben swung into view, then vanished. On a second pass, they both appeared, locked in a clumsy dance pose. Ben bumped into Ellie, too busy watching his own feet to notice her change of direction.

"Remember dancing is like math," Ellie said. "There's a pattern and counting—"

"And I like math, so I must like dancing!"

Ellie towered over Ben, his head barely reaching her chest. Then, like an overlay, Sophia appeared, petite as ever, making her son appear taller. The vise crushing Olivia's sternum tightened. As Ellie filled the physical world—a hoodie draped over a chair, her scent on the sheets—Sophia intruded further into her thoughts and dreams. It had been a relief to go back to work after Ellie spent the weekend with them.

Olivia rubbed her eyes to dispel Sophia's outline, then stepped into the living room. "Hey guys, what's this?" Her voice came out flat. She pasted on a smile.

"I'm learning salsa! Did you know it's a dance *and* a condiment?"

"I did. Thought you'd be ready for bed."

"It's my fault," Ellie said. "He finished his homework early, so there was time for a dancing lesson. We ran long."

She sensed Ellie tracking her and ground her teeth. "The next day is hard if he doesn't sleep. Next time, stick to the schedule. It's easier."

"Excuse me? Stick to the schedule?"

"Are you mad?" Ben's question grated. Since when did he notice emotional undercurrents?

"I'm not mad. Let's get you upstairs and in your pajamas."

"But we weren't done—"

"You're done when I say you're done!"

"Olivia—"

"Don't." She stopped Ellie's protest with a curt wave.

"We were having fun!"

"Ben, if I have to tell you to get upstairs one more time, you'll have no computer tomorrow." She bit off each word. He fumed and pounded up the steps, and she followed, leaving a stunned Ellie behind.

"Olivia!"

She didn't—couldn't—break stride. The turmoil she'd suppressed these past weeks surged, leaving her with little control and even fewer words. She shook her head as she climbed the stairs. "Not now," was all she could choke out.

ELLIE PACED ANOTHER circle around the island. She'd stopped herself from chasing Olivia up the stairs, but barely. Olivia's remote moodiness had infected the whole house this week, and Ben didn't need to witness Ellie losing her cool on top of everything else. She ground her palm against her forehead. She had hoped to shield him from whatever this was, but she'd failed.

The morning after the breakdown in the shower, she'd been frightened but also relieved—Olivia couldn't possibly deflect after that. And yet she had, blaming it all on the flu. Ellie had been stunned. It was a terrible lie. Worse, Olivia knew it was terrible, and she said it anyway. In any other relationship, Ellie would've lost it right then, but Ben had burst into the room, all chatter and energy because she'd agreed to take him to school. She left the house wanting to scream, but as she wove through city streets, Ben humming in the back seat, she calmed enough to form a plan. Olivia had built wall after wall to protect Ben from her pain, but those walls were starting to crumble. If Ellie could act as the buffer, if she could take some of the burden, maybe Olivia would finally have the strength to help herself.

All week, she'd made Ben the priority, tackling as many of the practical demands as she could. All week she'd orbited Olivia without ever making real contact. She'd swallowed her impatience, her fear, her frustration—she had practically choked on it. Until tonight. There was no more shielding Ben; he'd seen it for himself. Olivia was crashing. One way or another, Ellie would find out why. Behind her, the stairs chattered, and then the floor creaked. She rounded on Olivia. "What the fuck is going on?"

"Can we not do this right now? I'm exhausted."

"What are *we* doing exactly? You don't talk to me like I'm some fucking nanny who broke the rules!"

"I had a rough day. I counted on him being upstairs. That's all. It caught me by surprise."

"That's all?" Olivia's forced blandness enraged her more than another lie. "That's fucking bullshit! Tell me what's going on!"

Olivia's face was an iron mask of silence.

"You yell at Ben. You push me away. And last weekend, in the shower…" Her indignation faltered when Olivia's face blanched. "I know you're not sleeping well, with the nightmares." Ellie stepped closer, but Olivia pushed past, toward the back door. "Where are you going? We're talking!" She grabbed Olivia's arm.

"Don't touch me!" Olivia wrenched herself free. "I need air. I can't breathe. I can't think!" She did look tired, the creases at her eyes and the lines around her mouth sinking into her skin, but there was something else, and it scared Ellie. Olivia seemed incomplete, as if a piece of her had been torn away.

"Why won't you look at me? I'm standing right here!"

"You're always right here! I need some goddamn space!"

"You said you wanted me here, anytime!"

"That was a mistake."

The words drove a spike through her gut. "You don't mean that."

Olivia balled up a fist and slammed her knuckles into the counter. "It's never just us! The way it used to be."

"You and Ben?"

"Maybe this isn't the time for change. It's too much for him. I can't make a decision based on what I want. It should be about Ben."

Ellie knew this script far too well. And she was sick of it. "Stop using him as a shield!"

"I do not *use* my son!" Olivia pounded the counter again.

Ellie yanked hard on the reins of her temper and lowered her voice. "To avoid talking about us, you bring up Ben. You're not the same since that night, and it wasn't the flu. The way you broke down in my arms... I didn't push you about it then, but you have to talk to me."

"I'll talk when I fucking want!" Olivia flung a finger in her face and spun away. Blood stained the white counter. Harsh, shallow breaths filled the kitchen.

"Olivia." She walked around the island to face Olivia where she stood, braced with one hand on the counter and the other clenched around the refrigerator handle.

"Olivia." Still, she avoided Ellie's gaze, as if her eyes might betray a secret she wasn't ready to share. Ellie wanted to cup her face, but it was a step too far. Instead, she wiped her finger through the smear of blood and held it up.

"I'm not scared of you, no matter how many times you pound your fist, but I am scared for you. You haven't been yourself, even before Sunday. We're so intimate, then a switch flips, and I can't get near you." While she spoke, Ellie could see the latches turn, hear the tumblers click as Olivia closed down.

"You need to go away." Olivia ground the words between her teeth.

"What do you—"

"I mean go away! Out of the house!"

"I will not leave you—"

"I'm not asking! Leave. Now!"

Ellie stared at the stony façade of Olivia's face. She was serious. She was actually serious. Of all the imagined scenarios, this possibility had never occurred to her. Olivia was kicking her out.

Ellie scrambled for any key to unlock the cage Olivia had trapped herself in. She came up empty. "I'll go now, but this isn't done. I love you, and whatever is happening in here—" She touched Olivia's chest with a gentle finger, and

Olivia flinched like she'd been struck. "—has to come out. This is it for me. You are it for me. I'm sorry if that's hard to hear, but it's the truth. I love you, and I'm in all the way. The funny thing is, I think you want to be too."

Olivia flinched again. Ellie almost caught her eye.

"You can lock your jaw and avert your eyes, but I'm more stubborn than you are. This isn't the end, not by a long shot."

"Just. Go. Away."

Ellie grabbed her purse and took slow steps to the front door. The painful silence stretched tight, broken by the click of the latch. She staggered onto the porch and leaned on the low wall. Her heart screamed at her to go back, to shake Olivia until whatever she was sitting on spilled from her frozen lips. Her shoulders made to turn, but her feet stayed anchored. The painful truth was, she didn't recognize this Olivia, didn't know how she would respond to a frontal assault. But there was someone who would know.

Ellie peeled her fingers from the cold cement, walked to her car, and sat behind the wheel. Part of her expected Olivia to burst onto the porch and call to her, but that faint hope died with the hollow thump of her door. She stabbed at the ignition three times before the key slid into place. Doubts from the past month flooded in, signs of Olivia's frustration she had ignored, hoping to find their earlier equilibrium. Anger and resentment simmered under her skin, but fear overpowered all of it. Fear for Olivia and what she was doing to herself. Ellie picked up her phone and dialed a number she'd never used.

"Arti, I need your help."

Chapter Thirty-Four

THE SPREADSHEET SHIMMERED on the screen. Cells spilled into rows and crashed into columns until the nursing schedule looked like driftwood piled up on a beach. Olivia closed the document and ground her knuckles into her eyes. She had driven to work on autopilot after dropping a quiet, twitchy Ben at school, seeking any distraction, but nothing worked. She glanced at her phone. Thirteen unopened texts. All from Ellie.

If you find yourself drowning one day under the weight of all you carry, do not drag my daughter with you. Please, if you love her, release her before you both are lost. Rosa's words had drummed in her brain since Ellie had left two nights ago. Since she had forced Ellie to leave.

Tick, tick, tick, tick, tick. The sound was faint, but rhythmic enough to pull her from her thoughts. Tap, tap, tap, tap, tap. Heels on tile, and with an insistent edge. Crack, crack, crack, crack, crack. She recognized that stride—persistent, determined, tireless.

Arti stormed into her office and towered over her desk, hands on her hips. "It's been thirty-six hours since you kicked Ellie out."

Olivia faced her monitor, pretending at a calm she didn't feel. "Didn't you get my text?"

"Are you referring to Monday night's 'I need time' or Tuesday night's 'Not now'?"

"Either. Both."

Arti ripped the mouse from her hand. "'Not now' isn't an option anymore! Either take me to coffee, or I'll get histrionic on you right here."

Two clerks performed a slow-footed, curious shuffle past her door, and she got up to close it, trapping Arti's energy in the cramped office. Ignoring her was a useless feint, one she had stretched to its maximum.

"What the fuck is wrong with you?" Arti didn't sit down, even when Olivia did. Her rings dug into the desk as she leaned on her fists. "You can't have a woman in your house, in your bed, almost every night, then tell her to leave with no warning!"

"It's hard to explain." Her chest knotted at the memory of Ellie's pained confusion.

"Well, you better try. I'm worried, and your girlfriend is losing her shit! Because she wasn't around the last time you lost *your* shit. She doesn't know what it looks like."

"I shouldn't have gotten involved with her." A prickling, like so many ants, crawled under her skin. She rubbed her forearms, willing the sensation to recede.

"Have you checked in with Dr. Williams? I know what this week is."

"It doesn't change the fact I made a mistake bringing Ellie into this."

"Your only mistake is driving away a woman who loves you!" Arti's voice climbed a frustrated octave. "You had the woman of your dreams for twenty years, and then...she's gone! But by some miracle you survive the accident that took her from you, and you survive nearly killing yourself with grief!

"Fast forward to now, and you meet another woman of your dreams—how impossibly lucky, since most of us never find one person like that. This woman adores you and your son, and you're going to shit all over it? Sophia would strangle you herself if she saw this!" Arti slapped the desk, and pens rattled in a mug. "I can't let you struggle the way you did after the accident. I'm scared...I'm scared you won't come back to us this time." A tear splattered on a folder, and Olivia forced her eyes to Arti's streaked face.

"This has to end, Olivia. See Dr. Williams, see Ellie, see someone, and tell them every single thing eating at you, including the shit you've kept from me. And once you've told them, burn it all and move on."

With those words, she acknowledged the only blank page in their friendship. Olivia had never lied about the accident, but she had tossed a shroud over the memories, rendering them inscrutable even to Arti's keen prodding.

Arti dropped to a chair and jerked a box of tissues off the desk. "I'm glad we stayed here. This would have been an ugly scene at a coffee shop."

Olivia was too stunned to laugh. "Why do you think I've kept things from you?"

"I'm not an idiot. You tell me everything, so I know when something's missing."

"Ben—"

"Stop it! This is about you. You've changed, and not for the better. Did you tell Ellie it's four years on Friday since the accident? And it always gets dark for you around this time?"

"She doesn't need to know."

"You think no one needs to know about that day! It's not fair not to tell her."

"What's fair to me?" Olivia smacked a palm on her desk. "What if four years isn't long enough for me?"

"What if ten years isn't enough, or twenty? How long will you do this?"

"As many years as I fucking want!" She spat the words at Arti. Anger was a bright, welcome flare in the miserable haze of this past month. She tried to hold it, to feed it, but it guttered and died in the face of Arti's gentle, knowing smile.

"Yell all you want. At least you're letting yourself feel something." Arti leaned forward and rested a hand on hers. She ran a finger over Olivia's bruised knuckle. "I will love you tomorrow, and next week, and if you never talk to me again, I will still love you. Ellie feels the same way, but you won't let her in."

"It's too much." She choked on the words.

"You have to risk feeling too much if you want to be happy."

"Maybe I don't want to be happy."

"Sophia wouldn't want that."

"Then she shouldn't have left me."

"Olivia…" Pain marred Arti's vibrant face. "*Ben* needs you to be happy. These past four years you've been there for him even when you couldn't be there for yourself, but this version of you, it's a half-life. Eventually, it will catch up to you…and him."

Arti's words hit the one nerve she couldn't ignore. Ben. Space from Ellie let her escape the chokehold of her emotions, but he didn't want space. He wanted Ellie. After Sophia's death, their shared misery kept them in lockstep. Now, his needs had hewed from hers, and she couldn't find a way forward for both of them.

"You should tell Ellie about the anniversary. If you're going to be stupid and end it, do the decent thing and tell her why." Arti stood and perched huge sunglasses on her puffy face. "Do you need me on Friday? For Ben?"

"Mom's got it. You have that big show in Wisconsin." A hollow weariness engulfed her, and she slumped in her chair. She couldn't remember the last time they'd truly fought.

"We'll talk when I get home? Sunday?"

"Sure." When Arti came around the desk to hug her, she stood up and mechanically returned it. "You're my best friend. I love you."

"You're the one twisting the knife. Please stop." Arti planted a big kiss on each cheek before heading to the door. As she opened it, she turned back. "See you soon?"

Olivia raised her hand in a silent wave.

BURNT GARLIC STUNG her nose for the second time, and Olivia tossed the smoking pan into the sink with a growl. She stalked a circle around the island. Arti's outburst had worked its magic. She'd spent the rest of the day squirming between the sharp teeth of grief and recrimination.

"Do you hate Ellie?" Ben appeared in the doorway, his question yanking her from her spiral.

"What?"

"Do you hate Ellie now? You won't talk about her."

"No, I don't hate her! I could never…" She grabbed a box from the cupboard. "We're having cereal for dinner tonight. I burned the—"

"Is she sick? In the hospital?"

"I would tell you if there was anything wrong. It's been a busy few days, and I haven't been feeling well—"

"That's not the truth!" He stomped a foot.

She threw the box onto the island. "It's as much truth as you'll get! Some things are meant for adults only!"

Ben kicked a stool, sending it crashing to the floor.

"We are not having this fight again. Pick up the stool, and sit at the table."

He scowled and threw himself into a chair, ignoring the stool. He took his phone out of his pocket.

"Pick up the stool. And you know the rule—no phones at dinner."

He ignored her, tapping his thumbs on the screen.

"Ben."

"I'm texting Ellie. She'll tell me the truth."

"Do not text Ellie." She moved to the table, using her height to loom over him.

"Why?" he shouted up at her. "She's my friend too!"

"I'm your mother, and I'm telling you to pick up the stool, and put down the phone!"

"It's my phone!"

"Put down the goddamn phone!" She snatched it from him and flung it across the kitchen. It hit the wall with a crack and fell to the floor. Ben clapped his hands to his ears and cried.

Shame crashed over her. "I'm sorry. I'm so sorry. I lost my—"

"I hate you. You ruin everything!" He bolted from the kitchen and ran upstairs, but she didn't have the strength to follow.

She crossed the kitchen and picked up the phone. The case was in pieces, but somehow it turned on. The home picture was Ben, Olivia, and Ellie sprawled out on the couch for a selfie, their faces distorted by the shattered screen. She hurled it a second time and slid to the floor.

Chapter Thirty-Five

"ELLIE! ELLIE! ELLIE!"

Ellie clenched a fist and pressed it to her mouth. Olivia must have caved and brought Ben to the TTC party after all. She'd ducked into another room to avoid a scene, but his frantic voice reverberated down the hallway. She stepped through the open door. "Ben!"

"Ellie!" Dark bangs clung to his sweaty forehead, and he fell into her arms. "Mom said you were okay, but I didn't believe her because you wouldn't leave if you were okay."

Olivia rounded the corner at a jog, stopping when she saw them.

Ellie picked him up. He was a coiled spring in her arms. "Let's go in here, buddy. Shhh, I've got you." As she carried him into a small meeting room, Olivia followed.

"Where were you?" Ben pressed clammy hands to her cheeks.

Her planned response dissolved in the face of his wretched confusion, and she glanced at Olivia, searching for any hint of what to say. But like their fight in the kitchen, she wouldn't meet her gaze. Whatever Olivia was hiding, it boiled so close to the surface she didn't trust her control with even that scant connection. If they'd been alone, if Ben weren't trembling in her arms... "It's hard to explain, but I promise I haven't forgotten you."

Ben's breath slowed, and she set him on his feet. He threw himself at her waist and buried his wet face in her shirt. "Was it me? I'm sorry. I'm sorry if it was me."

"Oh, sweetie, it wasn't you."

"It's not you, Ben." Olivia finally cracked. Even with this storm inside her, she wouldn't let Ben blame himself. Tiny as that spark was, Ellie clung to it. "It's me. It's my fault. I asked her to stay away."

"Did you fight? You said if you love someone, you always say sorry, and they always forgive you. You said so!"

"It's not forever. Just a break. I need time to think."

Ben launched himself at Olivia, landing wild punches with his skinny arms. "Time to think means no! Why did you make Ellie go away? WHY?"

Olivia knelt and grabbed his shoulders. "Ben, we can't stay. I made a mistake bringing you here. Ben! I'll pick you up if you don't stop!" He thrashed against her, refusing to give in. Olivia's shuttered eyes were blank as she lifted him in her strong arms and left.

A repressed scream scalded Ellie's tongue, and she lost control of her own tears.

"Ends of the Earth, Ellie. You said! Ends of the Earth!"

Their song, their lullaby. Ben's plea forced her feet into motion, and she ran down the hall.

"Ben. Ben!" When she caught up, Olivia stopped but didn't turn around. Ben faced Ellie over her shoulder, and she cradled his hot cheeks. Enough with Olivia's stubborn reticence. She couldn't watch him struggle anymore. "I'll see you this weekend. On Saturday, okay? I will visit this Saturday, and we'll talk about everything."

Ben reached over Olivia's shoulder to wrap his arms around her, with Olivia pinned in between. Ellie fell into the embrace, absorbing the press of Olivia's warm back against her chest.

"Go with your mom now, okay? Take care of her until Saturday."

Olivia stepped forward, jerking Ben away. He clung to her as she turned the corner. Curious stares dotted the hallway, and Ellie hid from them in the nearest empty room. High and tight in her throat, a pressure swelled. She'd been choking it down, hiding it from Ben, but now, like a balloon inflating, it lodged under her jaw with painful intensity. The first sob was a wet gasp, her body fighting to breathe both out and in, but after one shuddering intake, it all burst free. She collapsed into a chair, sobbing until there was nothing left.

Chapter Thirty-Six

ELLIE LIFTED THE squirming toddler onto the yoga ball and kept a tight grip on his waist in case he pitched himself sideways. A knock drummed, more insistent than she might expect when she was in session. Shelley stepped into the room, tentative but concerned. The staff had been tiptoeing around her after the scene with Ben yesterday. She waggled a phone.

"Let's have three minutes of free time, Aiden." Ellie set him by a pile of cars and walked to the door. "Is that my cell?"

"I'm sorry, but it kept ringing in your desk drawer. It's Ben. You take this. I'll stay here."

Ellie took the phone and walked toward the offices. "Ben?"

"Mom promised to call at three. At three!" His shrill tone pierced the speaker.

"I don't understand, buddy."

"She left me with Grandma and promised to call by three. It's the day!"

"So you're in Joliet?"

"No. Grandma is here. Because it's the day. She said to wait, but you have to help Mom!"

"I will help, but I don't—"

"The day. The DAY!"

She slapped her hand against the wall. Ben was spinning. "What day? Take a breath. I can't help if I don't understand."

He gulped air on the other end of the line. "The day of the accident!"

The world crashed to a halt. How had she not known? There'd been vague references about summer, but she'd been careful not to press. She ground her palm into her forehead. Too careful.

"Mom went away, but she promised to call by three."

Ellie made it to her desk and grabbed her keys. "It's a quarter after, buddy. Maybe—"

"But Mom promised—"

"Okay, okay, I'll find her. I'm sure she's fine."

"She's not fine!" Ben choked on the words. "She's so sad about Mommy, and now she's double-sad about you. I told her, don't go when she's double-sad!"

"Maybe it's her battery. Hang up, and tell Grandma you called. I'll call Thea Arti, okay?"

"Okay. Okay. It's the day, Ellie. The day," he muttered as he hung up.

Heart hammering, she bolted for the front door, dialing Arti as she went. The first call went unanswered, as did the second. She flung herself into her car and started the engine before trying a third time.

"Ellie—"

"We can't get Olivia on her phone. Have you heard from her?"

"I saw her on Wednesday. Why?"

"Ben called. Today's the anniversary, isn't it? Of the accident?"

Arti took a sharp inhale. "Yes."

"Does Olivia go somewhere special?"

"I don't know."

"What do you mean? You have to know!"

"Every year, she goes off by herself, but she's never said where. The rule is no calls unless Ben's in the hospital. Oh my God, he's not, is he?"

"No, but he called me freaking out because Olivia promised to call by three and didn't."

"Fuck me." The quaver in Arti's voice drove a spike of fear through her.

"Arti! Tell me something. Anything!" Ellie pounded the wheel.

"We need to think. Where would she go?"

"How the hell should I know?" For the hundredth time this week, she cursed herself for not barging back into Olivia's house Monday night.

"I remember at the one-year mark, she said she needed space to reflect on the accident and what she was going to do now that Sophia was gone."

Beyond the dashboard, a decorative stone bridge spanned the middle of TTC's garden. "Where was the accident?"

"West on twenty, out by TTC, but farther. Her mom would know the exact spot."

"I'll head that way. Check with Alice, text me the name of the river or anything else that would help. Ben's right to be freaked out because she didn't call?"

"Oh, he's more than right. Olivia wouldn't say it if she didn't mean it."

"Do you think she'd say it as a cue to start searching if she'd..." Ellie dropped her voice as if speaking too loudly would make it true.

"She wouldn't...Ben...fuck. Call me when you find her."

Chapter Thirty-Seven

ELLIE FLEW ALONG the highway, her stomach turning with each empty overpass. Clearing a long curve, she spotted the Subaru parked up the next hill, but as she pulled in behind it, blank sky framed the empty bridge. A sour bubble of fear popped in the back of her throat. She threw herself out of the car and ran to the railing. Counting one breath, then another, then a third, she finally peeked over the edge. Olivia's blondè hair swirled in the wind, and panic roiled before Ellie's mind could register that she was alive, sitting on a large rock next to the river.

With clumsy fingers, she texted Arti. *Found her. Going to talk. Give me time.* She silenced her phone and walked to where the railing stopped. Wet grass slithered beneath her feet as she skidded down the steep ditch. Olivia had talked about the car rolling, but now, standing at the bottom, Ellie couldn't imagine how it had held together at all. She picked her way to the rock. A litany of hurt and fear and anger surged against her lips, but Olivia's sorrow-ravaged face stilled her. Grief had carved new creases onto her serious features with ruthless efficiency. Silence pressed in, broken only by tires hissing on pavement overhead.

"The patrolman said we were lucky." Olivia sneered at the word, her voice a rusty croak. "If I hadn't clipped the railing, we might have crashed in the river, and we all would have died. I wanted to claw his eyes out. He knew Sophia was dead, and still he said...lucky."

"When I saw the empty bridge I thought you—" Fear smothered the rest of Ellie's thought.

"I was sitting on the hood of the car, but I needed to get closer. I've never climbed down here before." She shook herself roughly as if waking from a dream. "How did you—"

"Ben called when he couldn't reach you."

Olivia dug in her pocket for her phone. *No service* sat in the corner of the screen. "Fuck. I lost track—"

"It's okay. I texted Arti when I got here. She'll tell him."

"He must be freaking out—" Olivia rolled onto her hip, but Ellie stopped her momentum with a hand on her shoulder.

"He can wait this one time." Coiled muscles trembled under her palm like Olivia might resist, but then she sank back.

"I'm sorry. This isn't what you need."

"What I need is to understand."

The bridge rumbled with the thunder of a passing semi. A crow's caw split the air.

Olivia's reticence, that brittle enemy they'd fought this past month, asserted itself until finally she lifted her head and pinned her gaze to the horizon. "Sophia was an early riser. She would poke me awake, call me her hibernating bear."

Ellie snorted with false humor to keep the story from dissolving into silence.

"We'd lived together awhile when one morning I woke up to find her still in bed, staring at the ceiling. She'd been doing it more often, saying she couldn't sleep in, but she wasn't ready to be apart from me yet. I asked her what she thought about in those quiet moments. And she told me. It became a private daily ritual. I loved it." Olivia squinted and rubbed her mouth. "The morning of the accident, she was already gone, letting me sleep in while she prepped for the trip. It happened occasionally, no big deal."

How many last moments had passed unnoticed, camouflaged by the monotony of daily life? How many nights did a grieving Olivia sift through uncertain memories, hoarding as many precious "lasts" as her mind could conjure?

"I'd give anything to ask her what she was thinking about one last time. Like her answer could make the rest of that terrible day make sense."

"Is that why you're here? To make sense of it?" Ellie asked the safe question, unable to voice her grimmest thoughts.

Olivia clenched and unclenched her hands. "Those first months, I couldn't escape the idea of killing myself. It was always there, lurking. It got to the point where it affected my focus on Ben. I needed somewhere to put those thoughts, some way to deal with them. One day, when it was really bad, I snuck out here. I stood at the railing and made myself imagine what it would take to actually end it. To leave everything. To leave Ben."

"You didn't tell your psychologist?"

"No. If he hospitalized me, it would've devastated Ben. And it helped, being here. It made it a concrete thing. In the middle of the night, when you're drowning in grief, the idea can feel seductive, like a release." Olivia's eyes drew a lazy arc from the railing down to the sluggish water. "But here, in broad daylight, it became a choice. So I set a date, once a month, to come here and confront that choice. Anytime a stray thought intruded, I tucked it away in a corner of my mind where it could wait for the next visit."

"Did you ever come close? To doing it?"

"The one-year mark was especially hard. I thought I hadn't loved Sophia enough if I could live a year without her."

"Olivia…"

"I only came yearly after that. It scared me, how much I had come to need this place. How connected it made me feel to her." Olivia's eyes slid to Ellie's for the first time before gliding back to the river. "I never truly considered it again until today."

"But why? It was going so well."

"Too well."

"I don't understand."

"I pretended my feelings for you weren't as intense, as real as they were with Sophia. It was safer. But that night in the shower there was a moment when you filled every space, every thought. For the first time, I couldn't imagine not having you in my life. Then Sophia popped into my head, and it all came crashing down. Your presence is built on her absence. To be happy with you meant I had to be okay with her being gone. What kind of person does that? Who pushes aside the love of their life?"

"You didn't push her aside. You took a step toward a new life. A life Sophia would want you to have. Her death was a tragedy, for you and Ben, but you're allowed to come to terms with it and find some peace."

"I can't have peace. Not after losing her the way I did."

The bleak tone under the words stopped Ellie's protest. "What do you mean?"

"I've never told anyone about the accident, not even Arti." Olivia released a shaky sigh. "I blacked out after we rolled. When I came to, Ben was screaming in the back. I couldn't get to him—the steering wheel had me pinned. Each breath was fire. When he went silent, I couldn't tell…I didn't know…

"Then I heard him breathing, shallow and soft, and I knew he was still with me. Sophia, though...she was so still." Olivia dug her fingers into her knees until the knuckles went white. Her wedding band glowed on her clawed hand. "And then her head moved. I wanted to laugh with relief, but the pain was too much. I could just reach her hand, and I grabbed it. She turned slowly, like she was underwater. She was in so much pain, but she held my eyes. She tried to talk, but when—" A dry heave bent Olivia, and she spit into the grass. The story tore itself from her throat as she continued. "When she opened her mouth, it was full of blood. Her teeth were stained this terrible bright red. She was choking on it, choking to death. It poured out of her mouth in this thick stream—"

Horror fixed Ellie's tongue to her mouth.

"All I could think was, 'She's dying, and I can't help her. I'm right here, and I can't help her. I'm a fucking *nurse*, and I can't help her!'" Olivia shouted the last sentence, and Ellie's heart wrenched. "She touched my hand with one thumb, looked right at me, and then she was gone. Her eyes were open, but she wasn't there. I shook her, yelling, trying to bring her back." Olivia's jaw rippled as she fought tears, and Ellie wrapped her in a hug, grateful she allowed it. "I still see her face—blood rushing over her chin, down her neck. Sometimes...sometimes it's the only way I can remember her."

Ellie buried her face in Olivia's hair. "How long were you there before the ambulance came?"

"I have no idea. I passed out for good as they cut me out of the car. When I woke up in the hospital, I told them I remembered the drunk driver's car. Nothing else."

"And they told you Sophia died instantly. She didn't suffer."

Olivia let out that horrible, dark laugh, the one Ellie had come to hate. "I wanted to scream at them, 'But she did suffer. And all I could do was watch!'"

"When you dream about the accident, this is what you dream—her death."

Olivia nodded, and Ellie cradled her again. The wind blew through them as the minutes passed, until Olivia's shoulders released, and her clenched hands slacked.

Ellie kissed Olivia's temple. "You don't have to struggle alone. It might feel hard, and dark, but we can get through it. I can wait as long as you need."

"You don't understand. The night you found me in the shower? I'd had the dream again, more intense than in years. It was all the same, the wheel crushing me, Ben screaming, but when I grabbed Sophia's hand, it was you who looked at me." Olivia grabbed her shoulders with painful intensity. "Your mouth filled with blood, your eyes with that dead stare."

"It was just a dream. I am right here."

"But I'm not! Part of me is forever in that car. I barely survived losing Sophia. If I lost you...there wouldn't be anything left."

"I'm not going to—" Ellie couldn't make that promise, not to this woman. "So you're closing yourself off from me, from anyone, because of what might happen?"

"I've *lived* what might happen. It's agony. If I could go back, I would never—"

"Never what? Meet me? Meet Sophia?"

Olivia's eyes widened, and Ellie grabbed her forearms. She saw a chance now, a way to cut through this fog of grief. "Tell me you'd give it all up—kisses in the dorm, Sophia taking you to bed for the first time, her pregnant body. You spent twenty years with her, and you'd sacrifice all of it, you'd sacrifice Ben, to avoid this pain?"

Olivia yanked away, pushed herself off the rock, and stalked toward the ditch.

Ellie dashed to catch up and flung herself in front of her. She slapped a palm on her chest. "Tell me! Tell me you'd lose twenty years with Sophia to wipe that image from your brain. Tell me you'd give up twenty years, or forty years with me!" She pushed Olivia hard. "I wasn't in that car! Please don't walk away from me, from us."

Olivia's heavy breath chopped through the swirling wind. She dragged watery eyes from the ground and back to Ellie. "Ever since I dreamed about you instead of Sophia, I can't keep things straight. In the nightmare, I never know whose face I'll see. Sophia's in my head, but in the house, there's only you." Tears slipped from her cheeks and stained her shirt. "I don't know how to let her go."

"You don't need to let her go. You just have to let yourself truly start living without her."

"That's why you should walk away. From me, from this. I don't know how to stop being afraid so I can—" The wind tossed Ellie's hair in front of her face, and Olivia reached out to tuck it behind her ear. "You deserve someone who can give you everything."

Ellie grabbed Olivia's hand and kissed the palm. "You are everything I want in life, which is the most anyone deserves. You're so hard on yourself. The trauma you experienced, trapped in a car, forced to watch your wife die... You are so much stronger than you realize."

"You see things in me that aren't really there." Olivia choked on a sob.

"I see all the incredible things you won't let yourself see." Ellie wiped damp tracks from Olivia's cheeks. "You said once you didn't have room for anger because there was only grief. And no wonder. You were so busy caring for Ben and the demands of his grief you never dealt with your own. But it can't be only grief, stretching out to forever. Maybe that's what you've been doing these last few months—making room for something else."

Olivia turned from her to face the river. She clenched her fingers around the back of her neck. "I thought this was the place of my biggest fear—watching Sophia leave me, but today I realized how wrong I was. The worst fear came later. The first night in the house, Ben clutching my shirt with a nightmare, alone. That was terror. How could I ever parent without her? And the first time I laughed again, I was so afraid. Afraid I was losing her. The grief made me less afraid. Because if I was grieving, she was still with me. But if I was happy...she truly was gone."

Her hands dropped, and she stuffed them into her pockets. "You could meet a woman your own age, maybe have your own children. Why choose me, and Ben, and this screwed-up life I've made for us?"

Ellie finally took a real breath. Olivia tossed the old argument out there, but her heart wasn't in it. Ellie came up behind her and wrapped her arms around her waist. "Because I love you. And I love Ben." Her voice broke on his name. "Sophia will always be with you, with us, but let me help you. Let me love you. We can get through this together."

Olivia stood stiff and brittle in her arms for long seconds. Then she unraveled, resting her temple against Ellie's with a sigh. Ellie reveled in this soft intimacy, one body fused to the other, and waited. Rustling grass streaked the silence. The river's damp, mossy scent licked their skin. When a flock of birds burst from a tree, Olivia's head shifted to follow them. Her ribs expanded under Ellie's arms as she took in a deep breath, then she leaned forward, pulling her fists from her pockets. The gold band shone on her left hand.

"I took this off after Sophia's service. I wore it on these days in case I went through with it. I wanted a piece of her with me." She removed the ring. "But it's time to let it go."

Ellie guessed at Olivia's intent. "If you do this, you might regret it, years from now. Or maybe Ben will want it later."

"I saved Sophia's in case, one day, he wanted to give it to someone. Sophia would want me to have that dream for him." She rolled the ring between her fingers. "Mine represents something I used to need, but not anymore." With those words, she tossed it. It winked in the light as it spun before splashing into the muddy river. Ellie didn't know what to think, but it was already done.

Olivia turned her back on the dark ribbon of water and took Ellie's hands. "I kept returning to this spot, but I never jumped. Because of Ben, of course. And because deep down, I knew Sophia wouldn't want me to. Each time I came here, Sophia helped keep me safe. But today was different. Do you know why?"

She shook her head.

"Because today, I knew *you* wouldn't want me to. *You* helped keep me safe."

Olivia cradled her face, and the warmth of that touch sent fresh tears down Ellie's cheeks. "I love you, Ellie. I love you with all I have. I'm sorry I didn't say it sooner. If I had, maybe it wouldn't have come to this. I love you more than I thought would ever be possible again." She brushed a gentle kiss against Ellie's wet lips and buried her face in her neck. Ellie wrapped her arms around her, wanting to never let her go.

Chapter Thirty-Eight

BEN WRENCHED FREE from Ellie's arms the second Olivia came out of the bathroom in her pajamas, and the two of them snuggled into her bed, his slight frame plastered to hers. When they'd arrived at the house earlier, he'd thrown himself at her and refused to let go. Alice and Arti hadn't been far behind. Ellie understood the clinging need. She'd insisted on driving Olivia home from the bridge, unwilling to be more than an arm's length away. They would collect her car later.

Now, the three of them were home with plans to see everyone tomorrow. Ellie grabbed her own pajamas and stepped into the bathroom. Her tired reflection, all wind-snarled curls and shadowed eyes, stared back from the mirror as she brushed her teeth.

"Why didn't you call?" Ben's thin voice leaked through the crack she'd left in the door. He'd already asked that question countless times. His desolation reinforced the pressure Olivia had been under to always have the phone nearby, to be available whenever he needed her.

"I was selfish. I'm so, so sorry." Thick regret filled Olivia's voice, as it had every time she answered.

"Because you were double-sad."

"Double-sad?"

"Because it was The Day. And because Ellie left."

"Ellie didn't leave. I pushed her away."

"But it didn't work."

Olivia's chuckle was quiet, but it was genuine. It had been so long since Ellie had heard the sound, and her chest ached. "Do you know why?"

"Why?"

"Because she doesn't give up on the people she loves. Even when other people make it hard for her."

"Why would you make it hard for someone to love you?"

"Oh, buddy." Olivia cleared her throat. "That's too big a question right now."

"But you're not pushing Ellie away again? Because I was scared when she left."

"I won't push her away, and I'm sorry for scaring you."

"S'okay." Ben yawned, a drowsy drag in his voice. "I decided I definitely love Ellie."

Ellie spit quietly into the sink and took a soft breath. *Love.* It was the second time today she'd heard that declaration.

"I definitely love her too."

"Did you tell her?" he asked.

"Yes."

"Oh, good. Maybe I'll tell her."

"Whenever you're ready."

"Mommy would want us to love her," Ben said. "She told me."

"What? When?"

"Before the accident."

Silence settled in the bedroom. When Olivia finally spoke, it was in a harsh, strangled voice. "I don't understand. Can you explain a little more, buddy?"

Entranced with his story, Ben didn't read the emotion in her question. "When Jonah's dad died, and he got a new dad."

"You mean when Jonah's mom remarried?"

"Jonah was so sad. Mommy said it was because he missed his dad. She said when a person dies, the people left behind are sad. Then you get less sad, and maybe you find a new person to love."

"She said this?" Olivia rasped the question.

"She said something else. I never told because I thought you'd be mad."

"I won't be mad. I promise."

"I told Mommy to promise to never die, but she said she couldn't." A weepy quaver blurred his words. "But she said if she did die, and you got lucky like Jonah's mom, I should work hard to love that person too. She said you would never love someone who didn't love me."

"Oh, Ben, your mommy was the best person in the whole world. She loved you so much."

"Did I cause the accident? Because I asked Mommy to promise, and then she did die!"

"No, no, no. You didn't cause her death. She would never want you to think that."

"You didn't cause Mommy to die either." He sniffled through the words.

"Why would you say that?" Olivia's stricken tone took Ellie back to the river, the devastation on her face.

"I heard Thea Arti tell Grandma you thought it was your fault because you were driving. But it wasn't. The bad car was in our lane. It was too fast. You asked about lunch, and Mommy said she didn't want greasy food, and BAM!"

Ellie twitched when he yelled the last word.

"You remember all this?"

"Sure. You do too."

"How do you know?" Olivia sounded so shaken Ellie almost went to her.

"Your dreams. You yelled sometimes, after the accident. It woke me up. You yelled about the blood." His voice grew soft, hesitant. "I saw it too."

Ellie cupped both hands to her mouth, holding in a pained sob. All three of them had been conscious. For one fragile, final moment, they had been together.

"You never told me."

"I thought it was a secret. Because you never said. I thought it was so secret you could only talk about it in your dreams."

"Is there anything else you remember?"

"I was scared when you shook Mommy and yelled. I thought you were hurting her."

Olivia made quiet shushing noises while he cried. "Buddy, no. I was pinned, and I couldn't get to her. I wanted Mommy to come back. I wanted her so desperately not to be gone."

"I know. I told Dr. Allison about it, about the shaking, not the blood. She said you were scared, and Mommy was already dead. That you would never hurt her."

"I love you so much. And Mommy loved you. I'm sorry you remember all of that."

"It's okay." Ben's voice faded.

"Sometimes, I hold things inside when they're hurting me, and I shouldn't. We have to talk, you and me, about everything, okay? Ben?" A light snore rumbled from the bed. He'd given out, exhausted by the emotions of the day.

Ellie fumbled into her pajamas, then peeked around the door. Olivia waved her over.

"I never thought...I didn't even suspect—"

"Shhh... It's been a long day. It's time for rest." Ellie nodded at Ben. "He needs you. I'll sleep in his room."

"But I need you. Will you stay? Please?" Olivia's eyes were glassy with fatigue, but there was an openness, a vulnerability Ellie hadn't realized was missing until now. For the first time in a month, she could *see* Olivia, all of her. She slid into bed and pressed herself to Olivia's open side. It took only a few breaths for Olivia to unravel in her arms. A light snore, a twin to Ben's, matched his rhythm. Ellie buried her face in Olivia's hair. It smelled of the wind and the river, and she shuddered as she started to cry.

Chapter Thirty-Nine

DENSE HEAT OOZED across Olivia's skin. Sunlight scalloped on aquamarine water. Shrieks and splashes and tinny music crackled in her ears. The pool's energy was bright and buoyant, almost painfully so, but she let it wash over her. She'd huddled at the edge of the world too long. She needed to remember how to be in it.

Grief, for her, had always landed like a fist, but this time had been different. It crept up, subtle and insidious. A pluck at her hem, a tug on her ankle—small miseries she tried to kick away. But one tug became ten, and ten became a hundred, all dragging her down a long, slow, sickening slide into what Ben always called The Day.

Marco...Polo...Marco...Polo. The peeps and chirps skimmed across the water as children bounced around an eyes-closed, grasping friend. Past them, Ellie stood waist deep, encouraging Ben to submerge himself. Her bronze skin collected the dense sunshine, where his pale arms, crossed in stubborn refusal, could only reflect it.

"If June keeps pretending to be August, she's going to lose her status as my favorite month. Ninety-two degrees is ridiculous." Arti plopped an enormous bag on a deck chair and pulled it closer, feet screeching against concrete. "How long has Ellie been trying to get him to dunk his head?"

"Ten minutes." Olivia leaned over to exchange kisses, Arti's perfume whispering against her cheeks. Citrus and rose softened the bite of chlorine.

"And you told her he's never gone underwater, not once?"

"I did, but she's determined."

"Thank God, with the two of you." Large silver circles flashed on her ears. More discs in various sizes floated on her sea of cleavage. "So what are we celebrating—the end of sixth grade or the end of your don't-scare-me-like-that-again spiral into darkness?"

"Both?"

"Fair enough."

It had been a week since they'd last seen each other. That kind of gap would never have happened after the accident. Arti was her watchful shadow then, both support and shield as Olivia fought her way back. But this time, she'd left some space between them. Space a couple would need to find stable ground again. Space she trusted Ellie to fill. Arti appeared all brass and bluster, but Olivia knew the depths of her insight, her grace, and she had never been more grateful for it.

"How's our boy doing?" Arti lifted her chin in Ben's direction. "We're three weeks out now."

Ben took one step deeper, then another, until the water reached his chest. He turned, searching for Olivia. Ellie pointed in her direction, and she waved to catch his attention. He waved back, then began bobbing. This was his favorite depth. It provided the sensation of swimming without the risk of being submerged.

"He's better. But still clingy."

"And you're still wearing a guilty expression every time you look at him. How long's that going to go on?"

"Until he's back to being himself."

"Plus an extra month because you can't help yourself." Arti's earrings jangled as she shook her head. "And how's Ellie?"

"Better than I deserve after everything."

"There's the guilty expression again. You know it's not about the fight anymore. It never was, really."

"How did you know—"

"Because you still carry around every fight you had with Sophia. All four of them."

"I hurt Ellie. Badly."

"No, you scared her. Badly." Arti let her sunglasses slide down her nose. Shrewd brown eyes stared over the top rim. "And I know *that* because I was the one she called right after the fight."

"Hurt. Scared. It doesn't matter which—"

"It does matter. It matters a lot actually. If you're thinking 'I hurt her' while Ellie's thinking 'She scared me,' then you're going to put all your energy into apologizing when what she really needs is reassurance." Arti nudged her oversized glasses back into place with one manicured nail and turned to the pool.

Olivia rubbed at a knot in her jaw. Apologies had poured out of her since the bridge, but maybe it wasn't enough. "Why am I paying a psychologist again?"

"Because he gets to do all the dirty work, leaving me to drop these bon mots into your lap at just the right moment."

Ben's orange rash guard flared in her peripheral vision. He trudged up the slope of the zero-entry area alone.

"Where is—" Olivia's words slipped away as a dark head surfaced right in front of them. Ellie hauled herself up the pool ladder, water rushing over her breasts, which stretched her blue tankini to its limits. Olivia's shuttered libido stirred. Sparks of yearning had started to return, but for all the work they'd done to reconnect, the sexual piece hadn't clicked yet.

"When did you get here?" Ellie pressed a damp kiss to each of Arti's cheeks.

"Just now. Nice suit."

"Thanks! I was going for a bit more coverage, but I couldn't say no once Olivia saw me in this one. A slack jaw is every woman's dream compliment."

"My jaw was not slack!"

Ellie tossed her a wink. "Ben went to the bathroom. I'm going to make sure he doesn't get lost in the locker room again." She sauntered off, damp suit hugging every curve, and another tendril of desire snaked through Olivia's brain.

"That was some reasonably playful banter. Things can't be too bad."

"Nothing is 'bad,' but this is the most she's flirted since it all went south."

"Really?"

"I mean, she's been tender and sweet and warm and absolutely supportive, but she's also tentative. Physically, I mean."

Arti's lips bowed in a thoughtful pout. She scratched her chin. "How are you going to handle it?"

"With exactly what she gave me—patience and understanding."

"And clear communication about your needs?"

"I'm only now getting back myself. 'Needs' might be a strong word."

"Look, I know sex is usually the thing that saves you from talking, but this time might have to be different."

A long sigh leaked between Olivia's teeth. Physicality, intimacy, sex—they'd always been a refuge when words failed her. The idea that she might need words to find her way back to sex...

"You should bring it up with Dr. Williams. How's therapy going, by the way? Overall?"

"Good. I stepped away too soon the last time. I won't repeat that mistake."

Ben skipped across the cement. "Thea Arti!" He gave her a quick peck as Ellie camped on the end of Olivia's chair.

"My sweet Ben! Will do you do me a favor?"

"What?"

"See the long line for concessions? I'm giving you this ten-dollar bill to buy me a lemonade. If you can stand in line and politely wait your turn alllllll the way to the front, you can use the leftover money for yourself."

"Yeah?"

"But I'll be watching from here, so I'll know if you cheat. No pushing into someone's personal space and no loud complaining about how long it's taking. Got it?"

"Easy-peasy!" He ran for the line.

"Walk!" Olivia shouted at him. He slowed to the fastest speed walk imaginable, waving when he reached his position. She returned the wave, then poked Ellie with her toe. "I'll take the next pool shift whenever he's done digesting the junk he's about to buy."

"Sounds good." Ellie raised her eyebrows, looking from her to Ben. "This seems like the perfect chance."

There were a dozen people in front of Ben, who was distracting himself by creasing Arti's bill into thin accordion folds. Olivia slumped in her chair and sighed. She didn't know which was more painful, telling Arti the truth, or admitting she'd kept it from her at all.

"What's going on, ladies?"

"Dr. Williams suggested if I've held information back from the people who love me, I should tell them. Clear the decks, as it were." Olivia glanced over her shoulder. Ben was bouncing now, vibrating with the effort to be patient.

Ellie patted her calf. "I'm going to keep him company. Take your time." She stood and wandered in his direction, leaving them framed in the shadow of the umbrella.

"God, your expression, Olivia." Arti pushed the hair from her face with her sunglasses. "Not that I'm not curious, but are you sure you want to do this now?"

"He suggested picking somewhere less serious so it didn't feel as threatening." Olivia tossed her own sunglasses on the towel at her feet. "There are only two things I have ever kept from you."

"Both about the accident."

"You know me too well."

"Just well enough." Arti flashed her best smirk. That glimpse of their decades-old banter released some of the tension in Olivia's chest.

"When I went to the bridge, it wasn't just to process the accident. Each time, I thought about what it would mean to end it."

Arti nodded once, her grin fading.

"You knew."

"Not at first. But later, I suspected. I just wouldn't admit it to myself."

Olivia pivoted on the deck chair to fully face Arti, resting her elbows on her knees. The hot concrete throbbed against the soles of her feet. "The second thing I lied about is not remembering the accident. I remember most of it. Sophia didn't die instantly."

A muscle twitched in Arti's jaw, but she stayed silent.

It was only the third time Olivia had revealed the truth. She'd kept it in so long that with Ellie, at the bridge, the words had torn themselves from her body, piece by piece. With her therapist, the story hadn't sliced to the bone, but it still hurt. Describing Sophia's death to Arti was its own exquisite kind of pain. She could only watch as the realization played out on Arti's expressive features, as her memory of a close friend was altered. Olivia was reopening an old wound and making it deeper. Bloodier. Uglier. This was why she'd kept it a secret. She knew what it was like to live with that memory, and she'd been desperate to spare anyone else the agony.

Arti swung her own feet to the ground, going knee to knee. "This is what's been destroying you? That Sophia was hurt. She was dying. And you watched it happen? Why didn't you say something?"

"How do I tell someone who knew Sophia, who loved her, that she died next to me, in pain, and I could do nothing to help her?"

"Oh, that's where you're wrong, kardiá mou."

The rare expression pulled Olivia's eyes up from the concrete. *My heart.*

Arti took her hands. A tremor rippled through their shared grip, and then Arti squeezed, hard. "No one should die the way Sophia did, but if she had to die first, at forty or at eighty, she wanted your face to be the last thing she saw. She might have been scared or hurting, but she wasn't alone. It's your gift. You can make someone feel like they're the only person in the world. I'm sure that's all Sophia felt, at the end."

Their final moment had always seemed so certain, but Arti's words muted the horror enough to allow for another possibility. "I never thought about it that way."

"Because your curse is you aren't generous with yourself the way you are with others. You can't know what was happening inside Sophia. The one certainty is you were with her. Would you want to be anywhere else, given what was happening?"

The idea of being absent, of Sophia dying alone... Olivia pressed her lips in a thin line and gave a single, curt shake.

"Then you did all you could."

"It doesn't feel like enough."

"Knowing you, it never will. Blame your tender but oh-so-serious heart." Arti tapped Olivia's forehead with a finger. "And your thick skull."

"I'm sorry I didn't tell you."

"It's fine. We're fine. Maybe this secret wasn't meant for me."

"What do you mean?"

"Do you remember what I said when you asked me if it was really over with Jen? I said any woman who didn't fight for you didn't deserve you. Ellie fought—for you, and for the secret you locked away. I think it was hers to pry loose."

"I can't believe I could get so lucky. Twice."

"The common factor is you. You're easy to love. Hard to talk to sometimes, but—" Arti lifted her shoulder in a tender mimic of Olivia's reflexive shrug. "Keep it simple from now on. Sophia loved you, and she would be thrilled that Ellie loves you too."

"Sophia always said if she went first, I should find someone to be with because I'm terrible at being alone."

"She was an exceptionally smart woman."

"As are you." Olivia lifted Arti's hands and pressed a kiss to her knuckles. "You've been my best friend for forty years. I know the last four have been the hardest, but thanks for not giving up. Thanks for always being there for me, even when I couldn't be there for you."

"Olivia, being your friend is the easiest thing I've ever done." Arti drew her in until their foreheads touched. "And you didn't have to tell me, but I'm glad you did."

She squeezed Arti's fingers again. "Me too."

Chapter Forty

OLIVIA TOSSED HER book on her nightstand and set her reading glasses on top. Next to her, Ellie flipped a page, lips in silent concert with the words. Reading together was a recent routine, a gentle unwinding before bed. Olivia held in a sigh. Ellie had been nothing but gentle. Gentle with her words. Gentle with her attention. And gentle with her touch. Olivia understood, now, the fear behind that gentleness, and she had been picking her way around the edges of it. Their sex life had taken an encouraging step forward—a few intimate nights, quiet orgasms shuddered under a cocoon of blankets—but just as quickly, it had plateaued.

She stroked Ellie's smooth, round thigh. In the past, this would've been signal enough, but Ellie only turned another page. Olivia nuzzled her shoulder, then planted soft kisses up the arch of her neck and along her cheek until she reached the corner of her mouth. Ellie's dimple creased beneath Olivia's lips as she quirked a smile.

"What are you up to?"

Olivia answered the question with a kiss, thrilled when Ellie responded with a trace of her old hunger. Then a hand pushed lightly against her sternum. When it didn't fall away, she slumped back to the headboard, Ellie mute beside her. Olivia opened her mouth. Closed it. Opened it again. Failed a second time. Before her mouth could snap shut a third time, she forced the words out.

"Can we talk?"

"Of course."

"It's been six weeks since the bridge."

Ellie set her book aside, her expression guarded. "I know."

"I appreciate you being available while still giving me space, but I'm doing better, and I've been trying to show you. To get back to where we were before all of this." She painted a line down Ellie's bicep with her fingertip.

"What do you mean?"

"Our physicality, it's tentative. You're being careful with me, with our sex life." The words were heavy in her mouth, but she fought to get them out. "With all that's happened, it's understandable, but I miss you. I miss us."

When Ellie's eyes dropped to the bed, Olivia's heart dropped with them.

"Do *you* miss it?"

"Yes."

"Then why hold back?"

The corner of the sheet twisted in her hands. "I'm not sure how you'll react."

Olivia voiced a recent suspicion. "Because of the night in the shower."

Ellie nodded, head still low.

"I'm so sorry I scared you. Is there anything I can do, anything I can say, to help you feel safer?"

"I don't feel unsafe. It's just..." Ellie looked up and blew out a shaky breath. "That's when it all fell apart. That's when I lost you."

"You could never lose me. I just lost myself, for a bit." Olivia pried Ellie's hands from the sheet, cradling them in her own. "At some point—and maybe we're not there yet—but at some point, you have trust I won't break. So many walls have come down recently, but the physical one is still there. I need it to fall too." She pressed her lips to Ellie's palm, choking on the next words, the ones she feared the most. "I need to know you still want me. That I didn't ruin it for us."

Ellie looked up at her quiet plea. "You haven't ruined anything."

The kiss Ellie gave was gentle, at first, exploring, and Olivia didn't push. But as the pressure deepened and Ellie let slip her eagerness, Olivia opened wider, craving the wet rush of searching tongues. When Ellie matched her, her heart leapt. She straddled Ellie's lap and yanked her own T-shirt over her head. The desire in Ellie's eyes sent her pulse racing, but then sadness muddied that beautiful face.

"Hey, what is it?"

Ellie ran careful hands between her breasts and around her ribs. "You're starting to look like yourself again."

"I told you I'd get it back. It was just the stress and not eating." Olivia cupped Ellie's cheeks. Her smile seemed more melancholy than relieved. "Isn't it a good thing?"

"It is, but..."

She drew Ellie close, cradling her to her chest. "If you don't want this right now, it's okay."

"That's not... I was thinking if I'd spoken up sooner, maybe we could've avoided..." Ellie's words swam in a river of emotion. "But I was afraid of pushing too hard, driving you away. My fear kept me from seeing what you needed."

"You can't help someone who won't let you. And you've always seen me so clearly." Olivia pressed a kiss to Ellie's temple. She'd shared so many stories recently, hoping to erase the pain her silence had caused. But they were all from a time before, a time tinted with heartache and loss. Ellie deserved a new story, one all her own. "I learned that our first night together. You were warm and kind and absolutely gorgeous, and I wanted you so much, but I was scared you'd find the damage too overwhelming."

Ellie shifted to protest, but Olivia held her close, continuing the story above her head. "When you kissed my scars—I thought feeling so safe, so cherished again was impossible. Then you made love to me, and I came, and... It's my favorite thing, to be kissed in that moment."

She hovered the words by Ellie's ear. "You kissed me, and you saw all of me. And that was it. The moment your eyes met mine, I was in love. I was yours."

Ellie dragged her lips up Olivia's neck to the shell of her ear. "I'm yours too, always." Then they kissed with a desperate possessiveness, grinding their open mouths together. Olivia could have wept with relief. This was her Ellie.

Ellie's hand coasted across her scars and down her belly, slipping through her curls into that aching, wet space. The intimate gesture dragged a low moan from her, and she ground her hips, hungering for more. Their chests were heaving when they broke the kiss.

"Tell me what you want." Ellie's husky desire sent a shiver down her back.

Olivia hesitated. Panting breaths filled the silence. She had brought them this far. "I had an idea, to make a new memory."

"Tell me."

"It might be easier if I show you." Pulling herself out of the straddle, Olivia stood and went to the dresser. She took out an object they'd never used together—a harness with a dildo already inside. "I want you to use this. On me. In the shower."

A candle of fear flickered on Ellie's face. Olivia hated that she'd put it there.

"I know what happened the last time, but with this, we can be face-to-face. We can check in with each other, stop anytime." Olivia's voice trembled. "I hoped, if we did this new thing in this...complicated space, we could make it feel safe again. And nothing would stand between us anymore."

Ellie stared at her in pensive silence.

"I'm sorry. I shouldn't have brought it up so soon—"

"No, it's okay. It just caught me off guard. You're right about the shower, about everything. I haven't been able to get past it. And I want to." Ellie blew out a long breath, then tossed off the sheet and strode into the bathroom. Olivia waited until the hiss of water started before she followed.

Ellie stood with her back to her, framed in the open door of the shower. Her hand drifted back and forth under the spray. "I haven't been able to take a shower in here without thinking about it."

"I wish you'd told me."

"I was half afraid if I did, you might tear it out one weekend and replace it with a tub."

Olivia winced. It wasn't an inaccurate picture. "That sounds like a thought I might have at my most guilt-ridden."

Ellie gave the temperature knob one last tweak and turned. Her eyes were clear and steady. "You're sure?"

"Only if you are. I want you to be one hundred percent okay with this."

"That's a pretty serious dildo." A real bit of humor tugged at her lips.

Olivia took a risk and gave a flirty grin. "If you can dish it, I can take it."

Ellie's smile broadened. "Let's get a little wet first."

The water streamed heat down Olivia's spine, but it was nothing compared to the furnace of Ellie's palms, the torrid path of her tongue. Olivia latched on to the soft sweep of Ellie's neck, sucking hard at the racing pulse. She traveled the landscape of Ellie's expansive, yielding flesh with feverish intent. How could there be so much of this woman and still not enough?

Olivia scrabbled for the harness on the floor and held it open as Ellie stepped into it. The dildo jutting out from Ellie's voluptuous body, the straps digging into her full hips, sent a charge through Olivia. She slipped her fingers under the harness, and Ellie twitched.

"Jesus, what are you doing?"

"You forgot the bullet vibrator." Olivia pressed a discrete button, then eased her fingers away. "Now, fuck me. Please."

She didn't have to ask again. Ellie thrust into her, and that first exquisite fullness brought a quiet sigh to Olivia's lips.

"Everything okay?" Ellie whispered.

"Go."

Ellie gripped Olivia's legs and drove her off the floor, tiles stuttering up her back as water arced down her calves and dripped from the bottom of her swinging feet. She'd always been the taller partner, the stronger lover, so this sensation of erotic suspension—her entire weight staked precariously on another's body—dragged a cry of desire and awe from her.

Worry rippled Ellie's features, but Olivia dug her heels into those thick thighs. She grabbed a mass of curls. "I want you. I trust you. Give me everything." Then she devoured Ellie with a kiss. Ellie groaned into the shared space of their hungry, wet mouths and began to pump her hips. The steady strokes added new urgency to the initial fullness, each movement a spike of intensity. It was as if with each thrust, Ellie blissfully tore her apart, and with each retreat, she mended her. The rhythm had a slick satedness Olivia couldn't control. As Ellie pushed deeper, drove faster, she slid closer to the edge.

"Come with me," Ellie said. "I'm so close."

"I need more."

"Tell me. Anything."

"I need you to fill me everywhere." The words slipped through their damp kisses.

Ellie cupped a hand around her ass and eased her middle finger in. Olivia bucked against the tender invasion before relaxing. The warm ache low in her belly climbed to a relentless throb, each small pulse of Ellie's finger timed to the pounding between her legs. Part of her wanted to stay pinned for hours, but her body roared for release.

Grabbing Ellie's face, she forced their lips apart, and when Ellie opened her eyes, so close, Olivia tumbled into space, crying out for her. Ellie kissed her then, swallowing the sound of her own name, drinking in every moan and whimper until she came as well, gasping into Olivia's mouth. When it ended, their foreheads touched.

Olivia could feel the wide grin creasing her face—one of those sloppy sex smiles that couldn't be contained—and Ellie laughed as she lowered her to the floor. The dildo slipped free, leaving a hollowness in Olivia. She almost pulled Ellie back into her.

"Your laugh, what was it for?" Olivia asked.

"That smile. Seeing it after sex again makes me happy."

"You make me happy."

Ellie turned off the vibrator and dropped the harness. After fiddling with the jet controls, she backed Olivia against the cool tiles, facing out, the jet of water thrumming between her cheeks. The pressure sent her pulse racing again.

"What are you doing?"

Ellie kneeled, her own wicked grin flaring. "I'm keeping a smile on your face. All night." She hooked one of Olivia's legs over her shoulder and raked her tongue up her slick length before sucking on her clit, hard.

A belly-deep groan rattled Olivia's teeth. She scrabbled for purchase on the tiles, and all coherent thought trickled from her brain as another orgasm crashed through her.

Chapter Forty-One

FADING AUGUST LIGHT streaked through gaps in the sky-scrapers, glazing windows until they gleamed. Amber, gold, butter, saffron, ochre—Ellie ran out of words before the panes ran out of color. She loved Chicago in summer. The long days and warm nights were a lover's kiss after the bleak, frozen sleep of winter.

Through the town car's tinted glass, the pedestrian crowd was shifting, families with sleeping toddlers weaving back to their hotels as young women in short skirts and young men in tight shirts flowed to their first spot of the evening. She tried to guess her destination, but downtown was still a maze to her. Growing up, Chicago architecture meant two-flats and bungalows and incongruous terra cotta flourishes above the currency exchange her family used as their immigrant bank. The Loop was more postcard than place, the Hancock and Sears Tower looming guardians for the city's wealth, its whiteness. When she finally visited on a high school field trip, the canyons of blunt modernism and ornate stonework had awed her.

Her teenaged self would laugh to see her now, gliding through evening traffic in the capable hands of a driver, wrapped in the earthy, tobacco smell of leather, wearing a dress that screamed sex. And all for a date with a woman. When Olivia asked if she could plan a surprise to celebrate the anniversary of their meeting at TTC, Ellie was thrilled. Their relationship had shifted this past month, as if they'd been fumbling through a massive key ring since that day at the bridge, unlocking door after door, until the final one swung open. Nothing more stood between them.

She readjusted her neckline, which plunged right to the edge of scandalous. It had been a while since she'd poured herself into a dress like this, race-car red with curves to match. It was her only contribution to the surprise. The style was Olivia's request—old school glam. When Ellie had been tasked with choosing Olivia's outfit in return, it took all of five seconds to decide—butch rock star. She couldn't wait to see what Olivia had come up with.

Olivia had left earlier with her garment bag and Ben, to drop him at Christina's before prepping on her own. Anticipation trilled down Ellie's spine, along with a twinge of nerves. It was the first time since the bridge Ben was willing to be away from Olivia for the night. They'd conferred with his psychologist, who felt it was a good time to take this step, and laid out a plan, but there were no guarantees. She clicked her phone screen on—no notifications—and then shook her head with a snort. The maneuver was a mirror to Olivia's, one she'd seen so often in their early days. At the time, Ellie didn't understand how bone-deep the reflexive need to check could go. Now, it was part of her as well. The car rounded one last corner and pulled up in front of the restaurant the two of them had visited after the December fundraiser.

She caught the driver's eye as someone opened the door. "It's taken care of, miss. Have a nice evening."

"Thanks!" A hand appeared, offering support—her heels would be the death of her—and she started at the contact. It was Olivia, but no version of Olivia she had ever seen.

"Hey, beautiful. You look indescribably gorgeous." Olivia raked a fingertip across her cleavage.

"Olivia—"

"Yes?" The right corner of her mouth curled into a sexy grin.

"You look fucking hot! I know that's crude, but Jesus!"

Olivia's outfit was butch rock star personified: skin-tight black leather pants tucked into scuffed motorcycle boots, hair tied up with leather cord, wrists bound in leather cuffs, and a sleeveless white denim shirt unbuttoned a step past decency. Ellie lingered on the thick cuffs. The slight kink they added made her shiver. Her mind wouldn't stop imagining what they could do with them later.

"Are you not wearing a bra?"

Pink shaded Olivia's face. "Guilty."

"Call the car back."

"Why?"

"Because I'm going to rip all this off you in the back seat and do something very indiscreet."

"It's a miracle I got these pants on in the first place. They can't come off until we're done for the night."

"Which is when?" Her hand found the warm skin of Olivia's exposed chest. With her thumb, she traced the curve of her breast.

"Several hours from now." Olivia held a bland expression with frustrating ease.

"Will you at least tell me the plan?"

"No, but it starts here." Olivia grinned, pivoted away from Ellie's attention, and held out her arm. "We were interrupted in this restaurant eight months ago. I want to finish the date the way you deserve."

"Then let's get started. Because I already know how the night ends—you in nothing but those cuffs."

THE TOWN CAR braked as a just-released theater crowd spilled into the street, shifting Ellie closer to Olivia. She stroked a leather-clad thigh, intoxicated by the supple layer between her palm and Olivia's skin. She'd spent half of dinner pawing her. "How about one little hint?"

"Nope."

Ellie took Olivia's fingers and slid them along her own inner thigh. "Not even if I tell you I removed my underwear in the restaurant bathroom?"

"Nope." Olivia played it cool, but her grip tightened. "Where are they?"

"You said no purse, so I ditched them."

"Naughty woman." Olivia peered out the window as the driver stopped, her skin soaked in the lurid red and orange of a neon sign. "We're here."

The nightclub from the fundraiser bustled beyond the glass.

"But you hate clubs."

"I have fond memories of this particular one." Olivia helped her from the car and led her past a long line of trendy twentysomethings. They drew plenty of stares—Olivia was a biker's Amazonian wet dream—but she noticed none of it, her relaxed confidence clinging like a sexy second skin. She nodded at the doorman, and he let them through.

House music blasted. Ellie's molars throbbed with bass. A sour-sweet fog of sweat and alcohol hovered over the humid press. A club used to make her feel young; tonight, she'd never felt older. Olivia lingered by the dance floor, her eyes thoughtful as first blue, then red, then purple strobed across her face.

"What is it?" Ellie leaned close to be heard.

Olivia captured her mouth in a long, languid kiss, stroking until Ellie wobbled on her heels. She dragged her lips away and put them by Ellie's ear, her warm breath another kiss. "A different person walked into this club last December. You made everything possible. I will be forever grateful."

The soft admission in this hard place surprised her. Tears welled, and one slipped free, warm on her cheek. Olivia wiped it with her thumb before tugging her through the crowd to the VIP lounge. Again, she nodded at the bouncer, who held the door, then shut it gently behind them. The heavy bass retreated, replaced by the mellow shimmer of Adele's voice. At the bar, framed by a soft circle of light, were two stools, two glasses, and a bottle on ice. The rest of the room held downy shadows nestled among faint pockets of illumination.

"We have the whole space?"

"You are the definition of a VIP."

Ellie ran her hand along the cool brass rail. It hardly registered as the same place she'd flipped bottles in December. "I'd never been so distracted tending bar. With my eyes glued to you, it was a miracle I didn't serve tequila in the old-fashioneds and bourbon in the margaritas."

"Tonight the pressure is off because I'm serving the drinks. And if we're talking distracted, try focusing on non-profit statistics with a tall, sexy bartender nearby." Olivia tipped champagne into each glass, its foaming effervescence a match for Ellie's own feelings—bubbly, bright, and hard to contain.

She took the offered flute, surprised by its dense crystal weight, and touched it lightly to Olivia's. A small clear chime rang. "I can't believe you arranged all of this!"

"I wasn't in the best place, before, to give you the romance you deserved. I'm making up for it, starting tonight."

"You don't have anything to make up for. I told you—being with you is all the romance I need."

The smile that bloomed on Olivia's face was full and easy. Ellie hadn't realized how little she'd seen it during those difficult weeks until it reappeared like a shot of sun through the clouds.

"What is it?" Olivia asked.

"Your smile. I'm so happy it's back."

An even bigger smile filled her face. "There's one thing you can do to keep this smile here forever."

"Name it!"

"Say yes." Olivia brought her left hand forward. Her fingers held a small, square promise Ellie hadn't dared hope for. The velvet box tickled her palm when Olivia placed it there. "I'm sorry it took so long to say I love you, but I do love you so much. If you give me the chance, I'll say it every day for the rest of our lives. Isabella Vasquez, will you marry me?"

Light-headed, suspended on a thread of disbelief, Ellie cracked open the box. A simple gold band winked at her, and where diamonds might have been, there were three roses engraved in an old-fashioned style.

"Abuela's...how..."

"Your father gave it to me when I asked for your hand."

The ring glowed in the low light, and memories of it on Abuela's hand flooded her. Ellie had touched this ring so many times, studying the delicate outline of each rose. "I can't believe it."

"Which part?"

She swung her eyes around the room, absorbing every romantic detail until she ended where everything had begun, with Olivia's intent hazel gaze. "All of it."

"You haven't answered my question. Should I be nervous?"

"Oh my God, yes! Yes, I will marry you. I'll marry you tomorrow, next Tuesday, whenever you want. I love you, Olivia Northman, and I will marry you." Her lunge almost knocked Olivia off the stool, and their kiss squeezed the air from Ellie's lungs. A tremulous mix of happiness and shock shook her.

"Let's put it on." Olivia slipped the ring from its box and slid it on her finger.

"How does it fit? Abuela's hands were tiny."

"Remember when you modeled pieces for Arti's jewelry portfolio? She checked your size then. I wouldn't trust this ring to anyone else."

She grabbed Olivia's forearm. "Arti helped you with this? When?"

"The last few weeks. Why?"

"I just...can't believe she didn't give it away."

"Arti's an excellent secret keeper, for a loudmouth."

Ellie grinned and kissed her again, loving the way the ring pressed into Olivia's cheek as she held her face. "How did you get the idea to ask Papá?"

"Sophia and I were together long before legal marriage, so a proposal was kind of beside the point." Olivia handed the glass of champagne back with a smile. "Since this would be my first, I didn't want to ignore any family traditions. 'Berto let me know your father would expect to be asked."

"What did he say?"

"At first, he was so quiet I thought I'd screwed up the Spanish. Your mother kept looking from him to me, like she wasn't sure what to do. Then he left the room, and I thought I was screwed."

"You would've asked me either way?"

"Of course. But he returned with the ring. He said before his mother died, she told him to save it for you because the right person would come asking for it."

Any time Ellie considered marriage or rings, she never pictured this, and Abuela had never hinted. But now, with this artifact that held so much life sitting renewed on her finger, ready for more decades of love, she couldn't imagine it any other way. "She always had a little magic."

"As does her granddaughter."

"Olivia..." She leaned in for another soft kiss.

"The roses in place of diamonds are a lovely touch."

"Abuelo was too poor for diamonds. He couldn't even buy her a ring until years later. The roses are for my father and his two brothers." Ellie twined her fingers through Olivia's. "When did this happen? Talking to Papá?"

"A couple of weeks ago. I couldn't stop thinking about the night when I kicked you out. I didn't know if you'd marry me, but I wanted to show you it was our life, our house, and I wouldn't push you away ever again."

"I like that—our life, our house."

"It's true, for as long as you'll have me."

"How about forever?" Ellie slipped from the stool to wrap herself around Olivia, the ring already warm against her skin. The mellow patina gave the illusion of it being on her finger for years, not minutes, and as she clutched Olivia tighter, she sent Abuela a silent promise to wear it as well, and as lovingly, as she had.

Chapter Forty-Two

KICKING THE COMFORTER off, Olivia arched her back with a loud crack. No amount of stiffness could suppress her self-satisfied smirk. She hadn't planned a surprise this complicated in a long time, and it felt good to put her energy into looking forward after years of looking back. Last night had gone perfectly, and with an unexpected bonus. Her smile grew as she remembered Ellie checking the supply room before they left the club, her grin when the handle turned. Her orgasm in the small space sounded even better than Olivia had imagined.

"This is exactly how I like you—wearing nothing but a satisfied grin," Ellie said, returning from the bathroom. She dug a leather cuff out of the sheets and tossed it next to its sibling on her nightstand.

"You liked what I was wearing well enough last night."

Ellie moaned as she crawled across the bed. Her breasts swayed with the movement, sending her large, dark nipples into transfixing orbits. "That outfit. I love your scruffy, sexy vibe—"

"Is that what they call it, my lack of style?"

"But you in leather...it gets me wet just thinking about it." Ellie's kiss swept her away—a snick of teeth, champagne-faded breath, the slick scour of tongues. She opened wider, taking in more until nothing was left but the thrust and the swallow, until Ellie's moan vibrated in her own teeth.

"Kiss me like that, and I'll wear anything you buy me."

Ellie's eyes twinkled. "Since you offered." She held out a small box, a twin to the one Olivia had used last night.

"What—"

"I wanted to propose, but you got there first. I needed you to know nothing would keep me from you. It could be next year or ten years from now or never, if you couldn't see yourself marrying again, but I was absolutely committed to you and Ben."

Stunned, Olivia cracked the box open. Inside was a matte metal band flanked by bright platinum strips. Two square stones were set flush in the middle. "Arti..."

"I asked her to design the perfect ring. She must have been working on this while she was adjusting Abuela's, the sneak."

It was sheer bravery, Ellie approaching Arti about this, a request for permission in her own way. And the ring was a perfect testament to her open heart, gracious to include Arti, not threatened by their decades of friendship.

"The band is steel edged with platinum. The ruby is Ben's birthstone, of course, and the diamond—" Ellie's voice grew thick. "She said the diamond is forged under intense pressure that would have destroyed anything else, yet it comes out stronger, like you."

"Dammit, Arti." Olivia choked back tears.

"The steel band is—"

"—is you. Right? Keeping Ben and me safe."

"Those were almost her exact words."

"And the platinum?"

Ellie laughed now, a burble of joy popping the heavier emotions. "She said if it didn't sparkle, how would you know it was from her?"

"I love its weight, how indestructible it feels."

"So, Olivia Northman, will you marry me?"

She rained tender kisses on Ellie's eyelids, her cheeks, her lips. "Yes, I will marry you."

Ellie took the ring and slid it on Olivia's finger. The cool circle warmed quickly, and she stared at this new symbol. It was nothing like the ring she had worn with Sophia, but the weight felt familiar. It felt like home.

The rings clinked when Ellie threaded their fingers together. "I love that sound."

"Me too." As Olivia kissed the back of Ellie's hand, the compass in her mind swung to the fixed constant of her world. "It's been an incredible twelve hours, romantic and sexy and wonderful, but we should talk about—"

"Ben." Ellie pushed her softly to the bed and curled against her side.

A question hovered, one Olivia had pondered in the peaceful gaps before she followed Ellie into sleep each night. She took a deep breath, Ellie's pillow-tossed curls shifting with the motion. "In case he asks—"

"I want to adopt him after we're married, if you both agree."

Her heart clenched at the certainty. "If something happens... Becoming a single parent unexpectedly is—"

"Harder than you will ever admit."

"There's no guarantee he'll live on his own, and I'm ten years older than you, so there's a decent chance—"

"I'll be alone with him?" Ellie rolled to her stomach and rested her chin on Olivia's shoulder. "Do you think I'd leave Ben, no matter the circumstance?"

When Ellie asked that way, she had no answer but the obvious one. "No."

"Then it's settled. I'm in all the way with you. And with Ben. What do you think he'll say?"

"I'm not sure. He adores you, obviously, but adoption... Please don't be hurt if he says no."

"Oh, I'll be a little devastated if it happens, but I'll understand. Did you warn him about the proposal?"

"Last night. Any earlier, and he would've spilled the beans. We stopped for ice cream on the way to Christina's, and I explained the plan."

"What would you have done if he hated the idea? You had it all arranged."

In her heart, Olivia believed Ben would be fine about the proposal, but her practical side, honed by years of "if this, then that," had demanded backup. "If he was ambivalent, I'd still propose, so you would know how I felt, but we'd keep it private until he had time to adjust. If he hated the idea, I would've cancelled the club. I booked an alternate reservation at a rooftop bar to make the night feel special, if I couldn't propose."

"Can I tell you how sexy this planning brain of yours is?" Ellie pressed a firm kiss to her forehead. "Since we're here, I assume he was fine."

"You've been all but moved in since July, so it doesn't feel much different. But you know him. He'll blow up in a few weeks because he's been stewing on it."

"Why does that sound familiar?"

"Zip it, you." Olivia took a playful bite of Ellie's shoulder. They had a small window until the real world asserted itself. She wanted to fill it with love and lust and peace. Nudging Ellie to her back, she nipped her way down the curve of her breast and the soft ladder of her ribs until she reached the valley where her leg met her hip. She buried her face in it and inhaled. Musk. Salt. Ginger. Hay. The exact scent of Ellie remained an intoxicating puzzle. "I can't get enough of you."

"Good. Because everything I have is yours."

She nuzzled Ellie's stomach. "I love you."

"I'll never get tired of hearing that."

"I love you, I love you, I love you." Olivia punctuated each declaration with a soft kiss. When her phone pinged, she sighed into Ellie's belly button. "We're supposed to have two more hours."

Ellie grabbed it from the nightstand, squinted at the screen, then held it away from her like it had grown fangs.

"What?"

Ellie turned the screen to show a text.

I am at Christina's to see Benjamin. If it is convenient, we could bring him home whenever you are ready. Then we could congratulate the two of you in person.

"Nonna?"

"Yeah." Olivia took the phone from her. Only three days back from Italy, and she was making her presence felt.

"They both know?"

"It was unavoidable. To keep things contained, my first choice would've been Mom, but she and her cousin are on that cruise. Arti would've done it, but Ben's never stayed overnight with her. Christina was our best chance for an uninterrupted evening."

"And you didn't want her finding out from Ben and not you. When did you tell her anyway?"

"A week ago, when we set this up. Nonna wasn't even back from Italy yet, but I told Christina she could either fill her in or wait for me to see her."

"Looks like she filled her in." Ellie raked a tangle of hair from her face and sighed toward the ceiling.

"I can't blame her. If Nonna found out Christina knew but didn't tell her..." Olivia gave a helpless shrug. "I'm sorry so many people were involved, but I couldn't organize the surprise any other way."

"It's okay. The text just threw me for a second."

Her phone pinged again.

OMG I just found out Mamma texted you. Not appropriate. So sorry. I'll call her off.

Olivia passed the phone to Ellie so she could read it. "Christina's on it. Just type 'ok' and hit send. I'll follow up with her in a bit."

Ellie snorted a laugh. "You can't stop an immigrant grandmother. You can only hope to contain her. Hey, do you think Nonna planned this, or is it spontaneous?"

"Oh, it's planned. Nonna's letting me know she's not happy being left out. She should've met you back when I met your family, but her last-minute trip to Italy derailed things."

Ellie plucked at the sheets, her face thoughtful. "Of course she's not happy, she hasn't met the woman who's going to be part of her grandson's life. Abuela would've been beyond upset." She handed the phone back. "If it's okay with you, tell Christina they can come over."

"Really?"

"I was never not going to be anxious about meeting them. This way it's only a few hours, instead of fixating on it for a whole day or a week or whatever. Let's say eleven o'clock, to give ourselves some time."

Meeting Nonna had not been part of her plan, but if Ellie preferred this to any alternative, she wouldn't stand in the way. Olivia pecked out a response, then held up the phone. "Last chance to change your mind."

"If you can survive Mamá's dark portends, I can survive this."

Olivia tapped send, then tossed the phone on the nightstand. "Since we've given ourselves some time, as you say—"

Ellie clapped a hand on either side of her face, stopping her before she could work her way lower. "Oh, no. I cannot focus on sex knowing those two women will be here soon."

"I'll be really fast."

"No."

"But—"

"No." Ellie grinned now, but she still didn't release her face. "Shower. Tidy up. And a quick trip to a bakery because we have nothing decent to serve with coffee."

"Fine, fine." Olivia rolled from Ellie's grip and headed for the bathroom. "When you say shower, you mean together, right?" A leather cuff flew by and bounced off the door jamb. "Can't blame a woman for trying!"

Chapter Forty-Three

"WILL YOU TWO be okay here? I'm sure his computer just needs a restart." When Olivia paused in the kitchen doorway, Ellie forced a nonchalant smile. Christina leaving to see Ben's Minecraft demonstration had been one thing. Olivia leaving was quite another.

"We're fine. Go, go." Nonna shooed Olivia, then shifted her attention to Ellie, who tried not to squirm. She'd been riding the high of their twin proposals when she suggested this meeting. Now, alone and face-to-face with Nonna, she felt more impulsive than brave.

Ellie had seen photos of Sophia, and Olivia had mentioned the resemblance, but it had still been a shock when Adrianna walked through the door. The woman was both a living reminder of Sophia and a snapshot of her lost future. Ellie knew she was being superstitious, but even the house seemed to recognize her. Or at least the resonance of Sophia within her. And as it turned toward that memory, it turned against Ellie. The silverware drawer jammed when she went to close it. The cabinets flustered her, revealing the wrong contents every time she opened a door. Even the espresso maker rebelled, the threads refusing to line up until Olivia took over.

Ellie spun her cup slowly in its saucer to avoid drinking her espresso—her stomach couldn't handle its bitter bite right now.

"Add milk. There's no Italian law for drinking it black."

She startled when Adrianna guessed her thoughts, then smiled, reaching for the creamer.

"You have a quick smile. I like that."

"Thanks." Ellie smiled again, as a reflex, then blushed.

"My grandson is fond of you."

"I love him so much." The words burst out, betraying her. She almost swallowed her tongue trying to get them back.

Adrianna's mask of appropriateness didn't slip. She set a biscotti on her plate. "My daughter would be happy knowing he and Olivia are not alone."

"It must be hard, seeing me in this house."

"I'm old. I have seen much. This is not the hardest thing, not by any measurement."

"Sophia."

"To bury a child. There are no words."

The espresso swirled and clouded as Ellie stirred. The chime of spoon on ceramic marked the silence. "I love Olivia and Ben, but I have no intention of taking them away from you. Not that I could, I mean, but I want us to be comfortable." She bit her lip. "I'm not saying this well."

"You think I'm upset you will replace my daughter?"

"Judging from the stories, she's irreplaceable."

A glinting smile carved Adrianna's face.

Ellie set her spoon down. "I want the three of us to be a family, but it doesn't mean leaving all of you behind."

Adrianna pierced her with a shrewd glare. The smile flattened, grew sharper. "You are leaving something—how do they say it—on the table."

Ellie's words had spun away from her, and she couldn't reel them back. It didn't matter anyway. Nonna had already guessed. She just wanted to hear Ellie say it. She swallowed hard. "We've talked about my adopting Ben after the wedding, but only if he wants it."

Silence again. And Adrianna's unshakeable stare. The sticky-sweet smell of Ellie's untouched Danish grew cloying. Her stomach churned.

"My Sophia carried Benjamin."

"I know."

"She will always be his mother."

"Of course."

Adrianna sipped her espresso. Some of the steel left her expression. "It is hard to imagine him calling anyone other than Olivia...mother."

Ellie took a slow breath, remembering Abuela's admonition, and measured her words. "I'm sure it is, but Ben should know I'm committed to him as much as Olivia." She leaned back in her chair and waited. Adrianna was different from Abuela—more blade, less hammer—but the fierce love for her family was identical.

"It is the right thing for Benjamin," Adrianna said, finally. "But it will never be an easy thing for me."

"Thank you." Ellie tried not to slide off her chair in a puddle of relief.

"May I see the ring?"

"Of course." The marvel of this ring on her own finger hadn't faded. "It was my abuela's."

Adrianna cupped Ellie's hand in her own clawed fingers, then lifted her reading glasses from their chain to study it. "Three roses?"

"For her three sons."

"And now for another family of three." She let her reading glasses drop.

Ellie almost burst into tears at the gift of those words, at their tender acceptance. She drew in a long, unsteady breath and nodded.

Adrianna patted her hand, then released it. "You must miss your abuela a great deal."

"She was the first to accept my being gay. Knowing she loved me meant everything."

"Then she was a wiser woman than me." Adrianna interlaced the gnarled branches of her fingers and rested them on the table.

"But you and Sophia were close."

"Eventually, yes, but after she first told me, a strain grew between us. It was over thirty years ago, a different time. There was no thought of marriage, or children, for women like this." Her bent knuckle rapped the table. "You're an immigrant. You understand."

Ellie nodded.

"I said it was a terrible mistake. I almost told her to leave the house and never return, but I knew my daughter. She would do it. With Christina, maybe, I could threaten this, but not my Sophia."

Olivia and Christina hovered in the doorway, but Ellie said nothing to break the story.

"I withdrew from her. Only the light things, the small things, we discussed, for a year. Before university, she came to me. She said I didn't know what she would be giving up, to stay in the life I wished for her. She said—" Adrianna's thin voice cracked. "Sophia said she would have to give up her very soul."

"So you accepted who she was."

"I said I would try, and I did, thank God, because if I had not—" She crossed herself. "A few years before her death, Sophia and Olivia organized a surprise party for me here, filled with people. Every moment was perfect. Olivia was so devoted to my daughter, so considerate of me. Watching them together, I felt such shame. My stubbornness might have kept them apart, if Sophia hadn't defied me. Or I could have lost them all, living a life separate from mine. To imagine it even now—"

Olivia touched her mother-in-law's slight shoulder as she and Christina sat on either side. "Sophia knew you loved her."

"I pushed her away when she needed me to draw her close."

"She understood you needed time. She was never angry at you. Not for one second."

"My dear." Adrianna touched her cheek. "That is what makes it shameful. The daughter should push away and be angry. Her mother should know better."

Olivia's lips stretched tight, the way they did when she pushed a smile through her pain. "I wish Sophia could—" She shook her head.

Ellie knew that shake, the way it erased the words to come. She'd seen it too often in those weeks leading up to the bridge. Worry fluttered in her stomach like a moth. Olivia had been concerned this meeting was too soon for Ellie. But she hadn't seen Adrianna since before the breakdown. Maybe all of this was too soon for her.

"You wish she could see him now." Adrianna finished Olivia's thought.

"Sophia believed in him, more than I ever did. As a nurse, I clung to the realistic, the practical, because it felt safe, but she saw all of this for him. And the way he's blossomed with Ellie makes me wonder if my grief kept him from being happy." Even as her eyes watered, Olivia forced a flat, measured tone.

"So I understand when you speak of shame; when you say a mother should know better. To protect Ben from more pain, I withdrew and took him with me. Sophia wouldn't have done that." A deep sorrow threatened Olivia's painted calm. She buried her face in her hands. "I've always thought, for Ben, that the wrong parent lived."

The whispered admission shocked Ellie, but before she could reach for Olivia, Nonna peeled her hands away and lifted her chin. "You both needed the same thing—time to step out of this world until you could face it again without her. You see so much of my daughter in him that it blinds you to how much of you is there as well." She patted Olivia's cheek.

"When Sophia first told me about you, do you know what she said? That she had never met anyone who forgave others so easily but could never forgive herself. I thought it was a strange way to describe someone—I'm Italian, after all. We hold our grudges."

Olivia chuckled through her tears. The wry sound soothed some of Ellie's worry.

"I did not fully understand her until this moment. Sophia never doubted you as a parent. Always remember that." Adrianna hadn't forgiven Olivia, because there was no need, but she had granted Olivia permission to forgive herself. As Sophia's mother, it was a grace only she could give. "And if you do not remember, I trust Ellie will."

"I will, Adrianna."

"Nonna," she said, mock-scowling.

"Nonna." Ellie pulled Olivia close, kissing her temple. She'd never heard her talk about this poignant regret, and she ached at how hard Olivia could be on herself.

"Is it always like this around here?" Christina teased, breaking the somber mood. "I've lived on testosterone island so long, I'm out of practice."

"I said I was getting emotional in old age." Wiping her face, Olivia released a jittery sigh.

"And I said wait until menopause. Not that some of us have to worry about it for a while." Christina gave Ellie a playful kick under the table.

She laughed and pushed back in her chair. "Let me get you an espresso." Ellie squeezed Olivia's shoulder as she got up; fingertips brushed across her knuckles in response. With the murmur of voices floating behind her, she crossed to the kitchen. The silverware drawer opened with a smooth glide, and she let out a long, slow breath as she reached for a spoon.

Chapter Forty-Four

CHILDREN SWARMED OVER a giant wooden play structure, too intent on stealing every minute of fun from their last school-free week to mind the suffocating heat wilting the adults. Ben tramped across a wood-planked rope bridge, absorbed by the deep rattle in his legs. Each stomp set off a grinding clatter of board against chain. Ellie couldn't decide if the activity was a sign of frustration or regulation. Not for the first time that week, she wished for Olivia's intuition, her ability to read Ben like a map. She eyed a sullen thundercloud pinned to the horizon. The wet-pennies scent of ozone made her throat itch.

"How long do you think we have?"

"Awhile yet." Olivia squeezed her hand. Humidity fused their tacky palms. "How are you feeling?"

"Nervous. It's a little awkward between us right now. What if this makes it worse?" Her stomach clenched remembering their adoption discussion. Ben's rejection stunned her. He'd been clear that the engagement was fine, a wedding was fine, but adoption caused him to shut down, and no amount of explaining or reframing could get him to talk. Since their conversation, he'd withdrawn from her—not fully, but enough that she felt it.

"Your gift is incredibly thoughtful. I know you're still tender about last week, and you've been so good not letting him see that, so trust—"

"I'm thirsty!" Ben leapt from the bridge, then bounded over.

"Lucky for you we brought this." Olivia gave him a water bottle, and he chugged half of it. She glanced at Ellie, who swallowed her trepidation and nodded.

"Hey, Ben, I have a late birthday present for you. It took longer than I thought to have it made. Want to see it?"

"It's here? In the park?"

"Yeah, come with us." The knot in Ellie's stomach eased when Ben tucked a hand in each of theirs. They followed a sidewalk away from the playground, and the children's shrill cries faded into the mechanical whine of cicadas. Nestled in a corner of the park, shielded by a wall of reeds, sat a small wetland area. The smell of it, mud-dark and mossy, masked the metallic sting of the coming storm.

"This is where Mommy and I counted the ducks! And turtles!"

As they approached the lily-speckled pond, Ellie eyed the bench, relieved it was empty. When she'd brought Olivia here last week, they had to walk three loops of the park before an older couple finally left.

"This bench is new!" Ben yanked free of their grips, sprinted up a slight rise, and stumbled to a stop in front of it.

Ellie scrambled to catch up, then put a careful hand on his shoulder. "This is your bench, Ben, yours and Mommy's. I wanted to give you a place where, when you're missing her, you can come talk to her."

He reached for the back of the bench, which was covered in a collage of photographs, and touched an image in the center. "It's my selfie with Mommy." Their last selfie. Ben, smaller, slighter, with his quiet smile and middle-distance eyes; Sophia grinning and windblown, poignantly alive in a way only the dead can seem. When Ellie had asked for a picture months ago, for a surprise, she'd been stunned, and so moved, that Olivia shared this private touchstone of hers and Ben's.

"Around it are photos of other families who lost someone to a drunk driver. The sign at the top explains it. Every time a person sits here, I hope they remember to drive safe, so no one else loses their mommy the way you did."

Ben climbed on the seat and touched his mother's radiant face. Olivia sank next to him, available but waiting as he looked from Sophia to her several times, processing, absorbing. Nervousness bubbled, sharp and sour, in the back of Ellie's mouth. She couldn't read Ben. And she couldn't rush him. The time he needed was the time he would take. Finally, he scooted next to Olivia and buried his face in her shoulder.

"Our being married doesn't mean you'll leave Mommy behind." Ellie sat on the other end of the bench and gently squeezed one bony ankle. "You can come here anytime—"

Ben's head popped up, and he launched himself at her, shoving her against the armrest. "I'm sorry I didn't say yes to the adoption. Please don't leave. I love you!" He burrowed under her chin.

"Oh, Ben, I love you too. I'm not leaving, ever." Her throat nearly closed over the words, and she cradled him loosely.

"I don't know how to give up Mommy to let you be Mommy."

Olivia rested a hand on his back. "We told you before that you don't have to give up Mommy for Ellie."

"But Jonah calls his new dad, Dad. So now his old dad isn't Dad anymore! I want Ellie to adopt me, but she can't be Mommy. So she can't adopt me!"

"Is that what you're worried about, what to call me?" She smoothed the hair from his face. All week, she and Olivia had weighed what might be bothering him, but Ben had found the right words on his own.

"There are lots of names for family," Olivia said. "You have Grandma and Nonna, right? Ellie doesn't have to be Mommy."

"Spanish for Mommy is Mamá. You could call me that."

"And Mommy could stay Mommy?"

"Always, Ben. Always."

He lifted his head. "Can I change my mind about the adoption?"

"Is it what you want, in here?" Ellie tapped his chest over his heart. "Because you will always be my son, no matter what a piece of paper says." She'd never said *son* out loud before. Her voice cracked on the word.

"I do want it. I want you to be my Mamá."

Ellie crushed Ben to her.

"Too tight. Too tight!"

Kissing the top of his head, she relaxed her arms. He wiggled free and turned to the bench, his finger tracing other images. She hiccupped a laugh, which freed a trickle of tears. As they threatened to become a rush, she jerked to her feet, hoping to shield the flood of emotions from him. Olivia encircled her from behind, solid and silent. Clouds had scudded east, but strips of blue still fluttered among the gray. Ellie leaned into Olivia's steady presence and released her relief and joy into the wide summer sky.

Chapter Forty-Five

"THE PHOTOGRAPHER'S READY. Do you want to participate?" Olivia took a few steps into Ben's room and shut the door, muffling the noise from the caterers downstairs. His space was the only area left untouched for the reception, and she had to pick her way through a sprawling Lego subdivision to get to him.

"The same photographer as yesterday? At the courthouse?"

"Same one."

Ben lay on his bed, knees bent, feet pattering a muffled rhythm on his comforter. One shirttail hung free, a bedraggled flag of surrender. "Why do weddings need regular pictures? Why can't they be selfies?"

"There's forty people here. You'd need a really long arm to get everyone in."

"Or the world's longest selfie stick."

"Even then, it might be tough. Plus, you'd be stuck taking selfies the whole party. When would you play with

Jamal? Or eat barbeque? Or cake?" One last careful step brought her to the edge of his bed.

He squinted up at her, gnawing on his crooked tie. The light blue fabric had stained dark at the tip. "You're tall in those shoes. Like, taller than usual."

"I suppose I am."

"I don't like you in them."

"Me either."

"Then why do you wear them?"

She tapped a boot heel on the floor. "Sometimes they make the most sense with my outfit."

"Have you ever worn a tie?" He yanked at his collar.

"About as often as I wear heels. I'm not a dressy clothes person."

"Me either."

"We're the same that way."

His forehead furrowed, and he spit out the tie. "Are we the same in other ways?"

"Sure." Olivia squeezed next to him on the mattress, her feet hanging off the end. On the ceiling, freshly painted leaves filled long-abandoned branches. Four different artists meant the tree was a hodgepodge of styles, but Ben didn't mind.

"Tell me. About how we're the same." He put his legs out straight in a mirror of hers.

"Why do you want to know?"

"Because you always tell me how I'm like Mommy. But never you. How come?"

She paused at the edge of answering. She had to do this more often lately. What once were simple, shallow questions, a puddle easily stepped over with barely a thought for her response, had grown wider, deeper. She marveled at the change even as she was forced to find another way around.

"Well, Mommy carried you, gave birth to you, and was the absolute best Mommy in the whole world." Folding her hands on her stomach, she let out a slow breath. "I want to keep her with you, I guess. I want you to know a big part of who you are is because of her. And since she's not here to do it herself, maybe I try too hard."

"Can you tell me now? How we're alike?"

"I can, but there's also this party outside. If you're uncomfortable being there, I understand, but I'll need to leave soon."

He squirmed closer until his shoulder pressed tight to hers. "Tell me three things."

She drummed her fingers before putting one in the air. "We both love ice cream."

"That's true."

A second finger flipped up. "When I don't know what to say, I shrug instead. Especially to compliments."

"Me too!"

She lifted a third finger, and then curled her hand in a loose fist. "When my heart hurts, I have trouble using my words."

"You do?"

"Yes." She slipped her hand into his. "Mommy helped me, because she was good with words."

"So, when Mommy died, you lost your word person."

"I did. And so did you."

"But Ellie is a word person too."

"She's many wonderful things, which is why I married her yesterday."

"And why she's going to be my Mamá."

"Exactly." From the kitchen, a deep voice echoed, and Olivia sat up. "That's three. I promise to tell you more, but I have to get back to the reception."

"I'm coming too." He hopped off the bed. "Do I have to wear the tie?"

"No, but you look handsome in it, so if you wear it for the pictures, you can...set the darn thing on fire after."

"Really?" His eyes grew round, and he looked down at his tie with new zeal. "On actual fire?"

"Not while you're still wearing it!" Being spontaneous with him was always a risk. "But yeah, on actual fire. When we light the firepit, you can toss it right on top."

"Okay! Will you fix it?"

"Sure." She snugged the tie up to his neck and got half of his shirttail tucked in before he bolted from the room. Partway down the stairs, his footsteps were swallowed by the churn from the kitchen. She couldn't remember the last time she hadn't heard him hit bottom. With her hand on the railing, she paused, listening to the cacophony that had absorbed her son—silverware clattering, cabinets slamming, chairs scraping. And so many voices, rubbing cheerfully against one another, sliding for purchase in too small a space. Slowly, she descended, adding her own quiet steps to the bustle.

"YOU WERE RIGHT to rent heat lamps for the back yard." Light speared through the cracked bathroom door. Ellie's shadow fluttered past. The rasp of brush through hair mixed with her words. "I mean, it was gorgeous for October, but we did need them."

Olivia settled deeper into her pillow. "The firepit makes for good atmosphere, but it can only do so much.

"I still can't believe you let Ben burn his tie!" A gleeful cackle spilled into the bedroom.

"I probably went a little far with that bribe."

"Hey, it got us a non-selfie family photo. He could've torched his whole outfit, and it would've been worth it." The mirror creaked open, then clicked closed. The strip of light vanished. Ellie made her way through the darkness to the bed and slipped between the sheets with a groan. "I used to be able to wear heels all day. Now look at me, hobbled after five hours."

"You're just out of practice."

"They weren't even that tall—I didn't want to tower over Ben during our dance."

"I'm still amazed you pulled that off. Amazed and touched and..." She pulled Ellie into her, burying her face in her hair. Of all the mental snapshots of the day, their surprise was the one she kept turning over and over. "I couldn't take it all in before. Tell me the whole story."

Ellie's Cheshire cat grin curled against her chest. "We were watching clips of wedding receptions on YouTube, so he could get a sense of what to expect. There were some couples' dances, and in one, the kids joined in. Ben noticed, and I explained about blended families. Something about his expression made me ask if he was interested. The rest was all him—picking the salsa music, making it a surprise. I honestly didn't think he could hide it from you, but he wanted to try."

"I'm still not sure what shocked me more—the actual dance, or that he kept it a secret!"

"For a second, when I was introducing us, I thought I might lose him. I could see it on his face, how the reality of dancing in front of everyone came crashing down. But then the music started, and all his focus went to the footwork."

Olivia had latched on to Arti for support in those first stunned moments, when the surprise clicked into place. Ellie led, but Ben followed gamely, counting under his breath. With each step, he seemed to transform—the top of his head floating closer to Ellie's chin, his upright posture spreading his shoulders wide. For the first time, she could see the teenager lurking in her son's gangly collection of elbows and knees. "I was so proud. Of all of it—the practice it took, keeping the secret, the sheer bravery. And I think Nonna was almost as thrilled as me."

On one of Ben's turns, she'd spotted her mother-in-law, hands clapping with the music. The way she laughed, mouth open and eyes sparkling—it was so Sophia that for a moment, Olivia couldn't breathe. Adrianna's words at the kitchen table had returned to her. *I am Sophia's mother, and since she is gone, I must speak for her. It is a hard burden sometimes.* Olivia didn't believe in God, or that Sophia's spirit had floated above them, watching the dance. But Adrianna watched for her daughter, and today it wasn't a burden. It was a joy.

Ellie slid a hand up Olivia's neck and cupped her cheek. Olivia leaned into the pressure, then smiled against that palm as Ellie cracked a wide yawn.

"Sorry—"

"It's okay. It's been a busy few days." Olivia pressed a kiss to Ellie's forehead. "Close your eyes."

Ellie nuzzled under her chin, grip tightening around her ribs. "What was your favorite part of the day? Not counting my dance with Ben."

"Other than being with you?"

"Yes, other than being with me." Ellie's smile tickled her collarbone.

Olivia thought about her aunt's arrival and how her steady hazel gaze was an echo of her father she hadn't known she needed. Then she thought of the yard, how all the faces and ages and languages blurred into a roaring sea of love and affection. And she thought of the setting sun spilling across that sea, its rich light gilding smiles and burnishing cheekbones until each face glowed like a small bright mirror reflecting her happiness, her peace.

All of these moments were hovering on her lips when a sigh gushed across her chest. The head on her shoulder grew heavy. The arm around her ribs slackened. A hush cocooned them, absorbing her wife's soft, sibilant breaths as she sank into sleep.

Wife. Olivia mouthed the word into the dark. It was both astonishing and perfect to use it again.

Acknowledgements

This book wouldn't exist without my wife, Joanne. Falling for her made me believe in love stories, and having her support made me believe I could write one. She provided unflagging confidence, thoughtful feedback, and countless practical assists that gave me the most precious of writing commodities—time. Every writer should have a spouse like her. She's the best. This book also wouldn't exist without our son, who has given me so much simply by being himself.

One of the joys of writing this book was how my world expanded as I worked on it. The earliest versions benefited from the helpful comments and encouragement of Shirene Nourbash, Kristen Petrillo Majdanics, Melissa Briones, Laura Ozark, Maria Theodorou, Aubrey Parker, Elizabeth Pappano, Nancy Hollander, and Rosa Chevez. And thanks to Elizabeth Andersen for being an encouraging set of editing eyes.

I also discovered the Pitchwars community on Twitter, and while it was still early days for LGBTQ+ publishing there, I found nothing but kindness and support. Thanks to Helen Hoang, Laura Heffernan, Brighton Walsh, Rachel Lynn Solomon, Maxym M. Martineau, and others for their feedback, along with an endless supply of double-entendre GIFs. A gigantic hug to Annette Christie and Lindsay Landgraf Hess for being especially stalwart cheerleaders all along the way.

Rochelle Karina—you're a pro at being both supportive and direct, and I appreciate that so much. Elyse Årring—I can't believe I found my doppelgänger on Twitter of all places, but your insight, consideration, and utter joy for language were exactly what I needed.

Jazmine Aluma, I'm so grateful you took the leap to form a writer's group and let me in on the fun. You, Jody Burke-Kaiser, Kathryn Hayden, and Allison Wehrle have all had a hand in bringing this book across the finish line.

Finally, thanks to my parents and sister, who have known me for the bookworm and word nerd that I am longer than anyone. I can't remember a time when I told my parents "I want to be..." or "I'm going to...", and they weren't supportive. That's about the best gift you can give a child, and it's one I hope to pass on to my son.

About Anne E. Terpstra

Anne E. Terpstra (she/her) writes heartfelt, sex-positive fiction that is grounded in realism and centers LGBTQ+ characters. *Beyond Any Experience* is her debut novel.

Anne graduated from the University of Missouri-Columbia and has degrees in journalism and technical theater. She has worked as a copy editor/proofreader, and she is a member of the Chicago Writers Association. In addition to being an author, Anne is a potter and photographer. In all of her pursuits, she enjoys exploring the unexpected angle or unappreciated detail.

Anne and her wife live in Chicago with their son. When she isn't writing, throwing pots, or taking photos, she procrastinates by baking and gardening.

All of Anne's other works can be found at her website, aeterpstra.com.

Email
aeterpstra@gmail.com

Facebook
www.facebook.com/anneeterpstra

Twitter
@anneeterpstra

Instagram
www.instagram.com/aeterpstra

Pinterest
www.pinterest.com/anneeterpstra/_saved

Connect with NineStar Press

www.ninestarpress.com

www.facebook.com/ninestarpress

www.facebook.com/groups/NineStarNiche

www.twitter.com/ninestarpress

www.instagram.com/ninestarpress

Made in the USA
Las Vegas, NV
11 July 2022